Balancing Acts

Balancing Acts

a novel by

Eddra Marchand

MZV  Publishing, Inc.

Published by MZV Publishing, Inc.

ISBN: 0-9742974-0-2

Library of Congress Control Number: 2003110263

First Edition
First Printing, August 2003
10 9 8 7 6 5 4 3 2 1

Book design by Afi Holmes

www.MZVPublishing.com

This book is dedicated to my mother,
Sandra B. Marchand.

Acknowledgments

There are so many people who supported me in this "from the heart" endeavor. First, however, I want to give thanks and praise to God, in whom my faith has never wavered.

There are so many people who gave me the encouragement and support to follow this passion of writing. At times when I did not believe it would come to fruition, their kind words enabled me to keep moving forth. I would especially like to give thanks to my parents who instilled within me the confidence to know that I could accomplish anything I desired if I put my trust in the Almighty. I love you mom and dad.

I must thank my husband Norbert, who has supported me since I was a lanky teenager in high school. He provided me with the love and stability I needed to pursue this once unforeseen dream. Thank you to my wonderful sisters, Kimberly and Melanie, who have always been my anchors at every stage of my life. You all provided a balance to my sometimes overwhelming life moments. Thank you to my brother Wendell, who provided the unconditional support I needed to make several aspects of this project move from paper to infinity. Thank you to my brother Edward Jr. for his unending support and laughter. I must thank my wonderful children, Mallory and Zachary for their patience when mommy had her "homework" to do. I love you both from the bottom of my heart.

Thank you to my wonderful editing team...Alexis, Cori, Denise, Geralyn, Kim, Mel, Leslie, and Sharon...you guys were brutally honest and helped so much in this wondrous journey. Thank you to my editor Ty, who always kept it real, no matter what. Thanks to Afi, for the wonderful cover design and insight. Thank you to my publisher, MZV Publishing for believing in me. There are a multitude of other people who contributed to this journey towards "Balancing Acts". Thank you and May God Bless you all.

Prologue

"Grandma! Grandma!" She looked at me, eyes piercing with a silence so loud. "Mommy. Why are they taking my Grandma?" I cried uncontrollably, unable to stop my frail body from trembling. My mom just held my head close to her bosom, and stroked my plaits and bangs out of my eyes. Grandma was yelling all these cuss words that I had only heard on TV when I slept by my cousin Rashid's house.

"Leave me alone you assholes."

Mom unsuccessfully tried to cover my ears while repetitively saying, "It's going to be alright, Cass. It's going to be alright."

But I heard every word escaping grandma's mouth perfectly as if it were being broadcast through a megaphone. "Assholes, Mother F'ers." Oh, I can't even make myself say that last one in my head. I was so confused and felt like everyone around me had lost their minds. How could everything be okay when three men were dragging my grandmother into a van? I felt I had no choice. So I escaped my mother's grasp, and ran to my father yelling, "Daddy. Stop them! Stop them," feeling sure that my father would be the savior of the day and stop this nonsense. It was if my words fell on deaf ears because he continued to point and delegate to the very men committing this heinous crime. "Am I the only one who's not crazy?"

As the van drove off I futilely ran after it until the red lights became faint. My father knelt down in the middle of the street next to me, consoling me, as I stood there breathless and unable to contain my heavy sobs.

"Grandma will be back. She just has to leave us for a while."

That little while soon became a faint memory as weeks went by with nothing being said about the incident. Every time I asked anything about that awful day, I was quickly hushed. Finally, one day when I asked the forbidden question mom finally said something. It still made no sense to me but at least I was not hushed yet again.

"Grandma was alone and lonely and those men took her to a place to help make her happier." All of my further probing was quickly stifled yet again. Finally, one day we went to Grandma's house and there she was sitting in her favorite chair. I ran over and gave her the big bear hug that she always loved and all I got in return was this clumsy hug without the giggling and the tickling that usually accompanied it. "I'm so glad to see you grandma."

Grandma said nothing. She just stiffly smiled and patted my back. It wasn't until a few years later that I learned the whole truth in the most inappropriate of settings. I was innocently playing with some friends and my anger got the best of me as I began screaming at the top of my lungs for the ball.

"Girl you better give Cass that ball, before she does one of her grandma's numbers."

"What are you talking about, Pam?"

"We don't want you to end up in a looney bin like her," laughed Derrick.

"What are you talking about?" I began to cry and further probed.

They both began to laugh hysterically. "Your grandma whipped that pistol out and aimed it at your grandfather." They continued to laugh making gestures like they were shooting a gun. "Thank goodness she's a bad shot, or her ass would be on death row."

"Stop lying. Stop it!" I began running as fast as I could away from them with their ongoing taunting.

"Everybody knows."

I finally reached my house in what felt like an eternity and ran to my parents' room. "How could you? How could you not tell me the truth about Grandma?" I felt so betrayed as my mother came over to hug me. At first I resisted but I needed her comforting arms around me to tell me everything would be okay.

"We didn't know how to tell you and we just kept waiting for the right time. We did not want you to find out like this."

Now I knew where the hole covered by plaster in the wall had come from. A bullet, not a secret vault opening like I had been lied to about for years. My dear grandmother had a nervous breakdown that escalated when my grandfather left her. It was that day when he returned to retrieve his last belongings that my grandmother aimed that nine mm at him and pulled the trigger. I almost couldn't blame her. Why would a seventy year old man leave his dutiful wife of forty years for anyone else? Especially when they were so happy. At least they appeared to be. He had the audacity to leave her for a twenty year old hussy with no history and no knowledge of the struggles he endured through the fifties and sixties because her ass wasn't even born. My dear grandmother has never been the same since.

I try to remember the times when we walked into their house and instantly smelled the aroma of fresh biscuits and pies. I try to remember my grandma's sassy saunter as she came out of her kitchen proudly displaying her delicious menu for the day. Now the house emanated that smell of old moth balls and of stale oxygen that had been breathed too much. Now my grandmother's playful banter was transformed into a dull and emotionless presence rarely camouflaged by the antipsychotic drugs now part of her daily repertoire. All she continued to emphasize to me and my siblings was that there was no novelty in getting old alone. It was almost as if those words had become branded on my soul. The mere thought of being alone had become almost a mortal sin to me. I believe that it affected me more than my siblings because I witnessed the unequivocal transformation from loving grandmother to medicated zombie. Not to mention the fact that for as long as I remembered, everyone commented on how we looked and acted so much alike. I was afraid that I was destined to travel her same course.

Balancing Acts

From that time on I vowed that I would not grow old alone. It became an unrelenting mission of mine to not follow the same path. To me, being my grandmother equaled being alone and medicated on drugs. Before I went to sleep at night my last words after my prayers for many years were, "I will not be branded by my past. I will not evolve into the shell that has become Sallie Mae Nicholas."

One

"   ove you, baby."

"I love you too, mom," Cass whispered as she hugged her mom tightly and turned to enter the corridor leading to the airplane. Cass could not believe that a tear was trying to escape from her eyes. She always tended to become exceptionally sentimental when she was leaving her security net at home. She prided herself upon being very strong and worked hard to eliminate any display of sensitivity which she knew so many perceived as weakness. It was a barrier she had to build to move up the ranks in the male dominated field in which she excelled. But at home she enjoyed being able to remove all of her protective shields and transform into the loving and playful self that had become a relic of the past. The human woman who had true feelings and a sensitivity so rarely penetrated. Outside of those borders, she exuded confidence easily teetering on arrogance. She quickly and inconspicuously wiped the tear that slowly streamed down her cheek and began to focus her attentions on fighting off another ever-present challenge—claustrophobia. Cass could feel her palms start to sweat and her heart begin to race as she stored her luggage in the bin above her seat. She tried to get her mind off of her current circumstances and instead began thinking of all of the misfortune involved with her move back to New Orleans after business school ten years prior, and how grateful she was that she was finally returning to Hotlanta. She laughed and thought, "Was that not the worst mistake of my career?" She then more insightfully corrected, "of my life," remembering she also had briefly moved back into her parents home, which stripped her of all of her once overlooked freedoms. Cassandra, however, promptly corrected that oversight and moved into her own apartment three weeks later. Needless to say, after far too many unannounced visits from her mother she truly had to cut the "same city" umbilical cord lingering between them due to the constant interruptions of favorite TV shows, quiet book reading, and the rare but occasional fucking. Barely hanging on in N'awlins' for two years in the markedly racially stifled climate perpetuated by her job as well as her family issues, Cass finally received a respectable job offer and within a week made final plans to move to Philadelphia. Cass abruptly grabbed the armrest as the plane slowly began backing away from the gate.

"God, please watch over me." Cass wasn't sure when her profound fear of enclosed spaces developed, but at this moment it was quite intense as she opened all the air vents and directed them to her face. The middle aged African-American gentleman sitting next to her inquired, "Are you okay?"

Cass half smiled and answered, "I'll be okay. Once we land in Atlanta."

"Don't like flying, huh. We'll be fine," he shared and returned to reading his magazine. Unfortunately his comforting words did little to calm Cass's overwhelming fear. So, Cass again challenged herself to deluge her mind with pleasant thoughts. She smiled thinking about how exciting it was to be moving back down South to a place where the winters rarely included snow plows and salted streets but she couldn't dismiss all that she had learned and grown by working at Jackson and Brooks, a Black-owned firm in Philly. Of course, that move had its own issues. Primarily at the firm, in which the drama was not based on gender, ethnicity, or religious ties like in New Orleans, but still as preposterous. The issues were typically related to personality differences, personal choices, and erroneous gossip. Cass attempted to stay above all of the petty realities and by doing so quickly excelled and became a CFO of the company in the ensuing eight years.

Since she always knew she wanted to return to the black Mecca of the south, she began internet hunting for CFO jobs with larger firms, larger earning potential and premium bonuses. Cass was doing very well for herself, but knew she had not reached her financial potential. She also figured that prospects for an educated black man without too much ego or baggage might be better if the market in Atlanta was similar to that essentially a decade ago. Which raised the next big issue with her move to Philly—her personal life. She perceived that most of the northern men she had encountered tended to be particularly arrogant and well aware of the dismal statistics and ratios between men and women. Unfortunately Zachary, her current and transitional beau, had fallen prey to this knowledge and sometimes used it to his advantage. She usually always forgave him after much kissing up on his part because she was whipped and she subconsciously was thinking he quite possibly was salvageable compared to some of the guys she had dated while there. Plus they had invested far too much time, almost her entire tenure in Philly, to contemplate starting from scratch again in the same tired old city with the same tired old faces. But when the position with Hayes and Laden was posted on the web, she knew it might be a prime opportunity for her and she was determined to at least try to get on with the Fortune 500 company based in Atlanta. Now, she slyly smiled, here she was headed back to Atlanta with a $20,000.00 signing bonus, on top of a hefty six figure salary, and surrounded by new faces and new attitudes. The latter of which she hoped was accompanied by eligible black men.

Cass's thoughts were cruelly interrupted again as the plane began to increase its speed during takeoff. Cass peered out of her window briefly and felt herself becoming nauseated. To avoid actually throwing up she immediately shut her eyes and began holding her armrests tightly while quickly saying another prayer. She shook her head as she thought of how lately her relaxation in New Orleans had always been ruined by her family's inevitable broaching of the topic of her incessant singlehood at the ripe old age of thirty-four, quickly approaching thirty-five. She slyly glanced at the hand of her neighbor who had a band on his left fourth finger. Cass slightly envious queried,

"So, how long have you been married?"

"Almost three years."

"Was it love at first sight?"

"Hardly. We actually had no interest in one another at first, but after meeting up with each other by coincidence so many times, we figured we obviously had similar interests and things took off from there. Are you married?"

Cass stuck out her left hand and jokingly added, "Nope. You know I'm a career woman, and most of you brothers don't have the time of day for me."

"Don't be so quick to judge. My wife is very much career-oriented and that is one thing that I admire about her. Maybe you should look at what sort of messages you are sending out to these men."

"And what do you mean by that?" she promptly transformed into her defensive mode.

"See, that might be what I mean. I know what type of woman you are simply based on your response. Can I be frank?" he questioned while looking over the top of his bifocal glasses.

"Sure."

"I envision you as one of those career-oriented women who seldom sways. You rarely give in even if you know you are wrong. You don't show a sensitive side, which we brothers sometimes need to be able to stroke, much like my first wife."

Cass began to laugh as his comments now had less credibility since he had failed at marriage once already. "Well, maybe that somewhat describes me, but what's wrong with being a strong black woman?"

"Nothing at all, as long as you don't distort the meaning."

"What is your definition of a strong black woman?" Cass challenged.

"Well. A woman proud of her heritage. A woman who can make it all alone, but acknowledges that she needs a strong black man by her side. A woman who is going to stroke her man's ego even when it might sometimes bruise her own self esteem."

Cassandra held her hands in the air like a "T", "Time-out! You black men always have to have your ego stroked. I am not going to compromise my beliefs because you feel insecure."

"And that my dear," he conjectured, "is why you are still single."

"Touche'. And if what you say is true, I will probably be single for a long time to come," she woefully admitted while scanning his face. He was not a bad looking guy. He looked about forty-five. He had a mild receding hairline somewhat accentuated by the fact that he had no hair on his face. He looked like a typical Creole New Orleans guy, who in the winter could pass for white, but in the summer time his ass was definitely a brother. Yellow, but a brother nevertheless.

"Let me buy you a drink," he offered as the flight attendant approached them. At first Cass wanted to again establish her self-sufficiency but then resigned, "Sure."
He laughed as he recognized the uncertainty on her face. "I tell you what. If we get another round before we land, you can pay."

Cass quietly sat in her seat pondering her current life perspective that her family seemed to think was so terribly dismal. Forget the fact that she was about to begin her job as CFO at one of the largest and most prominent firms in Atlanta. That very weekend her sister Casey, seven years her junior, joked that she would end up like their Aunt Edna. Aunt Edna was almost sixty years old, approaching four hundred pounds, single and never married. She always wore excessive make-up and hit on any male that had the misfortune of making her acquaintance. Rumor had it that in recent years gender had also become irrelevant to Aunt Edna. Cass shook her head as she had to admit that the thought of being anything similar to Aunt Edna surpassed depressing. She began to laugh and was jolted alert by turbulence and inadvertently grabbed her neighbor's hand.

He smiled and replied, "See that's all we want, a little bit of sensitivity sometimes. Make us feel like we are needed."

While his hand was somewhat comforting, her ego did not allow it to stay there. "Yeah right." Cass certainly knew that she had no problems getting a man. She just had problems attracting a quality man. She had experienced alot of flings and sexcapades in the past, but that was all they ended up being. The few times in which chemistry seemed to abound, Cass somehow just wasn't ready for commitment or she discovered that the guy had evolved into a lust driven dog. She did love her current S.O., Zachary, but was unsure as to whether their past was too warped to build a future upon. She laid her head back on her seat as they prepared for landing, truly wishing that Zachary were there to hold her hand. See, she thought to herself, I am not totally without feelings.

As the plane finally reached its gate, Cass extended her hand. "Nice meeting you, uhhh...."

"William. William Morgan and you too..."

"Cassandra," as they exchanged business cards.

"Cassandra," while quickly perusing her card, "well, I may call you if I need to get my portfolio in order. Good luck," he smiled.

As they stepped off the plane she did a double-take as she saw William embrace and kiss an Asian woman who looked to be about ten years younger than him. How could he claim to know so much shit about a strong black woman when his ass was married to an Asian woman? And she had heard multiple stories about extremely submissive Asian women, but Cass didn't want to fall prey to stereotyping. She did figure though that his previous wife was probably a sister who wasn't putting up with his shit. Nevertheless, Cass still felt somewhat jealous as she rolled her luggage to her car alone. No one was there to greet her, but she surmised that would be changing since she had finally made it back to Hotlanta. She hoped it would turn out to be the Mecca of available and accomplished African-American men, like she had heard. When she was there twelve years ago at Emory business school, her mind was too preoccupied to really care much about the dating scene, aside from the occasional mentally sustaining screw. Now, she was in a totally different place, physically and mentally. Now she had ample money, could make the time, and had pretty much gotten her body into shape. With that she hopped into her car and headed to her condo in Buckhead, feeling self-assured and reassured that Hotlanta was going to be the place where her life changed. It would be the place where she would meet a legitimate man who knew how to treat and sweet a strong black woman.

Cass could not believe that she had not taken at least one day off to recuperate before her first day of work, as she let herself into her new home. It was already eleven o'clock and she definitely needed to start her first day out fresh and on time. Therefore, she decided she would take a shower in the morning because her bed was mercilessly beckoning her. She scampered around her hollow home trying to figure out which box contained her night clothes. She had emptied most of her essential boxes, but somehow the pajama box did not make it on that list. She figured she would sleep in the buff, which was how she usually liked to sleep anyhow but only when she had someone to share her bed. She then smiled as she climbed into bed and thought of the fact that Zachary would be present for the rest of the week for her to snuggle up to. No sooner than she lay her head on the pillow was she fast asleep, both eager and anxious about her day and her life ahead, respectively.

When the phone rang, Cass jolted awake and brashly grabbed the receiver, "Hello." She willed it not to already be morning, but she knew if it were her mom's voice on the other end of the receiver, it was definitely that time. Mom always called on the morning of any new job reverberating all the things she needed to do like eat a hearty breakfast and make sure her clothes were ironed. In almost a robotic manner she always responded the same, "yes mother", barely recalling what her mother had said just a few seconds prior.

"Good Morning," her mom sang out much too alert to be an hour earlier geographically. Cass uncrossed her fingers and said to herself, "Shit," resigned to the reality that her time was indeed up.

"Good Morning? What time is it, mom?"

"It is 4:27 AM my time, so that makes it 5:27 there. Shouldn't you be awake for your big day?"

"Well my alarm was set to go off at five-thirty, so I guess so."

"Well don't forget to eat a good breakfast for the brain and soul, and say your morning prayer. In fact, in that prayer book I sent to you there is a prayer specifically for the first day at a new job. You should find it and pray to Him. You know you have been very blessed."

"Yes, mom, I know. Wish me luck. I have to go or I will be late." Cass interrupted while quickly turning to shut off the annoying blare of her alarm clock.

"Okay, well call me this evening and let me know how things go. Did you prepare your clothes last night for today?"

"Yes mom. I will call you. Love you. Good-bye." Cassandra barely found the button to turn off the cordless phone and slowly pulled her pillow over her head shaking it as she wondered if someday she would become the epitome of her mother.

After her mother's well wishes for her first day, she lay there staring at the mirrored ceiling of her high rise condominium, wondering why its previous owner had chosen to add this interesting accent. She laughed out loud as she imagined the robust fiftyish woman engaged in something kinky. Startled by the effects of her voice on the empty spaces in her condo, she scampered to her feet to prepare for the day ahead. She knew that she needed to be sassy yet conservative, which was why she had planned to wear the blue suit with its long blazer that met the hemline of her mid thigh skirt. She was so excited that she could once again fit this suit, remembering that only six months prior, squeezing into it would have been a joke. Now the suit had some slack and she could afford to gain a few inches to fill out the size eight outfit. She remembered how one year ago she had no discipline, ate everything she desired and the word exercise was foreign terminology. She thought nothing of it until she heard someone describe her as pleasantly plump. It was then while working in Philly that she met Melanie, the sister who started a group called "Sisters in Shape." Melanie was a fine sister, a fact to which both genders could attest. A woman with a body so tight that you had to let all the jealousy and envy go and blatantly ask this sister, "How can I be like you?" That was exactly what Cassandra did and shortly after, Melanie began working with her and began to mold her conscience and empower Cass with the gifts she had perfected. Exercise became a household name and fried and fast foods became a remnant of the past, except on rare and special occasions.

Cassandra admired her body in the mirror as she jumped into the shower. Growing up, she was a flat-chested and lanky child who wore glasses that hid her penetrating dark brown eyes. During her evolution into adulthood her thin legs filled out and fit perfectly on her five foot six frame and she finally had some cleavage, now wearing a true C cup bra without padding. Glasses were also a thing of the past. With the invention of contacts, for which Cassandra was particularly grateful, she only was forced to sport her coke bottle glasses at night in the company of herself. The only thing left compromising her total contentment was having someone to share it with. Someone around when she needed to laugh, needed to vent, or wanted to fuck. She laughed at her callous and selfish sentiment as she sashayed out of the shower. Deep down inside she had hidden the sporadic feeling of desperation and powerlessness she had been nursing since she had turned thirty as a single woman. Now, she was finding it harder and harder to hide the blatant reality that she might grow old alone. She again looked in the mirror and said, "Grandma, God rest your soul, I love you with all my heart but I have no plans of perpetuating your burden. You carried it enough for us all." She hadn't said those words in a long time but felt some validation in claiming them aloud.

She then abruptly turned to get dressed and prepared for the new first day phoniness that she was to experience. The phony hugs, pompous hand shakes, and the high pitched "HI's" had become common place in corporate America, and Cassandra had mastered it well as evidenced by the other women who ultimately began to despise her. "Shit!" Catching a glimpse of the clock on the kitchen wall, she realized her time was limited and gulped down a warm cup of coffee. She then began to carefully apply her make up. She liked wearing earth tone colors that seemed to accentuate her caramel complexion. She slowly lined her lips as she puckered them in the mirror realizing that this simple action actually made her thin lips appear fuller. As the phone rang she swept her hair into a simple bun, slipped on her blue broad-based pumps and reached for the phone without skipping a beat. On the other end she heard a sexy low-pitched voice say "Knock em dead, Sweetheart."

"Thanks sugar, I'll be at the airport on time. I promise." Mistakenly slamming the phone onto its cradle, Cassandra hurried out of the door ready to impress her new colleagues.

As Cassandra drove into downtown Atlanta, she could feel the butterflies begin to consume her stomach. She was glad she didn't live too far from the office in light of the fact that the traffic was moving at a snail's pace-- a fact which she had not calculated into her time schedule. The slow drive allowed Cassandra time to allay the nervous jitters, quickly replaced by anger and adrenaline as she blew her horn, pointed her middle finger and yelled, "Asshole," at the redneck in the semi truck boldly displaying the Confederate flag. He barely missed her front bumper while trying to squeeze into her lane despite her attempts to prevent it. She continued listening to the upbeat gospel on her radio and laughed at the irony of the words she was singing and the gestures she was exhibiting. She was excited and well aware that both New Orleans and Philly had their place in her life and both played a huge role in her transition into the financial guru she had become, but she was certainly glad to be back in Hotlanta.

"Finally!" she exclaimed pulling into her designated parking space barely two minutes early. When she exited her car she lengthened her stride and held her head tilted at an ever so slight angle. She had to abbreviate her usual smooth style as the cold wind readily slapped her face, but her motions remained strong and effective. This exaggerated gait was her way of controlling nervous jitters. Outsiders typically perceived her as either cocky or confident, usually depending on the gender of the observer. She was actually a lot of both traits, her nervousness only surfaced because of the unfamiliar. Not knowing who to trust and who had your back. These were essential factors that she tried to delineate very early on. She finally reached the building and was temporarily embraced by its warmth. This warmth was quickly transformed to the typical callous nadir of the corporate world as her palms began to lightly perspire. She caught the elevator to the twenty-third floor and was immediately greeted by Ted Randall.

"Good morning. Welcome aboard!" he nearly shouted. Clad in slightly too tight pin striped pants accented with burgundy penny loafers, Ted lightly embraced Cass and patted her on the back, which she hated. Ted was a scrawny white man who had worked his way through the hierarchy of the company. He only sported a B.A. on his wall of merit, but held one of the top office posts due to determination and a huge knowledge base. It also didn't hurt that he had been with the company since its inception twenty years earlier. As he opened the massive glass doors lined in gold accents bearing the company name and logo, he pulled Cass in to introduce her to her colleagues.

She first met Cindy the blond receptionist, who preferred to be called the office manager. Cindy jumped to attention as she and Ted walked in. "Ms., Nicholas, hi. Would you care for a cup of coffee?"

"No thank you," Cass answered wondering who she was sleeping with at the office. The skirt friendgirl had on was much too short and her energy overwhelming. Cass knew she would be keeping her distance from her. Ted then successively introduced her to the other four upper level men at the Buckhead branch office, three of whom seemed quite down to earth considering. The fourth man, Blake Reed, who happened to be the only brother, was another story. He was particularly uptight and arrogant. He had impressive credentials, having graduated from Harvard undergrad and subsequently Harvard Law, but he lacked significantly in the personality department. As Cass was introduced he blandly said hello barely looking up from his paperwork. He didn't even stand up to shake her hand. Blake was not an ugly man and he had a domineering presence, made more pronounced by his mingled gray hair and his similarly colored well-groomed beard. Cassandra could not help but notice the picture of his family that was proudly displayed on his desk. Cass thought, "Oh no he didn't," and then more insightfully corrected that thought to, "It figures," as she looked in disgust at the picture featuring him flashing an Uncle Tom smile hugging his blond wife and two sandy haired sons. Cass knew that this would not be one of those situations in which there would be a special camaraderie between the only two African Americans within a branch of the company. She was used to that attitude and woefully had to dismiss the feeling of discord that seemed to be unfortunately affecting many brothers and sisters who supposedly had "made it".

Finally, she met the two other women of the firm, Sharon Douglas and Linda Culpepper. "Oh, no," she thought, "here come the phony Hi's". As if on cue, Sharon exclaimed, "Hi!" in a high pitched voice along with a half hearted, soft-touching, hand shake with a pat on the back.

"Hi," Cass screamed back.

"Nice to meet you."

Sharon was an assistant broker who had been with the company for nine years. She was a large woman who exuded uncertainty in every word she uttered. She appeared unkempt, but wore very fashionable clothes. She just needed the clothes maybe one size larger. The gossip Cass had learned during her extensive interviews was that she was a divorced mother of two who had been bitter ever since it was finalized. She seemed pleasant enough to Cass, and despite her reputation, Cass figured she possibly could be quite resourceful. Linda, on the other hand, was quite the opposite of Sharon. She was exceptionally tall for a woman, sporting a stylish easy to manage short do. Her make-up was perfect and her fingernails were well manicured, Cass noticed as she extended her hand to meet hers. "Hello," she said in a curt manner, "Nice to meet your acquaintance." Cass responded similarly, "Likewise," as she forced a fake smile. Cass knew they would get along fine as long as they allotted one another their space.

The day went by fast as Cass tried to organize things in her new plush corner office with a beautiful view of the skyline of downtown Atlanta. Sitting in her swivel leather chair and childishly spinning it 360 degrees, she thought about how far she had come from being reared in indigence in the lower ninth ward of New Orleans. She was now a corporate financial officer. A fucking CFO at a top brokerage firm, she arrogantly smiled. Her eyes softened as she thought of her mother, who played such an integral role in her successes. As she began to dial her mother's number, John one of the other officers rapped on her door. Hanging up the phone, she prompted him to come in.

"Hey, some of us guys are headed out to get some brewskys. Why don't you join us?" Cass laughed out loud and thought this should be interesting.

Reluctantly, Cass feigned excitement and said, "Sure, why not. Just let me get my coat." Turning to grab her coat, she promised herself she would call her mom the next day, remembering she had to pick up Zac from the airport at seven sharp. She smiled as she envisioned his arms hugging her tightly and his lips gently caressing hers. She reemphasized in her mind. Yes. I must be on time as she slyly grinned.

Cassandra was feeling particularly good as she left Copeland's restaurant in Buckhead in route to the airport after sharing a few drinks with her new colleagues from the office. She had already decisively proven that she was not just one of the gals as she agreed to accompany the group of four guys. She already had probably succeeded in placing a wedge between herself and the other two women at the firm, which was exactly how she wanted it. She had learned years earlier that she did not get along well with women which is why she only maintained a friendship with one girlfriend from grammar school. Although that relationship was sometimes strained, she and Keisha were always there for each other. In fact, it was Keisha who taught Cassandra that a classy woman is more recognized being fashionably late rather than early. Looking at her watch, she realized that she had certainly far exceeded the fashionable part of being late. She really did mean to be at the airport at seven o'clock to pick up Zac, but unfortunately for him she was learning too many insider tips and hot gossip with the guys and figured that Zac could surely wait a bit.

Two

Zachary Bradford Taylor stood at the baggage claim of the Atlanta's Hartsfield International Airport looking immaculate in black tailored slacks and a white satin shirt peering through his long black wool coat. The shirt's first two buttons were open revealing a bit of the curly hair on his chest and the silver chain that Cass had bought him two years ago. He was becoming irritated as he looked at his Britiling watch and realized that Cass was already forty-five minutes late. She had never been particularly prompt during their on again off again whirlwind relationship, but more recently she seemed not to care. He believed some of her tardiness was passive aggressive behavior as she wanted him to be aware that she had total control of this relationship and that he was lucky that she still dated him after some of the games he had played. He didn't think he had played any games though. He honestly loved Cass and except for a few miscues and bad choices, his record was clean. As he paced the floor anxiously, he saw Cass approaching in her classic style, as if she were fifteen minutes early. He tried to remain angry and focused, but each step she made closer to him was melting away every negative emotion within him and despite how he tried he could not help but reveal those perfectly straight and brilliant teeth. He cussed himself as he always gave in too readily to her charm. He had to shake his head and admit to himself that he was undeniably whipped.

Balancing Acts

Two years earlier Cassandra had become quite insensitive to his feelings after discovering from a mutual friend that Zac was continuing to see his ex-girlfriend while the two of them were supposedly in a monogamous relationship back in Philly. Cass refused to believe it, however, until she unequivocally witnessed him with her own eyes at a club laughing and embracing this woman in much more than a casual fashion. She looked like a wannabe model with her thin, sleek frame, long wavy hair and no ass. She remembered it all too well. She walked over to him and yelled, "What the hell are you doing here? I thought you were going to be at the office late today?"

"I could ask you the same thing," he taunted back while trying to stand straight and gain his composure.

"And what the hell are you looking at?" Cass questioned with a subtle roll to her neck, looking up at the woman who towered over her.

"Look Susan, this is my woman now," Zac interjected before things could get too heated. Zac reached out to grab Cass who totally rejected his outreached arms. Almost immediately, two drinks adorned his face, showering him from both directions, as both women graciously made their exits leaving him standing alone. Since then they had both dated other people but always ended up back together, sexually if nothing else. Zac was like an addiction to Cass, no matter how unrelentlessly she resisted, he always concocted a way to ingratiate himself back into her world. She hoped that now since she was out of Philly, the addiction would lose some of its power. Cass had to admit that he seemed to be straightening up his act and had been focusing most of his attention on her in recent months and she was enjoying it and milking it for all it was worth. In fact, in the last six months they had essentially been a monogamous pair sharing most of their time away from work together including nights and weekends, a rarity in the past. His broad shoulders, six foot two frame and family jewels helped her to forgive and forget most of his transgressions. Cassandra was not naïve though and was well aware she couldn't change any man and refused to put herself in the same situation which so many of her friends had who claimed, "He's a changed man now that we are

28

married." Now most of them were either in divorce court or dealing with the same old bullshit. That was also one of her reasons for leaving Philly to start anew and leave that tired semi-relationship stuff behind. She did decide though that she would continue to use Zachary at will until she got more settled in Hotlanta, unable to elude the reality that she loved him.

When Cassandra entered the airport she immediately noticed the anger in Zac's eyes as she approached him in her confident yet demure manner. She saw his furrowed brow slowly soften with each step she took toward him, eventually disappearing and being replaced by his radiant smile.

She playfully approached him with her bottom lip poking out and softly snuggled up to him saying, "I'm so sorry, but I'll make it worth your while."

He chuckled with that deep voice of his and said, "I'll expect nothing less." Cass immediately felt the warmth of his hard body gently caress her after coming out of the chilled night. He almost instantly became consumed and soothed by the naturally sweet fragrance which her body seemed to emit and was looking forward to spending at least that night with her. The two of them hugged briefly in silence feeling almost like a trance had overcome them as they both secretly thought of the passionate love making each of their bodies yearned. After all it had been two weeks, which seemed like an eternity since they had been essentially inseparable of late. As they walked hand in hand to her car, she felt that something was different about him. While he was physically there, he appeared to be emotionally distanced. Cass tried to lighten the mood by exclaiming, "Zacky, if you don't lighten up, I'm not gonna give you any of this," as she subtly braised his hand against her groin over her thick wool coat. Zac sheepishly lied, "I'm sorry. Bad day at work today." He feigned a smile, gently but nervously squeezed her hand and added, "I'm sure you're gonna help ease my tensions," as he pensively continued to devise a rational scheme to break the news to her. They walked the remainder of the way to the car in silence, both unsure of what the upcoming week was going to mean for their relationship.

When the airport doors electronically opened the cold of the night abruptly hit them, making their slow loving pace quicken to a hardly cool gallop. As they reached her two-door Lexus, Cassandra by remote control opened the trunk and left him to himself as she slid into the driver's seat. He joined her shortly thereafter, having secured his luggage in back. He promptly leaned over and gave Cassandra a soft and sensual kiss, which eliminated any ounce of coldness that may have remained in the car. He then slyly proceeded to stroke her nylon clad thigh until he reached the point where her bare thigh greeted his hand. As he felt himself begin to rise, he too abruptly removed his hand and eagerly questioned, "Now how long is it from here to your place?"

Cassandra laughed and responded, "Not long baby" as she sped off trying to calm the tingling sensation that seemed to encompass every nerve in her body. She then quickly changed the subject and exclaimed, "I missed you so much, and I am truly sorry for being so late."

"I missed you too, baby. Just don't do it again," he playfully scorned.

"How was your flight? Did you have any layovers from Philadelphia to here?"

"The flight wasn't bad and you know I never book any flights with layovers. I hate flying as it is."

As she bounced to the music on the radio, partially for warmth and partially because she liked the song with its bass beat resounding through the car, she grabbed his hand and exclaimed, "I am so glad that you are here. You will be such a help with moving my things from storage and removing the cobwebs from my personal suitcase," she laughed. His eyes playfully teased her as he said "I don't know about moving things from storage, but I will be your personal bellboy sugar." She naughtily looked at him smiling and leaned over and smacked him with her lips on his cheek.

They were both glad to have finally arrived at her condominium as the sexual tension in the car was becoming quite overwhelming. As she drove into her space silence abounded as they both were anticipating what was about to happen on the thirtieth floor. She quietly said, as if reading his mind, "Sounds like a plan to me," as they hopped out of the car both with zealous fervor like two kids caught with their hands in the cookie jar.

The next morning as Cassandra lay in bed spooning with Zac, she hated the prospect of leaving his perfectly carved chocolate body in exchange for the imminently cold hard wood floors. As she thought about the night before, she devilishly grinned and was lulled back to sleep as she remembered the intense passion that had ended just a few hours earlier. For the second day in a row, Cassandra was jarred awake by the high shrill of her phone ringing. "Damn," she thought as she rolled away from Zac picking up the phone hissing into the receiver, "Yes!"

"Hey girlfriend. Did I wake you?" Normally Cassandra would say, "No, not at all," but this was Keisha her only girlfriend who she never faked the funk with. She exclaimed, "Hell yeah, what do you want?"

"Well, if you would listen to your voice mail and return people's calls on occasion, people would not have to call the only time they knew you would be home. Listen, though, can you help a sister out?"

"Is something wrong?" Cassandra responded in a worried older sister type of tone.

"No, no…not at all. I just have a favor to ask you. Do you remember my cousin, Rachel?"

"Vaguely. Isn't she the prissy little thing who was dropped by that NBA basketball player?"

"Yep, that's her. Well, she's having a big bash out here two weeks from now at one of the clubs somewhere on Peachtree street and I wanted you to promise you'd mark your calendar to come with me."

"You usually can hold your own at any social gathering, what's so special about this one?" Before Keisha could respond, Cassandra said, "I tell you what, I will check my calendar and get back to you."

"I need an answer by the end of this week. Why are you so damn cranky anyway? Wait a minute. Fine man Zac comes into town this week doesn't he? Is he laying there next to you?" she questioned. As the phone remained silent, she knew the answer was yes. "Well, you go girl! But tell him I said he must not be doing something right, because your ass should be belting out soft melodies and being particularly pleasant after a good orgasm."

Cassandra quietly laughed and said, "Bye girl. I will get back to you at the end of the week. And for your information, there were two wonderful orgasms and I am pissed because I have to leave this fine brother to grace the office with my presence. Bye woman." Without waiting for a response, Cassandra turned and hung up the phone.

As she briefly snuggled back up to Zac, she vehemently tried to concoct some feasible reason to miss work after having started only one day before. Cassandra then caught a glimpse of Zac's gorgeous body in the mirrors up above. He was lying on his side with one half of his body engulfed by the red satin sheets and the rest of his thin muscular frame totally exposed as if to tease her and command her to call in sick today. She almost truly had to call in sick because those satin sheets nearly caused her a concussion as she slid into her brass headboard during their sexual escapade. Softly snickering while rubbing the still sore top of her head, she made a mental note to get some cotton sheets to alleviate the slippery inconvenience of her current set. Cass anticipated much more love making occurring underneath her mirrored ceiling. Shaking herself back to reality, she totally dismissed the idea of calling in sick. After all, she did have him for the entire week. Cassandra slowly slid her unclad body from under Zac's heavy arm which encircled her waist and quietly laughed as his body jumped but then eased back into its restful state of sleep like a baby in its mother's arms. She quickly placed on her terry cloth robe to help decrease the chill that encompassed her body and headed towards the bathroom, but not before a brief detour to the kitchen to start the much needed coffee percolating.

Staring at herself in the bathroom mirror she couldn't help but laugh about how last evening she and Zac learned more about the creativity and flexibility of their sexual prowess through the aid of the mirrored ceiling which she once ridiculed. She, without a doubt, decided that the mirrors would remain a part of the décor, at least for now. She had to embarrassingly admit that the mirrors added another dimension to her sense of sexual adventure. After a quick hot shower, haphazardly french twisting her tangled hair, and applying a tad of makeup, Cassandra returned to the kitchen refreshed and eager for a cup of black coffee. To her surprise, Zac was there to greet her in his silk boxers.

"What are you doing up?" she questioned as she looked down towards his groin and realized that her question could imply more than one thing. Without responding, he walked over to her and laid a juicy and unrefined kiss on her lips and replied, " Good morning to you too. Would you like some breakfast?"

Glancing at the clock, Cass negatively nodded and said, "I'm running late, but how about we meet for lunch later this afternoon?" As Zac prepared to respond, Cass escaped to her closet to find an outfit that required no ironing. He raised his voice slightly and stated, "Don't you remember I have that luncheon today at the Lenox Marriot with the National Society of Black Engineers. Unfortunately, this trip is not all pleasure for me."

"That's right," she brooded as she slipped into her gray slacks and black cashmere turtleneck. It bore a few wrinkles but the houndstooth blazer that she added would hide that subtle fashion faux pas. "Well, I guess we won't meet again until this evening. I've got to go," she said as she practically fell while hopping on each foot putting on her black heels. "Here's my office number," which she placed on the small table in the black marbled foyer, "and the key to get in will be at the front desk for whoever returns first. Smooches!" she hollered as the door slammed behind her, muffling whatever Zac was saying. She figured if it were important, he would call her at the office.

On her way to work, Cassandra recalled the early morning conversation with Keisha. She wondered what that was all about. She knew that her schedule was open but took a passive role because usually when Keisha needed accompaniment to a social function it was with a man. However, this could mean that this function was going to be filled with eligible bachelors. Cassandra had much unpacking to do since she had only relocated to Atlanta the prior week, but figured it should not prevent her from being on the social scene in two weeks. She then consciously decided that she would go to this birthday bash, because she had a feeling that this might be the night that she met some perspective husbandkind. Cass briefly focused on Zachary as possibly being that man as she wondered what was going on with his aloof behavior. While their making love certainly seemed to loosen things up a bit, there was still something hidden which she could not quite grasp. She laughed as she thought, just like a typical nigga, now that my ass is gone from Philly he realizes how much I really mean to him. She whispered out loud, "This could be a deep week," she thought while anxiously tapping her fingers on her dashboard wondering what she would do if he wanted to move things to a more officially monogamous level.

When Cassandra saw Zachary Taylor at the twelfth street gym in Philly while working out with her personal trainer, she believed that he certainly met the physical criteria of the man of her dreams. He was pumping iron and she was on the treadmill getting her cardiovascular portion of her work out completed. Her trainer, Melanie, saw her glimpsing in his direction and silently smiled, "His name is Zachary. That's all I know." Cassandra laughed as she tried to get a look at his left hand while he continued to bench press. She saw no ring, and more importantly no tan line. Having become more aggressive in her late twenties, she decided that she would definitely speak to the brother before she left the gym that evening, after freshening up a bit.

She conveniently bumped into him at the water faucet and in her shy soft voice stated, "I'm sorry, how can I make it up to you?" He already had passed the first test by keeping his eyes on her eyes as they conversed. He kindly replied in his low sexy voice, "Don't worry about it. It's cool." And promptly walked away. Cassandra was pissed but challenged.

It was on the next visit to the twelfth street Gym that she was more direct and said, " I find you attractive and if you are not otherwise attached, I would like to buy you a drink some time."

In a boyish grin he smirked and said, "Sure. I was gonna ask you the same thing, but you beat me to the punch." Their relationship took off from there. They seemed to have so much in common. It was then that she learned that he was a homeboy of sorts. His grandmother lived in New Orleans, and he had obtained a degree in chemical engineering from Tulane University. He was thirty-three and did not profess being attached to anyone. Over the ensuing year she learned of one of his ex-girlfriends, Susan, who had a hard time dealing with their break up and basically refused to acknowledge that their relationship was over. Unfortunately, some time during their courtship, Zachary also conveniently forgot that they were officially apart and had a few lapses back into her arms. They parted for almost a year after Cass learned of his reckless indiscretions, but then initially reunited casually. Once things appeared more settled, they essentially resumed the role of monogamy, but since then, Cass felt like she could never truly trust him and had X-ed him off of her list of potential significant other. She did love him however, and wondered if spending the week together might change her perspective of him and their relationship.

The work day passed by quickly which pleased Cassandra, as she was eager to just chill with Zac and be his concubine for the night. On her arrival at her condo, she was surprised to find that the key was still at the concierge desk. She decided to initiate the fixings for a romantic evening for the two of them. She quickly hopped in the shower after putting the best of the Isley Brothers into her CD player. She put on the skimpy black teddy and garter belt that he had bought for her the prior year when they both had gotten heavy into sexual role playing together. She laughed as she thought of their police officer and slut routine. After lotioning her body with a sweet fragrance she began lighting candles throughout the condo. She already had chilled some wine and sprayed a peach linen fragrance on the durable cotton sheets. She figured that Zac would arrive while she was in the mist of preparing the place, but now she was just sitting twiddling her thumbs waiting for him. It was now ten o'clock and she was pissed. Why hadn't he called, she thought. She stormed around her condo blowing out the candles and settled onto her bed. She fell asleep seething to the song *Making Love Between the Sheets*, and was startled awake at one o'clock in the morning by the phone. She answered in a stale voice, "Hello." It was Zachary speaking in a barely audible whisper, "I'm so sorry. Let's meet for lunch tomorrow so I can explain everything to you. Again, Cass, I'm so sorry and we'll talk tomorrow to confirm plans." Before she could sit up good and roll her neck to start cursing him out, the phone was silent. Through the mist of tears, Cass saw herself in the mirror above and thought, "I deserve more than this shit." She would meet him for lunch the next day but anything short of telling her his mother died was going to unmask the gangsta mentality that she was forced to learn to survive in the ninth ward of N'awlins'.

Cassandra tossed and turned all night as she contemplated how she was going to respond to whatever he said. She had thought of so many scenarios that she felt like she was totally prepared for anything that could make its way out of his mouth. In every scenario her first sentence was, "Look you punk ass nigga, I don't have to take this shit from you or anyone." Those same words reverberated in her head until she was finally awakened by her alarm clock. Cass rushed off to work with her cell phone in tow as she anxiously awaited confirmation of her lunch with Zachary. Finally a foreign number appeared on her phone and she promptly answered.

"Hey Cass, it's me Zachary. Do you think we'd be able to meet at the Houston's across from the Marriott where my conference is at about twelve-thirty?"

Without trying to assume anything and to control her temper Cass simply responded, "Twelve-thirty, I'll be there."

Time seemed to be moving particularly slowly after Zachary's call at nine-thirty. Cass could barely focus on her work as she anxiously waited for noon to approach. She forced herself to complete some minute tasks, all the while fighting off flashbacks of some of she and Zac's past insolent encounters. "Finally twelve o'clock," she counted aloud as the second hand barely grazed the twelve on her watch. Cass grabbed her purse and headed out of her office filled with mixed emotions. She drove to the restaurant listening to some harsh rap music that was consistently degrading women which only served to heighten her anger which she figured she could probably put to use today as she drove into the parking lot.

Cass walked into Houston's and after not initially spotting Zachary questioned the hostess who pointed him out sitting in a secluded corner booth. As she approached the table she couldn't help but behold how incredibly handsome he looked with his deep blue mock turtle neck hugging his pecks, his totally smooth black skin, and every hair of his small afro neatly in place. A tiny part of her wanted to forget about the previous night, but she knew that she would never be able to just leave the issue alone and that he deserved his day in her court no matter what the repercussions. As she approached the table, he anxiously hopped up and gestured for her to have a seat. Cassandra's heart began beating faster as she felt deep inside that today might mark the end of their relationship. She instantly detected the tension masking his usually affable facial features and recognized that he did not even attempt to hug her or kiss her. She would have rejected him anyway, but she still resented the lack of effort.

"Would you like something to drink?" he questioned while nervously rubbing his hands.

"Zachary, let's cut the small talk and get to the reason why you stood me up last night."

"Well," he continued while slightly squirming in his seat, "you're not gonna like what I have to say Cass, but let me preface it by saying you know I love you and always have."

Cassandra interrupted as she felt her nerves taking over and proceeded to sit on her hands, "Just tell me Zachary. Cut the bullshit."

"You remember my ex-girlfriend Susan?"

"How could I not? What about her?"

"She's my wife."

Cassandra not totally comprehending what was just told to

her replied, "Come again?"

"Susan and I got married a little over a year ago."

Cassandra could feel her leg nervously bouncing under the table, "Married," she stuttered. "A fucking year ago?" Confused she asked, "What about the past six months when we were literally together all the time?" She could feel the tears beginning to form in her eyes.

"We separated six months into the marriage because Susan knew I was still seeing you when she informed me that she was pregnant with our twins. Then she basically gave me an ultimatum. I needed to make up my mind and figure out if I wanted you or my family."

"Pregnant," Cassandra clenched her teeth tightly as she struggled to maintain her composure.

Zachary tried to grab her hands and continued, "I am so sorry Cassandra. I know I should have told you a long time ago, but I loved you too much and I needed you in my life. I dragged this out as long as I could because I knew the time was rapidly approaching that I would have to say goodbye. My sons were born three months ago and I knew that it was well past time for me to make my decision."

Jerking her hands abruptly away from him she tried to refrain from screaming. "You sorry ass mother fucker," totally forgetting about her rehearsed speech.

"Cass, you know I grew up in a single parent home and I vowed not to have my kids suffer the same fate. So, I'm gonna try my damndest to be a good husband and father."

"Why now? Why did you come to my house and fuck me last night when you knew that you were going to become the fucking dutiful husband and the fucking father of the year."

"Make love, Cass. We made love. It was not supposed to happen that way but it did. I figured I would use your move here to Atlanta as the perfect time to tell you, especially since you were basically leaving me anyway. We both knew that we were at the end of us. You know we would not have survived a long distance relationship. Hell, we could barely keep it together in the same city. I just felt like I needed to feel your body next to mine one more time and maybe," he bargained, "we still could make something work out down the line once things get more settled at home."

Before he could finish Cass took the glass of ice water sitting before her and threw it in his face. "How could you do this to me?" she yelled as she stood to leave.

He stood and tried to embrace her to temper some of her anger and repeatedly stated, "I do love you Cass. I love you."

She escaped his grasp and slapped him with every ounce of energy that had surged within her. "Stay out of my life. Don't you ever, I mean ever, call me again," she tactlessly yelled and immediately turned walking at a pace akin to a jog.

Cass had no earthly idea how she was going to camouflage her distress at work for the remainder of the afternoon as she quickly hopped into her car without even acknowledging the valet attendant who stood before her. She began quickly wiping the tears which had finally escaped from her eyes while trying to make sense of what had just transpired. She began screaming out loud, "I cannot believe he pulled this type of bullshit on me. He used my black ass. He had the nerve to fuck me last night and for the past fucking year when he knew he was married. Oh hell no! Cassandra don't play this type of shit." She began fervently dialing his number fully intending to curse him out again but was greeted by his voice mail. Wanting his ears to actively hear her wrath, she promptly hung up the phone as she pulled into the garage at her office. "Okay, Cassandra. Pull it together girl. He was no good for you anyway," she silently repeated to herself. She looked at her swelled eyes in her rearview mirror and wiped the remaining black mascara from beneath them. She tried to reach Keisha for some venting and validation but was unsuccessful. She, in that short drive, decided that she was going to start having fun and forget about searching for a soul mate. If it happened— fine and if not— whatever. "Maybe I will grow old alone," she thought and then Sallie Nicholas popped into her head making her shudder to think of the very concept. "Maybe single, but not alone," she corrected. She then slammed her car door and headed to her office while trying to rationalize that her plight was miniscule compared to some others. She knew she was blessed and as she walked into her building Cass repetitively affirmed her faith that God had a plan for her and she was going to be patient and let Him guide her. While she entrusted in her faith, her pride had taken a nosedive and she was going to have to rigorously work to rebuild it. She figured one good way to start would be in spending some of that $20,000 bonus, at least the minute portion that she had not obsessively invested already.

Zachary gently rubbed his sore, red cheek. He sat in Houston's feeling totally dejected after Cassandra's abrupt departure. He purposely did not answer the phone vibrating on his hip because he knew without even looking at the displayed number that it was Cass. He had asked for the booth in the corner to minimize the scrutiny but was totally caught off guard when she hauled off and slapped him. He believed that he had done the manly thing by placing a priority on his family. He also figured she should be happy that he didn't tell her all of this over the phone, like so many dudes behave to avoid such spectacles of rage. He truly felt that he did the honorable thing by giving her the respect of telling her face to face. Now that night was not supposed to happen. He had no intentions of making love, but she was looking so fine he could not force himself not to hit that at least one more time. He silently smiled which almost instantaneously converted to a frown because deep down he knew Cassandra deserved more than that. She was not just a fling thing, she had been his girl for years and he respected their relationship for most of its tenure. As he continued to rub his cheek, surprised by the sting which still lingered there, he predicted that all of this would blow over in time. He would send her some flowers and by the time things got settled at home with him and the kids, maybe things could pick up where they left off. He sat there reminiscing for a moment while awaiting the return of his credit card. When the waitress finally returned he gulped down the swig that remained in his rum and Coke, slowly stood and headed back to his afternoon conference. He picked up his cell phone and called his hotel room, "Hello," Susan answered barely audible over the baby's cry.

"Hey baby. I'm just calling you on my break. We had a lunch conference and that's why I couldn't make it there for lunch. Can't wait to play with my boys since they were sound asleep when you guys got in last night. Are they okay?" he asked as the crying persisted in the background.

"Yes. They're fine. The question is, did you handle your business?"

"Of course I did. I told you I would. I'm ready to finally do right by you and the kids. Cass and I are officially over."

"That shit is long overdue. You still never told me why you didn't answer my calls the night you arrived."

"Baby," he lied, "I told you after Cass and I met and I told her that we were over, I met up with my boy Derrick. We had a few drinks and I just came to the room and crashed."

"Okay Zac. But you know I am not tolerating your games. I will leave your ass and take my sons with me."

"Susan, I told you. I love you and I am not going to hurt you again. Now let's leave that bullshit alone. I have to go to my conference. See you later." Zachary angrily hung up the phone and wondered if he was truly capable of monogamy. He instinctively knew he was not yet ready as he already had begun formulating plans in his mind of how to cajole Cass back into his life. With that, he called the florists to start putting his thoughts into action.

Three

etting through work that evening and the next day was a chore for Cassandra especially since she was unable to vent with Keisha who was nowhere to be found during her time of need. She hadn't slept well the previous night and was eager for the day to come and go. Cassandra who usually never wore her feelings on her shoulders, must have subconsciously revealed that something was wrong, as evidenced by her colleagues silly attempts to make her laugh. Nothing worked, however. Cassandra felt that she deserved to be an ass today. After all, in a few quick seconds, she realized that she was truly the lowly and forgettable mistress. As she shook her head in disgust her secretary rang in, "Line one is for you."

"Would you please take a message?" Cassandra said in an irritated tone. She busied herself for the remainder of the day, taking two hours to complete a task that would usually require only twenty minutes. As she prepared to leave the office almost having forgotten the events of the day before, she saw that Ms. Charlotte, her secretary, had placed her messages on her clipboard. There were three messages from Zac and one from her sister Stephanie. As her eyes welled, Cassandra threw the messages in the trash and thought to herself, "Why me?" She then quickly walked to her car and headed to her empty Condo all the while wondering if Zac had ever really loved her. She figured that the way he treated her must have been an indication that he never loved her and the mere thought affected her deeply. It seemed to penetrate her very core literally and figuratively. She had been having major cramps and diarrhea for the past two days since Zachary had shared his secret life. But she was done with her crying and self-pity. She was going to convert all that negative energy to something positive. Exercise. While she usually ran on her treadmill nightly for an hour, she knew that she would be running on it much longer that night to help release all of her unsolicited anger and futility.

The drive home seemed longer than usual. Probably partially due to the fact that she drove home in total silence, which only gave her more time to ponder the meaning of life. She tended to be so dramatic. She reached for her car phone to call Keisha again. After ringing three times, Keisha's voice came over the phone in the form of a message with the mellow music of Sade softly playing in the background. She hung up without saying a word. Since Keisha had all the modern phone amenities, such as caller ID, Cass figured such a gesture would be unnecessary. She finally arrived home and was met by Jessie, a handsome white guy who had been eyeing her since she moved in. As she stepped into the elevator he asked, "What floor?" She said nothing and simply pressed thirty. As the elevator smoothly moved up, Cass was hoping that was the extent of his verbalizing.

He then boldly queried, "Do you have plans for this weekend, because…" Cass rudely interrupted and said, "I don't do white, so please save your breath." Fortunately, he lived on the fifteenth floor, because a longer ride in the elevator would have been rather awkward. He gave her an evil look but to Cass's surprise said nothing more. He simply stepped off at his floor. As the doors closed behind him, Cass released a sigh of relief and felt no guilt for the way she berated him. She had tried white a long time ago and realized that their backgrounds were too different. Simple concepts like affirmative action, ebonics, and being "African American" instead of "Black" plagued their union from its inception. She was tired of feeling like she had to watch what she said and how she said it. And while the sex was pretty good she always felt like she was betraying the brothers by sleeping with their nemeses. Cass also plainly had a hard time getting beyond the wrinkled pink balls as she laughed for the first time that day while exiting the elevator.

Cass unlocked her Condo door, and subconsciously looked around hoping that the previous two days were a bad dream, and that Zac would be in her kitchen cooking his delicious Cajun Jambalaya. Instead she was met by a cold, dark and empty room. Without taking off her coat she flopped down onto her black and white velvet sofa and placed her hands into her coat pockets like a child who was angry with her parents might do. She felt something roll under her right hand from within the coat pocket. She pulled her hand out and there lay a bedi. She wondered where it had come from because as she recalled she had not worn this particular coat since New Year's Eve and she didn't smoke. Then she remembered the source. That New Year's Eve, she, her sister Stephanie, and Keisha had decided to celebrate the New Year in the Big Apple. While there, they met three brothers from Jamaica who they hung out with for the duration of their three day excursion. Cass was supposed to be hooked up with Edwin, who was a little shorter than she was used to, but kind of cute with long eyelashes, which accentuated his light brown eyes. His sense of humor was what had won her over. She recalled that on the day after New Year's, she and Keisha had decided that they would go out alone with their respective gentlemen callers, Edwin and James. Poor Michael, who was Stephanie's guy the previous evening, was stuck out. Since Stephanie was married, she refused to put herself in a position that she might later regret. She was not going out alone with that suave, fine Jamaican who was ten years her junior. Instead, she went out on fifty-fourth street and did some major shopping to keep her mind off of the excitement she inevitably would be missing.

Cass and Keisha, however, were a lot more carefree and had a totally different frame of mind. They were both single and determined to have a good time. Their philosophy was that of one of the morning shows which they listened to religiously in the mornings in regards to the island of Aruba. "What happens on the island stays on the island." Their island just happened to be New York. Edwin and Cass decided to eat dinner at the renowned small hole in the wall in Harlem called

Sylvia's which was known for its delicious home-style soul food. But the stereotype of the Jamaican being a consummate worker always with some hard earned money on hand obviously was not in effect because girlfriend had to pay for the entire cheap ass meal. This Jamaican brother was "in transition". Cass had no problem paying but it was the fact that she had to pay that irritated her. After dinner, Cass did not want Edwin to think that they were going to spend an entire night on the town at her expense. Now, her only selfish goal was to establish if at least the one other thing she had heard about Jamaican men was factual. She had already disproved the work issue, now she only hoped that his prowess in bed and his penile endowment would justify his true Jamaican descent. Not prepared for any further surprises, she promptly escorted him back to her hotel room instead of his to get better acquainted. He was great at foreplay, knowing exactly what to touch and kiss and did so masterfully. However, when it came to the actual sex, Edwin unfortunately was hardly packing and apparently had problems with that premature ejaculation shit. She endured the almost three minutes for his sake only truly cognizant that things were over when, with his sexy accent he proudly whispered "Was it as good for you girl, as it was for me?" Cassandra abruptly stopped her rigid grinding which was more pronounced because she was putting every effort into trying to feel his presence within her, but to no avail.

Cassandra, now realizing that all of her preconceived notions turned out to be myths, disappointedly responded, "Yeah man. Totally," mocking his only authentic quality.

He then pulled out a bedi, a tobacco leaf rolled with tobacco inside, and smoked it hoping it would at least relax her taunt pelvic muscles. Unfortunately, it only served to accentuate her sexual desires. She, now totally eager for him to leave so she could enforce her self-gratification rules, feigned sleepiness and fortunately he took the hint.

Before he left she inquired, "Edwin why don't you leave me one of those here for later?"

"Only if we can smoke it under the same circumstances

tomorrow."

"That would be great," knowing full well that her train back to Philly was leaving bright and early in the morning.

He placed the bedi in her coat pocket and said, "Later, mon. See you tomorrow," winking as he closed the door.

Cassandra could not think of a better thing to do that evening than smoke the bedi. She needed something to get her out of her awful mood. As she reached for the matches that lay next to the candle that had glimmered so brightly the night before for naught, she remembered that she needed to call Stephanie. She dialed her sister's number, and just when she was about to hang up, a man's breathless voice answered the phone.

"Richard, is this you?"

"Yeah it's me. Cass?"

"Yeah it's me, is Steph around?" she asked flatly.

"Yes, she's getting some groceries out of the car, let me get her for you. Is everything okay?"

"No, but I'll get over it."

"Okay then, hold on," not trying to get in the middle of his sister-in-law's issues which always tended to be a disaster anyway. Fumbling to the phone after what seemed like an eternity, Steph said, "Hey, Cass. What's going on?"

"Well, I was returning your phone call from the office today."

"I was just calling to check on you, since your trifling tail had been here for a week and hadn't called. I don't even have the phone number to your apartment."

"First of all it's a condo, and the number is…"

Stephanie interrupted Cass and said, "I have it now, it's on my caller ID box. And why are you in such a funk?"

"Well, Zac and I broke up," Cass tearfully responded while flashing back to the very nauseating discussion a few days before. After holding it in for what felt like an eternity, she exhaled the first puff of the bedi out of her mouth.

"That sounds like good news to me. Are you smoking?"

"I sure am, doc," she snapped back.

"You mean you have let his ass drive you to that? Pardon my French," Stephanie scorned.

"Calm down, it's just the left over bedi that I had from when we were in New York. This is not a new habit. I just needed to cool down a bit. He pissed me off so bad. Get this, after he fucked me he decides to tell me that he is married with fucking twins."

"You have got to be kidding. Are you okay? How could you not know about that? There must have been some hints or something, Cass. You were just blinded by his damn dick. I told you about getting caught up in the sex and not the substance of the man. This isn't something that just happens overnight. I told you good men like Richard are out there, you just have to go to the right places. Maybe you are just destined to be alone."

"You're no help, good-bye," Cass barked as she hung up the phone. The phone rang three consecutive sequences of five but Cass just let the answering machine pick up. She knew it was just Stephanie calling back to chastise her more. And chastising was not what she needed right then. She didn't need to be made aware of the dismal prospect of her future isolation.

Stephanie had that holier than thou attitude ever since they were growing up. Only three years older than Cass, she always exuded much more maturity and discipline. Stephanie was the one who was high school valedictorian, while Cass was only an average student. Stephanie was the one who received a scholarship to Xavier University in New Orleans and subsequently went to medical school graduating from Johns Hopkins AOA. It took Cass six years to finish undergraduate school but at least still with a decent GPA. Now a successful Ob/Gyn, Stephanie had the American dream with a beautiful home, a successful marriage to her college sweetheart, two kids and a dog. "Isn't that disgusting," Cassandra thought. She loved her sister immensely, but sometimes her success with no apparent failures, had made her arrogant and insensitive. As she finished the bedi, she felt tired and listless, so she pulled off all of her clothes and fell asleep on her sofa until the next morning.

The next two days of work seemed to drag on. Fortunately,

Cassandra's schedule was very busy so she was able to keep her mind off of the dismal aspects of her social life, or rather the lack thereof. She looked forward to the weekend to relax but she also had to get someone to help her move her things from storage. It was almost the end of the month, and she did not want to pay any more money to store her things. As she pondered the thought of who she would snag to help her, there was a knock on her office door. "Come in, "she shouted. As the door opened all she saw was two dozen of her favorite roses coming toward her.

The lanky delivery guy clumsily placed them on her desk and asked, "Are you Ms. Cassandra Nicholas?"

"Yes, I am."

"Well, these are for you."

"Is there a card attached?"

"Why yes there is ma'am," he stuttered as he handed it to her. Cassandra reached for the card and the delivery boy turned to leave. She prompted him to stay for a moment as she quietly read the card. "Missing you so much. I love you. Please forgive me, Zac."

Throwing the card in the trash, she asked the young man, "Do you have a girlfriend?"

His face flushed as he happily exclaimed, "Yes, I do."

"Well, why don't you give her these roses."

"Are you sure?" His face brightened.

"If you don't take them, they'll just go into the trash."

"Thank you so much, ma'am," he said as he picked them up and scurried out of the room. Cass felt good because this was her first step in accepting that Zachary would remain a remnant of her past. Back in the day this simple gesture of roses and a loving card usually might get him back into the door depending on how large the infraction. This time the infraction was insurmountable. His ass was gone for good this time she determined as she slid the one pink petal that had fallen onto her desk into the trash. As she prepared to leave the office, she still wondered what sucker she could get to help her get her things from storage. The only person she could think of who would do so on such short notice, and more importantly not expect anything in return was Robert Cason, a guy who adored her when she was in business school. As she drove home she could not remember whether she still had his number, but she figured if she did, it was worth a try.

Four

*R*obert Cason was preparing to go out for the evening. He was so pleased with himself for sticking with his personal trainer for all of those months. He had a renewed confidence since he had lost fifty pounds and had actually turned his fat into muscle. He was so happy that women were now looking at him and finding him physically attractive. He no longer had to flaunt his lucrative business ventures to get a date. As he sprayed on his Cool Water cologne, he turned to leave. Just as he was pulling the door closed, he heard the phone ringing. At first he opted not to answer it, but then his compulsive nature cajoled him back inside. "Hello," he melodically answered.

"Robert?"

"Yes, this is Robert," he said with his soft tenor voice. "Who may I ask is calling?"

"This is Cassandra."

"Cassandra who?" he said knowing full well that it was Cass Nicholas. He had a major crush on her when they both were completing business school. Back then he had to admit that he was the essence of geek. Fat, with glasses, a receding hairline and fucked up teeth. However, since he last saw Cass three years ago, he had undergone a major metamorphosis. He was at his ideal body weight, had exchanged the glasses for the Lasik surgery, had his braces removed and had shaved his head for the bald look that was considered particularly sexy at the time. They had gone out a few times to lunch and dinner since graduating, but despite his wishes, no romantic chemistry ever existed between them. At least not for her.

"Cassandra Nicholas" she said, beginning to question her decision to call.

"Oh Cass, hey, how are you? Are you in Atlanta for the weekend?"

Yes, fat ass is what she was tempted to say but modified that which she thought and said, "Well, actually I have accepted a job here. Which brings me to my next question."

"Yes," he responded in a curious tone.

"Since I just moved here, I have a lot of things in storage and I thought if you weren't busy this weekend, maybe we could kill two birds with one stone." She was beginning to feel guilty for her blatant ulterior motive, but continued. "You know, we could catch up on old times and move the things from storage at the same time." The phone was silent for a moment and Cassandra crossed her fingers.

"Well this is late notice but I guess I can rearrange my schedule tomorrow. But only on one condition."

Damn, she thought, well he certainly ain't getting none. "What's that?" she sarcastically replied.

"That after all the work is done, you will let me take you to dinner." She figured she could endure him for one day and conceded to his request. She gave him the directions to her house and lied saying, "Can't wait to see you."

"Same here," but he meant it. He knew that she was in for a big surprise.

Cass awakened early the next morning after her first restful night in days. She wanted to get dressed fast and go downstairs to the lobby, because she didn't want to have to invite Robert up. They were scheduled to meet at ten o'clock and it was now eight-thirty. As she turned to get out of bed she noticed her voice mail light was flashing with a whopping eleven messages. Wow, she thought. She pressed play and first on the machine was her sister Stephanie apologizing for being so insensitive the previous night and begging her to call. The next eight were from Zac, pleading for her to call him and apologizing profusely.

"Cass," Zac said, "I love you and I do need you in my life regardless of my circumstances. I don't care if it is just as my friend or lover. I need you." She fast-forwarded through most of his remaining sob story. Next was her mother saying, "I thought I told you to call me and let me know how things went. Well, I hope it all went well. Your mother shouldn't have to be chasing after you. Give me a call young lady as soon as you hear this message."

Her last message started, "Heffa, I told you I needed an answer by Friday. Call me please. Did you get your fill of Zac? Bye. Call me."

Cass did need to call Keisha back and let her know she would attend the birthday bash with her next weekend. And she had been so preoccupied since she had been unable to reach her previously, she didn't realize that she had neglected to share with her the Zachary saga. However, she put calling her mom and Keisha on hold so that she could prepare to leave. Cass threw on her old FUBU warm up suit, pulled her hair back into a ponytail, and put on her old and worn tennis shoes. She grabbed a glass of orange juice and quickly made an egg white omelet with wheat toast. By the time she finished, it was almost ten o'clock so she headed downstairs and sat in the lobby awaiting Robert's arrival. As she gazed out of the window, she realized that despite the cold, it was a beautiful February day. She frowned at how she would be spending it and who with. While embracing the beautiful day, she saw a fine brother pull up in the two door Mercedes that she was planning on purchasing with her next bonus. She had never seen him there before, but based on his physique she definitely wanted to find out a little more about him. She laughed and thought maybe there was something to what Stephanie said about wrong man prioritizing. But judging by the way he looked she assumed that he was definitely not available. She sighed and tried to mentally prepare for a boring and uneventful day with Robert.

Still admiring the driver of the Mercedes, she saw him walk up to the concierge's desk and while eavesdropping she thought she heard him ask for her. She wrote it off as wishful thinking until the concierge pointed in her direction. The fine brother began walking toward her and Cass fought an expression of shock as she realized that the guy she was admiring was Robert Cason.

"Hello Cass. Can I get a hug?"

Cass, still in shock, tried to hide her surprise but her voice gave her away. As she attempted to respond, her voice cracked and she had to clear her throat. "Robert, wow, look at you!"

He jokingly questioned, "Do you approve?"

Ignoring the question, she said, "You sure have changed."

"So what about it?"

"What about what?" she confusedly questioned.

"My hug, woman."

"Oh," she replied as she extended her arms to oblige him. As she hugged him, she hoped he wouldn't feel the perspiration which now lightly coated her skin. She could feel that this brother was not mush under his blue jeans and Emory sweatshirt. He was firm. As the embrace ended, Cass thought it might be an interesting day after all.

He opened the passenger door for her and quickly walked around to the driver's seat. As Cass watched him she could still see some of the nerd in his awkward gait. But she had to admit friend boy had come a long way. As he clumsily hopped into the car, he asked, "So what's been up, Ms. Nicholas?"

"Well, I basically got tired of the East Coast and wanted to get closer to home. So when a head hunter told me about a position as CFO at a firm here that had a lot of perks, I figured if I was offered the position, it was God's way of telling me to head closer to home. So, here I am. You remember we talked briefly when I was with that hideous firm in New Orleans and I could not wait to leave that racist place and then I ended up in Philly, dealing with a slew of other issues. Honestly, I am not sure how well I will like being back in White corporate America after being out of it for so long. I know that I like the money though."

"When did you become religious?" he quirked and continued. "Well that was one of the reasons I had to start my own thing, to not have to deal with ridiculous nonsense in either corporate structure. I am my own boss and loving it. You should consider doing the same if things don't work out as planned."

She shooed him away with her hand as if she were aggravated by a bug, "I might just do that. So, how have you been? You're looking good."

He confidently, bordering on arrogantly, responded, "Well, my business grossed over one million dollars after taxes in the last fiscal year. I'd say that means I am doing quite well. I've been learning to listen to my inner self and my therapist tells me I've come a long way, and I feel like I have. I have been able to channel the negative things in my life into something positive."

As he continued to speak, Cass thought, "Different package, but same old confused, dull ass man." She still figured she might be able to work with him and mold him. Thinking about this, she began to smirk.

He then said, "Am I boring you?"

Cass tried to conceal a yawn. "No, not at all," she lied. "The UHaul storage place is up here on our left past this light." He gently guided his car into the parking lot. As she hopped out of the car to obtain the key he sat in the car bouncing his head periodically off beat to an oldies but goodies station. He already figured he had impressed her and was feeling good vibes in regards to the likely possibilities that lay ahead.

The day flew by going up and down with packages to and from the thirtieth floor. They actually shared some laughs in the process and Cassandra thought the day was hardly as grueling as she had thought it would be. However, her body was screaming along muscles that she did not think existed after completely unloading the UHaul. She offered him some water and although she had enjoyed his company for the most part, she hoped that they could postpone the dinner because she was exhausted. He plopped down on the sofa after gulping down his water and began massaging her shoulders. "So what are we going to do for dinner?" he asked.

"Aren't you tired? Are you sure you want to do that tonight?"

"You are not going to renege on me tonight, Ms. Nicholas."

She, while feeling her shoulders loosen up a bit, pleaded her case. "You live all the way on the other side of town. By the time you get back to pick me up, every decent restaurant will be closed."

"Well actually I brought a change of clothes with me because of that fact. If you would be so kind as to let me shower here, that won't be an issue." As he said this, his large hands moved down from her shoulders to her lower back. Cass couldn't lie, the massage was feeling very good, and she couldn't help but be curious about the remainder of the evening.

"Well, Mr. Cason, it looks as though you have all your bases covered. So I guess it's a done deal," said Cass with both reluctance and intrigue.

He simply smiled as he pulled her T-shirt out of her pants and began to massage her bare back. Cass was unsure where this was going but as she felt the tension escaping her body she decided to let him continue. He gently massaged every crease and crevice of her back. To the point at which she was turned on. It seemed like ages since she had been caressed so tenderly. Especially since all of her planned intimate activities came to an abrupt halt together with the fact that any prior intimacy with Zachary had been purposely erased from her mind. By her calculations that meant she had been celibate for six years. Just as she was becoming more comfortable and rationalizing that it was okay to go further, he broke the mood by lightly slapping her back and saying, "Okay, kiddo, go take your shower and when you're done I'll take mine." Startled, Cassandra opened her eyes and expressed a face of disgust which she hoped was not obvious.

Feeling a little cheated and pissed, she reluctantly raised her body from the sofa and stretched, trying to imply that the massage was just mediocre. She slowly walked to the shower, moving a little more gracefully than usual as she felt his eyes on her. Robert laid back on the sofa smiling, while he watched her ass sway as she slowly moved toward her bedroom. He felt himself rising to the occasion and using his pet name said to himself, "Later Buster, later." He arrogantly smiled because he knew he had her just where he wanted her. He interlocked the fingers of his hands behind his head and closed his eyes as he was eager to see what the night's end would bring.

The hot water felt wonderful as it bounced off of Cassandra's achy body onto the gray slate like ceramic tile that surrounded the shower. Cassandra wondered exactly what Robert had planned. She did know one thing, it felt damn good being pampered and she was going to enjoy it. She smiled as she retreated from the shower and thought to herself, "If you play your cards right tonight, Mr. Cason, you might get some of this," especially since she was terribly horny. She quickly slipped on her robe, walked out into the den and startled Robert awake. "It's all yours." While he was in the shower Cass contemplated what she should wear. She thought something sexy but subdued. She then knew the perfect outfit. But before she pulled out the long sleeved but backless red dress, she figured she needed to find out what type of restaurant he had in mind. She certainly did not want to overdress if this brother's idea of fine dining was equivalent to *Po Folks*. She called out to him, "Robert, where are we dining, so I can dress appropriately?"

He slid the bathroom door open only clad in Calvin Klein boxer briefs and said, "How does "*Chops*" sound?" Trying not to give him the once over she turned away and said, "Sounds great!" While putting on the red dress, Cass couldn't help but flashback to Robert standing in the door in those underwear. His bare chest glistening with beads of water on his bulging pecks. Embarrassingly, she had to admit that his pecks were not the only thing she noticed bulging. "Damn," she quietly whispered, "Brother got it going on."

After making sure that everything was in place, Cass seductively stepped out of her bedroom to find Robert impeccably dressed in a perfectly tailored gray pin striped suit. As he turned to face her she noted that he had traded his contacts for a pair of square shaped Giorgio Armani glasses which balanced off his smoothly shaven head. He looks so good she thought and broadly smiled at him.

"You ready?" he asked, giving her the once over and then stating, "You look great!"

"So do you," she said as they walked out of her condo. Shutting the door, she decidedly thought, "I'm gonna get me some of that," subtly flailing her arms behind him excited about what the remainder of the night would entail.

On the way to the restaurant, Cass felt very comfortable with Robert. They laughed about old times and used this laughter as a means of contact between one another. She would laugh and touch his arm. He would chuckle and rub her leg. They knew the game that they both were playing, and they each were enjoying their roles. As they pulled up to "*Chops*" the valet opened her door and Robert quickly came around to take Cassandra's arm as they entered the restaurant. They started off with drinks and appetizers at their secluded candlelit table. Cassandra still was shocked that she was eating dinner with Robert Cason *and* seriously contemplating fucking him afterwards.

"So, Cassandra, I really am glad that you have moved to Atlanta. Maybe we can get better acquainted again."

Cassandra looking directly in Robert's eyes and said, "I would like that," and she really meant it this time. By dessert she had already begun to flirtatiously place the cheesecake into her mouth, giving him hints of her post dessert plans. He was enjoying her teasing but gave her no clue that he was aware of her motives. While they were awaiting the check, a chic young lady walked up to them and exclaimed, "Robert, Robert Cason! Fancy me running into you here."

Robert nervously chuckled, "Gail, how are you? This is my old friend Cassandra Nicholas." Cassandra smiled and extended her hand as she tried to figure out the weird dynamics going on before her.

Gail ignored Cassandra's hand and angrily stated, "Why didn't you return any of my calls? Is this your latest conquest, you asshole? You better watch out for his games. He ain't nothing but a player," she stated looking directly at Robert the entire time.

"Gail, let's talk about it some other time, okay."

"Fuck you," she quipped as she turned to leave.

"Well, well, well," Cassandra laughed, "I see you have been busy here in Hotlanta."

"It's not what you think. You know me Cass, I've never been a player."

"You don't have to prove anything to me, old friend."

"I apologize for that," Robert stated as the waiter arrived with the bill. "I hate confrontations."

"It's okay. Really," Cassandra silently laughed as she replayed what had happened. Shortly after their waiter brought the card back to the curiously silent table, Robert briskly pulled out her chair and said, "Let's get out of here." During the drive home, Cass figured she needed to rethink whether she wanted to go there with him or not because she had certainly experienced her fair share of players and just wasn't mentally prepared to deal with B.S. so soon. Although she presumed they would never really be a love connection, she figured they could be bedroom buddies, maybe. She had practically abandoned the concept of love anyway and decided that her goal would be to have fun safely because she needed to preserve her emotional well-being.

As they arrived at her condo, Cass asked, "Why don't you come up for a drink?"

"Well, you know it's late. If I come up there, I don't plan to be coming out in the cold again tonight," he smiled. This was Cassandra's very first time really noticing how nice his smile was and she said, "So, what are you waiting for? Let's go up," she guessed her rethinking this issue had been decided. She was indeed going to go there with him. In the elevator, there was some nervous tension, which Robert broke by cracking a bad joke that was so ridiculous, she could not help but laugh. As they arrived at her floor, they were falling over one another with laughter and Cass tried to gain some control, because she did not want to awaken her neighbors yet again. She had already been reported once before. She figured that would not be a good record since she had only lived there for a week.

As they entered the condo, Cass said in a soft tone, "Have a seat and I'll be right back." Robert took off his coat, the jacket to his suit and his tie, and sat down on her plush new wave sofa. He chuckled out loud thinking about the events of the day as he looked around her condo. He then noted her CD player and decided to put on some music. He found a Joe Sample jazz CD and decided that he would play it. As he placed the CD cover back in it's original position, he could not help but notice the empty condom wrapper that lay behind the speaker. He thought, "Damn, her ass has been busy, and she's only been here a week. Well, at least she's practicing safe sex." This concerned Robert some, because lately he always liked his women almost virginal and that's why he usually dated them significantly younger than his thirty-six years. He also dated them younger because now he could. He took pride in attending functions with a young and beautiful woman on his arm. He did have boundaries though and took sexual encounters seriously and never engaged in them unless he was truly emotionally involved. At least most of the time. He had no desire in scarring these women like he had been scarred in his past. Robert had his heart broken so many times before, he vowed he would not put anyone through the hurt he had experienced. He believed that once sex occurred, the entire dynamic of the relationship changed. His thoughts then went back to Gail. He never did the sex thing with her because he was not feeling it for her. She was very young at twenty-three and on many levels much too immature. One day she had planned the perfect romantic evening and tried to seduce him. Robert turned her advances down, and ever since then she had remained bitter and implied that he must be gay. Robert had nothing against gay folk, but gay he was not. His thoughts were promptly interrupted as he saw Cass coming toward him in too short cut off jean shorts and a sports bra. She had pulled her hair back into a ponytail and was very comfortable.

"My, my, my, I did not realize that you were as fine and sculpted as you are. Damn girl."

As she walked toward him, she purposely had forgotten to go to the kitchen to get the White Zinfandel. She wanted an excuse to go back to the kitchen to allow him to catch a glimpse of her ass, which was peeking out from the strands of jean material that remained at the bottom of her shorts. Robert definitely looked as she abruptly turned around to return to the kitchen. She asked as she secretly smiled, "Will some White Zinfandel be okay?"

"Sure," as he unbuttoned the first couple of buttons of his shirt and began to take off his shoes. She returned with two glasses of wine and gently sat down next to him.

"So, Mr. Cason. I must thank you for turning this mundane day of work into something fun."

"It was definitely my pleasure," he said, as he turned toward her and looked her in the eye. "You know that I have always liked you a lot, Cass. I just am glad that you thought to call me, although at the last minute. I hope this can be the beginning of a new friendship." With that he raised his glass and said, "To new beginnings."

"Yes," she joined in, "to new beginnings." As their glasses met, Cass took this opportunity to meet his full lips with a kiss. He eagerly participated. As they kissed, Cass began to unbutton his shirt further, so that she could stroke his bare chest. Once his shirt was open, she pressed her body closer into his and he held her tightly while stroking her hair. He then eased away from her lips and slid down to her neck where his tongue quivered lightly and playfully. Cass was still trippin' that she was actually being intimate with Robert Cason and enjoying it. As he kissed her neck, she gently squeezed his nipples, making him lightly moan and prompting him to softly bite her neck. They began to exchange moans regularly as if they were creating a melodic song. As Robert lifted her sports bra and began to pull her nipples into his mouth, Cass could not help but arch her back and push herself closer to him. She then fumbled for his belt and could feel him get even harder underneath the touch of her hand. She unbuttoned his pants and pulled back the elastic that blocked her from reaching her destination. She then began to firmly slide her hands along his bare skin feeling his body tense up. He then laid her on the sofa and placed his body on top of hers and again moved his lips to hers and affectionately kissed her. Their bodies were immersed in a ride of their own, as they rocked passionately and deeply meeting each other at their primary contact points intensifying their arousal. They each could feel the heat emanating beneath their clothes as their bodies begged to be released from their captivity. Cass fervently picked up the condom package that lay on the floor at its preplanned hidden location while Robert politely pushed her hand away and continued to kiss her and stroke her erotically. She thought, "I know that this brother does not think we're gonna go further without an umbrella." He then gently lifted her up and carried her into the bedroom. He lay her on the bed and pulled off his pants which revealed his well endowed family jewels. He then unbuttoned her jean shorts and pulled them off, which left her with only her red thong underwear on. He turned her onto her side and began to climb in bed next to her.

She interrupted the moment and said, "You really need to wear the condom." He quietly laughed and said, "No, I don't," as he pulled her close and hugged her tenderly. He had always been emotionally there with Cass, but definitely wanted to take it slow. She, in so many unspoken words, had broken his heart in the past. Cass soon realized that it was the end of the road. They were not going to make love. They were just going to cuddle. "What's the sense of having a perfectly hard and ready dick cradling my ass? Ain't this some shit?" she muttered as she forced herself to enjoy the closeness with a damn bone sitting in her ass. Fortunately, it eventually softened which allowed her to then slowly drift off to sleep. Robert on the other hand was enjoying himself, but was quite shocked by the image of him and Cass on the ceiling, "A kinky woman," he thought. He then snuggled his face into her neck and fell asleep, also relieved that he was able to exercise some major self-control and not let "Buster" take over the evening. He wanted Cass to feel just a little rejected in retribution of how she had dogged him countless times in the past, if only for one night.

Five

Cassandra awakened early the next morning to an empty bed. She quickly got up thinking, "Isn't that sweet, he must be making breakfast." She walked into the kitchen smiling and expecting to find Robert there, but all she found was a note attached to the refrigerator, "I enjoyed the evening Cass. Had a lot of work to do today. Call me. Robert." Cass disappointingly sighed and thought to herself, "It was a nice evening until that fucking cuddle shit at the end." She laughed as she thought how so many women crave a man who would just cuddle and be sensitive. Cass was no different and appreciated those characteristics as well, but she admitted that last night she wanted a roughneck. She wanted to be ravished. With all those sensual thoughts pervading her mind she abruptly turned and headed to her bathroom to take a cool shower and calm the erotic sensations that now readily teased her. Once in the shower, Cass decided to forget the cool shower, she was going to single handedly complete what was started the night before. Shortly after beginning to caress her body with the soap lather she felt her legs begin to buckle underneath her so she braced herself on the shockingly cold shower walls. "Yaw!" she yelled as she laughed almost uncontrollably at her weakened state. She stepped out of the shower feeling somewhat gratified but vowed that the next time Robert was there, he was not going to leave it up to her to finish the job. Cass thought she had heard the phone ringing while in the shower, but at that moment she was otherwise preoccupied and wasn't sure whether it was the phone ringing or her head. Drying herself off, she walked to retrieve her messages but there were none. So she pressed star six nine and the number quoted was Keisha's. She sat on the edge of her bed and dialed Keisha now simultaneously feeling exuberated and tired.

"Hello."

"Hey there woman," Cass excitedly said.

"Is this my long lost trifling friend?" Keisha jokingly questioned.

"Yeah it's me. You will never guess how I spent my evening."

"Well, I am waiting. Don't keep a sister in suspense."

"Do you remember that guy I told you about in business school that was crazy about me?"

"Do you mean the guy who you dogged?"

"Well, I wouldn't say all that, but I think we're talking about the same one. Well, anyway we kind of got together last night."

"What do you mean got together? I know you have not reached that desperate of times. Are we talking about the same guy who needed his therapist to tell him how fucked up he was?"

"The one and only, Robert Cason," Cass screamed. "Girl, he is a changed man. If you could see him now, brother is fine. And can you believe we got all the way to the point of being hot and heavy and damn near nude and brother decided to cuddle. I couldn't believe that shit. I had to handle my business this morning to release my sexual frustrations." Cass and Keisha both laughed hysterically.

"Maybe he couldn't get it up?" Keisha managed to say in between laughing.

"No sister, believe me, that was not the problem. I had trouble trying to get to sleep because of that damn bone sitting in my ass. I started to turn over and give him a blow job just to get that ongoing temptation out of my damn crack," she laughed. "I believe he just genuinely was not quite ready to go there with me."

"Wow! But I guess so after the way you dogged his ass in the past," Keisha exclaimed. "I guess Zac didn't take care of you then?"

"Girl, that's a whole nother story. Suffice it to say, he and I are no longer an item and that's going to be a permanent arrangement.

Eddra Marchand

His ass is married with children! Anyway, I am not even going there right now because I have too many positive things happening for me right now to waste all that negative energy. Speaking of which, I did not dog Robert too bad." After thinking further, "Yeah I did. But we both are mature adults now and can let bygones be bygones. I hope."

"Yeah right. But girl, you have got to be kidding! Zachary is married with children? Well you know ain't nothing wrong with being a mistress ho as long as the getting is good. But you gonna have to tell me about that drama later, I gots to go to get my hair done. I called to find out if you're going to hang with me next weekend at my cousin's party."

"I sure will. Just remind me Friday. It's Saturday right?"

"That's right, will do. Later." Cass hung up the phone still laughing. She then got dressed and wondered if she should call Robert. She decided not to appear desperate and opted not to call. "I'll let him call me," she confidently stated to herself. Looking at the clock, she realized that it was just a few minutes before her mom left for church. She always liked to call her mother when there was a finite amount of time available for talking, and mom never liked to be late for church. She dialed her mother and the phone rang longer than usual. She thought, "Damn I hope I didn't miss her." Just as she was about to hang up, her mother answered the phone in an exasperated tone, "Hello."

"Hi, mom," Cass exclaimed, "just calling to touch bases."

"Now Cass you know I am about to leave for church. You know I have to be there early to conduct bible study. Cass, are you going to church? You know you need to make Him a priority in your life?"

"I know you need to go to be on time. I love you, and I do make Him a priority."

"Love you too baby. Will call you a little later. Bye."

After calling her mom Cass set out to put her condo in order, since things were just thrown around in boxes after removing them from storage. So she poured herself a glass of wine, put on her Janet Jackson CD and bounced around while putting things in place. Amidst

65

the loud music, Cass barely heard the phone ringing, and picked up the receiver just before her answering machine message was ending. "Hello," she yelled above the music. "Cass, Cass. I'm so glad you answered the phone." With the music blaring in the background she could not decipher who she was talking to. She figured it must be Robert since the day was nearing its end. As she lowered the music she exclaimed, "Hey, how are you?" in one of her sexiest voices.

The other caller responded, "So you have forgiven me?"

"Forgiven you?" and then her smile quickly reverted to an angry grimace. Silent as she was shocked that it was Zac on the other end she reached for the flash button to hang up but she didn't.

"Cass please. You know I love you and I know we can make us work. After all, you live there and I am in Philly. I have several conferences there and Susan never has to know. I need to feel you."

"Look, you trifling ass mother fucker. I am not gonna be your little sometimes ho. I cannot believe that you have the audacity to call me after the bullshit you have pulled. You go on and work on being a husband and father, 'cause I don't want anything to do with your sorry ass." Cass, without waiting for a response, quickly hung up the phone before he wasted another breath. The phone rang a few times immediately after she had hung up. She knew it was just Zachary trying to plead his case. Suddenly all of Cassandra's exuberance had faded away as she slumped down onto the floor shaking her head and trying not to let herself get pulled into a mini depression. She picked up the phone and began to dial Robert's number. As the phone rang, Cassandra began to perk up until she heard a woman's voice on the other end. "Hello," she said. Cassandra quickly hung up the phone and then thought, "Shit, I hope he does not have caller ID." Then no sooner than Cassandra could put the phone on its receiver it rang. "Damn," she mumbled, "Ain't this a bitch." She swallowed her pride and answered the phone with a flat hello. "Cass," she heard Robert's voice softly say.

She embarrassingly responded, "You caught me. Yes it's me. I'm sorry."

"What are you apologizing for? I just happened to have a

client out in your area and wanted to know if I could maybe pick up some Chinese food or something and come by and get our grub on."

Cassandra a little bewildered responded, "You mean that you are not home?"

"No, why?"

"No reason," wondering if she had dialed the wrong number. She quickly changed the subject and said, "Chinese sounds good to me. I would like the stir fried vegetables with grilled chicken over brown rice."

"Okay, I should be there in say a half an hour."

"Great!" Cass had now become very curious about the woman that answered the phone. She was almost sure that she had dialed the correct number. She wondered if she should bring it up or leave it alone. First and foremost, she picked up his telephone number again and carefully dialed each number and again a woman answered the phone. "Sorry wrong number," she yelled and promptly hung up the phone all the while wondering who the hell it was. She rationalized that Robert was not her man so what if he had some woman shacking up with him. "Yeah right," she thought and instead deterred her attentions to dressing to please Mr. Cason. She knew exactly what she was going to wear. Her "easy access" short mini dress. It was so cute and revealed all of Cassandra's curves and accentuated her cleavage. She quickly placed it on, dabbed on a little make up and let her long bob flow down her shoulders. As soon as she sprayed a little of her perfume in the right places there was a buzz from downstairs. Cass thought, perfect timing as she picked up the phone and instructed Fred at the concierge desk to let him up. Cass unlocked the door and sat on the sofa at such an angle which exposed just enough leg and cleavage to catch the eye of any man who walked into her foyer. When she heard the barely audible knock, she loudly but sexily called out, "Come in." After a few seconds the door wasn't opening and she replied even louder, "Come in." This time Robert clumsily entered the door wearing plaid pants, a yellow shirt and ugly white shoes. As soon as Cass noticed all the things he was carrying, she quickly hopped up to help, but not before the bottle of Chardonnay he was carrying slipped from his grasp and splattered all over her marble floor.

"Shit," he exclaimed. "Why didn't you open the door?"

Cass, now totally having had her plan ruined, lied and said "Sorry, I was in the bathroom," as she took the bouquet of roses he had and got the paper towels out of her pantry to wipe up the mess.

"Where's your broom? I'm sorry. I was just trying to carry too many things. Be careful without shoes on, there's glass down there."

"No, no, that's okay. You have a seat and I'll clean this up. You can get us something to drink out of my fridge. I don't believe I have any wine. I do have a few Coronas though. Maybe I should get them too, they're made out of glass," she laughed.

"Oh, okay. You gonna dog a brother out. That's cool though. I can handle it."

"I'm just joking," Cass laughed as she finished sweeping up all the glass and walked over to the kitchen table. "Are these for me?" she smiled, as she finally had a chance to admire the lovely yellow roses since the commotion had settled.

"Yes they were, but you're gonna have to work to get them now after dogging me out," he snided. She leaned over toward him, knowing that she revealed quite a bit of cleavage in her braless state and gave him a wet and passionate kiss. He pulled her close and said, "They're yours, Babe," as he gently kissed her again. She silently laughed thinking, " Sister girl won't have to finish the job today because that was way too easy."

As they finished eating Cass surprised herself when she asked, "So who is the woman at your place?"

"Woman, what woman?"

"Nigga, don't play with me. You know who I am talking about."

"Do I sense a bit of jealousy?"

"No, I am just curious," Cass said feeling a little embarrassed now by her query, especially since they had only been seeing each other a few days.

"Well, for your information, not that it's your business, every Sunday I have a maid come in to clean my house. Cleaning is not one of my fortes. Any other questions?"   Cass truly was embarrassed and quickly changed the subject, "I figured as much. So how was your day today?"

"My day was great! I had the chance to brush up on my golf and I believe I succeeded in getting some more major league players to back a project I believe will put me into the Fortune 500. I couldn't ask for more. How about you? What did you do today besides get jealous about my maid answering the phone," he smiled while placing rice in his mouth with his chop sticks.

"Why do you use those things? It's so much easier to just use a fork."

"Culture my dear, I enjoy learning about different cultures and I like the challenges adopting some of their customs provide," he arrogantly stated.

"You are such a damn nerd," she laughed, "and those ugly golf clothes don't help the issue." They continued to laugh as they cleared the mess from the kitchen table and began to move to the den when Cass yelled, "Ouch!" Robert quickly turned around and noticed the blood on the floor and Cass scorning while clinching her foot.

"I told you not to walk in here barefoot." Robert picked her up in his arms and gently walked over to and sat her down on the sofa. Without saying a word he went to her bathroom and came back with a cold towel to place pressure on her foot. Cass, pouting in a puerile manner, softly whined like a child who was disobedient might, "I'm sorry." It was a small cut, but Cass decided to be a little more dramatic. "Ouch, it hurts so bad. It must have severed one of my foot nerves. Ouch," she exclaimed again as he continued to place pressure. Covering her face to shield her laughter, she continued to cry out in agony until she felt moisture surrounding her toes. She looked down and saw that her toes were in his mouth. Her cries of agony abruptly changed to whimpers of excitement. "What are you doing?"

"Would you like me to stop?" he asked looking at her with a devilish grin.

"No, actually it seems like your technique is mending those severed nerves," she chuckled as she began to relax and enjoy the wonderful sensations which he was arousing. He continued to sensually caress and kiss her feet and slowly moved atop her body to rest his mouth on hers. Their bodies were intertwined and she could feel how aroused he was. It was now that Cassandra decided to take control of the situation, because she did not want to take the chance of this ending in a cuddling session again. She stood up slipped off her panties and turned him onto his back. She then took out a condom and casually unbuttoned and unzipped his pants. She was not interested in foreplay today. She wanted to feel him inside of her. She then slipped the condom onto him, began stroking him and asked, "Do you want me, Robert?" Without a word, he pulled her panty-less body on top of his and they began making love. First, Cass on top moaning and commanding his attentions while he vigorously kissed her breasts. He then slid her to the floor and began to decisively take control of the situation. They transitioned there easily with drizzles of perspiration forming between them as he continued to forcefully conjoin their bodies. All the while looking her in her eyes still amazed that he was making love to the woman who had headlined many of his sexual fantasies of years past. He then quickly pulled out as he was getting too aroused and slowly licked her from her breast to her navel and then to her throbbing midsection gyrating slowly to meet his touch. Once reaching his destination, he pulled her hips up with his strong hands until he was able to feel her warmth. He then caressed her with alternating rhythms of his tongue, fast and slow until he felt her hips begin to tremble in his hands. He then gently laid her on the floor and slowly but forcefully entered her again until they both simultaneously succumbed to their body's ultimate gratification. After their sexual endeavor ended, no words were spoken. They just held one another tightly fearing that the slightest movement might disrupt the perfect tranquility of the moment. Before they realized it they were sound asleep both lulled there by the consummate energy emanating between them.

Cass again awakened feeling abandoned, as Robert had yet again slipped away without her knowledge. She was already tiring of those refrigerator messages. She angrily swiped the note off of the refrigerator door reading, "Cass, you looked so peaceful, I decided not to wake you. I have a business trip and will be gone for the week, but I can't wait to see you when I return. Will try to call you while I am away. If not, I definitely will be thinking of you. Robert "Buster" Cason." Cass laughed as she thought, "Yet another man with a name for his penis." She had to admit, as she slowly walked to her shower feeling somewhat achy and gapped legged, he had earned his title. "Buster," she silently whispered as she smiled and hopped in the shower and for the first time in a long time wondered if she had finally found her soul mate. Robert encompassed so many of the traits that she eventually matured to endear. He had always been very sweet and trustworthy from back in the day but back then she was blinded by juvenile criteria which prioritized looks over everything. Now he had transformed into a wonderful specimen of a man and proved that everything functioned well beyond her expectations. An honest, handsome, charming and rich Christian man. "What more could a girl ask for?" she questioned as she mischievously smiled and added, "And a good fuck too."

Six

The work week was moving quickly as Cass was becoming acclimated to her job duties and enjoying her position of authority. Cass tried not to abuse her powers, but sometimes felt the need to let some of her counterparts know who was boss. She blatantly denounced a colleague's idea and told him that she wanted a full report on the next business day of all the clients that they had lost in the last year with their completed portfolios. Cass knew full well that to have such a project ready on such short notice would require stamina, determination, and an enormous pot of coffee. Sleep would not be had on that night. Cass was being exceptionally evil because she was pissed that it was already Thursday and she had not heard from Robert. She sat at her desk tapping her fingers curiously wondering if the woman who confronted Robert at the restaurant was telling the truth. Maybe Robert really was a player. At that moment her secretary buzzed in and stated that there was a party on the line that would not leave their full name and only announced themselves as "Mr. B." She thought, "Mr. B, who in the hell is that?" "Put them through," Cassandra curiously responded.

"You miss me?"

"Who is this?" Cassandra questioned not catching the voice.

"This is Buster," Robert laughed.

As she got up to close her office door she said, "Oh, Robert.

I do miss you. It has been a terrible week. Why didn't you call me sooner?" she chastised as she flopped down into her chair.

"Cass, I miss you too. I realize that more since I have been away. I know we have only been seeing each other for a little over a week, but it feels like a lifetime. I have something special for you. I will be driving back into town Sunday. Can I drop by then?"

"Sure, Buster, I can't wait to see you. I mean Robert, of course. My foot nerves also need some more mending." They laughed and hung up. Cass felt like things were moving fast and she was enjoying it. She thought she could be falling in love with Robert Cason. Then as if a teenager in puppy love she began writing on her pad "Cassandra Cason" repetitiously. She thought that sounded catchy. "I like that." She smiled and prepared to leave her office for the day.

On the ride home, Cassandra did not feel like cooking and stopped at a fast food restaurant and decided to indulge in one of her cravings. She forced herself not to feel guilty as she ordered the large fries and burger with extra mayo. She reasoned, "I am in shape and exercising, I can splurge sometimes." She finally arrived at her condo and quickly went upstairs hoping her fries would still be hot. They weren't. She figured, "That's what I get for trying to eat this trash." She sat there quietly eating and reminiscing about her evening with Robert and how amazing he was in bed. She also was thinking about how close they had gotten in such a short period of time. It was almost as if they had been seeing each other as a couple since business school. Their relationship quickly blossomed without infantile charades and the love they shared was a mature love. In the past, Cassandra admired Robert and appreciated only his intelligence and wit. Now, except for a few kinks, she liked the entire package. If she were honest with herself, she knew that as much as she had matured, if Robert had come to her house looking like the Robert of old, after he had helped her move her things, Cassandra would have left him, his intelligence, and his wit right on the curb outside her condo. Cassandra chuckled guiltily to herself.

Cassandra was smiling at the thought of spending her Sunday with him when she was jarred back to reality by the phone.

"Hey chic."

"Who is this?"

"This Carl. Girl you know you remember me and how good I banged that ass." She wondered what trifling guy would be calling and addressing her in such a manner. And how did he get her number?

"Carl who?"

"Carl Washington. Remember. I am Keisha's cousin. I ran into her today and she told me you was here and kind of lonely. So I figured I could, you know, hook you up."

Terribly offended by his brazen arrogance and lack of tact Cass retorted, "Oh, yes, I remember now. Carl, how could I forget you? You're the one with the miniature dick. Thank you but I'd rather spend my time cuddling with a good book."

"You must got me confused. 'cause ain't nothing on me mini...mini...small," he stuttered. Girl you know I could make you feel good. Here's my number in case you change your mind."

Cass promptly hung up the phone without bothering to pretend that she had any interest. Oh yes, she remembered Carl, a fine brother who had the brains of a mouse on crack. He could do a good strip tease dance and looked sexy as hell doing it. He just had a problem transferring all of those wonderful moves into the bed. He was not terrible in bed if you just had to get you some, but Cass's mind was only on one man, Mr. Robert Cason. Before drifting off into Cason's land, she remembered that she was supposed to be peeved with Keisha and decided to call her immediately and cuss her out for giving out her number. She dialed Keisha's number and after only one ring, Keisha picked up.

"Hey there, girlfriend. What's up?"

"Bitch, don't you be giving out my number. Your stupid ass cousin called me and offered to hook me up," Cassandra laughed.

"I was worried, you're starting to show the signs."

"What in the world are you talking about?"

"Girl, the first sign of true desperation is dating your own leftovers. I thought Carl might be a good distraction. You keep trippin' about this being alone shit. Get over it. You don't have to settle down with the first man that asks you out."

"Keisha, seriously. Robert has changed. And I really think I am falling for him. Hard."

"Oh Lawd! He has you whipped already. Damn. When he starts trying to bring you to his counselor to help explain the meaning of your relationship, you gonna wish you had my simple ass cousin by your side. All he wants is some grits in the morning and some coochie at night." They both boisterously laughed.

"No, but really, I like him a lot and I want you to meet him really soon. He also has gone through a transformation. Brother is looking good now."

"See, ya'll silly ass women just think that after these so-called transformations a brother is looking all good. But what about the kids! Your ass gonna be upset when you have all those bucktooth, fucked up kids looking just like their pa pre-transformation. I don't want that shit. If you ugly, come at me ugly so I won't be trying to figure out if you are really the father of my ugly ass kids. Anyway," she continued to laugh, "but on to bigger and better things. I'll pick you up at nine o'clock sharp Saturday to go to the party. It's not too far from your house and we need to get there before ten to avoid the cover charge. So be ready!"

"Girl. Your ass is crazy! What should I wear?" still trying to control her laughter.

"Just casual but no jeans. Girl, I gotta go change my pad. If we don't talk before then, I'll see you at nine. Bye," she yelled as she quickly hung up the phone.

Cass laughed and thought, "That was more information than I needed to know." She then ironed her clothes for Friday and tried to go to sleep listening to the waves tape that her sister Casey had bought her because she believed that she was too uptight. She started to feel as if she was in an infomercial touting the usefulness of the stupid tape and abruptly shut it off and opted to listen to the tape situated on the opposite side of the dual cassette boom box. She then clutched her pillow tightly and was lulled to sleep by the mellow voices of Luther Vandross and Cheryl Lynn singing *If This World Were Mine*.

Cass was feeling good at work and knew that nothing could mar her wonderful mood. She then ran into Blake Reed. "Cassandra. I understand that your report done earlier this week was missing some important elements especially from the legal perspective. If you need my assistance with coordinating the information more objectively just ask. I believe my knowledge base far exceeds yours in the field of law seeing as though I have a law degree. Plus, we men tend to see things more objectively than you ladies when it comes to money matters," he snided.

"Well, Blake. I believe that you have gotten your information from an inept source. My project for expanding our client base and their respective portfolios has been accepted and we will begin implementing it within the next several weeks. I know you have had a difficult time dealing with a woman with such an expansive degree of knowledge backed by impressive credentials being a part of the team here. But you might as well get used to it. If I need your legal expertise, there is no doubt that I would come to you. I hope that you would give me the same respect in turn as you no doubt will need me. And next time you want to know what's going on with me, come to me. I don't have a thing to hide."

He shrugged his shoulders in disbelief and promptly walked to the secretary to get a copy of the memo. Cassandra could not believe his balls to approach her in such a manner. She was even more so in a good mood after raining on his parade. When she returned to her office, she called Stephanie who she had been evading ever since they had their fall out. When her secretary picked up Cass stated, "Dr. Jordan please, this is Dr. Nicholas." She learned that the only way to get her sister to the phone quickly was by acting as if she were a doctor. Stephanie came to the phone shortly thereafter and stated in too perky and snobby a tone, "This is Dr. Jordan."

"Hey there Dr. Jordan."

"Cassandra?"

"The one and only."

"How are things? Why haven't you returned any of my calls? Let me first say I am sorry for being so insensitive to your feelings, but you know how I feel about your dating patterns anyway. But I'll leave that alone. Are you okay?"

"I'm fine. I believe that you would approve of the guy I'm seeing now. The guy you were trying to get me to take seriously years ago, but I just wasn't ready."

"Are you talking about that guy, what's his name?"

"Robert, yes the guy from business school," Cassandra interrupted.

"Yes, Robert. The little wholesome and sweet fella. Good. Maybe now you have your priorities straight. Looks aren't everything sis. You all should come over to the house some time soon. I can prepare a meal and we can get to know him. He's not married is he, Cassandra?"

"No he isn't and he is very handsome these days. You wait and see, but we can talk about it later. I just wanted you to know that I have forgiven you for being you. I love you. Bye."

"Love you too, Cassandra. I'll call you later."

It was not quite five o'clock, but Cass was too ready to leave. She packed up to go and purposely passed by Blake's office and smiled a smug smile and waved good-bye through the glass windows. She knew he was now even more pissed at the written reality that she had overstepped him in so many words. He quickly averted his eyes as if he did not see her. So, Cass opened his door and politely said, "Have a great weekend," and gave one of her biggest and phoniest smiles. She turned around without giving him a chance to respond and strode away in that confident stride which so many had come to despise. Cassandra was exhausted when she arrived home and did only the essential things like taking a shower and brushing her teeth. She quickly slid into bed and escaped into dreamland amidst only the darkness that shrouded her room. The darkness usually seemed to unmask her loneliness, which is why she always made sure there was some degree of a light source nearby. That night, however, she felt unaffected by falling asleep without a small light on in the hallway. She now realized the difference between being alone and being lonely. Cass was alone in body but not in her spirit. She could feel Robert's presence in her heart which made everything so different. Cass closed her eyes and thanked God for sending this wonderful man back into her life.

Seven

Saturday flew by as Cassandra completed the tidying up of her condo since her move. She finally had everything the way she wanted it with the dimmer lights on her plants and her candles in specific places; all of the subtleties that could readily turn a ordinary day into a romantic escapade simply by the flip of a switch. She also had her favorite books laid out on the coffee table such as the Delaney Sisters' book and a few books from the Oprah Book club. Cass definitely had to have her Essence magazine in place for those special days when she needed grounding. The *In the Spirit* column always helped her feel good about who she was and helped validate the decisions that she made throughout her life. She reminisced briefly about when she was away at grad school and was depressed because she was not doing particularly well and her relationship with her high school sweetheart was losing its battle with distance. She knew then that she and Glenn were slowly drifting apart from each other. He was remaining stagnant in New Orleans while she was being exposed to so many new adventures and so many things that life in New Orleans could not offer. She was trying desperately to hold onto the relationship when she read one of Susan Taylor's columns about loving yourself and recognizing when you are being steered away from your destined path. It was then that she decided not to prolong the inevitable and she mustered up the courage to end their four year engagement. She then entered the wild phase of her life, filled with party hopping and casual sex. She quietly laughed as she thought of some of the things she had done. If her mother were made privy to those escapades, Cass was sure she'd damn near have a heart attack. Cass sometimes wondered if breaking up with Glenn was the best thing, because now he was married with kids and had the stable family life that she longed to have. Cass then detached herself from the past, looked up at herself in the mirrors above her bed and exclaimed, "Where I am now in life is where I am supposed to be. Even if I am almost thirty-five and alone." She often found herself quoting many other self-affirmations she had learned from watching the Oprah reruns with Ms. Vanzant. Sometimes it was the only thing that sustained her during the breakups with Zac and her occasional self-pity drama.

"Shit," she exclaimed as she hopped up recognizing that she had only fifteen minutes to get ready for the party.

Cassandra now wished that she had not agreed to go, because she was currently no longer on the prowl. She knew who she wanted and was going to put all her efforts into letting him know it. She believed that Robert was the man who she could likely spend the rest of her life and she did not want to put herself in any nonsensical situation that might jeopardize the continuing growth of their relationship. Too much valuable time had already been lost and her goal now was to adjoin the rare positive times of their past with the freshness and newness of their present. She was well aware that their past history, albeit overflowing with youthful ignorance, played a significant role in their almost too easy transition into coupledom but now she had to nourish it rather than stifle it. A job which she was now determined to accomplish. She rationalized that once you've reached a certain age in life that the long courtships are not a necessary prelude to a successful and loving relationship. "Yep," she thought, "I just might marry that man," as she prepared to wear something cute, casual and unrevealing. She decided on a pair of black jeans which she had recently bought, a black turtleneck, and a hounds tooth blazer with her black boots. She pulled her hair up into a ponytail with a small velvet-looking scrunchy and applied a tad bit of make-up. She figured she looked decent enough and was not particularly concerned in any case. By the time she was ready it was a little after nine and no word from Keisha yet. This certainly was not unusual. It was nine forty-five before the desk called up. "Your friend is here and she asks that you hurry up and come down." Shaking her head, she responded, "I'll be right there." Cassandra locked her door, headed downstairs and hoped that her mood would improve. The only positive thing about spending the night out, she surmised, was to help pass the time until she saw Robert again.

As Cass walked out of the elevator she saw Keisha in her SUV prompting Cass to hurry up. As Cass opened the door Keisha exclaimed, "We have only ten minutes to get there before the cover charge goes into effect. Lawd knows I don't have no extra twenty dollars to spend just to get into the damn place. You're looking cute."

Before Cass could buckle up good her head snapped back as Keisha sped off around the curve of the complex. "Damn, girl. If times are that bad I'll pay the damn money. Let's just try to get there in one piece. So what's up with this party? Why you want me tagging along? I hope you're not trying to set me up with anyone because I think I have found my man. He was standing right in front of me all these years and I am just realizing it."

"Spare me all that lovey-dovey bullshit," she laughed. "You wouldn't be saying all this "right in front of me shit" if he was looking as fucked up as he did back then. It's all good. I guess. I just never saw the two of you as a couple, looks aside, but whatever. And as far as why I asked you to come with me to this party. Let's just say, I think it will be a… uhhh, a learning experience for you."

Ignoring her on point comments about Robert and his looks, Cassandra continued so as not to give any credence to her words, "Learning experience? I don't know what your ass is up to, but I know pay back can sometimes be a mother fucker. You just remember that." Keisha just laughed and turned up the music as she bounced to some rap song to which she knew all of the words while Cass sat there holding on for dear life as she prayed that they would safely arrive at their destination.

83

As they arrived at the club, Cass noticed that there seemed to be nothing but women entering the club. She told Keisha, "Damn, it's a good thing I am not looking for a man. The ratio of women to men judging by the crowd out here must be ten to one." Keisha laughed out loud and thought, "I think it will be less than that." As they entered the club, Cass offered to pay for Keisha as it was one minute after ten and the club owners were not letting the fact that only one minute had passed alter their decision to charge full price. As Cass paid, the girl at the window looked at her and smiled. Cass felt somewhat awkward at how the woman peered at her, but could not place her finger on the exact reason why. As they entered the club, Cass noticed two women playing pool as they bounced to the beat of the music playing. She found it to be quite odd that in the midst of this club there was a pool table. She shrugged it off assuming that she had been out of the club scene for much too long. She and Keisha walked to the bar and each ordered their favorite drinks, a Long Island iced tea for Cass and vodka on the rocks for Keisha. They sat down at a table hidden away in the corner; in perfect position to view everyone who entered the club.

"So," Cass inquired, "what's going on chic? How was your day today?"

" It was fine, just fine," as she looked around the club anxiously.

"Where is your cousin?" Just as Cass asked the question, Keisha started waving at a couple beckoning them to come over. They began to walk over hand in hand looking so much in love and Cass just smiled wanting to tell them, "I know what you are feeling." As they got closer, Cass tried to hide her surprise when Keisha exclaimed, "Cass you remember my cousin Rachel."

"Yes of course," Cass responded while extending her hand uneasily.

Keisha went on to say, "And this is her partner, Chante'. I did pronounce that correctly, right?"

"Yes" Chante' responded in a markedly deep voice.

"Nice to meet you," Cass responded as she darted Keisha the evil eye.

84

Rachel then exclaimed, "This party should be happening tonight. Make sure you guys stay until the end because there will be a big surprise. This is a very special occasion because not only is it my birthday but it is the anniversary of when Chante' and I moved our relationship to another level." Cass observed the glimmer of excitement bouncing in Rachel's eyes as she stroked Chante's chiseled face and kissed her on her cheek. Cass tried not to stare as she curiously looked at the happy couple. Rachel looked the same as she had years ago when Cass met her at that NBA function with her fine ass man. Cass couldn't imagine what he must have done to her to make her hop on the other side of the fence.

Rachel was very pretty, Cass inquisitively noted, with her petite yet shapely frame. In New Orleans she would be considered a red bone with her yellow complexion, hazel green eyes and her flowing hair. Her hair was cut in a cute style that framed her face perfectly. Her partner, Chante' was quite attractive as well with her sleek and svelte body. Her thinness seemed to make the height difference between she and Rachel much more pronounced. Cass noticed her stunning olive complexion, which was accentuated by her catlike eyes and her full lips. Her hair was perfectly cut and lined in one of those very short curly dos that accentuated every facial feature. If you were pretty it worked, if you were ugly it was very apparent. For Chante', it worked. It was her lack of any distinct femininity that led Cass to believe that she and Rachel were a heterosexual couple as they were approaching. Chante' had on a well tailored suit that looked as if it could have come straight out of GQ magazine with tie and all. And Cass was amazed to see the Stacy Adams shoes which Chante' wore to complete her outfit. Cass presumed that Chante' must be the "man" in the relationship and just as she was beginning to feel more uneasy at the thought she was abruptly pulled back into the conversation when Rachel asked, "Are you family?"

"Family," Cass queried back in a perplexed tone. They all began to laugh as they realized that Cass had already answered the question in the negative by her response alone. With that, Chante' smiled and quipped, "Nice to meet you," as they walked away to greet their other guests.

Cass, still confused looked to Keisha and angrily yelled, "What's so got damn funny?"

Keisha still laughing responded, "Family means are you a lesbian, silly."

"Oh, well they are aware that I am not of the homosexual persuasion, right?"

"The homosexual persuasion," she condescendingly mocked, "what the hell are you talking about? You need to lighten up, girlfriend."

Then Cass quickly stepped back and gave Keisha the once over then stated, "Is this your way of trying to tell me something?"

Keisha laughing even louder as the music was ending, "I don't have anything against lesbians, but you know I gots to have my dick." Eyes began to dart in their direction as the word "dick" seemed to echo off of the walls in the silence of the room. They laughed shamefully and promptly headed to the restroom to hide their sheer embarrassment.

Once gaining their composure, Cass, as if totally shocked stated, "They are both beautiful women. Why can't they find a man?"

"Did you ever think they might not want a man? You are a typical homophobic who believes the stereotype that in order to be a lesbian a woman must not be able to get a man. You'd be surprised at the number of "straight" women who have had a piece of coochie."

Cass turned her mouth up and whispered, "Have you been with a woman, Keisha?"

"What difference does that make?"

Cass inquisitively looked and probed further, "I'm just curious. Honestly, have you?"

"Only once when I was in undergrad," Keisha finally admitted after endless prodding.

Cass screamed, "You've got to be kidding! Were you the man or the woman?"

"There your fucking ass goes with those damn stereotypes. No one necessarily is trying to be a man or the woman. There are no set rules or roles."

"Interesting," Cass exclaimed as she stood there in amazement trying to figure things out. "But Rachel had that fine man that she was dating. What happened to him?"

"It's a long story but suffice it to say that Chante' stole her from right under his nose."

"You mean that Rachel gave him the boot?"

"Basically," Keisha retorted. As Cass attempted to piece the story together in her head, Keisha broke her trancelike state by saying, "Enough dyke 101, let's get back out there and drink and have a good time."

Cass tugged at Keisha's arm anxiously before walking out of the bathroom and questioned, "What do I do if one of them asks me to dance?"

Keisha laughed and said, "Hell, if you find her attractive, dance."

They walked out of the bathroom, and Cass's usual confident demeanor was transformed into an awkwardly demure presence. Before going back to their table Cass pulled Keisha with her to the bar to buy her second Long Island iced tea. She needed something more to settle her nerves a bit. Keisha just shook her head and tagged along willingly, since she realized that she had been less than honest with Cass when she invited her to the party. Immediately on arrival at their table a woman approached Keisha and asked her to dance. Keisha accepted the request to Cass's dismay. Cass sat there uneasily peering at everyone around her and sipping continuously at her drink in attempts to mask her anxiety. Now she realized why the woman at the entrance smiled as she paid Keisha's way. She playfully gagged at the thought of she and Keisha being a couple. Keisha was her ace, but she knew that if she did bounce both ways, Keisha would definitely not be her type. Keisha was just a little too hoochie, with her always slightly too tight clothes hugging her pleasingly plump frame. As teenagers, Cass found herself jealous of Keisha because of her perfect shape compared to her own thin frame. But after too many poboys, gumbo, and genetics, Keisha's hour glass big fine curves were transformed into little mounds and hills by the time they reached college age while Cass filled out perfectly in all the right places. Keisha could still pull in the men, but always the wrong kind. As she thought of men, she again realized where she was and that she was not in the presence of any; at least not any straight ones. As she peeked up from the top of her quickly disappearing drink, she had to admit that she was quite surprised by the number of women there who looked just like her: professional and attractive women. Of course, she too noticed the women who could have passed for men and wondered if they had similar organs in the most vital areas. She tried to look in the crotches of some of the women to see if there was a hint of something there. She then quietly laughed to herself at her ridiculously childish curiosities. Cass almost fell out of her chair when she felt someone tap her on her shoulder. She tried hard to hide the true reason for the incident by nervously stating, "Whew! I guess I have had one too many of these," all the while knowing that she reacted that way because she was very intimidated by the setting.

The woman quietly responded, "You're okay. I was just wondering if you wanted to share your joke."

"Joke?"

"Yes, I was looking at you and noticed you laughing. I thought you might want to share it with me. My name is Lisa."

Cass clearing her throat, nervously chuckled, "Oh, that," she lied, "I was just thinking about something that happened earlier today."

"I see. And your name is?"

Cass briefly sat there in silence and wondered if she should lie or tell the truth. She had no idea why she was letting the environment intimidate her so. She then responded, "Michelle."

Lisa extended her hand and responded, "Well nice to meet you Michelle. Mind if I join you?"

"Well actually that is my girlfriend's seat. I mean, oh shit. That is my girlfriend as in good friend's seat. You see..."

Lisa interrupted, "No need to explain. I call my ex my girlfriend sometimes too. Old habits are hard to break. It's good that you two parted friends. That's fairly uncommon for us," she laughed. Cassandra in an exasperated tone responded, "No, you don't understand." At that moment Keisha walked up and intentionally hugged Cassandra and laid a kiss on her cheek.

Lisa promptly stood up and said, "Well, that is my cue. I don't have time for any drama. Nice meeting you Michelle. Take care."

Keisha laughing repeated, "Michelle, who the hell is Michelle?"

"Keep your voice down girl. That's my name tonight. I just feel very uncomfortable and I don't think anyone needs to know my real name."

"Whatever. Michelle," Keisha boisterously laughed.

Cassandra somewhat taken aback by Keisha's behavior but also somewhat relieved shouted, "Bitch, you better not leave me alone any more. If you want to dance any more tonight, it will be with me."

Keisha playfully responded, "Sorry, girlfriend. You are just not my type." Cass shooed her away with her hand remembering her similar thoughts about their lack of compatibility earlier and promptly changed the subject and stated, "A lot of women in here look quite normal. Like look at her over there sitting at the bar, she reminds me of your friend Lori from college."

Keisha noticed that Cass was getting more tipsy and relaxed by the second as she began to subtly bounce her head to the music. She then looked to the bar and exclaimed in surprise, "That is Lori."

"You have got to be kidding. Are there any straight women anymore? There used to be a line that people never crossed. Those lines seem to be totally obsolete these days. Chile, I guess you just never know."

Keisha just laughed at her friend who at least seemed to be enjoying herself a little more. "Well, I wonder what she is saying about you? Cass, look over there," she said pointing in the direction near the door. "That woman has been eyeing you since we got here."

"So what?" she uninterestingly yelled.

"Damn, I was just pointing it out. Look, I am going to go speak to Lori. Do you want a drink while I am over there?" Cass, now bordering on tipsy responded, "Why the hell not?"

Cass then curiously looked over toward the door to see the young lady that Keisha had pointed out. She seemed to be attractive from what Cass could see, sporting a nice red blazer and black slacks with a turtle neck. She had to admit oddly enough that she was somewhat intrigued by the thought of a woman finding her attractive. She quickly dismissed the entire thought and diverted her eyes over to Keisha to check out what was taking her so long as she was about to complete her drink and felt she needed another one. No sooner than she turned back to look towards the entrance, the woman who was checking her out stood right before her. Cass almost choked on her last swig of her Long Island iced tea. She in fact began having a coughing fit prompting the young lady to gently tap her on the back.

She then spoke in a soft tone, "I'm so sorry. I didn't mean to startle you."

Cass, totally embarrassed, finally completed her choking and said, "No," still clearing her throat, "it just went down the wrong pipe. Not your fault at all."

She took it upon herself to sit down and said, "Well, my name is Tanya." Cassandra still embarrassed softly responded with a slight smile, "My name is Cassandra," totally having forgotten her alias.

"Are you from Atlanta, or are you a transplant like most people?"

"I guess I am another statistic then. I am from New Orleans." Cass noticed Tanya's perfect teeth and her radiant smile as she laughed, "Well, I guess that means I am one of the few true Atlantans remaining."

Cass still nervous forced a slight laugh and said, "I guess you're right."

"So how long have you been here?"

"I actually just moved here about two weeks ago."

"Oh really," she smiled, "well I guess I'm going to have to show you around."

"I guess it would be more accurate to say that I just returned here, I was here some years ago in school." As she finished the statement she wondered if she was sharing too much information.

"School? Really? I just completed school one year ago. May I ask a personal question?" Cass wanted to respond "no" but figured that would be too rude. "You can ask, but that doesn't mean I will tell."

"How old are you?"

"That is a personal question. How old do I look?"

"I would say, um…," as she studied Cass's face. Tanya purposely was going to say younger than she believed just because she knew that's what women like to hear. She figured Cass was at least thirty but responded innocently, "Twenty-five?" Cass blushed while thinking I still got it going on. "I am actually thirty-four, why?"

"I was just curious. I am twenty-nine and dreading turning thirty. Maybe you can share with me how to make that transition smoothly."

Cass laughed, "Gosh, don't make me sound like an old lady. I still got the looks and the moves," she shouted above the music as she was beginning to feel more comfortable.

"I can see the looks for sure, but the latter remains to be seen. In fact, let's dance so I can see if the other half of that statement is true."

Cass flushed at her response and was hoping Keisha would come to save her yet again, but as predicted she was nowhere to be found. Cass knew that if it were a guy asking she would definitely dance because one of her favorite songs was playing. As Tanya sensed Cassandra's uncertainty she stood and prodded her more saying, "Come on. You know that's a jam." Cass finally stood and slowly moved to the dance floor, while praying that she would not run into anyone she knew. She began dancing stiffly at first and then as the music and her drink began to consume her she loosened up and her now flowing movements were captivating her dance partner. Tanya could tell that Cass was new to the scene and had probably been straight all of her life, a characteristic that she loved to take advantage of. She loved the challenge of getting a supposedly straight woman into her bed and really showing them what making love was about. Usually, after experiencing her, they forgot about all of their preconceived lesbian notions and made fools of themselves begging her to take them back after she had dropped them once she had gotten what she desired. She knew that there was so much trading off between women on the Atlanta gay scene, she wanted to reel in Cass before she became "tainted" by her gay counterparts. Too many women had already slept with ex girlfriends and it almost had become like an incestuous gay click. She did know she would have to take things slow and be patient, while guiding Cass into the lesbian world. She also knew that she wanted to make passionate love to Cass and leave her begging for more like she had done with so many women in the past. Her beauty was so innocent and a welcome change Tanya thought as she tried to reciprocally use her moves to begin enticing Cass.

Cass noticed the sensual moves which Tanya so eloquently displayed and was somewhat tripping on how smooth she was, but she also took this opportunity to truly observe Tanya. She really was a pretty woman, she thought. She had her hair neatly pulled back into a bun which made the diamond earrings she had on blatantly obvious. As Cass took notice of the diamonds' size Cass she wondered what this woman did for a living. Unless, of course, they were Cubic Zirconium. She then noticed her particularly expressive face, with beautiful and expressive eyes, which seemed to be hiding a deep and turbulent past. As Tanya caught Cass staring at her, she lightly smiled revealing her deep dimples which made her entire face glow. Wow, Cass thought while quickly averting her eyes, she is really attractive. As she looked toward her table, she saw Keisha who smiled and lifted her glass as if to say, "You go girl!" Cass then began to feel quite awkward yet again and was very eager for the song to end so she could escape the dance floor. It seemed like forever before the conclusion of the song. Cass felt herself on the wrong beat a few times which definitely indicated that she felt uneasy about the entire situation. Again, sensing her trepidation, Tanya grabbed Cass by the hand and eased her off to the side and said, "It was a pleasure dancing with you. Maybe you'll save one for me later." Cass smiled and said, "Maybe I will." As she turned to go, she heard Tanya say barely audible above the music, "You do have the moves too."

Tanya knew that she had to somehow get Cassandra's number before she left and she knew she had to make her presence known again before the night ended. As Cass quickly scampered over to the table, she noticed that Keisha had on a smirk that made Cass almost want to slap her. "What?" she questioned as she got closer.

"I told you she was looking at you, miss thing."

"Well, I told you not to leave me again. I couldn't be rude," she shouted. "Where's my damn drink anyway?"

"Girl, I ended up buying Lori a drink and sister ran out of money. I'll be happy to go get you one if you dish out the cash."

"Your trifling broke ass. Forget it. I'll get it my damn self." Keisha shrugged her shoulders as Cass pulled her purse and headed toward the bar. Tanya saw the entire interaction and wondered if Keisha was Cass's girl and if she would be an obstacle to her plans. Cass decided prior to buying her drink, she would explore the scene a bit and walked over towards the entrance where the pool table sat. She quietly observed the women around her again trying not to make any eye contact. She leaned against the wall and began feeling more comfortable as she watched the two teams of two women each try to break each other's concentration with playful derogatory remarks. It made her think back in the day when she played pool and how good she used to be. Cass however would not dare pick up a pool stick now since it had been over a decade since she had played. As she was reminiscing, a butch woman walked over to Cass and asked, "You play?"

Cass laughed and responded, "A long, long time ago, but not anymore." As they continued to have light conversation while they observed the game, Cass could not help but notice in the far distance Tanya lighting up a woman's cigarette while whispering something into her ear. Cass smirked and thought, "she must be a major player." Just as Cass began to turn away, their eyes met and Tanya winked seductively at her as she took a swig of her drink. Cass felt butterflies in her stomach as she instinctively smiled and quickly returned to her conversation. By the end of the conversation, the woman had introduced herself as Shawn and had persuaded Cass to be her partner in the next game of pool. Their turn had arrived and Cass was feeling a nice buzz as she bounced her head to the music. The game started out slow, but soon Cass had found her mark of the old days. As she sat along the wall letting her partner have her turn, Tanya walked over and whispered in Cass's ear "You did not tell me you could kick some ass in pool."

"Well," Cass unwittingly flirted, "you didn't ask." She slid off of her stool and had regained her confident stride as she called the winning shot, "Eight ball in the corner pocket." As she leaned over the pool table to make her shot, Tanya looked in delight at the perfect curve of Cass's ass. "Damn," she thought as Cass's prediction had proven true and the game was won.

Tanya then shared, "You know a better shot would have been to bank it off of the side and into this pocket," she arrogantly pointed out. "Here let me show you." She replaced the balls in their exact positions and slid behind Cass to let Cass still control the stick. As she leaned over Cass's body to point out positioning, their bodies met at the torso. Cass began to lightly perspire as their arms and torsos moved in sync as the stick slid between their hands. The breath of Tanya's words lingered on Cass's neck as she whispered in her ear, "Hit it slow and easy." Tanya's hands barely grazed Cass's hands as the white ball was hit into the eight ball. It all appeared to happen in slow motion as Cass's body sank back into Tanya's arms after the shot was made. Realizing this, Cass quickly regained her composure and turned herself away from Tanya's firm grasp and said, "Thanks for the tip," while walking away as she decided it was definitely time for her next drink. Tanya smiled and responded, "Anytime," as she turned to get her partner for the next game exclaiming, "Who's up next," trying to hide the excitement in her voice from that brief close encounter with her next conquest, Cassandra. "She sure does feel good," she quietly murmured as she watched Cass slowly disappear into the crowd of people at the bar.

As Cass began to order her drink she heard someone softly yell over her shoulder, "Make it two of those." Cass knew that it was Lisa who had escaped earlier in the night after Keisha had suggested by her actions that they were a couple. She gently rubbed Cass on the back and said, "This is my treat if you don't mind." Cass truly did not care at this point. She just wanted another drink and if Lisa wanted to pay for it, it was fine by her. Lisa then apologetically stated, "Sorry about my behavior earlier, but I have seen so many cat fights over silly bullshit like that."

"That's quite alright," Cass matter-of-factly responded. "Because she is not and has never been my girlfriend, which is what I was trying to explain to you."

"Oh, I see," Lisa excitedly responded while wondering if that meant the coast was clear for her to pursue. As two bar stools became empty, Lisa pulled out one and prompted Cass to take a seat. Cass reluctantly sat down but figured she owed this woman at least a brief chat for her drink and quickly retorted, "Thank you." The bar tender brought over their drinks as Lisa sat down and turned toward Cass while telling the bar tender, "Put it on my tab." Cass, thought, "Well, she must be a regular."

"So, Michelle, tell me a little more about yourself."

"What do you want to know?" Cass queried as she attempted to hide her surprise when Lisa called her Michelle.

"Well, for starters, where are you from and how long have you lived here?" Lisa questioned as she was obviously trying to pronounce every syllable of every word perfectly. Cass kept the conversation light and tried to appear interested, but this took more energy and effort than she could muster up in her tipsy state. Lisa also unfortunately was not easy on the eyes with her own eyes appearing to be spaced too far apart, her teeth needing much dental work, and her hair in a jerry curl almost allowing Cass to see her reflection off of her forehead. While Cass sat there trying to scheme a way out of the situation without being rude, Tanya came to the rescue and said, "You did save this one for me, right?"

Cass certainly relieved yelled above the music, "You know it," as she politely popped off of her stool and said, "Nice talking to you." Cass, so desperate to end her conversation did not realize until she hit the dance floor that she had agreed to dance to a slow song. "Oh shit," she thought. "What the fuck am I supposed to do now?" Instinctively, Tanya placed her arms around Cassandra's small waist and pulled her close to her body. Cassandra resigned to the fact that she had to do this and so she lightly placed her arms around Tanya's neck and begin to move to the beat of the song. As they danced Cass could smell the perfume that Tanya wore. It bore a sweet yet strong scent. Still tense she just observed the other couples around her and wondered if anyone else was in her predicament. Tanya was surprised that Cassandra had accepted her offer to dance, but she sensed that Cass was not interested one bit in her conversation with Lisa and figured that was as good a time as any to intercede. She could also tell that Cass was very stiff so she pulled her even closer to her and tightened her grip around her waist. Cass somewhat tired and tipsy unconsciously rested her head on Tanya's shoulder and let herself be taken by the music. Her stiffness began to subside as her body fell smoothly into the natural curves of Tanya's body. As the song slowly faded out, their embrace similarly ended as the next song was beginning. Tanya looked Cass in the eyes and said in a soft yet commanding tone, "Thank you Cassandra. It was indeed a pleasure." Cass was speechless and let Tanya glide her off of the dance floor into a secluded booth. "So Cassandra, tell me more about you and what you do."

Cassandra felt at ease with her and decided that she would be honest, "Well. I told you that I attended school here. I got my MBA from Emory and I now work for a brokerage firm."

"Oh I see. That's great. You are in the money field," Tanya responded as she was becoming more captivated by Cass by the minute. She liked her women smart because it made the conquest that much more savory. She gently smiled and made eye contact with her. Cass averted her eyes momentarily to avoid the stare and queried back, "So what do you do?"

"I am a physician. I just recently finished my residency in Ob/gyn." Cass became nervous as she thought about her sister and if she might know this woman. She knew Stephanie with her self righteous ways would have a fit if she thought that Cass was "in the family". Cass knew that their conversing would definitely now not leave the confines of this room. Tanya continued to be charming and finally she posed the question. "I really like talking to you and I would love to see you again. Will you give me your number so I can call you some time?"

Cass shook her head and said, "I'm sorry. I don't give out my number, but it was a pleasure meeting you and maybe we'll cross paths again sometime."

"Why leave it to chance. We can make sure that we cross paths. I tell you what. I will give you my card and I will write my home number on the back. I will leave it in your hands to call or not, but I hope you do." As she gave Cass her card she gently caressed her hand and affirmed, "It was definitely a pleasure meeting you. Call me." Cassandra arose from her chair unsteadily and said, "We'll see," as she slipped the card in her blazer pocket, "and thanks for the drink."

Tanya walked away pissed because no woman had ever denied her. She now knew that she would make it her business to cross paths with Cass again. As Cass reached the table Keisha was there with keys in hand and said, "Let's go, you flirt." Just as they were preparing to leave, the lights came on and Rachel and Chante' stood on the stage embracing one another as Chante' took the mic and said, "All of you are here to celebrate Rachel's thirty-sixth birthday. First, we would like to thank everyone for sharing in this wonderful occasion. This day also is our one year anniversary," she stated as she turned away from the audience and looked intensely into Rachel's eyes, and said, "It is on this day one year ago that my heart realized the true essence of love. You made me feel for the first time the intensity that such a bond could bring. It was not until I met you that my life became complete." She gently wiped the tears that began to roll down Rachel's face as she stated, "I love you, Rachel and it is on this day one year from now that I want us to commit to one another in the presence of our friends and family." The crowd began to thunderously applaud as the happy couple embraced.

Rachel then took the mic and said, " I love you too, Chante', but why so got damn long," she laughed. "Sister got to wait a whole damn year." The crowd laughed. Just at that moment, some scantily clad women began rolling out a cake which appeared to have hundreds of candles garnishing it and Chante' started the crowd in the singing of a soulful rendition of *Happy Birthday*.

In the glimmer of the candlelight, Tanya again allowed her eyes to meet with Cass's as she clapped at the completion of the song. Cass did not avert her eyes this time. She boldly stared back and gently met her smile with a smile. It wasn't until the crowd began shuffling before them that their visual contact abruptly and prematurely ended. Cass sat there immobile while trying to decipher the meaning of the awkward feelings stirring inside of her. She was submerged in thought and was not aware of the expression on her face until Keisha startled her back to reality stating, "Don't worry, your man will be back tomorrow."

"What made you say that?"

"Well, you had this look of longing on your face." Cass silently pondered Keisha's response realizing that Robert was hardly on her mind at that moment. She was glad that this point did not linger as her thought process was interrupted by Chante' who then exclaimed, "Thank you all. Ya'll get some of this cake and enjoy the music and drinks. The next round is on us," with that they walked off the stage with a piece of cake amidst the crowd of people surrounding them and congratulating them. Once they made it through the crowd they exited the club in grand fashion with a chauffeured limousine awaiting them. Cass sat there in a daze as she addressed Keisha and said, "What the hell just happened? Gay marriages are not legalized." She rambled on, "But they do seem to be so happy. I am happy for them, I guess. Can we go now?"

"Sure let's get out of here, but let me get a piece of cake first." Cass remained seated while Keisha retrieved her cake. Just as Keisha was returning, Tanya walked up to Cass and said, "I am gonna go catch some z's. I am on call tomorrow and need to be of sound mind. I hope to hear from you soon, and it was a pleasure meeting you."

"Likewise," Cass responded as Tanya walked away. Keisha laughed and said, " I see you have an admirer. I should catch her and tell her don't hold her breath with your homophobic ass." Cass laughed uneasily as they exited the club because she was bewildered by the unusual feelings she was experiencing. Cass was somewhat intrigued by this Tanya woman. She quickly and purposely dismissed the entire thought as the chill of the night hit them full force. They drove home in silence as each of them reflected on the events of the evening. Keisha was wondering what Lori was really doing there, while Cass was wondering if being intrigued by a woman and dancing with a woman made you gay. She was jolted awake by Keisha yelling, "You're home. Do you need me to help you get in?" Yawning, Cass slowly opened her door and responded, "No, I'll be okay," as she was pulled forcefully back into the car by the restraint of the seat belt. "Shit," she laughed, "it might help if I unbuckle the damn seat belt."

"You sure you don't need any help?"

"Girl, go home. Call me when you get there. I'll be fine." Cass quickly ran into the building as the cold air entangled her. When she arrived to her door, she thought, "Home sweet home." She quickly threw off all of her clothes and hopped into the cold bed. She was shocked that she did not immediately drift off to sleep. She decided to do what always helped her get to sleep. She began thinking of Robert and how much she missed him. She began to slowly caress herself. Soon her picture of Robert faded out and was converted to the shadow of a woman. She continued to gently caress herself and explore different parts of her body with an emotional depth that she had not experienced in the past. Her hands began to tremble as the intensity was mounting and the ambivalent shadow was replaced by a vision of Tanya. Cass began to perspire as she was about to reach her sexual peak and she found that she had to force herself to think of Robert. She used her pillow to muffle her gasp as her body uncontrollably shuddered more intensely than she had in a long time. She lay there feeling confused about what had just transpired. She thought, "I have apparently had too much to drink. That's all." She forced the thought out of her mind, closed her eyes, and focused on Robert's return, which could not happen soon enough as far as she was concerned.

Eight

The next morning Cass felt awful. She knew she had drunk too much the night before but as she jumped out of the bed and ran to the toilet retching, she could not believe how much she'd had. She continued with the dry heaves over the toilet and finally was able to pull herself together. As she returned to her room she glanced at her clock and was shocked to see it was after noon. "Shit," she yelled. "I have to get ready, Robert will be here any minute." Just as she was beginning to tidy up the place and pick up the mess from the prior night, her phone rang. "Hello," she bellowed into the receiver.

"You have a guest down here. Shall I send him up?"

"Already," she resigned, "yeah send him up." Cass scurried around her condo hiding things anywhere to lessen the disarray, while trying at least to find her satin robe instead of her old favorite robe that made her look homely with its colorful flowers embroidered in its pink flannel layers and the holes that completed its design. Her hair wasn't combed, she hadn't brushed her teeth, but when she heard the knock at the door she joked, "Well, he'll have to realize I'm not perfect at some point." She walked to the door, opened it and decided to feign sickness. "Hi, I'm sorry I look so bad. I just am not feeling too well," she sniffled.

He smiled broadly, "You look beautiful to me," as he grabbed her and hugged her. "I missed you," he honestly admitted as he snuggled her neck. Then he abruptly pushed away from her and laughed, "Your ass ain't sick. You been out drinking and you are hung over. You smell like a brewery."

Cass bashfully smiled, "Guilty as charged. Why don't you have a seat and let me pull myself together so I can greet you like you deserve to be greeted." As she turned to go to her room, he patted her on her ass and said, "Yes, why don't you do that while I get some coffee on to brew. Or better yet, give me the key so I can just come back up. I'm gonna go get us some cappacino and bagels, okay?" Cassandra yelled as she quickly moved to her bedroom, "My keys are on the table in the foyer." Robert left and Cass thought, "He has got to be one of the sweetest and most considerate guys I know." She then glanced at herself through the misty mirror and thought, "Damn, I look like shit." As she disrobed and stepped into the shower she began to think about what happened on the prior evening. She had to shake her head as she thought about the intense orgasm she had experienced. She felt a need to rationalize the entire incident to protect her once unwavering inherent sexuality. She attributed it all to drinking far more than usual and the environment that she had been present in for the entire night. She knew also that the thought of her being gay was ludicrous just because she was so in love with Robert Cason. She laughed and placed the thoughts of the previous evening exactly where they belonged— in her subconscious memory. She was sitting on the floor lotioning herself when Robert returned. "I hope you like cinnamon and raisin bagels, because that's what I got." "That's fine. Actually one of my favorites," she lied as she lifted herself from the floor and pulled the belt to her satin robe more snugly to her body. She walked over to him and hugged him and gave him a soft and wet kiss. He eagerly returned the kiss and said, "Now that's the type of welcome I like."

She gently smiled at him and said, "There's more where that came from. What do you want to do today?"

"Well, to be honest, I am a little tired from that road trip. I'd like to just relax and hang out here and spend some quality time with my baby. Maybe we can go out for dinner a little later this evening."

"Sounds good to me," Cass responded as she felt exactly the same after having retched and regurgitated what felt like her intestines earlier. She and Robert lounged around all day watching television and cuddling. Cass did not answer her phone at all. She left that duty to her answering machine. She was enjoying and devoting all of her time to Robert. They read the paper and had some insightful discussions about the world economy and laughed together at their shared geekiness. They eventually fell asleep and Cass awakened, surprised to find that the room was entirely black. She quietly slipped from under Robert's grasp and thought about awakening him to go out for dinner as he had suggested earlier. She then saw how peacefully he was sleeping and decided to surprise him and cook a simple meal. Cass was not a gourmet cook she woefully admitted to herself while shaking her head as she tried to determine what she could cook that would not require much time or talent. She decided to make spaghetti with a salad. She had made this combination several times in the past and knew that she could not go wrong. She put the pasta on to boil and put the ground turkey in the microwave to defrost. As she was beginning to prepare the meat sauce Robert sneaked in behind her and kissed her on her neck. Startled she jumped and spilled some of the wine she was drinking onto her chest. He laughed and remarked, "Sorry, baby. Let me get that for you," as he smoothly licked every drop of it from her chest and tried to open her robe a little more to expose her breasts. She promptly stopped him in his tracks and said, "Maybe for dessert, but let me finish this because I am starving."

"Okay," he unwillingly accepted as he quietly walked away like a child that had just been scolded. He turned on the TV and began watching the Sunday night football game on ESPN. Cassandra finally finished the meal and was somewhat disappointed with the finished product. She had mistakenly let the meat sauce cook too long when her mind had drifted to the evening at the club and the weird sensations which she had experienced. Fortunately, she was able to salvage some of it. She placed the food on the table and lit a candle, as she attempted to hide the burnt clumps of meat on her plate. She had scraped the top layer of the meat sauce off and gave that portion to Robert. He thought the food was delicious as Cass tried to force down some of her less than savory dish.

The rest of the evening passed by quickly as they watched a documentary on Malcolm X on the public television network. They joked around as Cassandra began preparing her clothes for the next day and Robert then questioned, "So, where were you last night?" This was a topic that Cass did not care to discuss in depth so she quickly answered, "Keisha wanted me to go with her to a birthday party for her cousin. It was alright, but I was just counting the hours until I could see you," Cass winked.

"Sure you were. Where was this party held?"

"Oh, some club on Peachtree Street. I forget the name." Cass immediately changed the subject asking, "So how did your meetings go?" She knew that he was such an arrogant little nerd that this question would inevitably lead to a thirty minute one-sided conversation as he was so proud of his business and how much he had accomplished. But this time it was fine with Cass; anything to get off of the topic of her prior night's outing. Before they realized it, they had talked until the wee hours of the morning and Cass grabbed his hand and said, "Let's go to bed. We both have busy days tomorrow." Robert regretfully pulled her into his arms and stated, "I have an early morning meeting on the other side of town. I think it would be best if I hit the road tonight to avoid the traffic in the morning."

Cass poked out her lip and whispered, "Robert, please. You have your own business. You make the rules. Stay with me tonight and we will set the alarm so that you can beat the traffic. Please," she childishly begged.

"I wish I could Cass, but this is a very important account. In fact I should have done some more studying on my client's portfolio tonight." As Cass begged she gently snuggled up to him and placed her hand firmly on his groin prompting him to sigh and exclaim, "Cass, why do you insist on attacking my vulnerabilities?" Shaking his head, he slid off his shoes and sheepishly followed her lead into her bedroom. Once there he turned her around to face him and stated, "So you want some of this," as he playfully nudged at his groin. He then commanded, "Set the clock for five A.M. sharp."

"As you wish master," Cass coyingly obeyed while smiling at how easy it was to persuade him. "Just like a man," she thought. Robert loved the sound of her uncharacteristic submissiveness and commanded, "Now get over here and turn around," while dropping his pants to the floor. Cassandra turned around right before him as he continued, "On your hands and knees," after pulling down her shorts and underwear with one stroke. Cass becoming more excited and eager to feel him promptly bent over onto the bed on all fours. "You sure you want this," he again teased. She knew exactly what she needed to do to end this prolonged cadence and get into the actual rhythm which she desired and whined, " Please sir, please." With that they began erotically marching to a flagrant theme as Cass enjoyed his animation and feeling him more forcefully than ever. "You feel so good baby," Cass moaned. Robert continued to make love to his woman responding in turn, "Oh baby. I missed you so much." Eventually, they collapsed after the rigorous activities and slept holding one another fitting together like a perfectly carved sculpture but not before he whispered, "I love you, Cass." Cass smiled and snuggled closer to him and eagerly responded, "I love you too, Robert," as she quickly closed her eyes to not allow the tears forming in them escape.

Nine

anya sat at the desk quickly trying to complete the notes on her patients after a horrible night's call. All she wanted to do was get home, take a hot shower and sleep. She had been in a zombie like state since the third of seven admissions. Today, however, she could not seem to focus. Her thoughts though begotten with fatigue kept drifting back to Cassandra who she had met exactly four months ago. It was fucking May and her arrogance would not let her digest that Cassandra had not even attempted to contact her despite the chemistry she knew she felt. All of her attempts to find out Cassandra's whereabouts had been futile and Tanya was considering hiring a private investigator to speed the process along. She had thoughts of Cassandra every day which had played a role in the failure of her three mini relationships since they met. She had placed Cassandra on a pedestal of perfection and none of the women she met could overcome or live up to her vision. Things had gotten to the point at which Tanya had to envision Cassandra's face to reach a climax in place of whatever woman she had selected to entertain her on that day. Defeatedly, she shook her head realizing that the image of Cass's face was becoming less and less distinct as the subtle, adorable features branded in her head were rapidly fading.

Finally completing her notes, Tanya slowly commanded her body to move to get her belongings so that she could get out of the door. Just as she turned to go, Dr. Jordan beckoned her into her office. "Tough night, huh?" she questioned.

Tanya lied, "It wasn't too bad but I am ready to catch up on some sleep."

"I'll bet. Well I just didn't want you to forget about the money that's due for the banquet. The deadline is quickly approaching."

"I know," Tanya haphazardly responded and began to spin around when she glimpsed at a picture on her desk. She then thought, "Goodness I am seeing images of this woman even with my eyes open, damn." She then shrugged her shoulders while preparing to leave and noticed that what she had seen was real, it was a picture of Cassandra and she presumed the rest of the family. Observing a surprised look on Tanya's face Stephanie exclaimed, "Is something wrong?"

"No, no" she stuttered, "I was just admiring your family. Is that your sister," she pointed at Cass, "because she looks familiar."

"Yes, that's Cassandra, but she's only been out here for about six months so I doubt that you have seen her before especially since she's a workaholic."

"A workaholic," she prodded hoping to retrieve some more information.

"Yes, she works for some firm out here, I forget the name but it's in downtown Atlanta." How vague could you fucking be, she thought, as she forced a smile and realized that further questioning would be inappropriate. "I see," she said as she turned to go.

"See you at the banquet, Tanya. Go get some sleep." Tanya walked with more pep than she had as she felt like fate was on her side. She slyly smiled, as she seemed to have unmasked some newfound energy and information. As she trotted to her car she quickly began the task of how she would use Dr. Jordan to get to her sister. As she hopped in her car she figured one of the easiest things she could discover is whether Jordan was her maiden name or not. She blasted her radio both to keep her awake and to bounce to the beat because she felt like now she was closer to her objective of seeing Cassandra again and the mere concept made her day, post call and all.

Ten

C ass would not have believed last year in Philadelphia that her life would be so different so soon. "Six months. Thank you Lord," she exclaimed while stretching her arms. On holidays she used to wallow in self-pity living the classic life of a thirtyish single woman. She remembered it all too well. Lying in her apartment bed alone barely recognizing that it was a holiday and wishing that she had gone home to at least be around live humans rather than the fake ones on TV. She would typically be so depressed during those times that she would almost inevitably call one of her bedroom buddies, usually Brian, who would at least fake like he cared before they fucked and he left. Brian was a tall and relatively attractive but uneducated guy who she could always count on for a good fuck. Yes, he was one of the few married men who she had allowed into her world, but it was only during the rarest of times. He lived in the same apartment building and therefore was easily accessible. She would never let anyone know that she was sleeping with the maintenance man at her apartment building. Not even her ace Keisha knew about him. All she had to do was page him and put in 1337, her apartment number, and shortly thereafter he would arrive to take care of her problems, which usually amounted to horny isolation.

They had met when she moved in and she needed some assistance getting some things into her place. He quickly came to the rescue with his tight jeans on hugging his tight ass and showing the imprint of his ample tools. It didn't matter that his country ass couldn't formulate a full sentence correctly. Brother was fine. Cass tried not to go there but after he had been there three times and was obviously flirting with her by winking his gorgeous dark eyes, she gave in to the temptations. Especially since Zachary was up to his trifling games at that time. So, Cass paged him one day and when he arrived, she blatantly told him that she wanted to fuck him. He told her he was married from the jump, and Cass truly didn't care at that time. He had been teasing her too long and she wanted him bad. She always felt so guilty afterwards as she always seemed to inevitably run into his wife at the mailboxes and she seemed to be so sweet. Always saying hello and smiling, readily driving the guilty stake deeper into Cass's heart. It wasn't until several encounters later that Cass learned that his winking eye was a nervous tic and that he never was flirting with her in the first place. Cass then rationalized that it was a means to an end, which they both ultimately enjoyed. Since those most desperate of times, Cass always prayed that in the next year God would be more merciful and help her overcome her dismal social life. She had no idea that her prayers would be answered so soon. She smiled broadly as she turned over to find remnants of Robert's cologne next to her on the pillow.

The previous months had been a whirlwind affair filled with romantic dinners, exquisite weekend getaways, culturally stimulating events, and passionate lovemaking. On Valentine's Day, Robert not only sent the typical bouquet of roses but the card attached stated, "Meet me downstairs …now. " As if by clockwork her private line rang and his voice exclaimed, "I'm waiting …come on down." He apparently had arranged things at her job to have the afternoon off as well as the next day. A limousine whisked them away to the airport and they caught a flight to the Bahamas. He had bought her an entirely new wardrobe for their three-day excursion. Ever since that trip Cass had essentially become a permanent fixture in Robert's beautiful home. She had become practically a Suzy Homemaker trying to cook a variety of different meals and even occasionally doing the laundry. She never had been particularly domestic, but lately she had been doing things simply because it felt so good to be sharing all of the everyday mundane tasks with someone else. The only major adjustment for her had been making the commute to downtown Atlanta from way North almost every day. However, going to sleep and awakening in Robert's strong arms always made it worth it. She laughed out loud as she thought about how love sick she sounded. If one of her girlfriends had made similar comments in the past, she would have gagged. But now the shoe was on the other foot, and was fitting perfectly.

Cassandra had never been so pampered in her life and she was getting terribly spoiled and loving every minute of it. Now, in a few days they were going on a planned trip to Aruba. Keisha was all but convinced that on this trip Robert was going to propose to her. She had mentioned it so much that Cassandra was convinced of it as well. She was trying not to jinx herself and get too excited, but everything had fallen so perfectly into place that she knew that a proposal soon was almost inevitable. They had even briefly discussed things like marriage and children, both of which they desired, coupled with the fact that they were not getting any younger. Throughout the next couple of months they had become practically inseparable and she had begun to casually and purposefully leave various portions of her wardrobe and toiletries behind. It started out with a toothbrush and make-up and gradually escalated to include almost half of his closet. She laughed as she turned over again and caught a glimpse of Robert's reflection in the bathroom mirror as he carefully and methodically shaved his head. She watched his biceps smoothly contract with each stroke while his pecks responded similarly. She found it hard to believe that God saw it fit for him to reemerge into her life after the many years she overlooked him and was down right mean to him. But she still had to admit that he did not fit the classic mold that Cassandra had always imagined would encompass her soul mate. She however was not remiss in thanking God every night for placing this wonderful specimen of a man into her life.

Cass had always envisioned herself with a chocolate man but Robert was a golden yellow. She had always stipulated that her dates be taller than six feet which she thought was the perfect complement to her five foot six frame with or without heels. Robert was pushing five foot ten. She had grown to be biased to the thinner framed men after her cousin had informed her years before that they were the ones who had the length and the width to reach the spot. Cass, of course initially had no idea as to what her cousin was implying until she was schooled during her senior year of high school when she slept with lanky ass Darryl. She muffled a laugh as she thought about how she was walking gapped legged through school for the next week. Startled, Robert turned around as his towel fell to the floor and exclaimed, "Hey sleepy head. So, you finally are awake, huh?" He leaned over to pick up the towel and Cass quickly retorted, "No, leave it down. I like to look at your bare ass." He obliged her and continued shaving his head. He is no Darryl she giggled silently while observing Robert's fine compact frame, but he is certainly packing enough for me as she recalled the several times that brother had a sister feeling like she had a dry tampon in place.

Robert then broke her peaceful tranquility after framing his goatee' perfectly around his mouth, "If we're to make it to eleven o'clock services, we need to get moving," as he picked up his towel from the floor and threw it in her direction. He walked over and placed a kiss on her cheek, tapped her ass and said, "Come on. Get up while I get some breakfast started." Robert was very much into church ever since he was a kid. His need and desire to be in church was consistently reinforced by his psychoanalyst whom he saw regularly, which also served as a form of therapy of sorts. Going to church served to keep him grounded so he would not succumb to the worldly possessions and desires that arose with being rich. He always needed to remember where he came from to help him stay on track and not fall into the depression which he had in the past. Cass was hardly an atheist but she always had felt growing up that church was a chore rather than a pleasure. Now, partly due to maturity and a reverence for a superior being but also due to a renewed sense of self and respect for life's hidden gifts, she had now begun to develop a genuine liking for the church. This simple acknowledgment received much acclaim from her mother who was ecstatic that she was now seeing a churchgoing guy. Cass was now attending church at least three times a month as opposed to the once every other month only after being coerced by her guilty conscience.

Realizing that her time was truly limited, she bounced out of bed and detoured from her original route to the bathroom and proceeded into the hallway to ask Robert to bring up her purse. Just as she leaned across the iron rail she shrieked as she found herself totally nude staring in the face of another man galloping up the stairs. Not even averting his eyes he exclaimed, "Hi, I'm Jason, Bobby's brother." Too embarrassed to respond Cass ran back into the bedroom slamming the door to muffle the chuckling which followed. She retrieved her bathrobe as Robert slowly opened the door. "Sweetheart, I'm sorry. I guess you met my brother, Jason," as he walked over to console Cass while trying not to laugh at her flushed face.

She hit him and yelled, "Nothing is funny. Your brother just saw me totally nude."

"Don't worry. It's okay. I forgot to tell you. He came in last night. He's going to house sit for us while we're away in sunny Aruba." She jerked her purse from him and shooed him away while traipsing into the shower. She figured she might as well get over the embarrassment as she was sure to be seeing a lot more of Jason at the rate that the relationship between she and Robert was intensifying.

Keisha a few weeks prior helped Cass shop for some appropriate attire including sexy lingerie and a subtle engraved silver bracelet for Robert to also have as a keepsake after he proposed and placed a beautiful ring on her left hand's fourth finger. While thinking of the vacation ahead, Cass smiled and extended her left hand into the stream of the shower and imagined a large pear shaped diamond with its shiny platinum band which she expected to be surrounding her fourth finger over the course of the upcoming week. In fact, she and Keisha were going to the spa the next day to assure that her fingers were perfectly manicured for the occasion. Cass smiled and shortly thereafter was interrupted from her pleasant thoughts by the sound of Robert's voice yelling for her to hurry. So, she scurried around quickly to get ready all the while beaming and recognizing that for the first time in years, she was stable in all aspects of her life. She might be able to finally erase the shadow of her grandmother that loomed over her, taunting her almost every day since she had turned thirty. Mocking the fact that she was still alone and searching. But now she was at a new peace emotionally, spiritually, professionally and personally and she could not ask for anything more except another pair of nylons to replace the ones she had just torn. "Shit," she exclaimed as she looked for the clear nail polish and was grateful that she was wearing a particularly long skirt that day as she ran down the steps to start her day with Robert.

Eleven

While standing in the long line at the airport, Cass looked down at her nails to admire her beautiful French manicure. Keisha's ghetto ass tried to get her to get palm trees painted on her nails. She wisely chose not to make that fashion statement and quietly laughed at the mere idea of it. Robert pulled her close to him, smiling and said, "What's so funny?"

"I was just laughing about the palm trees I told you about." He just shook his head and questioned, "How can two such close friends be so different?" Under his breath he added, "Thank God."

She nudged him replying, "She's truly a good person. So I guess that's one characteristic we share."

"That is indeed debatable," he laughed while laying a gentle kiss on her lips. Cass could feel the Ativan begin to take effect as she sought her seat on the airplane. She would usually be a basket case, anxiously awaiting takeoff, but now she was the epitome of calm, even sharing pleasantries with fellow passengers. As they slowly began their departure Robert gently squeezed and rubbed her hand. That gesture alone probably did more for her than any pill could do. With that, she closed her eyes and lay her head on his shoulder as she thought of the sunny coast which awaited her.

Robert, contrary to Cass, loved flying. As an indigent child in the back woods of Georgia he had always dreamt of flying as a reprieve from the many pressures which seemed to embody him. Growing up in a single parent home the eldest of four siblings, he had become the provider and disciplinarian at far too young an age. Growing up for him was encompassed by betrayal and a rapid realization of innocence lost. His external environment filled with drugs and violence played a large role in destroying his childhood, but the most detrimental offender occurred very much within the confines of what was supposed to be his place of comfort. His own home.

Robert's mother had always been a very independent women, and ever since his father left them when he was five years old, she worked several odd jobs to make ends meet. It wasn't until Reginald, his mom's boyfriend came into their lives that she was able to quit one of her three jobs and have a tad bit more energy and time to spend with them. At first it was great. Hot home cooked meals replaced the Spaghettio's alternating with ramen noodles daily. When Robert's mother would leave for her night shift job at the hospital, Reginald watched the kids and essentially took on the role of provider taking much of the pressure off of Robert who was only eleven years old at the time. Robert's job as the eldest was to help his younger siblings complete their homework and tidy up for bed. After they were put to sleep, Robert and Reginald would drink beers and watch a variety of porn flicks, all of which his mother was unaware. However, this secret was one which Robert treasured as a growing adolescent boy. And he was going to protect what he had recently learned was his indelible right as a man. At least that was how Reginald made him feel. Like his buddy and friend. Everything was cool until one night after Robert had put his siblings to bed Reginald was not sitting in his usual spot waiting for their nightly ritual. Robert then went to his mom's room where he suspected Reginald had dozed off and opened the door and was immediately silenced when he saw him fucking a woman who was not his mother, in his mother's bed. Robert's heart began beating at a rapid pace as he forced himself to run out of the room. Because if he didn't he thought he might have been capable of killing him and he didn't want to follow in the footsteps of his father who was in jail for doing just that. Killing some guy who stepped on his shoe. At least that was the story on the streets. "How could he?" he thought after his mom had provided his sorry ass with shelter and food, amongst other things. Reginald came out of the room and chastised Robert. "Boy, you never just walk in a room without knocking."

"This is my house mother fucker and I walk anywhere I fucking please."

"Listen, bruh. Are you a man?"

"Yeah I'm a fucking man," Robert angrily responded.

"No," Reginald challenged, "Are you a real man?"

"What's your point?"

"As a man, it is our duty to please our women. No real man has only one woman, you have to spread the love and you would know that if you were a real man. Now there is something I want you to do if you claim to be a real man."

Robert being sucked in responded, "What?"

"Go back into that bedroom, right now."

"For what?"

"Just go." Robert hesitantly walked back to the room where the scantily clad woman walked over to him and began to unbuckle his pants. He felt his manhood begin to rise, despite his commands to do otherwise. She knelt before him and pleasured him until his legs felt like elastic. "Shit," he thought, as he quickly pulled up his trousers and silently left the room passing Reginald on the way who patted him on the shoulder laughing and saying, "Now that's my boy." Robert, confused, not having felt anything that intense except in the setting of a wet dream quietly lay in his room and rapidly fell asleep.

Shortly thereafter, Robert graduated to having sex with the women that Reginald brought by the house. They would either each have their own bitch as Reginald put it or they would take turns with the same one. This began to occur almost weekly and Robert had immeasurable mixed emotions. Deep inside he knew it was wrong and he wanted to tell his mom, but he was enjoying being a man and screwing these older women. All of which would cease if his mom found out. So he kept rationalizing that Reginald's definition of being a man was right and that it was their duty to please these women and to always have more than one. Again, in the blink of an eye, his perception of Reginald and all his manhood talk was changed forever when one night he and Reginald were hanging out waiting for the women to come over.

Reginald in his drunken state, walked over to Robert and said, "I'm going to find out how much of a man you are."

Robert shrugged it off and laughed saying, "You want to see how many bitches I can screw in one night? Come on, it's on."

"No," Reginald brazenly retorted, "You're gonna be my bitch tonight." With that he pinned Robert down and raped him. When he was done, he stood up and teased, "You ain't no man. You just a little bitch too. You my lil bitch. Now get cleaned up and go to bed and stop that crying. Oh, but before you go, change those sheets so I can have a fresh pair to fuck your momma on." Robert lunged at him and futilely yet steadily punched him. But Reginald was a large man at six feet tall and roughly two hundred fifty pounds who just laughed at Robert's fruitless attempts to combat him. Eventually, Reginald dragged Robert to his room and left him on the floor silently weeping. Robert felt totally confused and dejected while trying to decide what he was to do. Finally, he realized that the only thing he could do was confide in his mom or he would end up spending the rest of his life in jail, and he did not want to become yet another statistic.

"Robert, I don't want you to become another statistic like your pa and half of the other niggas out there. You're gonna be different," he could vividly hear his mother say whenever he did or said anything out of line. Robert prayed harder than he had on any night in his life asking for forgiveness. He eventually mustered up the courage to share this horrible revelation with his mom, who expressed disbelief, but never doubted him. The day after he told his mom, Reginald was out of their lives and she was forced to resume her previous unrelenting work schedule once again.

Robert never got over the guilt he felt for his actions. He knew that his mom had taught him the morals and values to be a good man and he abused them horribly to his advantage. Then when his manhood was compromised he spoke up and she never even questioned him or challenged other possible motives he might have had. She took his word and by doing so had to restructure her life for the benefit of her family. He never forgot her unconditional love and one of the first things he did when he finally got a descent paying job was buy her a new home.

The turbulence jarred Robert back to the present as he quickly wiped the tear rolling down his left cheek. He was happier than he had been in a long time and had finally come to terms with his past, a trait which his psychoanalyst finally helped unveil after countless years of therapy. He had problems believing that he deserved any happiness. Now that Cassandra had come into his life, he more than ever felt a need to resolve those issues if he was going to be man enough to do right by her. He then gently rubbed her cheek which lay on his shoulder and thought, "I truly love this woman," while wondering if she shared his heartfelt feelings. His pleasant thoughts were interrupted by the words, "Peanuts, sir?"

Cass slept through the flight and only awakened when the rubber on the wheels hit the pavement in Aruba. "Wow," she thought, "we're already there. I guess that pill Keisha gave me really did its job." Robert groggily responded, "Yep, you wouldn't even wake up for our delicious meal of turkey, mashed potatoes and gravy. With the appetizing peanuts that followed for dessert," he joked. Cass could not believe how beautiful it was as she stepped into the limousine awaiting to drive them to their hotel. She slid her sunglasses down out of her mangled hair and exclaimed, "Oh, Robert this is beautiful." Looking over the top of her glasses she sincerely said, "I love you Robert Buster Cason." He laughed and smiled as he snuggled her closer and said, "I love you too Cassandra." They rode off in one another's arms— Cassandra thinking about what month they would marry, and he thinking of the beautiful eighteen-hole golf course which awaited him.

They had a wonderful night with dinner over candlelight at a restaurant with a gorgeous view of the horizon. Cassandra wondered if Robert would begin the trip with his proposal or end it with the proposal. She quickly shook her head to force herself not to be overly zealous about something which she wasn't even sure was going to happen. "What are you daydreaming about?" Robert questioned.

Cassandra laughed, "I'm just looking forward to my day at the spa tomorrow. I can't wait to be pampered."

He squeezed her hand and winked at her and responded, "I expect to be doing some pampering of my own tonight. I plan to fulfill all of your desires." Cassandra slid off her sandal and boldly placed her foot into his crotch and countered, "I expect nothing less." As their bill was paid Cassandra began to stand and Robert said "Sit down a minute, will ya?" She eagerly sat down and thought "Will this be the moment? Is he going to get down on one knee?"

She slyly smiled and exclaimed, "Yes, Robert." He began to awkwardly tilt his head and stated, "We're not quite ready yet." Cass had no earthly idea what he was referring to, "What do you mean, Robert?" she asked, thinking this was still a scheme to entice her.

"Buster and I aren't ready yet." Trying to hide her disappointment, she quietly sat down as she realized that her foot in the crotch ploy had gotten Buster up and would be quite apparent if he stood up at that moment. She faked a smile and waited for his cue to leave. They rode home in silence. This silence was quickly replaced by moans as they made passionate love in the hotel. Cassandra thought about how Robert truly tried to fulfill all of her carnal desires while she was beginning to drift off to sleep. There was only one desire which he hadn't fulfilled— her desire to officially become the future Mrs. Cassandra Nicholas-Cason. Almost as soon as she had conjured up her new identity, she wondered how Robert would feel about her hyphenating her name. "I have worked too damn hard to earn my credentials as Cassandra Nicholas to throw it all to the wind now," she thought to herself. Not a second later she changed her mind. "What the hell? Cassandra Cason would be just fine." She then closed her eyes and snuggled up to her man.

Twelve

he next morning Cass and Robert had breakfast as they began to prepare for their separate days. Cass realized if she was to accept one flaw of Robert's it was his mixing of business with pleasure. She used to be almost as bad when she first entered the corporate world trying to be the best of the best. But after too many sleepless nights and missed opportunities she made herself transition from that type A personality to a type "me" personality. She still had much work ahead to get him into a similar frame of mind, but was up for the challenge. Today, he was meeting CJ for a game of golf to discuss potential joint business ventures while she was going to spend the day being pampered at the spa. They would meet up again at four o'clock to go on a tour of the island. As she continued to feed him the chocolate covered strawberries while she ate her bran muffin she smiled at him seductively. "You keep that up woman and you will miss your day at the spa." She looked at her watch and noticed it was almost ten o'clock and quickly stood up, "Shit, it's time honey. I'll see you in the hotel lobby at four sharp." She smacked him on the lips as she departed with his eyes gazing on every sway of her hips. She confidently turned around to him and stated, "Good Luck with your golf game. I hope you score well over par." All he could do was chuckle at her lack of knowledge of the game and exclaim, "Yeah. Thanks."

It was four-thirty, and there was no sign of Robert and they had missed the shuttle. Cass was seething. She finally decided that she was not going to let him ruin her vacation. She could not believe that he waited to get her on foreign land and stand her up. "This is some bullshit. And he knew how much I was looking forward to that fucking tour." She hopped in the elevator blatantly feeling teased by a couple laughing and embracing one another as she forcefully jabbed number six as the doors closed. She sat out on the veranda as the sun was beginning to set. Still no signs of Robert. She retrieved her messages from her cell phone fully expecting one of them to be Robert, but it was her mother wondering if she had made it safely and Keisha wondering if her left hand was any heavier. Finally, the hotel phone rang, "Hello," she answered in an exasperated tone.

It was Robert sounding as if he were under water, "Sweetheart, I'm sorry. I've tried to reach you but my calls would not go through. Can you hear me?"

"Barely, but I can make out what you're saying. What happened?"

"It's all my fault, business affairs took longer than I expected, but I am on my way to you honey. Don't be mad. Remember this trip was partly business and we can go on the tour tomorrow, okay? I love you."

Cassandra forced a smile and weakly responded, "I love you too." She was still angry that he stood her up, but she knew she needed to get over her spoiled inclinations. Finally, at seven o'clock, the door slowly opened and there was Robert waving a white flag and carrying some flowers. Angrily, she stuttered, "Well, it's about fucking time."

"I'm sorry sweetheart, I came very close to closing a deal and I could not leave with things up in the air. I am so sorry, but the deal did go through and I can be all yours tomorrow," he bargained while pulling her close to him with the corners of his mouth turned down in an exaggerated frown and his eyes pointed toward the floor.

She weakly tried to push away but quickly had to smile at his playful antics and replied, "All mine tomorrow, huh?"

"Yes sweetheart. One hundred percent yours. I can also make

it up to you tonight in the secret confines of our room," as he continued to firmly embrace her. She quickly turned out of his grasp and tried to hide the tears beginning to well up in her eyes. Cass could not believe she was about to cry. "Damn, I must be PMSing," she thought to herself. Instead of letting Robert witness her vulnerability, she picked up her purse and began to leave the room. "You men always think you can satisfy things with sex."

"Where are you going?" Robert, perplexed by her behavior, promptly followed like a dog obeying his master. She remained silent and continued on her way. They rode down the elevator in silence and he followed her to the restaurant for the buffet. They sat and ate in silence for most of the meal with Robert saying a variety of things in an attempt to make her laugh. Finally, Cassandra gave in. She figured he had suffered enough for his mistake and hopefully he had learned his lesson. She also hoped her feigning anger might help him justify proposing at that time. Just as she began to loosen up a beautifully tanned black woman with a flawless complexion walked towards them with her red halter dress with splits on either side that displayed her curvaceous legs with each stride. She walked over to Robert who stood up as she kissed both of his cheeks and he the same in turn. Cassandra graciously smiled as she awaited an introduction to "the bitch," and she then corrected her thought and changed it to "the woman." After all, she had no need to be intimidated by her.

"Robert, dear. Nice to see you again," she said with a British accent.

"The pleasure is all mine. CJ, I would like you to meet my friend Cassandra. Cassandra this is CJ." Cassandra tried hard to conceal her shock as she realized that this was the business associate bitch with whom he had spent the entire day. "Oh hell no," she thought as she extended her hand, "Nice to meet you." Cassandra sat there trying hard to maintain her composure as CJ and Robert shared some laughter about their day. Finally, CJ with her perfect teeth smiled back at Cassandra and stated, "Have a great vacation dear. I will try not to steal too much more time with Bobby." Cassandra smiled and was initially speechless and without thinking she said, "Take me home," not realizing that she was eating in their hotel lobby. "Shit," she thought, as she immediately stood up and walked away enraged. Robert stayed behind to pay the bill and quickly went to the bar to have a drink as he mentally prepared for what awaited him upstairs.

Robert entered the room to Cass angrily pacing the floor. "How was it?" she screamed. Robert hesitantly responded, "How was what?"

"How was it fucking that bitch all afternoon?" His eyebrows raised and his eyes widened as he angrily retorted, "You have it all wrong. Our relationship is purely business, and if you feel so insecure about us, you have a lot more growing up to do. If I wanted to fuck her, as you so readily put it, I would have left your ass in Georgia, and fucked her the entire week." Cassandra could not hold back her tears as she turned away from him pondering what her response would be.

"If your meeting was so innocent why didn't you tell me that CJ was a woman, a beautiful woman at that." Instead of waiting for an answer, Cassandra rambled on. "Why did you introduce me as your friend?"

He walked over to her and embraced her from behind. "I don't see her as beautiful. I see her as a potential client. She is not the woman I want to be with. I brought you here because I love you. I'm not ambivalent about my feelings for you. I'm in a field where I will be meeting with beautiful and educated women all the time, and if you are not secure in my love for you, then maybe we need to rethink us." Robert dared not mention to her that CJ was the only woman that he had ever broken his rule with a couple of years back. When he first founded Cason Securities, he had vowed he would never mix business with pleasure—until he met CJ. CJ was almost ten years older than him but her stunning beauty together with her sassy and sophisticated attitude became an insurmountable challenge. Eventually they shared a few sexual encounters but that was the past. Nevertheless, CJ was still a tad upset that Robert had brought Cassandra along because if it were up to her their sexual relationship would still readily exist. However, after realizing that he had lost significantly on the market because of his skewed priorities after mixing business and sex, Robert vowed never to mix the two again, and he hadn't despite the obvious temptations.

Cassandra turned around with her eyes wearied and red from crying, "I'm sorry Robert, I feel so incredibly stupid right now. I trust you. I do. It's just that you always seem to make me your priority and in this instance, for a change, I felt like I was playing second fiddle."

"I love you and only you Cassandra Nicholas, and I have loved you for a long time. And this time my love is being reciprocated and it feels great to finally feel loved by the woman I have cherished for so long."

Cassandra's tears began to flow again as she rashly wiped them away exclaiming, "Oh Robert, I'm sorry. Forgive me for being so childish. I am so happy and I guess I am afraid because I don't recall being this happy in my life. I'm afraid that I will wake up and find that this was all a dream." They embraced and kissed and continued to exchange those two simple actions throughout the night. That night they did not make physical love but rather intensified the emotional love that seemed to solidify the bond which they shared.

The week had gone by particularly fast and despite Aruba's aesthetic beauty, Cass and Robert spent much of their time indoors touring one another. Cass also made Robert promise that there would be no further interaction with CJ longer than two hours or a situation in which she could not access him. He originally denounced the whole idea as silly, but eventually obliged her because he figured that it was not a battle worth fighting. Cass was finding it harder and harder to be subtle as she was packing her bag to return to the states and her left fourth finger remained bare. "Robert," she queried, "You do love me don't you?"

"Of course, sweetheart."

"Do you think I am wife material," she stuttered, "because a lot of men seem to think I am too dominant and too independent for that lifestyle, but I can be docile and sometimes downright submissive, you know. I mean, I am a human being just like anyone else and us working women need lifetime companions too."

Robert kept his response simple as he tried not to laugh at her blatant curiosities, "You're good people Cassandra, and someday you're going to make somebody a very happy man." Seeing that she was getting nowhere and somewhat embarrassed she slammed her suitcase shut and defeatedly acknowledged that she was not going back to the states an engaged woman. "Whatever," she thought as she closed the room door for the final time, "he obviously doesn't recognize what a hot commodity I am."

They dropped their baggage off at the concierge desk and went to the restaurant to feast on the delicious brunch that was prepared. Cass still was in disbelief that Robert didn't take advantage of the perfect ambiance to ask her for her hand in marriage. Ever since resolving their conflict on the second day of the vacation, everything had been almost perfect. They had gone snorkeling and sailing and dancing. And of course they had the most wonderful lovemaking, including one night on the veranda with their sweaty bodies immersed in the heat as if they had just taken a long run on the beach. She got chills as she thought about it and slammed her legs shut as the sensation seemed to encompass her pelvic walls. Cassandra was so immersed in thought she did not see the little blue box that Robert had slid before her. Cass tried to suppress her excitement as she exclaimed, "For me?"

"Of course, sweetheart. Go ahead. Open it," he beckoned. Cass slowly began to open the box as she wondered why his ass was not on one knee. Her eyes became wide with surprise as she saw the beautiful diamond elephant pendant which she was admiring a few days previously.

Cass tried hard to hide her disappointment as she whimpered, "It's beautiful Robert."

Robert either was ambivalent or ignoring her as he exclaimed, "You thought I didn't see the sparkle in your eye when you saw it the other day, but I did and I sneaked back around to purchase it for you." As he sat there congratulating himself, Cassandra rolled her eyes and lied, "You are so observant." Without taking a breath she stated, "Are we ready?"

Robert rubbed her hand and smiled, "I love you baby."

Cassandra just feigned a smile as she stood to leave, because she could not muster the positive energy needed to reciprocate a similar response. Cass quickly dropped the box containing his bracelet back into her purse as she now had no desire to complement his trinket. As they landed on US soil Cassandra had procured a major disliking of elephants as she laughed at her childish resentment.

Robert then interrupted, "What are you thinking about woman?"

She flatly responded, "Elephants, Robert. Beautiful elephants." They rode off to her condo enjoying being back home. As they pulled up to her building, it felt like Cassandra hadn't seen it in much too long to be paying for it on a monthly basis. It was after midnight when they arrived and all Cassandra wanted was to take a shower and hop in her own bed, alone. As Robert prepared to go into the garage she stopped him and said, "Maybe you should go on home tonight. I feel like I need my space tonight," she lied as she was blatantly trying to punish him for not reading her mind and asking her to be his wife in the preceding days. Maybe this night away from me will help him realize how much he wants to share his life with me she thought as she hugged him and laid a flat kiss on his lips. He asked, "Are you sure? At least let me help with your baggage."

"No, Robert. Really it's okay. I got it," as she slammed the trunk shut. "Okay then," he resolved, as he opened the door to the building for her. "Thanks Robert. I love you and I'll see you tomorrow okay."

"Okay, baby. Love you too. Peace," he touted back in a deep tone like the kids were saying in Aruba. She turned and laughed responding similarly, "Peace."

Robert hopped in the car and could not help but laugh. He laughed until his stomach began to hurt. He saw the disappointment on her face after she opened the box with that cheap ass elephant in it. He then opened the locked glove compartment and pulled out the three karat diamond platinum ring which he had chosen several weeks prior with Keisha's help. Originally, he was going to ask her to marry him in Aruba, but after her ridiculous accusations about CJ he figured he'd leave her hanging just a while longer. He was planning on giving her the ring that night, but she opted for him not to come up, so he figured he'd allow her to suffer one more night. But, after that night, no matter what, he wanted her to know that he wanted to share everyday for the rest of his life with her. She was his soulmate and he couldn't help but smile warmly at the thought of finally being at peace with himself and his life. He closed the glove compartment and headed home listening to smooth jazz while wondering what month they would marry.

Thirteen

ass was not prepared for her alarm to ring when it did. She thought she had turned it off, since she had taken the day off from work to have at least one day to get her life back into some semblance of normality. She turned over to catch a few more winks of sleep and was jarred awake again by the shrill of her phone. "Shit," she thought as she quickly grabbed the phone, "Hello."

"Ma'am we are taking a poll and would like you to answer a few questions." Cass slammed the phone back on its cradle and yelled, "There's the damn answer to your questions," as she pulled her pillow over her face and through her fatigue couldn't help but laugh at her brazen lack of tact. She then turned over to sleep longer as she felt significantly jet lagged from the trip, but not before turning the ringer off on her phone. When she finally awakened she was shocked to see that it was three o'clock in the afternoon. She was shocked that Robert didn't awaken her as he now had a key to her place and could get up without buzzing in. She turned to call Robert and began dialing his number but rather decided to call her mother to at least inform her that she was back. She knew that her mother was one of the people on the answering machine which she neglected to listen to so late on the prior evening. Her mother quickly answered the phone, "Hello."

"Wow," Cass exclaimed, "You did not even let the phone ring, who were you expecting?"

"Cass?" her mother yelled into the phone.

"Yes, mother. It's me."

"Oh, I was waiting for your father to call. I just paged him because he got a phone call from that new office here that he is trying to get a part time position with. How's my baby?"

"I am fine ma," Cass disinterestedly responded, as she hated any conversations concerning her father. Her mother then said, "Hold on, baby. I hear a noise." As Cass waited she reflected on her relationship with her father. She had begun to despise him years ago when she found out about his numerous adulterous affairs. Their relationship was cordial but restrained. Cass laughed in amazement sometimes at how she and her father played each of their roles almost flawlessly. Cass sometimes had to force her daughterly behavior at the beckoning of her mother, such as acknowledging her father on holidays and such. She always was sure to buy the blandest of cards so as not to misguide him into thinking that she had forgotten his meandering ways. He was lucky that she even continued to communicate with him, as Stephanie and her older brother Dwayne had not exchanged words with him for several years. Poor Casey had been caught in the worst years of their parents' relationship woes. She had to endure the arguing and served as the peace maker most of the time. She still dutifully played that role and therefore did not take sides for one versus the other. She probably was the glue that held them together. Cass getting impatient sighed as she heard her mother fumble back to the phone. "That man, I am gonna kill him," her mother stated in an exasperated tone. "I bought him that beeper for important reasons like this and he leaves it here at home. I mean…"

Cass knew the routine well. Her father always did things like that when he did not want his whereabouts known. She attempted to console her mother indirectly by saying, "Well if it is meant for him to have the job, he will get it. He'll get the message when he gets home. Anyway, I just thought I should tell you that I am legitimately falling in love and I figured you should know. The trip to Aruba essentially solidified my feelings."

"Oh Cass, did it happen yet? Did he pop the big question?"

130

Just as quickly as Cass smiled while thinking of Robert, the corners of her mouth took a dive as she reluctantly cleared her throat retorting, "No, not yet." On that note, Cass decided to cut the call short. "Well, mom. I need to go. I love you and I will tell you all about the trip later. I bought you a souvenir that I'll express to you. Bye." As she was clearing the line she faintly heard her mother return her accolades as she hung up the phone.

Cass could not believe that Robert had not called or just come by. She figured his workaholic butt had probably gone into the office. She dialed his work number only to get his voice mail and therefore pressed star two for his home. After only one ring she heard a woman's voice on the other end. She thought to herself, "Now today is not Sunday. Who in the hell is this now?" growing more upset she angrily quipped, "Is Robert there?" As she waited for a response she heard many voices in the background and wondered if he was having a celebratory party because of his account. As she waited someone else came to the phone and said flatly, "Who is this?"

Cass becoming more aggravated by the second stated, "This is Cassandra." Another long silence elapsed and she could hear fumbling on the phone. Finally, another woman came to the phone and stated, "You are the bitch. You are the one to blame." Cassandra totally confused now queried, "Blame? Who is this and what in the hell are you talking about?" She yet again heard a fumbling for the phone and an elderly sounding woman came to the phone and apologetically stated, "I am so sorry. Forgive my daughter, we are all at our wits end right now. Robert," she stuttered as her voice quivered and broke into a muffled moan, "was in a terrible accident."

Cassandra's hand began to shake uncontrollably as she was trying to comprehend what was just told to her. She then said, "This is a cruel joke. I just saw him last night." Her voice began to tremble and she said, "So will you please put him on the phone." A male then came to the phone who sounded like Robert and as she was about to let out a sigh of relief he said, "Cassandra, this is Jason."

"Jason, would you put your trifling brother on the phone?" As he continued on it was obvious that he was putting much effort into remaining stoic. "Last night," his voice now becoming more inaudible as he fought to find the words and hold back the tears, "on his way home a drunk driver crossed the midline on the two lane highway, and Robert was killed instantly." Cassandra still confused and trying to keep her body from trembling stated in a barely audible tone, "That's not true. It can't be true. Please tell him I'm not mad," as she began to move into an upright position from the stool in her kitchen and felt her knees beginning to buckle below her. "Tell him I will cook a special meal tonight. We don't have to go out. Please give him the phone. Just give him the phone."

"Cassandra, are you okay?" She dropped the phone and slid down onto the cold marble floor almost pulling down her framed portrait while unsuccessfully trying to grab anything that might support her weight. She then let out a high pitched shrill as her body succumbed to it's trembling. She lay there on the floor entirely numb as she tried to awaken herself from what she thought was a terrible dream. The coldness of the floor was now replaced by the heat produced by the friction of her body's uncontrollable shivering. She lay there for what felt like hours in disbelief and subconsciously waiting hopelessly for Robert's knock at the front door. Cassandra eventually pulled herself from the floor and in a daze walked to her bathroom to retrieve her leftover Ativan from her recent trip. She quickly placed two of them into her mouth and moved toward her bed. She knelt down on her knees instinctively to say her prayers but abruptly rose to her feet. She felt God had dealt her a horrible injustice and any attempts at praying would have been futile and hardly heartfelt. She instead opted to lie on her bed and hold herself tightly while rocking to and fro to the rhythm of her tears falling onto her bed. She eventually fell asleep as dawn quietly approached.

The next morning Cassandra awakened to the banging of her door. Groggily she pulled herself up and saw that it was Keisha. As she opened the door, Keisha extended her arms around Cass and her body slumped into them as she began to cry. Keisha just stroked her friends back and comforted repetitiously, "Let it out. It's okay." Keisha had heard on the news earlier that morning about the horrible accident and rushed to Cassandra's aid. She guided Cassandra over to the sofa and stated, "Do you need me to do anything? Have you called work and told them you would be out?" Cassandra remained silent and shook her head in the negative. "Don't worry, I will handle it. I will call them." Keisha fought to hold back her own tears as she observed Cass's disheveled appearance and the dark lines which encircled her eyes. After calling her work and explaining to them Cass's tragedy, Keisha put the coffee onto brew and turned on the shower. "Come on Cass," as she gently tugged at her to get out of the bed and into the shower.

"No, please," were the first words which finally had escaped her friends dry mouth since she had arrived. "Please Keisha, I just want to stay in bed." Keisha having experienced true clinical depression knew that her role needed to be supportive but firm. She then explained, "Cass, this will be an awful ordeal for you, but you cannot let this terrible thing drive you into a frenzy. Now get in the shower." Cass slowly dragged herself into the shower as she felt hopeless and lifeless. The water trickled down her body and as it hit the shower floor sounded like a drum purposely taunting her horrific headache. Keisha played back Cassandra's messages while she was in the shower. One was from her mother who was totally unaware of Cass's recent woes. Two from her as she was trying to make sure Cass was alright after she heard the news of Robert's death, and one from a Mrs. Cason who beckoned Cass to call and was particularly apologetic about the previous night's exchange. She described that they were going to try to handle things simply and promptly as Robert would have wanted. As Cass stepped out of the shower, she could hear Keisha talking on the phone. She quickly dried herself off and heard enough of the conversation to know that Keisha was talking to her mother. She quickly grabbed the phone and as she heard her mothers soothing voice was moved again to tears as she longed for her mother's arms to comfort her. Cass felt like a young child as she begged, "Oh, mama. I am hurting so bad. Make it go away."

"Oh baby, I am so sorry. He is in a better place. He is with his Savior and Father. It is God's will."

"How can God be so cruel? How can He?" Cass's voice faded away as she tried to understand the justice in such a cruel reality. Her mother continued to comfort Cass, but realized that right now her words were falling on deaf ears. Keisha took the phone and reassured Cass's mother that everything was going to be okay. During lunch breaks and after work, Keisha made sure that Cass had eaten and dressed in the days leading up to Robert's funeral. Keisha was not going to be able to attend the funeral but made sure that Cass's outfit was prepared for the Saturday services. Cass's mom also could not make it to Atlanta because she was a matron of honor in her sister's wedding that weekend, but Cass felt that she needed to be alone anyway to truly grasp its reality. Cass had not returned Robert's mother's call as she felt that no apology was necessary under the circumstances but she had resolved that she would introduce herself to his family after the funeral and would prepare something to bring to the repass after the services. She felt that introducing herself to them before hand would have only served to interrupt her private mourning for Robert and make her the spectacle of attention to his many family and friends, who in some way seemed to indirectly blame her for his death.

Fourteen

Saturday turned out to be a rainy and windy day. Cass slowly dressed in her plain black rayon dress that Keisha had prepared for her on the previous evening. Cass looked at her friend soundly sleeping in her bed after staying up half the night consoling her and giving her the strength that she needed to get through this day. In some ways, Cass was glad that Keisha had another engagement because she felt like she needed to do this alone. She felt that to get closure she had to privately tell Robert good-bye without concern of the humanly pathetic distractions of how she might appear and how her exterior demeanor, usually so strong, would be quickly dismantled as she entered the services. Yes, she was glad that she had not yet met his family and could anonymously and without conservation mourn her lover's death. After dressing, Cass applied a little make-up, purposely excluding the mascara and eye liner that usually completed her ritual, as she knew that they would eventually become streaks of black adorning her face. She slowly picked up her keys as she was preparing to leave, now feeling more trepidation about the entire day ahead. Just as she was trying to convince herself to go, Keisha's hoarse voice rang out, "You're gonna be okay. Now go on and be strong. I love you." It was as if Keisha knew exactly what Cass needed to hear to get out of the door. Cass went over and kissed her friend, whose eyes were barely open, on the cheek and said, "Thank you Keisha. I love you too," as she quietly shut the door and obeyed her friends orders.

The harsh rain was limiting Cass's ability to see as she approached the site of the funeral, and she was surprised by the number of people already present. She was forced to park a few blocks away because the parking lot was already full. Finally finding a parking space, she felt her hand tremble as she turned off the car's ignition. As she felt herself beginning to hyperventilate, she took a deep breath and forced herself to open the car door while simultaneously and unsteadily trying to open her umbrella. Cass began walking quickly at first as the wind was brazenly hitting her in the face. Her body abruptly stalled to a halt as she saw the black hearse heading her way escorted by a fleet of police motorcycles. Her eyes began to water as she was beginning to realize the finality of it all. Cass no longer was fazed by the wind or the rain, now recognizing that she had to concentrate on her every step as her legs felt like they were ready to buckle beneath her weight. It was as if she had to mentally reinforce the nerve pathways that the brain so masterfully used to enable the process of walking. Finally, through much effort, she arrived at the entrance to the church and quickly found a seat near the back practically drenched but totally unaware of her physical state.

The church was beautifully adorned with what appeared to be hundreds of flowers. There was a huge choir singing accompanied by an organ, their voices and their movements echoing the feelings of everyone present as they slowly swayed to and fro in their gold gowns lined with black. It was hard to hold back the tears amidst the music and faint cries emanating from all areas of the church. Cass was stoic for the most part, silently crying as she thought of the last times she had shared with Robert. Finally, the pallbearers slowly marched in as the choir hummed a chorus of *Amazing Grace*. Cassandra now felt herself succumbing to her emotions as a moan escaped from her mouth. She quickly bowed her head as the tears began to flow more readily. It was then that she wished someone was there to hold her and tell her that everything was going to be okay. They finally placed the mahogany coffin accented with silver at the front and kept it closed while placing a wonderful picture of Robert on the stand. Cass barely heard the things being said by the several people who went up to memorialize

Robert, as she still felt like she was in a state of shock and denial. She had finally gotten her tears under some measure of control, but knew that she was barely holding on. The choir then began to bellow one of her favorite gospels, *His Eye is on the Sparrow*. She could feel her hands beginning to tremble yet again. As she tried to contain them, she felt warm hands envelop hers. She looked up to see a woman who looked particularly familiar but Cass could not place her. The woman's eyes were so warm and caring as she removed one hand from Cass's grasp and placed it around Cass's shoulders. Almost instinctively Cass laid her head on the woman's shoulder and began to cry harder than she ever imagined she would. It was as if the woman knew that a mere touch would give Cass the needed permission to let her feelings out and mourn Robert. Cass had no idea who the woman was, but at that moment it hardly mattered. She had unleashed Cass's initial phase of closure, as she responded to Cass's sobs by saying, " It's okay. Let it out," and that she did.

As the funeral procession came to a close, Cass began to regain her composure while the masses of people began filing out of the church. As she turned to thank the woman who had been so kind and compassionate, she was shocked to see that the seat next to her was empty. She was gone. Cass then began to question her own sanity. Wondering whether the woman had actually been there or was rather a figment of her imagination. Puzzled and a little paranoid, Cass stepped out into the crowd and quickly headed to her car so that she could follow the motorcade to the site of internment. Standing around the grave site, she unabashedly searched for the mystery woman but without success. She then bowed her head as the minister extended his final words and the casket began its descent into the ground. Cass amongst many others began to silently cry. There were two women up front who ran to the opening in the ground and fell to their knees begging for them to stop. Two men, including Jason, gently eased the women up and held them tightly as they cried and screamed uncontrollably. As the final patch of dirt was laid down, Cass walked over to place a rose and say her final good-bye to Robert. She recited a silent prayer and she gently smiled while thinking of Robert's wonderful hugs. As she turned to stand, Jason met her with a hug and said, "He truly loved you Cassandra and I'm sure I am not telling you anything you don't know." Cass just hugged him tightly and remained silent while tears continued to flow. "I hope you are planning to come to the house. The rest of the family is very eager to meet you."

Cass wiping her weary eyes responded, "I am. I know he would want me to meet everyone. It will be nice to place the faces with the names."

"Would you like to ride with me?"

"No thank you, but I'll be there, I promise."

"No problem. We'll see you there." They parted ways as Cass made her way to her car and proceeded to Robert's home.

Cass drove in silence to Robert's home and reminisced over their short time together. She was still puzzled by the woman who consoled her who seemed to disappear in midair. She was sure that she had seen this woman somewhere before and that she wasn't hallucinating. At least she hoped not. Finally having arrived at his home, she was in total disbelief that she wasn't going to be following her almost daily ritual of pulling into the driveway and quickly walking along the walkway into the home with her key and bellowing Robert's name. She inevitably would fall victim to his ridiculous hide and seek game having to always seek him out as he always liked to jump out and surprise her. "Wow," she whispered to herself and shook her head, "what a great loss. Robert was a successful African American man doing the right thing and now he's gone." Cass was still finding it hard to believe that such a tragedy could be God's will. Her spirituality, which had always been so firm and rooted, was being put to the test and Cass was afraid of the outcome.

As she mentally prepared herself to go into his home, Cass vaguely remembered a brief and not so pleasant exchange with one of his sisters several years ago when she and Robert were in business school. It was at a time when she was using guys to get her meals, sex and help minimally supplement her negligible income. Back then she was hardly interested in Robert intimately or otherwise. He had invited her to a social dinner for some special occasion, which she

138

could not recall at the moment; she just knew that it was a free meal. At the last minute, while getting prepared for the event, she received a buzz from downstairs. She thought that it was Robert a bit early, but to her surprise it was her casual supplemental sex partner and after a long week of tension and tests, hot sex far outweighed the lure of a hot meal. She let Mark upstairs and they barely spoke a word while they quickly hobbled out of their clothes and began old-fashioned fucking. No foreplay, no false innuendoes, just wild sex. As she lay there eagerly receiving Mark, the buzzer from downstairs began to ring. She knew it was Robert, but soon the sound of the annoying buzzing was quickly replaced by her moans as she had a wrenching orgasm. Eventually the buzzing subsided and Robert left. Cass did not attempt to call him. She figured he would get over it and maybe catch a hint that she was not interested. She eventually ran into him when his sisters were dropping him off for class that week since his car had died several weeks earlier. He must have told them right at that moment who she was. The younger sister immediately hopped out of the car and shoved Cassandra saying, "You ain't nothing but a whore. How could you stand him up like that?"

Robert interceded, "Leave her alone. I'm sure she had a good reason."

"Good reason my ass," she angrily responded. "If I ever see you again, I will hurt you. Nobody plays my brother like that. He could have invited anyone, but he chose your sorry ass," with that she turned and hopped in the car while displaying a lewd gesture with her middle finger. Cassandra felt awful after Robert explained to her that the evening was a special invitation only dinner commending his commitment to excellence in the Boys and Girls club in his community. He had paid one hundred dollars for her seat which remained empty and taunted him for the entire evening. Cass was ashamed of her behavior and vowed that she would make a change in the priorities in her life. Nevertheless, the growth and changes that she had vowed would not take effect for several years to come, as good sex continued to take precedence over and over again. Cassandra was terribly embarrassed by those childish years of her life, but she hoped they had all grown from those foolish years, and more importantly she hoped that his sisters had plain forgotten about the entire incident.

As cars drove up and distracted her from those old memories, she briefly glanced at herself in her rearview mirror, touched up her lipstick, and woefully admitted that there was nothing that she could do to conceal the swelling which had developed beneath her eyes. She was very dubious about how his family would receive her, but finally stepped out of the car because their meeting was inevitable. Immediately upon her entry into the home, she was greeted by Jason. "May I get you something to drink?"

Shyly Cass responded, "Yes please. Coke would be fine," she stated as her throat seemed to become dry the instant she walked through the door. As he poured her a drink he stated, "I apologize in advance if anyone is inappropriate. We all have had a terrible time dealing with this and sometimes emotions run high."

"Well, Jason, this has been very hard for me too. I keep wondering and questioning if there was something I could have done to avoid this awful tragedy." She began crying and admitted to herself that if she weren't being so selfish he would have stayed the night. However, that was a secret she would carry to her grave, because to admit that out loud would make the guilt she already felt more tangible, and that she could not handle. Then from out of nowhere a young woman sarcastically chided, "If your ass was a real woman, he would not have been trying to leave there in the first place. Didn't I tell you if I ever saw you again I would hurt you? Bitch!" she screamed as she lunged toward Cassandra. Speechless, Cass quickly jumped away from the open hand but could not avoid the cold splash of wine that slapped her face instead. Before she could form her lips to make a response, Jason found some napkins and began to help Cass dry off while he tried to calm his sister, "Nicole, please. We are all hurting here. No one is to blame. I'm sorry Cassandra. This is our younger sister Nicole."

Trying to be bigger than the stinging words and the befitting welcome, Cassandra extended her hand. Nicole promptly turned around as if no one stood before her. "Again, I am terribly sorry. She was particularly close to Robert, because he had helped her get back on her feet. Let me introduce you to the rest of the family." He gently grabbed her arm and took her to an elderly woman sitting on the beautiful love seat on which she and Robert had cuddled many nights. She alone however almost matched its size in width. "Mother, this is Cassandra." She prompted Cass to take a seat in the small area which remained available on the sofa. Cass did so and the woman placed her arms around her and said, "Don't you let nothing that's said here today faze you, chile. Robert loved you and I know that alone means that you come from good peoples." Cass felt the warmth and love emanating from his mother. "They call me Mama Lilly. Now you go and make yoself at home."

Jason pulled her to meet his two other sisters who were out on the deck watching their oblivious children playing in the yard. "Yolanda and Tammy, this is Cassandra." Tammy who was almost as robust as their mother was very pleasant and responded, "It's so nice to finally meet you. You're the first woman that Robert dated that he ever mentioned to me," she gently smiled. Tammy was the oldest of them all and exuded that maturity.

Yolanda on the other hand sighed and responded, "Ya'll better get that bitch outta my face. I ain't got shit to tell her ass." Cassandra could no longer let this antagonism go on, "Listen. I loved your brother. You can certainly choose to go on blaming me and allowing the past to influence your behavior, but I am not to blame. Robert and I had grown to cherish and love one another deeply. No one wishes Robert had stayed over that night more than me," her voice began to crack as she damned herself not to cry, "and that's the bottom line." Cass turned to walk away and find the nearest restroom to regain her composure. She was not about to let this turn into some torrid drama. As she turned the bathroom knob, she was immediately stopped in her tracks because the door was locked. Steaming, she leaned against the wall and took a few deep breaths as she waited for its occupant to exit.

As the door opened, Cass realized that she had not been hallucinating at all. It was the woman who was consoling her at the church. Cass was not going to let her escape again without thanking her. "Excuse me," Cass said as she tapped the woman on her shoulder, "I just wanted to thank you for lending me your shoulder to cry on." The woman turned around and as their eyes met, Cass knew that there was something so familiar about her. The woman simply responded, "It was no problem at all. I sensed that you needed that comfort and I was there to provide it. So I did." She touched Cass's hand gently and smiled as she retreated. Cass walked into the bathroom and shut the door. As she squatted over the toilet, she was puzzled because the voice sounded familiar as well. Cass almost fell into the toilet once she realized why this woman was so familiar. Her hair was down and she was wearing glasses today. That is why she could not place her before. It was Tanya. The woman who she had met several months before at the club. Cass was in shock and now a nervous wreck for different reasons. What if she told them that she was at a gay club? What if she mentioned that they had shared a slow dance? What if she mentioned that Cass had taken her number? "Shit," Cass muttered as all these thoughts repetitiously raced through her mind. "Talk about drama." Cass decided that she needed to make a quick exit in hopes that Tanya would not remember her, especially since she was not particularly welcome there. Let alone the fact that she felt like this in all actuality was she and Robert's home and irrationally felt like her privacy was being terribly invaded. This was the home they had shared for essentially three months and nobody really knew that fact as Robert's mother was from the old school and totally rejected living together without marriage. Although if anyone looked in his room or bathroom, it was truly evident that she essentially was living there. As usual Robert always tried to protect and obey his mother's wishes at all costs unbeknownst to her. She presumed at some later date she would retrieve her clothes and would likely have to purchase some for the upcoming work week since almost her entire wardrobe had been transplanted to his house. Again her eyes began to well with tears as she prepared to leave what was to be their home happily ever after. The happiness, which the home once exuded, was now replaced by intense sadness. Overcome by that reality, Cassandra rushed to the door for some air as she suddenly felt like the house was smothering her.

Fifteen

anya had immediately spotted Cass at the back of the church almost as soon as she entered. She wondered how Cass knew Robert, but figured it likely was through investing like her. She figured this had to have been fate. During the funeral proceedings she kept observing Cass's pew to determine if she was alone or with someone. When it became evident that she was alone, Tanya decided to make her move. She had hardly heard anything being said during the services, as Cass had become her primary thought and her primary objective. When she noticed that Cass appeared to be near her boiling point she used this to her advantage and slid over to comfort her. This hardly was a selfless act. Tanya had ulterior motives. She desired Cass and just touching her made Tanya horny, even in this most inappropriate of settings. She knew that if she played her cards right, it would at least get her a dinner invitation. Once at the house, she knew that she had to be very subtle because it was apparent that Cass was in the closet in a major way. But if she had to use bribery to get the dinner invitation, she would. She could easily threaten to expose Cass and definitely get her wishes but she wanted to avoid doing it that way, because it would make it all that much harder to get with her. So Tanya decided to keep her cool. Tanya presumed that Cass must have been quite close to Robert evidenced by her emotional breakdown at the funeral and she had every intention of preying on her vulnerabilities.

Cass, after regaining some composure, reentered the house which was cool now compared to the heat outside since the sun had parted the clouds. She knew that she had to avoid Tanya at all cost. She figured the best thing for her to do was to gracefully leave after once again expressing her condolences to Robert's mother. Cass, therefore actively looked for Robert's mother, who was no longer seated on the love seat. She did see Jason, however, and opted to ask him of her whereabouts and also tell him that she needed to head to her side of town. "Jason," she called out as he appeared to be going in the other direction. Turning away from the woman on his arm he responded, "Yes Cassandra. Let me introduce you to my fiancee, Julie. Julie, this is Cassandra. Robert's friend that I told you about." Cassandra trying to ignore the fact that she was lilly white as she was anxious to leave, she extended her hand and said, "Nice to meet you." Turning back to Jason she said, "I was looking for your mother, to tell her good-bye."

"I believe she's in the back room. Go straight through that door and make a left going all the way down the hall until you can go no more. What am I thinking, I'm sure you know exactly where it is. Anyhow, she should be in there." Jason proceeded to hug her and said, " Please don't be a stranger. Though it might not seem so right now, we consider you family." Cass returned the hug and responded, "Thank you so much Jason. I'll keep that in mind." Pleased that she had not yet run into Tanya, Cass rushed to the back where Mama Lilly was sitting alone. Cass knocked lightly on the door. Mama Lilly looked up and said, "Come on in chile. Come sit and talk to Mama Lilly." Cassandra tried to figure out how she could graciously excuse herself. Cass sat down uneasily and said, "It was such a pleasure meeting you. I can now see where Robert got his gentle spirit." Without taking a breath, Cass continued, "I'm exhausted and I believe it would be best that I leave since I have such a distance to drive."

"You could always stay here the night so as not to have to rush yoself."

"Thank you for your kindness, but I must decline," Cass stated as she inched into a standing position. Mama Lilly then extended her arms and sorrowfully beckoned, "Well come on and give me a hug. You come back and visit us once things is calmed down a bit. Okay?"

"I will be sure to." Cassandra responded as she turned to go. Cass breathed a sigh of relief as she closed the door behind her and began the trek to her car. Just as readily as she had seemed to disappear earlier at the funeral, Tanya appeared out of nowhere. "Now I know why you look so familiar to me," she said as she reached out to hug Cass. "How are you? I've been waiting for your call."

Cass embarrassingly sighed, "So much has happened in that time with Robert's passing and all. There has just been no time."

"I know. This was so sad and unexpected. Now that you see I am legitimate folk," she said while pulling out a pen and card, "write your number down so that I can call you and we can meet for dinner some time. I can tell that you must have been very close to him and it's times like these that we need diversions."

Cass, feeling like she made a good point, wrote down her number and said, "Sure. Give me a call." Upon taking the pen and paper back, Tanya's hand brushed Cass's on purpose as she winked and said, "I will do that. Drive carefully." Tanya turned feeling like she had accomplished her goal and decided she would leave too. She did not set foot back in the house. In fact she did not even know Robert that well. She followed the people who she knew would be going back to the house specifically for the purpose of seeing Cass and getting her digits. She smiled and patted herself on the back as she unlocked her SUV door and hopped in and blasted the same CD she had blasted en route to the house: Juvenile singing *Back That Ass Up*. She put on her shades and bounced her head in sync with the music, feeling that the long trip was well worth its while.

Cass hopped in her car and wondered if anyone had seen that exchange. She didn't resist giving Tanya her number because she wanted this obvious interaction to end as soon as possible. Especially if Robert's family was aware that Tanya was gay. Cass still thought it quite ironic that she had run into Tanya. She flushed as she remembered the last time she had thought of her. She was in a very compromising position. She shook her head as she began the long drive home. She begrudgingly admitted that she was still somewhat intrigued by Tanya for some reason. So feminine, she found it hard to believe that she was gay. She lightly giggled for the first time in a while as she recognized that Keisha would have reprimanded her for using such stereotypes. Cass was remiss in giving a fictitious number as she had done numerous times in the past, but part of her was interested in at least talking to Tanya a bit more. "I could talk to her and still never see her again," Cass rationalized with herself. She then turned on her radio and listened to classical jazz for the remainder of the drive home thinking of nothing at all. Just driving.

Sixteen

The next two weeks went by particularly slowly as Cass tried to return to her normal routine. Her days were consistently mundane, beginning with a hot cup of coffee, going to the office, doing the minimal required, returning home, taking a shower, and going to sleep. Cass seemed to have no energy. She had not gone to her mail box, and the ringer on her phone was set to the off position because she had no desire to talk to anyone. She had been remiss in checking her messages and only called those people who she knew would be worried if she had not checked in. Her life had turned into a vicious cycle of remorse and guilt. The highlight of her life now was the end of the work week, when she could stay in bed and not be obligated to anyone or anything. When Cass's alarm went off on one particular Friday morning, she was not startled because she had been up several hours. She had been having dreams of Robert throughout the night and kept awakening in the midst of tears. So finally after the last dream at four AM, she decided she would stay awake so as not to have to endure the replaying dream of she and Robert and their nuclear family being so perfect yet again. She just lay there looking at her reflection on the ceiling above until the sound of the alarm was a welcome diversion.

Cass was glad it was casual Friday since she had not prepared anything the prior night. She pulled on her blue jeans and slipped her silk blouse over her head. She looked at herself in the mirror and was startled by how worn she appeared. After washing her face and brushing her teeth, she pulled her hair back into a tight bun, applied some lipstick and a little blush and headed out the door. She stopped at McDonald's and got her mandatory cup of coffee and continued on her way to work. On her arrival to the office, Cass noticed that no one else was casually dressed. She had forgotten all about the late memo which she had received on the previous day revealing that there was a board meeting that day and that they were expecting a visit from the CEO. Cass immediately walked into her office and closed the door while shaking her head in disgust. As soon as she sank down into her chair there was a knock at her door. In an exasperated tone, she yelled, "Come in." It was Linda, a colleague who since Cass's arrival at the firm had kept her distance and at the maximum extent was barely cordial. Linda spoke firmly but in a softer tone than usual, "Listen, Cassandra, I do not want to pry, but you seem to be going through some changes here that are affecting your work. I know we have never talked much, but I enjoy not being the only woman here with a brain. And quite frankly I don't want to lose you. I have been on Prozac for the past two years and it has done me wonders. You might want to try it to help you get through whatever it is you are going through." She then extended her hand with a card in place. "Here is my therapist's number, use it if you like. By the way, I suggest you go on and leave for today and use a sick day. The CEO is on his way and you don't need to meet him in your current state. I will cover for you. Just get yourself together and call me if you need to. See you on Monday," she endearingly spoke while quietly shutting her door. Cass sat there silent during the entire exchange. She did not know if Linda was being sincere or not, but Cass knew that she was right and that was the bottom line. Cass picked up her things and did as Linda suggested. She left for the day, determined to get herself together no matter what it took. Though she realized that it was easier said than done, she knew she had to do it before she sank into a depression that required medications. Cass, being the egocentric woman that she was, did not usually wear her feelings on her sleeve. Now that her life was a shambles, it was evidently out of her control.

The fact that others not close to her were aware of this fact made Cass reevaluate her situation and made her determined to overcome this huge obstacle. As she closed the door to her office, Cass vowed that she would also close that chapter of her life and try her damndest to move on.

Bright and early the next morning Cass was awakened by the phone. She had forgotten what its ring sounded like as she had just turned the ringer back on after nearly a month. "Hello."

The surprised voice on the other end exclaimed, "Cass, hey girl, are you ready? I am so glad that I did not have to leave a damn message again. Come on down."

"Come on down? Keisha, what in the hell are you talking about?"

"Remember, I told you that Eric got those passes for a full day at the spa. Girl, let's go get those kinks pulled out of these rusty bodies, get our manicures and pedicures, and head out on the town. I left the full message on your machine last night. So come on!"

"Keisha, girl, I really don't," she stopped herself in mid sentence remembering what she had promised herself the night before. She then sighed and said, "I'll be right down."

Cass finally made it down to the lobby where Keisha was batting her eyes and smiling at the new security guard of the building. As she saw Cass approaching, she quickly smiled and said, "Nice meeting you, Deante." She grabbed Cass's arm smiling as he responded, "Yeah, you too. Later."

"Girl, is he fine or what?"

"I have never given him a second glance, but if you say so," Cass blandly replied. Cass always questioned her friend Keisha's taste in men, and today was no exception. Deante was one of those muscular guys whose bald head appeared to be a separate muscle all by itself and his neck was equivalent in size to it. He was the type of guy who you knew tried to make up for his short five foot five stature with his muscles, which only tended to make him appear even more stunted. But Cass had to acknowledge that if he had anything going for him it was his chocolate unblemished complexion only to be flawed again

151

when he smiled revealing his huge gap. He had one of those gaps in his teeth wide enough to fit a finger, but Keisha always described how she liked that in her men, because it was just the right size to latch onto her nipples. Nevertheless, Cass thought, "Whatever." Keisha acted as if she did not even hear Cass's response as she hopped into her car, put on her shades and drove off, as she had unfortunately become accustomed to her friend's unbecoming depressed demeanor. She was hoping that the weekend would change all of that. She knew in the past a weekend at the spa worked wonders. She just prayed that this time would be no different.

As they drove along Cass was shocked to see all the red, white and blue around indicating the ever quickly approaching Independence Day.

"Wow," she exclaimed, "is it really almost the fourth of July? Damn, I guess I have really been out of it. What is today's date," she asked, as she truly had no idea having been on remote control for almost the entire foregoing month.

"Girl, today is June seventeenth. And today is the day that we let go of the past and move into the future."

Cass smiled and gave her friend a high five and exclaimed, "Yes, indeed it is." Keisha silently smiled and exhaled a sigh of relief. Her friend was back. At least she hoped. Cassandra had lost nearly fifteen pounds during her bereavement and had essentially become a hermit. She was even going to work looking haggard which truly was not her nature. Cassandra did recognize her unhealthy patterns and deteriorating perspective on life, but she felt as if she literally had no control. She now knew what people experienced when depression abounded. She recognized that she had a lot to be thankful for, especially her loving family and friends. She now empathized even more with the homeless people they passed on the street who had no family and supportive structures in their lives. As they approached the spa, her eyes welled with tears and she closed them briefly with a reaffirmation of God's role in her life and quietly whispered, "Thank You."

As they entered the spa, Cass felt a sense of calm as the

beautiful earth tone colors, which surrounded her, together with the soothing music over the speakers enveloped her. They were immediately greeted by a handsome young fellow who brought them to a room where they were to remove all their clothing and change into thick white robes and sandals. Once securing their valuables they were escorted to separate massage rooms. As they parted, Keisha said, "Tootles, dear."

Cass partially smiled and responded, "Tootles." After Cass removed her robe and lay face down on the massage table, a small but well-defined Asian guy entered the room. He asked, "Do you have any particular preferences, Ms. Nicholas?"

"Not at all." He slowly applied lotion to her neck and began to gently massage her. His fingers seemed magical as they turned her face forward and began to caress the muscles of her face. She could literally feel the tension rising out of every pore. She made herself relax and think only pleasant thoughts. His hands slowly caressed every inch of her body and seemed to penetrate her very soul. Before she even recognized it she was fast asleep. She awakened to the smooth voice of Sade singing, *Cherish the Day*. Cass felt so peaceful at that moment and so rejuvenated. It was the first time in weeks that she had slept without her recurring nightmare, albeit short. She felt lighter as her feet met the carpeted floor beneath. Keisha was sitting at the pedicure station when she saw her friend approaching with a new bounce to her stride. She sipped on her red wine and thought, "Step one of this mission has been accomplished."

"Hey girlfriend!" She unabashedly shouted. "Come on and have some wine," she smiled.

"You know, I think I will," Cass smiled back. "I'm so glad that you made me do this, I feel so much better. You are a true friend, Keisha and I love you for that, for being there for a sister."

Keisha, while prompting the waiter to bring more of the same wine, replied, "Girl, don't you be getting all mushy on me. I know I'm the most wonderful person in the world," she laughed to hide any hint of emotion. As she poured Cass's wine she touched her hand and said, "I love you too, sisterfriend." They both walked out of the spa feeling invigorated and mellow. Keisha tugged at her friend and said, "So, are we gonna paint the town red tonight?"

Cass looked at Keisha with her relentless energy and said, "I'm better, but I am taking this a day at a time. I really want to just go and chill at the home front, ya know."

"I hear ya. Well I might come in with you if Deante is still on duty with his fine ass."

"Whatever," Cass laughed at her trifling friend who reigned as the queen of one night stands and commitment phobia. Keisha dropped Cass off at the front and looked for her to indicate with a nod of the head as to whether Deante was still there or not. Cass turned and nodded in the affirmative. Keisha promptly parked, puckered her full lips as she applied her favorite lipstick, spritzed a little of her musk oil onto her neck and bosom, and headed to flirt with her some Deante.

Cass felt as if she were floating up to her floor in the elevator, as she leaned her head against the wall with eyes closed. She could not wait to shower and slide between the cool sheets of her bed which were beckoning her. As soon as she opened her door she was greeted by the ringing of the phone. Almost tripping over the clothes that had mounted in the middle of the floor over the prior weeks, she answered, "Hello," in a rattled tone.

"Hi," she heard the response in a voice which she did not recognize.

"Yes?"

"Finally I reached you," the other person quipped in an aggravated tone.

Still not recognizing the voice and annoyed by this person's attitude Cass replied, "Look, who is this?"

The person's tone softened and she responded, "I'm sorry, Cassandra, this is Tanya. Remember me?"

"Oh," she melodically rang out, trying to hide her surprise, "Yes I do." Cass was certainly not ready to talk to her so before much in the line of a conversation could be started she interrupted Tanya's typical "long time no hear" queries with, "I am just walking in. Do you mind calling me back later?"

No sooner than Tanya could blink, her ear met the click of a hang up. "Damn," she smirked, "Talk about attitude," and hung up the phone. En route to her bathroom she threw her clothes onto the ever-growing mound accumulating on her floor. As she looked at her caller ID, she realized then that the number she had been seeing repetitively and had not recognized was not that of a telemarketer as she had presumed, but rather Tanya's. As she entered her shower she was amazed to recall the number of times Tanya must have called. Literally more than a dozen times in an hour's time on some days. She shook her head as she slid her body down into the warm candlelit aroma jacuzzi bath which she had prepared for herself that she had to admit was long over due. She forgot about all her worries and let herself be taken away by the moment. Yet again, she was interrupted by the ringing of the phone, which she opted not to answer this time. She finally exited the tub after what seemed like an eternity. The only thing she could envision at this point was her bed. As she reached her bed she saw the answering machine light blinking so she pressed to listen. It was Tanya yet again. "Cassandra, I am so sorry for my rude behavior. It's just that I really want to get to know you better. I too have recently lost someone special to me. Please give me a call. Here's my number again in case you have forgotten it." Cass cut off the machine at that point turned out her light and drifted off to sleep without a concern as to whether she ever talked to Tanya again. Cassandra was awakened to the phone ringing. She turned to look at her clock and she saw a blurred set of red numbers that looked to be two o'clock. Exasperated, she turned over to the phone thinking, "This better be damn good."

"Hello," she yelled.

"Cassandra, sorry to call so late, but I couldn't sleep not knowing whether you accepted my apology or not."

"Yes, I accept your fuckin' apology," she shouted and promptly hung up the phone.

Tanya sneaked back into her bed next to her sleeping lover now feeling gratified that she had spoken to Cassandra. She felt things had been cleared up and that Cass would definitely be calling her back. She turned her lover onto her back and began to kiss her and vigorously make love to her. She could feel her lover wince in pain a few times but she persisted until she had reached her point of no return and whispered, "Oh Cassandra, You feel so good." Her partner, still half asleep, did not hear her words and said, "I hope you enjoyed that bullshit, because I didn't." "Well, I did," Tanya responded as she placed her arm around her and whispered again with a smile, "I most certainly did."

Seventeen

Cass awakened Sunday morning feeling more energetic than she had in what felt like years. Aside from that one ridiculous phone call, it was a most restful sleep. She wondered if she had dreamt Tanya's call, but her caller ID confirmed it to be for real. She thought, "That woman must be crazy." She quickly hopped out of the bed and was shocked to see the disarray that encompassed her once prim and proper abode. She decided to clean things up and begin living like a human being again. She turned on her radio to some easy listening jazz and began the arduous task of cleaning. After about four hours of vacuuming, washing clothes, and dusting, she eased down to her now visible floor with an ice cold beer. She lay back and began to wonder where her life was going to take her. She felt like in her almost thirty-five years that she had endured her fair share of turmoil and pain. She held up her beer in midair as if to toast herself and solemnly said, "To a new and improved me." She took a big swig of her Corona, spitting a little up on herself as she was jarred by the loud ring of the phone behind her. "Hello?"

"Wassup girlfriend? Girl, Deante has one of the longest tongues I have ever had the pleasure of tasting. I can't wait to get a feel of it somewhere else, if you know what I mean," Keisha laughed, "A sister almost choked on that shit."

Cass interrupted laughing, "Enough already. I'm doing well, thanks for asking. And how are you doing too?"

"Girl I'm sorry, you know how I get all excited with new, uncharted territory. He's a young'in too chile. He's only twenty-three."

"I know you are not planning on going there with that young boy," she questioned, knowing full well that the answer was most definitely. Keisha had been with her common-law husband Hank for almost six years. And for almost that entire time she sought a new and younger challenge. Hank made descent money and loved Keisha, but he just was not the most attractive guy in the world. Hank was not ugly by any means though and Cass always found it hard to believe that he stayed. There was no way that he could not be cognizant of what was going on blatantly in his face. Cass knew that one day her dear friend's luck was going to run out and old dependable Hank will have had enough. But she surmised, until then, life as usual. Fucking around.

"You think I'm not. Girl this almost forty year old pussy needs a little rejuvenating. Hank's tired limp dick ain't doing shit no more. Sister got to practically lay entirely still like a damn mummy to feel if the shit is there."

"Hold on girl, that's my line," Cass clicked over in the middle of Keisha's gregarious laughter.

"Hello," she laughed.

"Cassandra?"

"Yes?"

"Hey, this is Tanya. You busy?"

"I am on the other line." She then remembered Tanya's comments about losing someone recently and she instantly became sympathetic, especially after recalling her heartwarming gesture at Robert's funeral. "Is everything okay?" She heard Tanya sigh in defeat, "Well, hold on a minute."

Cass clicked over to Keisha's continued laughter, "Look I hate to hang up since you are on a roll, but I need to take this call."

"Well, who is that?"

"None of your damn business. I'll talk to you later. Bye." Cass clicked back over, not giving Keisha the opportunity to probe any further. "Hey, I'm back. Sorry."

"No that's okay, I'm just so glad we finally have the chance to chat for a minute. I've been thinking about you a lot lately, especially since I last saw you at Robert's funeral."

"I am so sorry to hear about your loss."

Tanya began simulating a muffled cry, "Yes, it was my dear cousin Marcus. He was an innocent bystander in a drive-by shooting. He was only seventeen years old."

"I am so sorry, Tanya."

"I just feel like I need to get out for awhile so that I can stop thinking about him. You know what I mean?"

"Yes, I know all too well."

"So why don't we meet so we can both release some of this negative energy."

Cass thought about it and figured there was no harm in being sensitive during someone's time of need and maybe it would serve as a good diversion for her as well.

"Let's do it. How about the *Cheesecake Factory*?"

"That would be perfect. Five o'clock?"

"Fine I'll see you there, Tanya." As Cass hung up the phone, she felt like it might be nice to have an intelligent conversation with a woman who was not constantly talking about her latest fuck. Especially since that aspect of Cass's life was totally stagnant. At least with a human being. She still harbored mixed feelings about the engagement and hoped that Tanya respected the fact that she was not gay. Just to be sure, she decided that she would make that point clear at the outset. She then stood and viewed herself in the mirror. "Cassandra it's only dinner. Chill out." She then decided to take a shower and get dressed since she was particularly funky after cleaning and working out.

Tanya hung up the phone and took a slow drag of her cigarette and released it slowly as if trying to savor the moment. She knew that she had told a small white lie, but it accomplished her goal, which was all that mattered to her. Who really cared that she knew no one by the name of Marcus, as she laughed trying to etch the name in her mind in case she needed to recall it. She knew she now had the upper hand.

She had made so many straight women question their sexuality in the past after what started out with a simple dinner. She figured Cass would be no different from the rest. Initially shy and reserved, then becoming more curious as they realized that lesbian did not equate to someone scorned in the past by some man nor a woman who wanted to be a man. On the surface, Tanya knew she was as feminine as they came, but sexually, she enjoyed being in control and showing her women what true love making was from a woman's perspective. As she put out her cigarette she thought, "And Cassandra, you will fortunately be able to experience it first hand." She slowly ran her hand between her thighs and let it rest there for a minute. She then licked her lips as she stood to get dressed for her evening. She knew she had to be charming and smiled as she welcomed the challenge. At that moment her lover walked into the room, "What are you smiling for?"

"Don't worry about it. It's all good."

"Did you just finish masturbating or something?" she questioned with raised eyebrows.

"No. Give it a rest, will you?" she angrily retorted as she walked into the bathroom to get ready.

Cass took a quick shower as she knew that five o'clock was quickly approaching and she was starving. As she dried her body, she could see easily the weight that she had lost, and it looked good, but she still could stand to regain a few pounds. She went to her closet trying to decide what to wear. She did not want Tanya to get the wrong idea. She would avoid wearing anything revealing or remotely sexy, she thought. She first chose a nice pair of slacks with a turtle neck but felt that was too dressy. She then opted on a pair of loose fitting jeans with a turtle neck and her black boots. She then thought the boots might make Tanya think she was a quasi dyke or something. She finally ended up wearing the jeans and turtleneck with some cute flats that she had not worn before. She then curled her hair at the ends and put on some light make up. Before she walked out of the door, she instinctively dabbed on a touch of perfume and then thought, "Shit. I didn't want to do that." She quickly left home as the growling of her stomach and the lack of food was creating a major headache. Fortunately the *Cheesecake Factory* was only a few blocks away from her condo as it was closer to six than five. "Oh well," she thought, "better late than never."

Tanya sat there in the candlelit booth seething with anger as each minute passed. She brashly puffed on her fifth cigarette since she had arrived a little before five. She noticed her foot involuntarily shaking with angry anxiety. "Her ass better not stand me up. She doesn't know who she's playing with," she muttered out loud as she took a long drag of her cigarette. Finally, Tanya saw someone coming her direction that looked like Cassandra... and it was. Tanya quickly stamped out her cigarette and released her last bit of anger along with the smoke from her last drag. She promptly stood up and extended her arms to give Cass a hug. Cass smiled and gave Tanya one of those pat on the back white hugs which she hated so, but felt it was most appropriate in the current setting.

"Hi," she nervously said as she sat down feeling exactly like she did at the club, simultaneously anxious and exhilarated. "I am famished. I'm so sorry for being so late, the time just got away from me," Cass honestly added.

"No problem," Tanya lied, "I was running on CP time myself. It is so good to see you again," she smiled. Cass couldn't help but notice her striking beauty in her red cashmere V-neck sweater.

"Again, I'm so sorry about your loss, Tanya."

"Yeah. Thanks. Michael was a good kid. On his way to a very bright future."

"I thought his name was Marcus."

"You see how distraught this whole thing has gotten me," she cursed herself, "I can't even get names right. Michael is his twin brother."

"How sad."

"Yeah. But let's get off of the topic of death. I've been thinking about you so much lately and how beautiful you were when I saw you and you're looking even more stunning today. I've been wanting to share another evening with you."

Not wanting there to be any confusion Cass interjected, "You do know that I am not gay, right?"

"That's what your mouth says, but I didn't pick that up when I held you in my arms that night."

Cass flushed, "Well, that was all by default."

"Are you saying that you didn't enjoy yourself that night?"

"I'm not saying that, it's just that it was a new experience and now it's over. The novelty is gone," Cass stuttered.

"Girl we were vibin', you can't tell me that you weren't feeling it."

"I can tell you that I thought you were an attractive woman, and that frankly I was surprised that you were gay."

"One hundred percent. I have tried men before in the distant past, but they couldn't do a thing for me. It wasn't until I tasted the sweetness of a woman when I graduated from high school that I knew I was home. I think I knew it all the time, but all the societal mores and all kept me trying to give the men a chance. When I turned eighteen and was out on my own I basically said fuck society, I'm getting mine. And, long story short, here I am. Enough about me though."

Cass, feeling as though her comments were ignored persisted, "Listen Tanya. We still need to get one thing straight," as she laughed and put her hands in the air and put straight in simulated quotation marks. "I have dated men all my life and plan to continue. If you can respect and accept that I have no interest in being with a woman," she whispered, "then I am fine."

"I understand. But is it against the law for a straight and gay woman to have drinks?"

"No not at all. I just felt like the issue needed some clarification." Quickly changing the subject, "So how is the world of medicine coming along? You're OB/Gyn right?"

"Yep. I delivered seven babies the other night when I was on call. Talk about busy. I could have used a good massage after that grueling night," Tanya knowingly taunted Cass to keep her off balance.

"I can't even imagine," Cass responded as she uneasily perused the menu. She had to rest her hands on the table to prevent them from obviously shaking. She had no idea why she was so apprehensive.

"Look at me," Tanya stated catching Cass off guard.

"Excuse me?"

"Well, it's just that I think your eyes are a beautiful brown, and I wanted to see them again, since you seem to be consciously avoiding my eyes," Tanya chuckled.

Cass embarrassingly responded, "I'm sorry. I've never quite been in a situation like this. I am a little uncomfortable."

Tanya then called over the waiter and stated, "Can we get a bottle of White Zinfandel?" as she nodded at Cass to assure her approval of the request.

"Yes, that would be great. Good idea."

"I figured that might help you relax a little more. Don't worry," she slyly smiled, "I won't bite ya, unless you want me to, that is."

Cass flushed trying to ignore the last comment, "So, what have you been up to lately besides delivering babies?"

"That pretty much is the story of my life these days. I occasionally find the time to go out with special friends, but that is rare. Speaking of special friends, tell me, are you seeing someone right now?"

Cass slowly looked up in shock. She thought, she really doesn't know that Robert and I were an item. Cass then hesitated and said, "Robert and I were getting pretty close to one another." She then quickly added to reinforce her heterosexual status, "I think he was the man I was going to marry."

Tanya then shocked Cass by grabbing her hand tenderly and responding, "Cassandra, I am so sorry. I had no idea." Cass hastily removed her hand from Tanya's grasp as the waiter appeared out of nowhere to take their order. She hoped that he had not witnessed their interaction.

Cass gave her order to the waiter all the while thinking, "He thinks I'm gay. Look how he's looking at me. Dammit, I knew I should have cancelled this damn date." Tanya gave her order and interrupted Cass's mental dilemma by asking, "Would you like a smoke and do you mind if I have one?" Cass had quit that bad habit several years ago at the beckoning of her sister who had coaxed her into coming to the cadaver room during medical school and letting her see the healthy lungs and those of a person who had smoked. She did not need much convincing after that. However, despite that vivid picture, Cass wanted to have one of those cigarettes now more than she had in a long while. Nevertheless, she resisted and gulped down a bit of her wine for some pacification and then responded, "No, not at all."

The remainder of the evening was very nice and serene. They laughed a lot about each of their families and ridiculous childhood fallacies. Cass had relaxed a lot more as the wine began to take some effect. She had to admit that she was actually enjoying the conversation. She was intrigued by Tanya's wit and sometimes overbearing arrogance. As the sun began to set, Cassandra knew that she should be making her exit. She knew that the next day was going to be very busy at the office as she caught up with all of the agendas that she had basically ignored over the foregoing weeks.

She interceded before Tanya attempted to order another bottle of wine stating, "I really need to be going. I have a long day tomorrow."

"Oh, okay," Tanya decided to respect her wishes without a fight. She picked up the bill as Cass began to reach into her purse and said, "I got this okay?"

Cass firmly responded, "Hardly, I'll pay my half of the bill and won't accept it any other way."

Tanya was turned on by Cass's gentle yet assertive demeanor. "Okay," she conceded, "This time we'll go dutch. Oh, before you leave, answer me this, do you like poetry, Cassandra?"

"Well I enjoy some," she hastily stated while placing her twenty-five dollars on the table.

"Well there is a poetry reading at a bookstore in Little Five Points this Thursday. Why don't you come? It should be very nice and uplifting."

"When is the funeral?"

"The funeral?"

"Yes. Your cousin."

Eddra Marchand

"Oh," she stuttered shaking her head. "Uhh…tomorrow. Yeah, tomorrow at two o'clock. So will you consider coming to the poetry reading?"

"I have to check my calender. Sounds interesting, but I'll call you and let you know," she responded as she arose from her seat. Tanya stood and extended her arms again. This time Cass sincerely opened her arms as well and gave Tanya a true hug, without the pats.

Tanya then commented on her perfume stating, "I love that perfume. You should wear it next time we meet." Cass did not respond to that at all. She abruptly ended the hug and said, "Take care. Bye." Tanya sat back down and decided to have a celebratory drink. She knew that she had penetrated some of Cass's "straight" core and that Cass was totally oblivious to it. She gulped down the last swig of her drink and openly smiled thinking, "Girlfriend you are good." She knew that Cass was going to be at the bookstore Thursday. She could feel it. She knew that Cass would also be shocked and a bit angry when she discovered that the poetry reading was all lesbian erotica, but she'd get over it and she would be enticed by the words so eloquently spoken of intimate relations between two women. Tanya was confident that she would be able to abate Cass's fears and move her even closer to that fine line between the straight and gay worlds.

Eighteen

The next week was hectic as Cass tried to resume her previous role as principal broker on paper and in actions. Her confident stride finally resurfaced in place of the "woe is me" meander of the foregoing weeks. The sensitivity which her coworkers displayed then was rapidly transformed into the arrogant and cold indifference of the past. Cass knew that she must have been doing quite well as Linda passed her in the hall smiling and exclaiming, "I told you that Prozac does wonders. You look great." Cass decided it was not worth the effort to make it known that the return of the old Cass was not due to the wonders of Prozac. Although she knew that it must have worked well, as Stephanie, her sister, had been using it for years and had recommended that Cass try it several weeks earlier. Cass just lightly smiled and said, "Thanks for everything." Cass was pleased to find that Linda had been sincere when she had advised Cass to leave for the day. She had left notes regarding the changes that they had discussed at the meeting on Friday, which she certainly did not have to do. Cass thought, "I guess she has a semblance of a personality after all." When Wednesday arrived Cass was ecstatic that it was already hump day. She couldn't believe that she had done as much catching up as she had staying late on the previous two evenings. As she left the office, she was shocked to see that the sun was still shining brightly. So once she reached her car she decided she would call Keisha to see if she was interested in a quick drink and maybe dinner.

Cass's hurried walk to her car reverted to a stale and anxious pace once she noticed that the car parked next to hers looked exactly like Robert's. Her heart began pounding and tears began to flow from her eyes. She quickly wiped them in a futile attempt to scan the license plate. Her sensible self knew that it was not his, but her heartache allowed her to fantasize that it could be his and that she had just experienced an awful nightmare. Cass still thought of Robert several times a day and continuously punished herself for letting him leave that night. However, she had gained some measure of acceptance and was now able to relish the good times without sinking into a hopeless depression. After scanning the tag three separate times once she reached her car and acknowledging that the car next to hers was not his, she laughed at herself and thought of how Robert would have laughed at her pathetic gesture. She unlocked her car, hopped in and was absolutely sure that a drink was in order to help divert her thoughts from her childish wishful thinking.

Cass lowered her radio as Keisha's cell phone began to ring. Just before she was preparing to hang up Keisha answered in a raspy tone, "Hello."

"Hey girlfriend. Wassup, and why are you breathing so hard?" She could hear Keisha trying to cover the mouth of the telephone but to no avail as she heard her whispering, "Be quiet Deante. I'll be with you in a minute baby," as she struggled to muffle a moan. "Girl, I'm just chillin' at the pad," she fibbed.

Cass laughed, "What type of chillin' has your ass breathing like that?" knowing full well the reason after overhearing Deante in the background. Cass knew that this dinner invite would have to take a rain check but she decided to prolong the conversation just because, "I was just calling to find out if you wanted to have a quick dinner and drink."

"Girl, I'm sorry, but I am just worn out. Can I take a rain check?"

"Sure. But when do you think we should do it? I'm looking at my calendar," she lied "and I will just be so busy. Oh and girl," she tried to conceal her laughter, "we have got to go see that movie,

Shaft. A girl at work said it was too good to wait until the video."

Keisha quickly and rudely interrupted Cass, "Look, I am trying to get my groove on. Later." Cass laughed as she hung up the phone and decided that she would feast on the Chinese food leftover from the previous night and maybe check out a pay per view movie. Cass was so excited that she had an evening to herself that she could just relax and do literally nothing.

Cass walked into her condo and placed her brief case neatly in its place and was pleased that the stale odor which had penetrated her home previously was now resolved as she took in a deep breath. She trekked to her bedroom and was surprised to see that no one had called her. She flounced back onto her bed after hanging up her coat, and for the first time in a long while, she was shocked to realize that she was horny. "Wow," she thought as she gently pressed on her nipples through her blouse. She lay there for a while thinking of whether she was going to give in to her desires. She didn't have to think long as that thought was quickly interrupted when the phone rang and she laughed thinking, "Saved by the bell."

"Hello."

"Hey Cassandra. How you doing?" Cass recognized the voice instantaneously and fervently began trying to conjure up reasons why she could not go to this poetry reading. "Hey," she responded acting as if she did not recognize the voice.

"This is Tanya." Cutting to the chase she jokingly stated, "Have you thought about my purely platonic proposal?"

"You mean the poetry reading?"

"Yes, the poetry reading."

"Yes, I have, and I really don't know where this Little Five Points is and I have been so busy trying to catch up at work and putting in mega extra hours."

Tanya arrogantly prodded, "I know that you are a reasonably intelligent woman who can read directions, number one and number two, there's nothing like a good poetry reading to help you unwind from a long day's work. More importantly, it will help both of us redirect our thoughts from our recent losses. Anything else?" she dared.

"No, I guess not. Why don't you fax the directions to my office and if I can make it, I will be there. Seven o'clock right?"

"That would be correct," Tanya smugly smiled back while trying to hide her laughter at Cass's virtuous prowess.

"Okay, then maybe I will see you then."

"Oh so is that the extent of our conversation?"

"Yes it is," Cass boldly returned.

"Okay, then. I guess I will see you there. And don't forget about that delectable perfume," Tanya added as she hung up the phone. Cass shook her head as she tried to arrange her day mentally for tomorrow to not be able to feasibly make it to the event. She then lay there and tried to remember what she was planning to do before the phone call. She then remembered she was intending on some individual sexual gratification and quickly hopped up with a scouring expression, as she recognized that her desire had entirely dissipated. Tanya, on the other hand, chuckled out loud as she replayed Cassandra's blatant attempts to avoid seeing her again. "See you tomorrow," both literally and sexually she hoped.

Cass took a nice hot bath and languished there for a while enjoying the serenity. She felt as though she was moving in slow motion. She then put on her favorite pj's and sat in front of the TV clicking until she found something of interest. She ate her Chinese food with chopsticks, a task that Robert had insisted on teaching her. She finally landed on *"An Imitation of Life,"* one of her favorite movies of all time. While always knowing the outcome she could never refrain from crying at the end. That night she cried uncontrollably both because she was lonely for Robert and the inevitable ending of the movie. She eventually calmed herself and gradually moved to her bedroom where she decided to call her mom.

"Hello," she said as her mom screamed back into the receiver, "Cass, baby, is that you?"

"Yes, mom it's me," she quietly responded as she recognized that just the sound of her mother's voice made her feel better. They idly chatted for too long as Cass remembered how loquacious her mom could be. She relentlessly tried to end the conversation, but wondered why after all these years she had never realized that regardless of her efforts the call would not end until her mom was ready for it to end. Finally, her mom said, "I am so glad that my baby is back. I miss you and I love you."

Cass sincerely responded, "I love you too, mom." But as she was preparing to hang up the phone she could here her name reverberating off of the receiver, "Cass, Cass." She reluctantly placed the phone back to her ear and said, "Yes, mom."

"God shall keep watch over all of his angels."

"Goodnight mom," Cass could not help but smile.

As Cass hung up the phone, she was shocked to find that the earlier sensation of horniness had returned. However, after just getting off of the phone with her mom who had quoted biblical scriptures she felt terribly guilty about placing her hand into her underwear, but she did nevertheless. As she lay there gently rubbing herself she thought, "This feels so damn good," amidst the words, "You are a bad girl." Eventually, she futilely realized that she was unable to separate her sensual feelings from the teachings of her strict catholic upbringing that masturbation was a sin. As this bantering in her head persisted endlessly, she found herself awakening the next morning with her fingers affixed to her clit. She could do nothing but laugh as she thought, "Next time I am feeling horny, I will not call mom, at least until after I handle my business."

The next day went by fast as Cass noted that she had been particularly productive. "Too productive," she thought as she realized that she would have ample time to make it to the poetry reading. She diffidently packed up her things as she walked over to the fax machine hoping for some ludicrous reason that it was not working. She realized that she was being ridiculously childish in that if she didn't want to go, she could just not go. But she rationalized that she enjoyed Tanya's company last time and what harm could there be. She initially laughed it all off as she thought, "Going to a function with a gay woman does not make you gay." She then alternately thought, "Birds of a feather flock together." She then shrugged her shoulders in disgust at the fax machine's blatant disregard of her wishes. She swiped the directions up and indifferently sauntered to her car to head to Little Five Points.

As Cass arrived at her destination she figured it was a popular function judging by the number of cars surrounding the small quaint bookstore. She wondered how she would locate Tanya in the large crowd. She timidly approached the bookstore and found a seat located near the back as the introductions of the three original poets were being announced. She was not shocked this time by the number of women as she understood that a poetry reading was rarely a setting where men would be prevalent. It was not until one of the poets had gotten partially through her reading, caroling, "As she lay there naked, her body glistened amongst the candlelight. She was calling me, not by the movement of her mouth but by the sway of her curvaceous hips," Cass sat there in shock initially as she foolishly hoped that the poet had a lisp and her s' were not easy to separate from other consonants. As she went on it was evident that she was speaking of sexual affection between two women. Cass could not believe how gullible she had been as she tried to figure out a way to leave without drawing too much attention to herself. Just as she was starting to feel overwhelmingly intimidated by the setting, she was startled by the hand that lightly rubbed her shoulder. At that moment she felt Tanya bend to her ear and whisper, "Glad you could make it." Tanya could not help but smell the perfume which she had requested Cass wear, teasing her on her neck. Cass tried to catch Tanya's eyes to communicate her dismay. Tanya purposefully avoided Cass's stare as she knew it would be quite evil. She knew, however, that it would subside as she listened to the powerful words being vocalized so eloquently.

Cass resigned to the fact that she had been played and in a defeated mood, sat there determined not to give credence to anything being said. But she couldn't help observing the obvious couples surrounding her sharing intimately in the spoken words. They were not being raunchy, many were just looking at one another in ways in which no words needed to be verbalized. It was evident that there were some intense feelings amidst the women present. There seemed to be a certain camaraderie shared between them all as everyone listened intently as the vibrations of the words seem to echo off of the walls and into the very soul of their beings. Cass was stunned at the power that she felt in their presence. She eventually began to relax, still initially trying to replace many of the feminine pronouns with masculine ones. As she realized that this tedious task was a worthless effort, she allowed herself to feed off of the abounding energy within the room. As the last poet was completing her poem, Cass found herself clapping at the end of the tender story of two people in love. They just happened to be two women. She began to stand and turned to Tanya and exclaimed, "This was very insightful."

"I knew that you would either eventually come around to appreciating it, or you were going to never see me again," Tanya laughed.

"You know that both of those statements are not necessarily mutually exclusive," Cass playfully bantered as the crowd began to dissipate. Tanya frowned and said, "Please don't diss a sister like that."

"No, but I really do feel a slightly different perspective of gay women. I still don't understand it but to each *her* own. Thanks for inviting me."

"Is that it? How about a quick drink or dessert or something?" she asked as they began walking to her car.

"Number one, I have a full day at work tomorrow, and number two I have a ceiling fan that I promised myself I would put up tonight no matter what it takes."

"Well guess what?"

"What?"

"I happen to be very proficient at electronic and mechanical stuff like that. I could help and as you know two heads are always better than one."

"You just don't give up, do you? Follow me." As Tanya glided over to her car, she could literally feel the wetness that was beginning to envelop the crotch of her boxers. She knew that it had started to develop long ago as she envisioned Cassandra in many of the scenarios that were erotically described earlier. Tanya hopped in her car and flashed her lights as she approached Cass to let her know that she was there. As she followed behind Cassandra, all she could do was smile and wonder if tonight would be the night. She had intuitively brought some wine that she knew would play an essential role in the events of the remainder of the evening, if they were to go according to her plans.

Nineteen

C ass slowly drove home contemplating if her decision to allow Tanya into her home was a wise one. She had already emphasized on multiple occasions that she was not a lesbian and hoped that Tanya was smart enough to respect that. She pulled into her designated parking spot and prompted Tanya to park in the space next to her car, since her neighbor Lisa was out of town. There was an awkward silence as they approached the door to Cass's condo. For once Cass was glad to see Deante who had started addressing Cass on a first name basis since he was sleeping with her best friend. He broke the silence with, "Hey Cassandra. How you doing?"

"Fine Deandre, thanks for asking."

"And it's Deante with a T. You not gon' introduce me to your fine friend," he casually stated as he looked Tanya up and down. Irritated by his bold indifference to the fact that he was fucking her best friend, she said, "No." He shrugged his shoulders as he continued to look at their asses as they entered the elevator. Tanya looked confused as she stated, "Sometimes you make things a little more obvious by responding like that."

"It wasn't you at all. It's just that he has been seeing a good friend of mine and I thought that was very inappropriate."

"Oh, I see. I was tripping for a minute there," she laughed while clinging to her bottle of White Zinfandel.

"What is that?"

"What? This?" Tanya shamefully admitted, "This is some wine that I just happened to have in my car," as she purposefully looked down to yet again avoid Cass's eyes.

"So, you knew you were coming to my house tonight?"

"Well, I was kinda hoping." Cass just shook her head as the elevator doors opened to her floor. "This is strictly to install my fan," Cass reprimanded feeling like she was talking to a male counterpart whom she had to keep in place. Tanya just bowed her head as she entered Cass's open door behind her claiming, "I know. I know."

As Cass turned on her foyer lights, she grabbed the bottle of wine. "Make yourself at home. Would you like some of this wine?" As Tanya sat down onto the sofa enamored by all the beautiful decor with very subtle accents throughout she responded, "Yeah, sure." She then without skipping a beat added, "And you should have some too. Great place." Cass opened the wine and removed a single wine glass from her cabinet and proceeded to bring it to Tanya.

"There's a coaster right there next to the remote control. I'm going to get out of these work clothes and I'll bring you the instructions for installing the fan."

Tanya noticed Cass without a glass and inquired, "Where's yours?"

"I'm not really in the mood for a drink right now," as she shut her door to quickly slide out of her skirt and heels. Cass did not want to give any false pretenses. She wanted Tanya to be aware of her heterosexual orientation and wanted nothing to cloud anyone's judgment. Tanya used the remote to turn on the stereo and she quickly switched from the jazz station it was on to an R&B station that played multiple love ballads back to back. Tanya knew of nothing better to set the mood than that. She removed her shoes while trying to figure out how she could feign a reasonable knowledge of this electrical bullshit. She damn near called the service man at her apartment building to change her light bulbs, she silently laughed. "Oh well, as my mother always says, "Necessity is the mother of invention." Just as she was beginning to relax Cass returned with the instructions for installing the fan. As she brought out the paper, she said, "You can at least start reading this Ms. Electrical Genius and I'll be right back," as she turned to go to the bathroom. Tanya hardly had her mind on the ceiling fan as she sat there trying to concoct a scheme to get into Cass's panties. She silently thought, "Damn she looks good." Cass promptly returned in a black velour lounge wear pants and top set, and Tanya quickly picked up the instructions and tried to appear like she had been intently reading them. She then lied, "This should be easy. You know to do this we have to turn off the electricity to not electrocute ourselves and since it is dark, do you have some candles we can light?"

Cass lifted her eyebrows and said, "Would a flashlight do?"

"I'm sure it will but we still will need another source of light."

Cass sighed and responded, "Okay. Let me see what I can find," knowing full well she had practically an armamentarium of candles from big to small and skinny to fat. She retrieved a couple and asked Tanya to come into the bedroom because that is where the fan was being placed. Tanya was actually in the kitchen pouring herself another glass of wine and was trying to find the cabinet with the glasses so that she could bring Cass a glass. Cass returned to the den to find out what was taking Tanya so long and then stated, "Top right hand corner. Right there," she pointed as she figured one glass of wine might help her relax just a little. Tanya smiled as she began pouring Cass's drink while singing to an Anita Baker tune on the radio. "That's my girl, I wonder what ever happened to her," Tanya exclaimed as she walked out of the kitchen barefoot with Cass's glass.

"Thanks," she responded, "Now shall we get to work?"

As they moved into the bedroom, Tanya could not help but notice the mirrors on the ceiling above the bed. She silently smirked, "I know I gotta get a piece of this kinky sister." Cass knowing that her mirrors were always a primary topic of silent discussion, promptly dispelled any delusions about her sexual prowess by stating sharply, "Those belonged to the tenant before me. I just haven't found the time to get rid of them yet." Tanya winked and responded, "They're fine by me." Cass ignored the last comment and prompted Tanya to sit on the floor as she opened the box to get the pieces of the fan together. As they read through the instructions together, Tanya could not help but see a portion of Cass's bosom as she leaned over to get the various tools. She licked her lips and distracted herself by asking, "Where's your bathroom?"

"That door right there," she pointed. "Straight ahead." Tanya quickly stood to go to the restroom. As she closed the door she rested her body against it and told herself to calm down. She pulled down her zipper, pulled her boxers aside and placed her finger quickly inside of herself not surprised to find how wet she was and thought, "Oh Cassandra, I long for you." She then tasted her own juices wishing that they were Cassandra's. She pulled her zipper up and flushed the toilet although she hadn't used it. She exited the bathroom and reluctantly tried to focus on getting the fan up.

They laughed and talked while jointly dissolving the remains of the wine. They had put all the appropriate pieces together and it was time to turn out the electricity to hook things up. Cass went out into the hall and found the circuit breaker to her bedroom and turned it off. She yelled into Tanya, "Is it off?"

"Yes," she responded. Cass returned to her room and Tanya was on the ladder, "Okay. Hand it to me," as she thought to herself, "this really is quite simple." Cassandra handed her the fan and she hooked up the wires and asked Cass to turn the electricity back on. As she did, the fan began to spin. Cass shouted from the hallway, "Is it working?"

Tanya lied and said, "No, turn it off again." Cass turned off the electricity again, and walked back into the candlelit room, "So what do we do now?" Tanya slid from behind the door and said, "We kiss." And before she knew it Tanya's mouth was softly caressing her lips. Cass initially steadfastly resisted, pushing Tanya away with her arms. This only resulted in exciting Tanya more as she continued pressing her body into Cass's eventually pinning her to the door. Cass could feel the wetness of Tanya's tongue trying to pry her mouth open but would not allow herself to surrender to it. Cass finally let her arms fall to her side but still was not participating in the least. She felt Tanya's hands beginning to rub her back. Cass did not know what she was doing or what she was feeling, but she knew it felt good to be close to someone and she knew she felt helpless to contest her advances. Tanya began sliding Cass's top up and saw she was braless and that her nipples were hard and beckoning her mouth. She squatted while simultaneously sliding her shirt up and began pulling Cass's nipple into her mouth. Cass heard a quiet moan escape from her lips and still stood there as if she were in shock, not moving but not resisting either. Tanya continued to eagerly lick and kiss her breast while squeezing the nipple of her other breast. Tanya then stood up and began tonguing Cass hard, and Tanya finally felt Cass's tongue entangling her own. Tanya moved from Cass's mouth to her neck where she gently kissed and bit her. She pulled Cass's arms, which were pinned to her side, onto her hips and Cass allowed them to rest there. The heat was emanating throughout the room heightened by nervous tension and sexual energy. Tanya then found the elastic waist of Cass's pants and slid her hand down and felt the moisture through her panties. She eased her hand through the elastic that was barring her and then slowly tried to slide her finger into Cass's warmth and as if she had just hit a switch, Cass yelled, "Stop. You're going to have to leave."

Tanya stood there in disbelief and said, "But Cassandra."

"Just leave please," she shouted, totally avoiding Tanya's eyes in the glimmer of the candles. Tanya slowly walked to the den, put on her shoes and quietly shut the door behind her.

"Dammit," she shouted while punching the wall near the elevators. "I should have taken it a little slower. Shit!" she openly yelled as the elevator opened and the occupants glanced at her in a perturbed manner. She stormed into the elevator and punched the already lit lobby button, totally ignoring their presence.

Cass sat on her floor feeling totally confused. "What in the hell did I just do?" She pensively sat on her bed wondering why Tanya had such an effect on her. "I know that I am not gay. I have slept with too many men to be gay, besides you're born that way." She wanted to call someone, anyone who could validate her sexuality, but she could share this with no one. No one would understand. She felt dirty and unclean and began shaking her head in disgust repetitively asking herself, "What have I done, what have I done?" She then decided she was going to erase the entire evening's events from her mind. She blew out the candles and went back to put on the breaker for her bedroom. She was shocked on her return to see that the fan was indeed working. She was too distraught to even recognize that Tanya had fooled her and the fan had been working all the time. All she could think of was getting in the shower and washing away all the weird feelings that were strangely unmasked. Cass hopped in the shower and pretended as if nothing had occurred earlier.

Tanya reached her car and was pissed. She still longed to have Cassandra and hoped that she hadn't missed her golden opportunity. She then got into her car and sat there for a while with her head lightly banging against her seat. As she reached up to remove a strand of hair that had fallen out of place she could smell Cass's scent on her finger. She closed her eyes and began to unbutton her pants as she sat in the parking lot. She placed her hand into her boxers and felt her wetness. She began vigorously rubbing herself until her body began an intemperate writhing as she felt herself succumbing to her actions. She closed her eyes tightly and envisioned Cass being the actual provider and no sooner than she did that did she come. She screamed in ecstasy and gradually the pattern of her breathing began to slow down. She then, as if nothing happened, started her car, turned up her radio, and headed home.

Twenty

*C*ass awakened Friday to go to work and appeared to be more organized than usual since Robert's death. She arrived on time and was resolutely trying to keep herself busy. She was trying to distract herself from reliving the events of the previous night but was losing the battle. She would be in the midst of preparing a huge briefing and then her mind would flashback to she and Tanya and she would shake her head in disgust. Throughout the day she was questioning her faith, amongst other things. Though she was not a practicing catholic, she knew being reared catholic that her behavior last night was an awful sin. She knew she was not homosexual but couldn't help but question her sensual indulgence. "I enjoy sleeping with men, I could not be," she thought as she took out a legal pad and began listing the men she had slept with in the past. The list kept getting longer and longer and that concept only served to make her more depressed. "Have I slept with that many men?" she thought. Cass knew that she was hardly the model Catholic. But while she knew it was considered wrong to engage in premarital sex with anyone, she believed that the penalty was probably worse engaging in such with a woman. "Are there varying degrees of being wrong?" She questioned herself realizing that she was getting way to deep. Fortunately, at that moment she was distracted when her secretary buzzed in. She had been screening her calls all day. There were a select few people she could not fathom talking to that day, in particular, her mom and Tanya who both had called earlier that morning. Her secretary stated, "There is a Miss Johnson on the line for you."

"Put her through. Hey Keisha, girl. Wassup?"

"I got a favor to ask you," Keisha meekly retorted.

"I remember your last favor. So this one better damn well be a good one."

"Well, Deante has a cousin coming in from Detroit tonight for a gig. Chile he's an aspiring rapper and we wanted to maybe do the double date thing, ya know." Keisha was shocked that Cass without even hesitating responded, "Sure, what time?" Keisha was caught so off guard she stuttered saying, "Huh, oh ummm, how does nine o'clock sound?" she said as she shook her head in the affirmative to Deante who was sitting at the concierge desk.

"That sounds fine. Are we meeting somewhere in particular?"

"We'll pick you up as soon as we get him from the airport." Keisha, then worried about her friend's uncharacteristic behavior asked, "Are you okay?"

"I'm just fine," she lied and said, "See you then." Keisha albeit surprised, silently resolved that phase two of her mission to get her dear friend out with another man had been accomplished much easier and faster than she had anticipated.

Cass knew that she was not going to give up the opportunity to go out with any man to help reinforce her position as a straight woman. Hell, if the goofy, old ass Federal Express man who had been flirting with her for months had asked her to go out that day, she would have obliged him. She knew that she had to get over this and she knew she could never, ever see Tanya again. As she left the office for the evening, she saw that there were several messages left with her secretary by a Miss Grayson. That would be Tanya. She knew she had never given Tanya her work number, but figured she had easily deciphered it by playing with the last digit of the fax machine number that she had given her before. She quickly threw the messages in the trash and headed out the door. As she drove home, she thought about how foolish she was being by trying to prove what she already knew. She knew that the wine had affected her judgment and that was the bottom line. She was as straight as they came and no amount of dating men would change that or prove that more firmly. She was cajoling herself to inspire her confidence to the point that she considered calling Keisha to cancel, but she knew that Keisha would be pissed and she figured she could enjoy an evening out of her home, just for fun.

She went upstairs to her condo and saw that she had multiple messages. She listened and all but one of the twelve was Tanya begging for forgiveness and a chance to go out again. She erased all of them immediately and decided that she was going to be stunning that night and have a good time out with a man, with whom she belonged. Remarkably, Keisha was on time as she was buzzed up from downstairs at precisely nine o'clock. She put on her heels which made her calves look pretty darn good in her short black leather skirt. She decided to reveal a tad bit of cleavage too, accentuating it even more by wearing her hair up. As she got off of the elevator, she prayed that the guy standing next to Deante with the caramel pants, matching caramel shirt, and caramel sandals was not going to be her date for the evening. He was so tall and thin as he looked toward her smiling with a toothpick hanging out of his mouth. She graciously smiled as she approached them realizing she should not have expected anything more. Afterall, this was a relative of Deante's trifling ass.

"Hey Cassandra. This is my cuz and homeboy, Trey."

Trey gently pulled on himself before reaching up and twirling the toothpick in his mouth, shaking his head up and down, sucking his teeth and then smiling, "Wassup?"

"Oh Lawd," Cass thought, "Please tell me that ain't a gold tooth in brother's mouth." Keisha grabbed her arm and entangled it, "Girl, it's just for one night. Just have fun. He doesn't look all that bad. He's just a roughneck, and you know what they say about those skinny brothers." Cass looked at her friend with disgust and whispered, "You know you owe me big for this one."

Deante hopped in the driver's seat of Keisha's SUV and unlocked the doors for the rest of them. They sped off with the music blasting as Deante lit a joint. Cass had not touched that stuff since college, and was not planning on starting again, but soon the aroma began to affect her and she found herself laughing at every ridiculous thing being said. In that time she found out that Trey was a pretty well-known rapper in Detroit but he was currently working as mall security until his big break came. He had a few rap gigs which he performed on occasion and supposedly had one that evening at some no-name club in Decatur. She also found out that he was only twenty-two years old, despite looking maybe a hair older with his bald head and hoop earrings in each of his ears. He was not awful looking, he just certainly was not Cass's type. She hoped she did not run into anyone she knew. "Where are we going anyway?"

Deante turned and said, "Girl, We going to the bowling alley."

"The bowling alley. I'm hardly dressed for bowling." Then Trey quickly quipped, "Not to bowl, gurl. To eat. You know the bowling alley has the goodest food and cheapest price you could imagine." She rolled her eyes back and thought, "What have I gotten my ass into with these brothers?" Keisha looked back and smiled as she stroked Deante's leg when they pulled into the bowling alley parking lot. Cass hoped that they had a lot of food because inhaling those joint fumes that they were smoking had made a sister hungry.

They sat down at a table in the bowling alley watching everyone else bowl while awaiting their food order. Deante and Trey were some funny dudes, but as far as intellect or ambition, the brothers were totally lacking. She couldn't help but laugh as the reflection of Trey's gold tooth complemented the dangling gold medallion shaped like a bone around his neck, both engraved with the letter "T". She lightly talked with Keisha who was definitely high. She was not going to waste her time talking deep in this setting where the level of cognition was much too low. As she gulped down her hamburger and fries, she had to admit that it was kicking.

She gave Trey some more money to go get her another hamburger and beer. He responded, "No prob, girl. You gon hook a brother up too?"

"Sure Trey. Buy yourself a burger too." She had never been in a setting where a man could not buy her a damn hamburger. After they all finally had gotten their fill, they headed to his gig. It was a smoked filled club with more people inside than it looked like it could hold. There was a silver disco ball hanging in the center of what was supposed to be the dance floor and a small stage in the corner accented with red lights. Shortly after entering the club, Trey parted from them and went to talk to his drummer and bass player. Eventually, the woman MCing came to the mic and hollered, "Ya'll put your hands together! I said put your hands together for the rapping style of T-bone." With that Trey came bouncing to the mic now sporting a pair of sagging jeans barely gripping his ass and a t-shirt. He began rhyming some words to the beat to which everyone was dancing and appeared to be enjoying except Cass. Once his act was completed all the women there were surrounding him like pigs in a mud pile. All Cass could see was that gold tooth shining as he smiled, looked up and winked at her while the women continued to behave as though he was a renowned celebrity. Finally, he stepped out of the crowd and put his arm around Cass, who actually felt okay with it as she had all of a sudden become a focus of envy by all of the women, because she was leaving the club with the trophy. A trifling, thug, roughneck trophy whose company she would enjoy simply because he was a man in contrast to her previous admirer. She put her arm around his skinny waist as her narcissistic self allowed her to play along. Trey self-assuredly got out of the car as they reached her condo and said, "How 'bout letting a brother up?"

"Letting a brother up?" Cass mocked.

"Yeah, you know. So we could, you know, get to know each other a little better." Before Cass could respond, still fighting off the dilemma of her sexuality, Keisha and Deante quickly drove off and shouted, "We'll see ya'll later." Cass shrugged her shoulders and figured she couldn't leave him out in the cold.

"Come on up." As they rode up the elevator to Cassandra's floor, Trey kept looking at her up and down shaking his head and finally said, "You sure is a fine sista." As the elevator opened to her floor, Cass felt almost vindicated hearing compliments from a man, albeit a roughneck with incorrect grammar, but a man nevertheless.

As she opened the door, Trey looked around in amazement exclaiming, "You got some nice shit up in here."

"Thanks," Cassandra stated as she put on her dimmer lights and decided what the hell she was going to seduce this young dude. "Would you like something to drink?"

"You got some beer?"

"Yes. Some Coronas."

"That's fine," he said as he sat down on the sofa. As Cass brought over his beer, she could see a hint of innocence in him despite his hood mentality. He also exuded a certain masculinity and dominance in spite of his young years. Cass sat down next to him as he asked, "About how much do you pay for a crib like this?"

"Oh, I don't know. It's not cheap, I'll tell you that."

"Believe that, believe that," he laughed while nodding his head. She figured she better move fast because if she had to endure too much more of his ignorance and trivial conversation, she would be totally turned off. "My dog back in Detroit got a bad crib something like this." Cass, somewhat confused by that statement, later realized that dog was analogous to his friend. She smiled and grabbed his dick saying, "Look let's not play games."

"True dat, true dat. It's all…" Cass cut off his words when she placed a finger over his lips implying that brother needed to shut up. She unbuckled his pants and he stood up letting them fall to the ground revealing his skinny and ashy legs. However Cass was soon readily distracted from his ashy legs as he pulled down his boxers "Damn," she thought. As she stood before him, he began pressing down on her shoulders thinking she was going to give him head. "No, we are not going there."

"Alright cool then." He began sliding up her skirt and saw that beneath she had on no panties. She had taken them off shortly after they entered the house. He began rubbing his cock with his hand saying, "You not gon' wet my knob just a little."

"No," she responded as she handed him a condom.

"Oh hell no. I don't where them thangs. I likes to feel them juicy walls.

"If you want a piece of this ass, you are gonna have to put it on." He grabbed it and put it on, without contesting because he wanted her. Cass then pushed him down on the sofa and began riding him. His little ass could move those hips, she thought as she gyrated up and down. Before she knew it he had flipped her over on all fours.

"You my bitch and your ass is fine and it's all gon' be mine" as he plunged deeper and deeper while going to whatever beat was resounding in his head. In the mist of the heavy breathing and moans he began to wet his fingers and place them around her asshole. It was feeling so good, she didn't pay attention to the derogatory remarks escaping his mouth. "You my fuckin' ho and you want mo and mo," as he kept wetting around her asshole with his fingers. Cass wondered what he was up to. Then he pulled out of her vagina and rhythmically continued, "Now I'm gon plug this hole with my big long pole."

Cass's eyes immediately popped open as she quickly flipped over yelling, "Oh, no you ain't!"

"Damn girl, I'll take it slow. Come on now."

"Hell no!" As Cass no longer trusted him from behind, thinking he might try to sneak her, she hopped on top again.

"Girl I ain't even in the mood no more." She looked down shocked to see that his dick was truly limp. She said, "Well arouse yourself."

"I ain't gon do that shit if I got a bitch sittin' next to me with a working mouth who can do it."

Now Cass definitely did not appreciate his disrespectful remarks and shouted back, "I am not your damn bitch." He laughed out loud rapping, "Yeah that's right, you my fucking ho and you want some mo." Cass found herself somewhat tickled by his ridiculous rapping and responded, "Will you cut all that rhyming shit out and fuck me?" Cass found herself somewhat aroused by his ruggedness, and she could see that his dick had found it's way back up, so she didn't resist when he picked her up and brought her onto her kitchen table, wrapping her legs around his neck and began fucking her. She moaned as he pushed deeper inside of her. Cass came as she felt her legs trembling uncontrollably around his neck. Cass was shocked that he was still going. She had never outlasted any man. The perspiration was dripping off of his face and onto Cassandra as he kept penetrating her. Cassandra couldn't believe it when she felt her legs beginning to tremble again. She was coming again, but this time he with her. As he came he slapped her ass several times saying, "Who's ass is this? I know it's mine. I know you want mo but I must decline." Cass never responded as she continued breathing deeply trying to catch her breath.

He then questioned, walking away from her, his body entirely wet, "You got some water in this bitch?" opening the refrigerator as if it were his own. Cass gathered herself together and tried to stand feeling wobbly on her legs thinking, "Damn, his ass is good." She handed him a glass and said, "Right there." He refused the glass and drank from the container with his big lips and walked into the den plopping down on the sofa.

"Fix me a sammich," he ordered.

She thought, he is truly trippin. "No, you need to put on your clothes and get up outta here."

"You mean you not lettin' a nigga crash here for the night. I could have picked any one of those bitches to sleep with tonight and I chose you."

Appalled but knowing his statement was true she demanded, "No, put on your clothes, and go." He laughed and began flickering his tongue faster than she had seen anyone do while looking directly at her. She tried to ignore him and said, "What are you doing that for?"

"Come here and I'll show you," he smiled with his gold tooth shining brightly.

"You truly need to go."

"How am I supposed to get to Deante's house?"

"I don't know. Catch a cab." He stood up and began putting on his clothes, saying while moving his arms along, "You a cold sista, brotha gon get a blista. Walkin' in the cold on this long and windin' road." She just sat there laughing at his blatant ignorance in her satin robe waiting for him to leave unfazed by his truly lacking rap style. He began walking toward the door and she was behind him. Before she could get the door open, he turned around, dropped to his knees, opened her robe and began eating her. She said very loudly, "No, get your ass up." He persisted and she said it again, a little softer this time, "Get your ass up." She could feel his tongue flicker so hard and so fast. She was ashamed that she was letting this man get the best of her sexually. She then grabbed his head and pressed it into her as she felt her legs beginning to resist her very weight. He pulled her down to the floor and continued ravishing her until she exploded. She screamed out, "Oh shit, oh shit," as she tightly closed her legs beneath him. She had never recalled feeling any orgasms that intensely. She decided brother had earned his keep at least for the night and told him, "Okay. You can stay the night, but you have to sleep on the sofa." She was not about to let his ass hardly think that she liked him or that this was anything more than a one night stand. All she wanted to do was selfishly prove the point that she had orgasms with men which equated, quite simply to her, the fact that she was hardly a lesbian. She felt gratified both sexually and with her rationalization of her sexuality. She threw him a blanket, said goodnight, closed her bedroom door, locked it and fell fast asleep.

Twenty-One

She was shocked to awaken to some rap playing very loud on her stereo. She had forgotten that Trey was still there. She quickly slid on a pair of shorts and t-shirt and opened her bedroom door.

"What the hell is that?"

He smiled, "Girl that is my demo. That's gonna make me famous. You saw me last night. You know I got the juice and that's why they call me T-bone. These are some cuts I ain't shared with too many peeps yet."

She quickly lowered it as she heard all the profanities being shouted behind a very simple rhythm. "You like?" he smiled.

"Yes, it's nice," lying and hoping that he had good benefits at his mall job. Then trying to get rid of him said, "Well, I have a long day planned ahead, so you should be leaving."

"I just called Deante and he is already here to start his duty. He's gon let me borrow his rod while he works. You wanna fuck before I go?" he blatantly questioned while pulling on himself.

"No, I don't think so," although the idea was quite tempting after the great sex the previous night.

"Alright then," he said. Fortunately, before she could change her mind about fucking Trey again, the phone rang and Cass promptly answered it, "Cassandra," the other person questioned in a dubious tone.

"Yes," she responded above the rap music still playing in her cassette.

"What the hell is all that noise?" her sister Stephanie asked.

"Hold on just a minute." She placed the phone down, cut off the tape and handed it to Trey, who grabbed it and said, "You sure?" Cass shook her head up and down.

"Okay then, I'm out," quickly shutting the door behind him. Cass retrieved the phone saying, "Okay, I'm back."

"How are you doing lil' sis?"

"I'm hanging in there," she responded as she flopped to her sofa shrieking, "Ouch," feeling the soreness from the previous night's activities.

"What's wrong," Stephanie inquired.

"I just stubbed my toe on the sofa that's all."

"Oh, okay. Do you remember that delicious dinner which my office sponsors for the medical students who worked with us before they leave for the Christmas break?"

"Kind of. Why?"

"Well this year it will be held at *The Atlanta Fish Market*, who by the way has food to die for, and we have one extra space and I figured this was not a free meal you should pass up."

"Okay, when is it?"

"It's this Friday. We can make an evening of it. Afterwards you can come over and see your niece and nephew and we can watch some movies."

"That sounds good to me. Let's call it a date."

"Great. Can't wait to see you. Cassandra, Have you spoken to mother lately?"

"Yes, I spoke with her the other day. She was fine."

"Good, I need to call her. Ciao."

"Bye," Cass responded as she moved her legs in and out trying to soothe some of the achiness. "Damn, he put a hurting on a sister with his young ass," she laughed as she figured she needed to share this with Keisha.

As she called Keisha's house, Hank answered the phone. "May

I speak to Keisha?" In his deep voice he responded, "Is this Cassandra?"

"Yes," she hesitantly agreed.

"She told me she was sleeping at your place," he angrily retorted. Cass fabricated, "Well, she did but she left not too long ago and I thought she would have made it there by now. She probably stopped to get her nails done or something."

"Are you covering for her ass?"

"No, no," she quickly lied. "I'll call back later," she abruptly uttered while hanging up the phone. "I'm gonna shoot her ass for always putting me on the spot," Cass thought as she heard a knock at her door. She thought, "That better not be Trey." She looked through her peep hole and it was Keisha. Barely letting her open the door, Keisha pushed her way in saying, "Please tell me you have not called my house."

"I just did."

"Was Hank there?"

"Yes."

"Shit! Did you cover for me?"

"Of course I did, I always do." She hugged her friend, now relaxed and said, "So how was your night?"

"Girl my coochie is sore."

"So the myth is proven to be true yet again. So a brother is packing?"

"Yes he is." They both laughed and slapped a high five as Cass poured them both a glass of juice.

"Deante actually asked me if I would be interested in a threesome with the two of them."

"I know you are not considering that," Cass inquisitively responded. She knew Keisha was out there, but she did not think to that extent. Keisha looked up with a sly grin, "Well, I have thought about it."

"You have got to be kidding. Why don't you get rid of Hank if you gonna be doing all of this screwing around?"

"Cause Hank is my boo. You know that. He just is not enough

for me in the bedroom, that's all."

"Your ass is a damn nympho," she laughed while swallowing some of her juice.

"Call it what you want. Well, let me go ahead and get home to my boo. Thanks for covering for me."

"No problem." As they walked to the door Keisha hugged her friend, "Are you alright? Really are you dealing with things?" she sincerely questioned.

Cass gently smiled giving her friend a kiss on the cheek. "I'm taking it day by day but I really miss him Keisha. I really do. But," shaking her head to distract herself from crying, "I'm fine." Keisha grabbed her friend and hugged her. No words needed to be said as she turned to leave.

Cass honestly knew that she was moving somewhere in her life, but was scared about which direction she was moving—forwards, backwards. She pensively studied that question as she sat on her bed. The recent events that occurred in her life seemed to have placed her in a gray area where she felt uncomfortable and out of control. Prior to the past week, she felt like she was grounded somewhat despite the too recent emotional trauma she had endured. Now she felt less sure of every aspect of her life. Less sure of her faith, her sexuality, the very essence of Cassandra Nicholas seemed to have been lost somewhere, and this fact terrified her. She was disengaged from her trance when the phone rang.

"Hello." She heard an older woman's voice on the line, "Is this Cassandra?"

"Yes, this is Cassandra."

"Hey there baby, this is Mama Lilly."

"Hi," she surprisingly stated as she sat straight up in her bed.

"I think it's about time you pay me a visit. I want to share some things with you. I know this is late notice, but last night I cooked some turnip greens, sweet potatoes, and some turkey necks and you are more than welcome to come have some."

Cassandra, not sure if she was quite ready to face them again said, "I don't know, Mrs. Cason."

"Please chile, call me Mama Lilly. And I won't take no for an answer." After that, what could Cass say but, "Well what time would you like me to be there?"

"Any time after five would be fine sugar. Can't wait to see you baby. Now here are the directions to my house." Cass hung up the phone after writing the directions on paper and figured, "I needed to face up to them at some point." She quickly scampered around her house trying to prepare herself for her newfound day's outing.

Cass finally had pulled on some nice khaki linen pants with a matching button up linen blouse. As she exited the elevator, there was Deante manning the desk. "Hey Cassandra," he winked, "Come here for a second."

Annoyed, she moved toward the desk and said, "What, Deante?"

"My dog said you got it going on."

"Oh really," she said in an aggravated tone as she began walking away because she certainly didn't like her business on the street. Before she was able to get through the door he grabbed her arm and said, "How bout sharing some of your stuff?" he smiled. She yanked her arm away and shouted, "Piss off, and if you ever address me differently than you would any other resident here, I swear I will get your ass fired." He lifted both hands up as if he were under a policeman's gun and surrendered saying, "Chill out girl. I was just playing." Cassandra rolled her eyes and hastily left the building.

Twenty-Two

The long ride in the rainy and inclement weather to Robert's mother's house was not what Cassandra needed. She was not in the mood to contemplate the meaning of her life, which she tended to do on these long, nostalgic drives. Therefore to avoid the almost inevitable, she put on her book tape of *The Delaney sisters,* to divert her thoughts from her introspectively dismal existence. Finally she arrived and pulled into the driveway. Before getting out she sat there a minute wondering if she would need to be ready for another altercation with his sisters. She then thought, "Today is not the day." She reflected as she walked to the door and was almost driven to tears thinking of what could have been. She felt as though she was reopening old wounds which were barely healed as she approached Mrs. Cason's door. It was a lovely ranch style home with Robert's personality reflected in its subtle richness. Cass only found comfort in knowing that maybe this meeting would help bring more closure to her life.

Finally Mama Lilly opened the door and smiled saying, "I'm sorry baby. Come on in." Cassandra carefully eased her way into the house not sure of what to expect. Mama Lilly noticed her trepidation and chuckled saying, "It's only you and me chile. And I apologize for all that happened last time we were together, baby," she expressed while pulling Cassandra's light weight jacket off. "You have a seat.

Would you like some nice hot tea or something while I fix you a plate?"

"That would be wonderful. That weather is starting to change on us. It's starting to get a bit nippy out there," Cassandra nervously added.

"That's why I stay inside in this kind of weather. I had the pneumonia last year this time and barely made it," she confided as she wobbled over from the kitchen with Cass's tea.

"Thank you."

"I ain't had pneumonia ever before, but this time I let my doctor give me that pneumonia shot, and shonuff as I am sitting here today, I got the pneumonia."

"Well, I'm glad you got over that hurdle. Pneumonia can be pretty tough as you get older."

"Yes, chile. Go ahead and say it. When you get to be an old fart like me." She continued, "I'm alot better if I can keep these old bones from hurting."

Cassandra silently laughed and changed the subject, "So you wanted to see me, Mrs. Ca," she stopped herself midsentence and said, "I mean Mama Lilly."

"Yes I did. Did you know that my dear Robert loved you?"

"Well, I felt like we were getting closer every day, and we both recognized that fact. We were growing to love each other more every day."

"Had you two ever discussed marriage?"

"Individually, we both might have danced around the topic, but never anything serious," Cassandra blushed wondering where Mrs. Cason was going with this line of questioning.

Mama Lilly reached into her pocket and took out a pristine small blue box, "Well, my Robert was apparently past the dancing. This was found in the glove compartment of his car after the accident, in perfect condition," she said as she handed the box to Cass.

"May I?" Cass questioned before she dared open the box.

"Go on, open it." Inside the box was a huge three carat diamond ring encircled by a shiny platinum band. Cass began trembling slightly. "Was this for me?"

"Read the engraving in it, chile. Go on now," she implored.

"My Cassandra," she began softly and nervously reading aloud, "I love you always," as her voice began to crack and the tears silently rolled down her cheeks, "Your Robert". She fell back into the sofa and placed her trembling hands over her face quietly professing, "I love you too, Robert, I love you too."

By that time Mama Lilly had walked over to where Cass was and placed her full arms around her, "I know, chile. I know." She continued to cry in Mama Lilly's comforting arms until she felt like she had drained her soul. Mama Lilly interrupted, "Come on over to the table. Feed that little frail body of yourns." Cass lightly smiled at Mama Lilly's description of her and slowly stood, knowing that her mascara must be all over her face stated, "May I use your restroom first?"

"Sure, dear. And there are some face towels in the closet to the right when you get in there." Cassandra went to the bathroom and saw how awful she looked with black streaks canvasing her face. She turned on the water and reached in the closet for a towel. Why hadn't he just proposed in Aruba, guilt-ridden, she scorned. If he had, maybe things would have been different. "My God," she thought while briefly feeling dizzy and bracing herself on the wall. "Am I cursed to be alone for the rest of my life?" as she began wiping her face. "All I ever wanted was to have a good job and be independent, and that I have accomplished. But I also wanted to come home to someone who I cherished and who cherished me. I had that in Robert," she thought as she angrily wiped the newly forming tears. She then found herself trying to reinforce those nine words which had carried her along through many of her trials and tribulations, "Everything happens the way it does for a reason." With that, she walked out to eat some of Mama Lilly's food. The delicious smell encompassed the house.

They sat and ate and talked for some time. She found out that Robert's father had left them when he was only seven years old and was still alive but in jail serving a life sentence for murder. She discovered that Robert had no scholarships and had worked throughout college and business school to supplement his meager income. Mama Lilly also confided that Robert had always begged her to get him braces for his teeth, but she never had the funds to do so. That is why she always felt guilty because he had to deal with the taunting by other kids about his teeth as well as his weight problem. They looked at pictures of him in the photo album and laughed about some of the childhood pranks which he had cleverly devised. Finally after having a piece of Mama Lilly's delectable homemade sweet potato pie, she resolved that it was past time for her to leave. As she stood, Mama Lilly implied that she should not be driving in the rainy and windy weather, especially since they were under a flood warning but Cass knew that she needed to be alone. With that, she politely thanked Mama Lilly for everything. Mama Lilly handed Cass her jacket and as she reached the door Mama Lilly said, "Aren't you forgetting something," while handing her the blue box..

"Mama Lilly," which Cass felt was a befitting title that she would never forget to use anymore stated, "I don't know if that is appropriate. I mean Robert was not able to make it official, and maybe there was a reason for that."

Mama Lilly looked at her with tender eyes and said, "My Robert loved you. I believe the only thing that is appropriate is for you to take this ring and always remember the depth of his feelings for you," she placed it in Cass's jacket pocket while extending a warm and caring hug. "You go on now chile, and don't you forget about Mama Lilly."

Cass turned to hug her again and said, "Thank you, Mama Lilly. Thank you for everything."

Mama Lilly then added before letting Cass escape out into the weather. "By the way. Robert's house is on the market now and my Robert cannot fool me no matter how he tried. I knew you was gon be moving into his house long before you did. When you plan on picking up all those fancy clothes because I know they is some high dollar stuff?"

Cass flushed with embarrassment and innocently replied, "Well I still have the key so I guess I will stop by sometime during the week." She reached and hugged Mama Lilly again and turned and left in silence.

Cass briskly walked to her car trying to escape as much of the rain and harsh breeze as possible. She finally made it and quickly turned on the heat once the car was started. While waiting for the car to warm up, she reached into her pocket and pulled out the ring. "This ring is gorgeous," she thought and then became overridden with feelings of remorse and guilt. She replayed the events of the prior week and felt like she had not given Robert the reverence and respect which he deserved. "My God," she thought, "I damn near let a dyke seduce me and I slept with a fuckin' hoodlum. What's wrong with me? Robert has barely been gone a month." Although it had been three. With that she pulled off into the mist created by the heat of the car intermixed with the cold of the night. As she drove she couldn't help but continue to punish herself on account of her immature behavior. She even wondered if she should seek psychiatric help, because while she may have had a few flings in the past, she never let a woman touch her intimately. She shook her head as if to erase the feelings which she had experienced. She knew that she could not share the events of that night with anyone and wondered what she needed to do to avoid Tanya. Cass was not afraid of Tanya but rather fearful of the strange feelings which she had evoked. Tanya had been calling her several times daily at home and at work, and Cass had successfully evaded her thus far. But she knew this behavior could not last forever. She knew she had to talk to Tanya and basically tell her that she could no longer see her as a friend or anything else for that matter. Her night had gone so well, she did not want to ruin it by calling her, but she promised herself that she would do it before the weekend's end. For the remainder of the drive home Cass placed in her Delaney Sister's tape yet again, but for a different reason this time. She wanted to melt away the guilt that enveloped her so intensely and immerse herself into an entirely different reality.

Cass awakened bright and early Sunday morning feeling like she hadn't gotten enough sleep. However, she had set her clock early so as to make the morning mass. She had decided the night before when she got ready for bed that she needed to go to church and get grounded in her faith again which seemed to have dissipated significantly over the foregoing months. Cass hardly considered herself a saint, but undeniably felt like she had done a year's worth of sinning just in the prior week. Cass attended church when she was overridden with guilt and feeling shameful. She somehow had allowed herself to believe that this one simplistic act would "fix" things. She quickly got dressed in her blue, rather homely, dress and all its accessories and promptly headed out to seek forgiveness for her sins. Cass knew that these antics of going to church when she felt like she had an excess of sins on her plate was entirely ridiculous, but at the same time it made her feel better and more accepting of herself, and possibly that much closer to becoming a bonified Catholic Christian.

As Cass sat through the mass she couldn't help but look around and scrutinize the faces around her. She looked one direction and saw a young man with his wife and children thinking, "He is majorly in the closet," as she observed his feminine mannerisms. She looked another direction and thought, "You know he is fooling around on her," as she had seen a woman's husband glance at everything with a skirt that passed by. Cass scolded herself for being involved in such childish conduct, but she had been doing this ever since her parents used to take her to mass and she had to try to remain awake during the service. Most of the time it was inevitable that she would fall asleep and awaken almost screaming to her mother's pinch on her thigh. Cass sang the hymns and tried to actually participate in the mass, despite her occasional distractions. Cass listened intently to the homily which focused on the demoralization of society and how everything had become so acceptable. The priest implored his parishioners to become involved in their communities and thereby place Christ back into society. Cassandra was enmeshed with guilt after hearing the priest's words which seemed to directly address her actions. Eventually, the time which Cassandra dreaded had arrived. She faced this dilemma every time she walked into church. Communion or no communion. Cassandra had avoided confession for years, believing that telling her sins to a mortal man made no sense, she would rather just go straight to the source and pray to God for forgiveness. However, since she was supposed to be a Catholic, she knew she should abide by the Catholic doctrine, but had never quite accepted the principle of confession amongst others. As the usher arrived to her pew, Cass politely sat up and let the other people on her pew go by, as she felt she did not deserve communion this particular Sunday. The decision was made. She did however, solemnly pray for God's guidance in her tumultuous life, for Robert, and her family. The priest then joyfully exclaimed, "Go in peace to love and serve the Lord." Cass quickly bowed and exited the church.

While Cass rarely connected truly during any mass, she always felt much better afterwards. She knew that she had a connection with God and was innately good, she just needed it reinforced sometimes. As she hopped into her car, she sang the gospel songs on the radio feeling one step closer to her God. En route to home Cass decided to call her mom to whom she could for once respond "yes" when she posed the question as to whether she had gone to church as she did every Sunday.

"Hey mom," Cassandra gleefully shouted into the receiver.

"Hey Cass. What are you doing up so early?" her mom yawned.

She proudly smiled, "I'm just leaving church."

"Oh really. I am so glad that you went," she quickly moved on shocking Cass, "Before I forget, I received a letter from your high school about the class reunion." Cass interrupted, "You know I don't attend those things."

"Yes, I know you should at least respond Cass. It will be held during the Christmas holidays and you'll be here any way won't you?" her mom curiously questioned.

"Yes, mom. I will be there for Christmas, and I have no plans of spending my free time with people who I didn't like then, and surely won't now. I am in touch with the people I want to be from those days." Her mom sighed, "I still think it doesn't hurt to respond."

"Okay mom," Cass lied, "I am pulling up to my destination, so I must go. Love you."

"Love you too, baby. Bye."

Twenty-Three

Cass couldn't decide whether she wanted to have breakfast or not. She decided that she would head towards home and if the feeling hit her she would stop. Cass opted to go to *Barnes and Noble* and have a cup of cappacino and maybe read the paper or buy a good book. When she arrived she was surprised at the number of people there starting their days so early. On a typical Sunday she would likely just be turning over. As she sat and ordered cappacino she couldn't help but gaze down at the ring which now rested on her left hand's ring finger. She had to put it on just to see what it felt like to be perceived as otherwise spoken for. She then thought of Robert and how close they were becoming and found herself becoming angry that she didn't have the chance to really experience their love. She wondered if she would ever have the opportunity again to meet a man who would make her heart feel true contentment like Robert had. Afterall, she would be thirty-five in the upcoming March, and according to the latest statistics her prospects were very dismal at that age. Just as she paid for her drink a nice looking, scholarly appearing man sat next to her and began to order some coffee. As their eyes met, Cass smiled and he did the same. His mingled gray hair was perfectly trimmed around his smooth and hairless face. He looked to be about forty-five, she guessed while trying not to stare. She couldn't help but notice how sleek and in shape he appeared for his age.

She then noticed his hand extended before her face, and startled, she grabbed it firmly and stated, "Hello, I'm Cassandra."

His deep voice then rang out so richly, "Harrison, Harrison Chauncey. In case you didn't hear me initially."

She flushed and apologized, "I'm sorry, I guess I was daydreaming."

"Is this seat taken?"

"No, not at all," she smiled smitten by his immaculately white and straight teeth. They talked extensively about books they had read and the lack of things they shared in common, more due to age than interest. Despite their differences, there was a chemistry that drew her to him. Maybe his charisma or his indisputable traditional values. Maybe his sarcastic sense of humor. Whatever the source of her intrigue, she was open to the prospect of learning more about him. She also figured that based on her track record of late, good old conventionalism might be exactly what she needed. She discovered that he was a divorced fifty-six year old Professor of Literature at Clark-Atlanta University who had made Georgia his home for the past four years since his divorce. He then shocked Cassandra by stating, "So when are you planning on getting married?"

She smiled and flirtatiously responded, "I guess when I find the right man, Professor." He looked surprised by her response and she noticed him looking down at her hand. Embarrassed she said, "Oh, this. I'm sorry. It's a long story, but suffice it to say I am single." He laughed and said, "So you are a heart breaker."

"Hardly. Maybe if we meet again sometime I'll break it down for you," Cassandra responded expecting him to ask for her number, as she got up from her seat.

"Well, it was a pleasure meeting you, Cassandra, right?"

"Yes," she replied, as she decided to graciously go to observe some other areas of the book store. "Nice meeting you too," she turned to walk away totally tripping that he had left it at that. "I guess he wasn't interested." She slyly glanced back to see if he was watching her walk away, but then had to swallow her pride as he was engrossed apparently moreso by *The New York Times*. Cassandra waded through some other sections and decided she was about ready to go. She figured she had given Harrison ample time to approach her again, and he didn't so she chose to make her exit. As she was leaving she couldn't help but notice him sitting in one of the comfy chairs at the end of an aisle with his small bifocals on. She thought, "He looks so distinguished, and so cute. I'm gonna give this brother one of my cards, and if he calls great, and if not, whatever. I'm a grown woman, I can deal rather easily with either outcome," she rationalized.

"Harrison right?" he looked up and smiled while removing his glasses. "Here's my card," she said while scribbling her home number on the back. "Use it if you want to discuss further about our lack of commonality." He took the card from her and she promptly turned away to leave. She didn't look back this time, because she knew he was looking. She smiled and headed home.

She arrived and saw Keisha's SUV in the parking lot, and was wondering if her friend was there paying her a visit, then figured she must be there hanging out with Deante. As she approached the desk, she was surprised to find that Deante was not on duty so she asked his replacement, "Did you let a visitor up to my place. Number 3023?"

He looked at his log in sheet and responded, "No."

"Well is Deante on duty?"

He exasperatedly responded after pulling out the scheduling board, "Not until six o'clock ma'am."

"Hmmm," She thought "So what's Keisha's car doing here?" She decided to go leave a message on her car because she wanted Keisha to come up and see her ring before leaving. As she got closer to the car, she saw them in the back seat basically making out. She decided her news was important enough to interrupt so she knocked on the window. Deante startled looked up and then put his hands up as if to say, "It's not what you think." Cass then saw why as she noticed it was not Keisha beneath him, but the white stripper girl from the seventh floor.

She then screamed, "You better get her ass outta there right now."

He hopped out of the car pulling up his pants, "Brother has to get some young pussy sometimes," he arrogantly laughed.

"You punk ass son of a bitch. You need to tell Keisha by tomorrow, because it's gonna be a lot worse if I have to tell her, and I will, Deante. I promise you with your trifling ass." By that time Marcia, the hoochie jumped out of the car and smiled at Cass saying, "See you later, neighbor."

"You would want not to, bitch," she quickly hollered back. She gave Deante a look daring him not to tell her friend, as she turned to go back into the building.

"Whatever," he mumbled beneath his breath as he strolled over to Marcia and playfully continued to banter with her.

As Cass went into the elevator, she could not believe how much of a dog he really was. She knew Keisha sometimes got herself into these ridiculous situations, but she could not just stand by and watch it even if Keisha chose to be oblivious to these things sometimes. Cass was not going to waste her day thinking about all the dogs lurking around. She had a brand new day ahead. As she reached her door she wondered what she would do with it. She decided a little sleep never hurts anyone, as she stripped out of all of her clothes and hopped into bed. She lay there and first decided to read one of her marketing magazines on her nightstand which always put her to sleep. While it always seemed to create excessive somnolence, she felt that the little knowledge that she acquired in that short span of time kept her somewhat up to date on the latest changes in the marketplace. She began reading it and like clockwork promptly fell asleep.

Cass was awakened by the telephone, "Hello," she sleepily responded.

"Please talk to me. Do not hang up. Please." Cass heard Tanya pleading on the line.

"Listen, Tanya," Cass stated initially in a half alert state. "I'd be very happy if you didn't call me again. What happened the other night was a big mistake incited by intoxication and your disrespect of my lifestyle. I don't appreciate that and do not tolerate people in my life who can't respect my personal choices," Cass now fully awake angrily recited.

Eddra Marchand

"Cassandra, just hear me out," Tanya continued barely breathing in between words, "I used the misguided feelings I had for you inappropriately and I apologize for that. I thought I felt us vibing and felt like I needed to communicate in some way what I was feeling. I chose the wrong way, and for that I apologize too. Please, don't make this be the end of what could be a very good friendship. We have so much in common, and I promise from this day forth I will respect who you are and not force my realities onto you," Tanya begged through an entirely fabricated story. She knew Cass was teetering on the line regarding her sexuality, she just didn't know it yet and Tanya intended on helping it to resurface, just maybe more subtly at first. She had tasted her juices and planned on tasting them again.

"I'm sorry, Tanya, but please respect my wishes and don't call me ever again." Without giving Tanya a chance to respond, Cass hung up the phone hoping that her words would sink in. Tanya, shocked, hung up the phone realizing that this was the first time that those rehearsed lines didn't work on one of her straight conquests. She smiled and thought, "Damn, she's a tough cookie; just like I like 'em," as she took a smooth drag of her cigarette.

Cass slowly stretched and decided to lay there a brief while longer. She was surprised to see that it was already three o'clock. She finally got out of bed and decided to shower and maybe check out what was on the tube. After getting refreshed she realized that she was hungry and while walking to the kitchen she was startled by a knock on her door. She looked through the peephole and saw her friend Keisha and ecstatically opened the door eager to share her news. Upon opening it, her smile immediately disappeared as she noticed that it was Keisha and Deante.

"Hey girl," Keisha hugged her friend, "Wassup." Deante walked in avoiding any eye contact with Cass saying, "Wassup."

"Hey," Cass responded quickly sliding off her ring and sliding it into her robe pocket. She didn't want to share the touching events of yesterday with Keisha and Deante, she wanted to share that only with her friend.

"You don't have nothing to eat in here girl?"

"That's just what I was coming in here to do. Find something to eat, before I got rudely interrupted," she pretended to laugh.

"Girl just fix you a sammich or something and let's chill and maybe play a game of Whisk. We are trying to chill out before Deante goes on duty," she smiled lightly hugging him.

Cassandra trying to hold back a gag said, "Yeah, ya'll go have a seat while I do just that. Fix a sandwich." Cass pulled out her turkey ham and quickly put together a sandwich with lettuce and tomato.

She heard from the other room, "So what's been going on? Where were you all day yesterday?"

Knowing she was by Mama Lilly's she just responded, "I had a lot of errands to run. Did you guys want anything? A drink or something?"

"No thanks," Keisha continued, "Errands, what kind of errands?" Keisha playfully mocked.

Cass then asked ignoring her previous query, "How did you get here, if your car was here?," planning specifically to agitate Deante.

"Deante came here early today to handle some paperwork from last night, and he said he would wash my car and pick me up later. So now a sister's ride is sparkling," she exclaimed and looked up at Deante laying a big kiss on his lips stating, "Thank you, baby."

"No prob," he smiled as Cass rolled her eyes directly at him. "Who's going to deal?"

"I'll deal first," Deante announced removing his arm from around Keisha's waist to take the cards. Cass harshly handed him the cards. As they began playing, Keisha and Deante were practically kissing between each hand like pathetic hormone raged teenagers, which almost made Cass blurt out the truth about Deante's morning paperwork. As Cass was looking at her hand trying to decide what to do next, she was astonished to look up and see Keisha's bare breasts exposed and Deante sucking them as if she were not there.

She quietly exclaimed, "This is ridiculous." She threw her cards down as she stated on deaf ears, "I'll be right back, I'm going to the restroom for a minute." Cass walked into her bedroom in total disbelief. Especially tripping since he was literally doing that same stuff with another woman a few minutes earlier. "What a fuckin' dog," she thought after sitting there a couple of minutes and giving them ample time to compose themselves. She exited her bedroom at that moment only to see Deante's hairy ass pumping to and fro next to her fucking coffee table, and Keisha eagerly beckoning him on with her sensual whimpers. Cass could not believe that Keisha was behaving so nonsensical over this imbecile. She knew Keisha had a wild side but always thought she had some scruples.

She stood there for a minute and then angrily yelled, "Ya'll need to take that shit somewhere else!" She then turned in disgust as she heard Keisha exclaiming, "This is all yours, daddy. This is all yours." Cass shut her room door and sat on her bed pretending that she had no house guests. She seethed with anger as Keisha was being made a fool of and seemed to not know it or not care.

Cass had learned the hard way years before to not tell a girlfriend that their so-called boyfriend was cheating on them. She had lost one good friend before for that exact reason. It was her friend Erika in high school. They were both on the cheer leading team and of course Erika was dating a guy on the varsity football team. Cass had run into Erika's boyfriend at the drive-in with another cheerleader who at the time was blowing him. She informed Erika, who in turn presumed that it was all a lie simply because Cassandra wanted her man. Needless to say that friendship was consequently ruined, and they had not spoken since that day. Cass certainly did not want to take the chance of the same fate happening with Keisha and opted to threaten Deante to unmask his doggish ways. Although she did not truly believe that Keisha would let this child come between them, she knew whooped people had been known to do some crazy and irrational things, and Cass certainly didn't want to test her friend's loyalty now, especially judging by her current juvenile behavior. Cass, not realizing how much time had elapsed since she had begun reminiscing, was puzzled that she heard no noise emanating from the den, so she emerged from her room to see that no one was there. Only a note on her refrigerator stating, "Cass, I am so sorry. I know we got carried away. Please forgive me. Your horny friend." She cracked half a smile and decided that she would get her things prepared for work and have an early relaxing evening with her aromatherapy, corona, and maybe "buster", her friendly vibrator. But prior to that, she befittingly chose to sprinkle some carpet freshener on the area next to her coffee table and vacuum any remnants of what had happened there shortly before.

Twenty-Four

The next week went by fast as Cass had again become the workaholic she was known for being, especially since she had no real distractions at the time. She couldn't believe that Professor Harrison Chauncey had not called her. The only people she had spoken to were Keisha, with whom she finally was able to share the story of her beautiful ring and the inscription it bore; her sister Stephanie, who wanted to confirm the dinner invitation and collaborate on Christmas gifts and shopping for the family; and of course mom who wanted to talk much about nothing. She did speak to her baby sister Casey who believes she's in love with some guy at her college and wanted to set up a day for her to meet him, but otherwise, work had become the centerpiece of Cass's existence. As she headed home on that Thursday, she was pleased that she didn't have to cook since she had actually found time to cook a decent meal on Wednesday evening and had leftovers that she wouldn't mind eating for a change. As she entered her building, Sam the new concierge that had taken Deante's place, called her over, "Ms Nicholas?"

"Yes."

"You have a delivery. Since your hands are tied would you like me to bring it up?"

"A delivery. Yes, Sam that would be just fine."

Cass was so pleased to have a courteous concierge not making passes at every woman that walked into the lobby. Although she assumed the primary reason was because Sam was gay, it didn't lessen the effect of his much more appropriate demeanor. Poor Deante had been fired only three days prior. When he returned to work on Monday, he was greeted by the police and subsequentlly arrested. Shortly thereafter, all of the occupants of the building received a notice about what had occurred. Apparently, Deante, who had the master key for all of the condo's was using the key for other purposes than just routine maintenance. He had been entering various homes after the occupants were gone and taking little items that wouldn't be noticed such as jewelry, money, and a few articles of clothing. He was busted when a woman at the complex believed that her fiance' was coming home in the afternoon for secret rendezvous and had a camcorder set up to catch him. When she viewed the tape her fiance' was on it and was innocently planning a surprise party for her, but more importantly, Deante was on the tape taking some items from her home. As Cass reached her floor, she shook her head as she thought of what a pitiful sight he must have been on Monday. She did not like Deante, but she did not want a brother to go to jail. Cass knew that this episode probably reinforced in many of her neighbor's minds that all African Americans are all indiscriminately without morals and any common decency. This upset Cass, as she slammed her door when she walked into her apartment. She had worked so hard to get where she was, and all people frequently saw was the color of her skin and automatically began stereotyping because of stupid bullshit like Deante had pulled. Now Keisha, on the otherhand, cared nothing of Deante's plight or its consequences because she figured she got what she wanted and was finally all up under Hank within her confined world. She resolved that she would be faithful to her boo, because "a good man is hard to find." Part of her nonchalance was because Deante did tell her about his unscrupulous behavior and she was through with him after that. Keisha had always gonethrough the same vicious cycle and would be doing the same thing when her next play toy presented himself. Cass laughed at the drama which her friend inevitably created and endured.

Cass slowly walked into her bedroom feeling as though she

was forgetting something and began to remove her clothes. The knock at her door quickly reminded her that it was Sam bringing her a delivery that she had not remembered. She quickly slipped into a pair of shorts and T-shirt and opened the door. Sam was holding a dozen red roses. Cass smiled and exclaimed, "Isn't that sweet? Just place them right there," as she pointed to the table in her foyer. "Thanks Sam," she practically threw him out eager to see who the flowers were from. Excitedly, she removed the card and it said, "You are admired every day from a distance. I only hope that the distance becomes shorter and shorter each passing day." Cass smiled trying to think of who it could be. She didn't think it was Harrison because he didn't know where she lived. She knew it wasn't Trey's trifling butt and soon found herself intrigued by her secret admirer, as she poured herself a glass of wine. She was sitting on her sofa sipping her wine while her food was heating and was disrupted from her tranquil moment by the phone. "Hello," she smoothly said into the phone.

"Well hello, Ms. Nicholas," she heard Harrison's distinguished voice emit over the line.

Knowing full well who it was, she stated, "Yes, this is she. Who's this?"

"This is Harrison. We met briefly the other day."

"Oh, Yes. Hi Harrison. How are you?"

"Fine, thank you. I was wondering if you wanted to possibly get something to eat this evening. I know this is late notice, but I had a meeting this evening that was cancelled and I know that I have a conference this weekend and part of next week that will occupy my time. And quite frankly, I wanted to see you again before I leave."

Cass smiled as she sensed his sincerity, and against all her usual rules replied, "Well, you caught me just in time, I was about to heat up some left overs."

"Well, shall I pick you up or should we meet somewhere?"

"What area do you live in, that might make it easier to decide," she excitedly questioned knowing full well that she had already gone out on a limb by accepting such a late invitation and that she certainly wasn't going to make him aware of where she lived just yet.

"I live in Buckhead."

"Perfect, me too. We can meet somewhere in this area."

"What do you say we meet at *Mick's* and then take things from there."

"Sounds good to me. Let's say maybe in an hour."

"Sounds great. See you then," he stated with that sexy voice of his.

Cassandra hung up the phone feeling the butterflies in her stomach, a sensation which she hadn't felt since Robert. As she realized that fact she looked down at her hand and slid off the ring before she forgot. She walked into her bedroom and placed it in it's special place. She then looked at herself in the mirror saying, "Girl, now you know better. When a man calls you with such late notice, it's usually because another date had cancelled, or you're a last resort." She waved her hand at herself as if to say, "Whatever." After Tanya and Trey, how much worse could it get, she figured. To add to that, "He sounded so sincere," she smiled. Cassandra knew exactly what she was going to wear, her sleek black all-in-one pants suit. It bore a look of sexiness combined with class, which was just the look Cass wanted to exude. She quickly took a shower and curled her hair. She was going to wear it down, since the last time he saw her she was looking somewhat homely in both her attire and her do. She dabbed a little perfume on and make-up, and slid out of the door, planning to be her usual ten minutes but fashionably late.

Cass arrived a few minutes late as planned and saw Harrison sitting at the bar. He lifted his hand to beckon her in his direction. She walked over to him and was taken aback by his beautiful unflawed caramel complexion and his cinnamon colored eyes which matched perfectly as he, like the perfect gentleman, stood to greet her. These little simple gestures impressed Cass, because she always appreciated a man who treated his woman like a woman. He bent down and kissed her on the cheek and pulled out her stool. Cass thought, "Friend boy is getting more brownie points by the minute," as she sat and smiled captivated by him and his alluring cologne. She thought he looked even more handsome that night, with his khaki slacks, mock burgundy turtleneck, burgundy and beige sports jacket, and penny loafers.

"Hi," he radiantly smiled, "Glad you could make it."

Cass smiled back and said, "Me too."

"May I buy you a drink?" he questioned while lifting his rum and coke to his small but perfectly shaped lips.

"Yes. I think I'll have a margarita." In his charming manner, he called over the waiter and said, "This young lady would like a margarita, please." As they retrieved their drinks, the hostess called his name as a table had become available. He again pulled out her chair and escorted her to the table, gently placing her arm onto his. Cassandra was immensely enjoying his assertive yet gentle manner. They sat and talked extensively about one another. She discovered that he and his wife of twenty-seven years mutually agreed to a divorce because through the years they had grown apart. Their three sons were understandably upset, but since they had waited until all of them were out of the house, he described that they were all dealing with it much better, realizing they were still going to be their parents no matter what. He admitted that the distance had taken a toll on their relationship, because when he was appointed to his position at the university, his wife, who had been a stay at home mom, had just started profiting from a catering business she had started three years prior, and therefore, was not willing to relocate.

He went on to say, "Eventually, my male curiosities began to peek and I started seeing other women, only casually however," he assured. "I did not begin seeing any women intimately until my wife and I had agreed that divorce was the most appropriate next step for us."

Cass raised her eyebrow thinking, "Yeah right." "So," she inquired, "You're telling me that you had been here for at least two years and had not been intimate with anyone."

"That is correct," he laughed, "you act as if you find that hard to believe."

"That is because I do, especially a handsome man like yourself," she flirted.

"Now I did not say that I did not desire the closeness of a woman. It's just that I felt that waiting for the divorce was the noble thing to do after a long and mostly happy marriage." Cass smiled again and thought this man sounds too good to be true. She wondered what was wrong with him. She laughed at her skepticism and said, "So, where do you stand now in your journey since you are now fully and respectfully divorced?"

He smiled looking directly at Cass and said while grabbing her hand, "Now, Cassandra I am a gentle predator seeking my perfect prey. A beautiful woman who doesn't mind a conventional guy who appreciates the finer things in life. I am not into games and I want someone who can share those things with me." Cass sat there speechless for a minute as she did not know how to respond.

She then looked into his eyes and said, "I certainly appreciate your upfront honesty, and I guess time will tell whether I am your prey or not. We already know that I am perfect," she laughed.

He smiled and squeezed her hand stating, "I love your sense of humor." As they completed their meal, they both were sorry that the evening was coming to an end.

Cass then ended, "Well, Harrison this has certainly been an enjoyable evening. I know I have a long day at work tomorrow, so I guess this evening should come to its end." He stood and pulled out her chair and gave her the most gentle hug. "Cassandra, I enjoyed this evening too, and I hope that we can see one another again when I return from my convention."

"I would expect nothing less," Cass responded as they walked out to the valet area. As Cass's car approached Harrison surprised her by gently tilting her head up and laying a sweet and romantic kiss on her lips.

"I hope you don't mind my candor, but I have been wanting to do that this entire evening." He opened her door, tipped the valet and said, "Be safe, Cassandra. Thanks for seeing me this evening." Cass smiled and drove off thinking, "Something has to be wrong with him. He seems too good to be true." She drove home with easy listening on the radio in a very serene state eager to discover where this new and placid path would lead her.

Twenty-Five

$\mathcal{T}$he next day started out on a pleasant note as Cass was walking on air from her previous night, especially after she received the call from Harrison shortly after arriving home. He was making sure she had made it in safely and wished her a goodnight and day. Cass felt good emotionally and physically for the moment. She had started her morning early and jogged at the gym before her work day began. She felt more energetic than she had in a long while. At lunch time, Stephanie called to remind Cass of the dinner that evening and suggested that she not be late because the evening would start out with a slide presentation by one of the ob/gyn attendings and they would move onto the dinner from there. Cass sighed, "I will be there on time, I promise. Seven o'clock right?"

"Yes, Cass. See you then." Cass's day flew by and she was so proud of being on top of things at work again. She thought she would never reach the pinnacle after falling so far behind, but she was evidence that hard work and perseverance pays off. She then looked down at her watch and exclaimed, "Shit!" It was five until seven and there was no way she could make it to the restaurant by seven o'clock. She resigned that she would just have to disrupt the presentation a little. She quickly ran out of her office, fortunately having already been dressed appropriately to attend the event. She finally arrived at seven-fifteen and slowly walked into the restaurant and asked for the Physician dinner. They promptly reinforced the fact that she was late and pointed her to an area that was darkened and all she could see from her perspective were the flickering lights of a projector. She thought, "Oh well, here it goes." She tried to inconspicuously slide into the room and she heard the whisper of Stephanie along with the shadow of a hand requesting that she take the seat. As Cass sat she heard her sister quietly reprimand her, "I told you to be on time, but that's okay. I'll introduce you later. We have already ordered so when you see the waiter place yours if you can see the menu for your choices." She then became quiet as she listened intently to the speaker. Cass on the other hand wanted a drink to settle her nerves and she quickly grabbed Stephanie's wine glass and took a swig, disappointed to find that it was straight ginger ale. She should have figured as Stephanie held back a laugh and she grimaced in distaste. She fumbled through the menu and was able to decipher something that she wanted and ordered just as the lights were coming on. The speaker, after addressing some questions requested that everyone mingle until the food came. Stephanie didn't hesitate to admonish Cass again, then hugged her saying how glad she was to see her. Cass just laughed at her older sister who had never changed. Stephanie then proceeded to take Cass around the room introducing her first to attendings and colleagues, and then to the medical students, who appeared to be eager to please as Cass teased her sister about abusing her power. Stephanie then introduced her to the last young lady in the room who had her back to them smoozing with some other attendings. "And Cassandra last but not least, this is Tanya Grayson, one of our third year medical students who just finished our rotation." Cass felt weak in her knees as Tanya turned to shake her hand. Tanya was shocked as well, as she stuttered, "Hi."

"This is my sister."

Tanya interrupted and said, "Cassandra right?"

Stephanie confused stated, "You two know one another?"

Cass then quipped, "Uh yes, we met once before. She invested with Robert."

"Oh," Stephanie exclaimed, "Small world. Well, I will leave you here with someone you know while I escape to the restroom before the food comes." Before Cass could contest, Stephanie was gone. Cass speechless for a moment then said, "Listen, nothing is to be said of our encounter. That was all a mistake. And why are you lying to people stating you are a physician when you haven't even graduated from medical school yet. You truly need to grow up."

"I could ask you why are you hiding behind this straight façade when you know that you want a woman. You were feeling me that night and I know it. I mean, I had my finger in your pussy, which tasted very good I might add." Cass flushed in humiliation and anger as Tanya continued. "I had no idea that Dr. Jordan was your sister. I am embarrassed that I lied and I am sorry but I know I will be a doctor someday," she laughed, "at least there was some truth to it. Oh since you are here dear, I might as well ask in person, did you receive my flowers?"

Cass now getting more pissed by the second angrily stated, "So it was you. Now I know that being in medical school you understand plain English. Leave me alone. I have no desire to see you, smell you, hear your voice or receive anything from you." Cass tried to maintain her composure, "Please, Tanya. I want no part of your world. I will ask you one last time to please respect that."

Tanya slyly smiled as Stephanie approached, "It was good seeing you again. You take care now."

"She is one of our best medical students. Very aggressive and," Stephanie laughed, "very annoying." As Stephanie noticed Cassandra's less than jovial mood she queried, "What's wrong with you?"

"Oh nothing, really. I just will have to cut this evening short. Soon as I finish eating, I will have to leave. I will have to take a raincheck on the movies and stuff at your house."

"Are you sure you are okay? Did something happen?" Cass tried to feign a smile and said, "No, everything is fine." The food began arriving and everyone began taking their seats and Tanya sat directly next to Stephanie. Cass felt a lot of nervous energy which she tried to conceal while she hastily ate her food. Stephanie commented, "I guess you are starving, huh Cass." Cass smiled with a full mouth and continued to stuff her food down. Tanya then opened a conversation, "I think I've seen you somewhere else too. I just cannot remember where."

Cass almost choking on her food responded, "I don't think so."

Tanya persisted, "No I am sure of it. When I place my finger in it, excuse me I mean on it," she smiled as she meant that literally, "I will let you know." With that, Cass stood up saying, "Thank you Stephanie, that was delicious but I really must go."

"So soon, Cass. Okay. Well call me, okay. You're gonna miss the delicious dessert." Cass smiled, as she hugged Stephanie and turned to go. Tanya then stood up and extended her arms saying, "I feel like I know you. Let me give you a hug too." Cass begrudgingly patted Tanya lightly on her back as Tanya whispered, "You take care, sweetheart," smiling as Cass left.

Cass could not get out of the restaurant soon enough. She felt as if she was suffocating and the cold air outside helped her regain her normal breathing pattern. As she hopped into her car, she clicked off the radio because her head felt as if was blaring a beat of its own. There was a repeating pattern of what happened several nights before with Tanya and her practically threatening to expose Cass this evening. "She is truly crazy," Cass thought. "What am I going to do to tone her down and let her recognize that I am for real?" Cass knew she would get her phone number changed Monday and hoped that would deter Tanya's continued unfailing advances. As Cass arrived at her home, all she wanted to do was take some Tylenol and get rid of the horrific headache that had developed. She quickly got out of her clothes took a shower and hopped in bed hoping that her living nightmare would be replaced by pleasant dreams. As she began dozing off, her phone rang, "Hey Cassandra," Tanya stated. "It was so good seeing you tonight. Do me a favor." Before Cass could hang up Tanya said, "Check and see if your lips are wet." Cass hung up quickly with repulsion and reaffirmed that she would get her number changed Monday.

Twenty-Six

Cassandra was surprised that a good part of her Saturday was gone by the time she awakened. Cass replayed the events of her night and shook her head. She couldn't remember if she dreamt Tanya had called or not, but she certainly hoped it was a dream. She chose not to look at her caller ID to confirm or contradict it. She didn't want to know. She just knew that she wanted no drama and that meant she had to get Tanya out of her world with a quickness. She turned over to call Stephanie to apologize for her behavior. Her niece answered the phone, "Hello."

"Hey sweetheart," Cass cheerfully responded, "How are you?"

"Auntie Cass," she exclaimed. "Fine. When are we going to see you again and what are you getting me for Christmas?"

"Soon. I promise, and I'm not going to tell you that." Cass promised herself that she was going to become a more active part of her niece and nephew's lives because she sincerely missed them. She also had the selfish motive of wanting a little taste of motherhood since based on her current status she would not be having kids of her own. She quit reflecting on her dilemma and inquired, "Is your mom home?" Without responding Cass heard a sigh and then, "Mom," being yelled into the receiver. Stephanie came to the phone, "Hello."

Cass said while moving the phone to her other ear, "Damn, do you think you can teach your kids to remove the phone from their mouth before they yell for you?"

She laughed, "Hey Cass. Are you better? What happened last night?"

"I'm fine. I just remembered something that I needed to do before today, so I had some time constraints I had to adhere to."

"Oh for a second I thought my obnoxious medical student had run you off," she laughed. Cass seriously stated, "Why would you say that?"

"I was just joking Cassandra. What is with you?" Cassandra then told herself, "Pull up before you cast more suspicion on your behavior." Stephanie then volunteered, "You know that medical student Tanya. She actually should be out of school by now. She just had a hard time getting into medical school, and then passing the boards to get into third year. It was a matter of time though, because she has some serious connections."

"Connections?"

"Yes, both her parents are physicians, and one is the dean of some medical school up North."

"Oh really," she said out loud wondering if they knew their precious daughter was both crazy and gay. "Anyway," Stephanie continued, "When are we gonna make up for last night?"

"Well you know Christmas is only two weeks away and we need to get together to finalize our Christmas lists."

"You're right. Just let me know when you're ready." She then yelled, "Jasmine stop that right now. Girl I must go before my kids tear up my house. Talk to you soon."

"Okay. Bye."

Cass decided that she would work out that day and then maybe catch a movie. She did just that. After a forty-five minute work out, a shower, and washing her hair, she headed to the theatre to see something. She didn't actually care what movie it was she just wanted to get out of the house because this was one of those days that she was feeling lonely but yet wanted to be alone. She would have considered calling Keisha but when Keisha was in that phase where she was into Hank, she was literally at his beck and call. Cass reasoned that it was those times that influenced him to stay despite all of her shortcomings. Instead, she sat alone watching *Stepmom,* eating her popcorn and drinking a diet coke. Cass found herself crying at various parts of the movie through to the end. She enjoyed the movie and left out in the chill of the night to head home. Cass was eager to get there too. Home to her bed. She arrived home and quickly entered into her room while removing her clothes. She thought she stepped on something as she walked in the door but was too lazy to turn on the light. She figured it was probably the quarterly newsletter which they sometimes slide under the door, and she could certainly check that tomorrow. She had messages but chose not to listen. She would hear those tomorrow. At the moment sleep was calling her, and she was answering.

Cass awakened bright and early Sunday feeling well rested. She began listening to her messages. One was Keisha asking about attending their class reunion. One was her mom, and one was Casey. Cass was disappointed that Harrison had not called. She hoped he would call before she got her number changed so he wouldn't think that she was totally uninterested in him. Cass was going to complete all the errands today that she should have done the previous day like washing her clothes and cleaning house. As she got out of bed she walked into the kitchen to put some coffee on. She realized what she had stepped on last night was not the newsletter but rather a card of some sort. Cass hesitated for a minute and then picked it up. She opened the card and there was a picture of two women hugging. Her instincts were correct, she knew that it was from Tanya. She opened it and read, "Cassandra, I know you want me just as bad as I want you. Stop avoiding the inevitable. Love, me."

Cass looked in disbelief, "Love. You have got to be kidding. This bitch is crazy." She then immediately picked up the phone to call the desk. "Concierge."

"Sam?"

"Yes, Ms. Nicholas. How can I help you?"

"Were you on duty last night?"

He laughed, "Unfortunately, yes. I am pulling a double."

"Did you let someone up here for me yesterday?"

"Ummm. Yes. I did. It was your sister right? She said she didn't need to get in she just had a surprise for you. So I let her up."

"Well, Sam. I don't know if you want to be next on the list to be fired," she chided in an irritated tone, "but you are not to let anyone up unless you have my expressed permission, no matter who they claim they are. She was not my sister and don't let her or anyone else up ever unless you get a verbal okay from me."

Sam, apologetically stated in a low voice, "I'm so sorry, ma'am. But I thought I was doing the right thing. It will not happen again." Cass chided back, "See that it doesn't. Good-bye Sam." Cass could not believe the bold persistence of this woman. Cass felt a frightful chill go down her spine as she almost jumped out of skin when the phone rang. "Hello."

"Hey girl, wassup?"

"Hey Keisha, girl. I know you are not seriously considering going to our class reunion?"

"Girl, I think it will be fun seeing what has happened to our old mates. And we said that we would go one year and I figured since we'll be there anyway, maybe this would be the best year."

Cass sighed, her thoughts preoccupied with Tanya , "We will see," changing the subject. "Do you remember that woman that was hitting on me at your cousin's party?"

"You mean that pretty woman you slow danced with?" she teased.

"Yes. She has been aggravating me lately."

"What do you mean aggravating you. You all have been in contact?" Keisha laughed. "You mean you gave her your number? What's up with that?"

Cass sighed and said, "It's a long story, but suffice it to say she has gotten a hold of my number and she has been badgering me since. To add to that she is not a doctor like she claimed, she is a medical student who has actually worked with Stephanie."

"Damn, girl, and I thought my life had drama," she laughed. Cass responded seriously, "I'm serious Keisha. I think the bitch is crazy. In fact I am getting my number changed tomorrow."

"Have you been leading her on or something, Cass?"

"Please," she truly didn't think so. "You know I am all woman, and I need, well not need, but I want a man in my life. Period," she said defensively.

"Chill out. I know. Well do what you have to do. You know I have some connections that could scare her out of your world." Aggravated, Cass changed the subject again, "So what have you been up to?"

"Well, Hank and I have been enjoying one another. But girl, to be honest," she joked, "I'm thinking about going to see Deante for one of those conjugal visits. Child after having a young buck like that, my poor Hank is no contest. It's actually to the point where sister is faking. It's a good thing he's good at foreplay."

Cass interceded, "Speaking of older men, I met a very nice guy who is a professor at Clark. He is so handsome, and so debonair."

"All he's doing is trying to rope you in before you become aware of his shortcomings, if you know what I mean," she joked. "How old is he?"

"He is fifty-six, but he looks about forty."

"Fifty-six," Keisha screamed, "Girl you better let his old ass find someone his own age. When they are that age you gotta find out their medical history and shit. Trust me, I know. You know I have dated my share of older men and if they have high blood, or sugar, they can't get it up good, and you know at that age they have problems getting it up anyway. All I have to say is make sure you give him his vitamin V." Cass couldn't hold back her laughter, "Vitamin V?"

"Yeah, child. That Viagra," she laughed. Keisha's line clicked and she controlled her laughter for a minute and said, "Let me get this. But really think about the class reunion. Later."

"Bye," Cass laughed while hanging up the phone and deciding she would do some chores that day, but also head to the mall to knock out a little of her Christmas shopping.

As Cass returned from the mall it was dark. She had done what she always did and bought herself more Christmas presents than her family. Oh well, as she struggled in with her bags. Unfortunately, one of the women was manning the desk. So she would have to lug everything up on her own. She finally made it to her floor not having completed half of the tasks which she had set out to do. She briefly thought about doing some of it after she laid down her bags. But that remained a fleeting thought as she opted to get ready for her hectic Monday and snuggle up with a good book. She saw that she had no messages and thought, "Well, Harrison. I guess I will have to contact you when I think you're back in town." Cass took a nice bath and turned on some music and enjoyed her relaxing evening. As she slid into her bed, she turned over to her nightstand to get her book. When she opened the drawer, she saw buster. "Buster or the book," she thought. "Buster or the book." Cassandra lazily turned out the light as buster had won that night's competition. She felt her body feeling so tense and rationalized that buster would probably help her get a better night's sleep than the book. She lay there initially tense and slowly began to relax as her body was giving in to the erogenous sensations. Her body shuddered lightly and Cass breathed a sigh of satisfaction and turned over feeling gratified. She fell asleep not a minute later.

Twenty-Seven

*C*ass awakened early anticipating the work she would have to
get done for the day, both personal and business related.
She laughed as she hopped out of bed and headed for the
shower after her prior night's events. Cass knew one of the priorities
on her list for the day was to get a jump start on Tanya, and have her
number changed. Cass arrived at the office on time and before
attacking the stack on her desk, she called the phone company, and
agreed to all fees as long as her number could be changed as soon as
possible that day and continued as a private number. The customer
service representative stated that it all could be accomplished that
day and Cass gratefully thanked him and hung up the phone. She
hoped the saga would finally come to an end. Shortly after her mood
had been uplifted, Linda knocked on the door and readily took a seat
at Cass's desk. "Hey there. How are you?"

"Fine," Cass responded inquisitively as Linda had never ever
come by to just chat.

"I just happened to pass by the fax and saw this notice sitting
there, and I thought you should see it."

Cass read in shock as Tanya apparently had brought this thing
to an entirely different level. It was a letter that had been faxed
describing fictitious accounts of their life together living an alternative
lifestyle. Cass read in disbelief as it appeared Tanya again had the
upper hand trying to slander Cass's name. Cass responded, "I cannot
believe this. This is totally ludicrous."

"Now to me either way it is irrelevant about your lifestyle, but in the wrong hands this could get nasty. I don't know if anyone else has retrieved copies from the fax but I wanted you to have a heads up. By the way, if it's true, then we all should go out sometime," she winked as she stood to leave. Cass was speechless. She felt nauseated as she felt this situation was getting way out of control and she had no idea what she needed to do to get things in order. She didn't want to get a lawyer involved at this point or the police for that matter, because it would draw attention to her and put her sexuality into question. Cass figured this was a scare tactic and maybe it would end here, she prayed, especially after getting her number changed. Cass found herself making numerous visits to the fax machine that day, relieved that no more erroneous information was being sent.

Tanya sat in her medical school class obsessed with Cassandra and barely listening to the attending on her surgery rotation. She laughed as she thought of how Cass must have reacted to her fax. She wondered how many people had seen it. She knew that she had lost Cass for good, but she wanted to make her sweat a little, and if that meant slandering her name a bit then so be it. Tanya had a hard time accepting rejection being the only child of an affluent family. She did know however, her father would not be so inclined to help her get out of jail if she broke her probation. She had a restraining order placed by her previous girlfriend who had broken up with her because of her controlling, possessive nature and her lack of commitment. Tanya laughed while thinking about it. Her girlfriend caught her screwing around at their apartment and decided she was not accepting anymore of her promises, gifts, or apologies. Tanya had grown up doing whatever she wanted, and was accustomed to fixing her frequent mishaps with gifts, and various things that money could buy. Most of her women got caught up in the materialism and allowed Tanya to screw over them, but not her last woman, Paula. So when Paula tried to break up with Tanya, she wasn't having it and basically began stalking her and begging her for another chance. Eventually, her girlfriend took legal actions and Tanya was subsequently arrested for not adhering to her restraining order. Tanya had stayed in jail for a week, simply because her father was appalled by her behavior and on top of that he was in total denial about her lifestyle. He thought by making her see the consequences of living such a shameful lifestyle, she would turn straight. Once released, he told her if she was ever caught in something like that again he would bar her from her inheritance. So Tanya had tamed herself a little but still maintained her player status. She couldn't help that she enjoyed the challenge of the chase, but once she got them, it was inevitable that she would seek fresher pussy, while trying to keep the home pussy relatively happy too. She was known in all the gay clubs as a major player and she wore the title proudly. Tanya then abruptly scratched Cassandra's name off of her pad and said to herself, "Who's next?"

The next few days at the office were quiet for Cass. She had become an emotional wreck since the initial fax incident and was always on edge about people looking at her differently or making the least suspicious comment. She was pleasantly surprised that there were no continued signs of harassment from Tanya. Cass had to call all her family to give them her new private number, describing that it was changed secondary to some area code zoning changes. She knew the story might sound far fetched, but most everyone in her family tended to be quite gullible and no one questioned it. The only person who had some hint as to what was going on was Keisha, and she hardly had the full story, and Cass intended it to stay that way. Cass did realize that at least one positive thing had come from all of this. Linda was being much more open and friendly, thereby alleviating the cut throat mentality that they both had previously shared. Cass did not substantiate the story one way or another to Linda, but was enjoying their newfound camaraderie, which could work to both of their advantage. As Cass left the office that day, she felt like maybe Tanya had realized that her actions were bordering on stalking and that behavior on her record could potentially end her aspirations of being a doctor. Cass went home that day feeling a lot better and feeling as though things had normalized to some extent. Therefore, on her arrival home, she drank a wine cooler relaxed and decided it was time to give Mr. Chauncey a call.

The phone rang several times, and Cass had resolved that he must still be at his convention, but decided she would leave a message nevertheless.

"Harrison. Hi this is Cassandra. Remember me?" she laughed. "I don't know if you have tried to call me, but…" Before she could complete the statement she heard his sexy voice on the other end, "Cassandra, Hi. I just got in and yes I did try to call you and figured that I should reevaluate my dating tactics if I made a woman run from me like that," he laughed. "I have never had a woman just change her number on me."

"It was hardly on account of you. In fact I really enjoyed seeing you and look forward to seeing you again sometime," Cass flirted.

"Well, now that my ego is still intact, I think I could manage that. In fact, in exchange for your new phone number, I will take you to the opera this Saturday if you're free."

"That sounds great."

"I tell you what. We will talk later this week to confirm things, but I am bushed and jetlagged from that flight so while I would love to talk further, I need to get going. So, your new number please?"

Cass smiled and obliged him then stated unabashedly, "Can't wait to see you."

"You too," he flirted back.

"Bye." Cass hung up the phone smiling and then grimaced thinking, "What kind of black man goes to the opera?" She laughed realizing she had to call Keisha and share this with her. The phone rang and Keisha answered.

"Hey girl, wassup?"

"Hey. You remember that guy I told you about?"

"Yes."

"Well he just invited me to the opera Saturday."

"The opera? What kind of black man goes to the opera? I'm telling you he has a small dick, child. Mark my words," Keisha laughed.

"Well, I kinda enjoy the concept of a mature and cultivated man. I'm going to go and see how it is."

"You go girl," she laughed and changed the subject, "When are we leaving to go to N'awlins?"

"I figured that since Christmas is on Friday this year, we should just leave next Thursday after work."

"Nope, we can't do that. You need to take a half a day Thursday and we leave by noon. I need to get home by early evening."

"Okay. I'll see what I can do. That sounds feasible though."

"Okay girl," Keisha rushed, "I'm trying to get this quick dinner prepared before Hank gets home."

"Dinner," Cass laughed. "Since when did you become a homemaker?"

"Since I got my man a prescription of Vitamin V," Keisha laughed, "Bye girl."

"Bye," Cassandra laughed as she hung up.

Cass figured she should also call Stephanie and ask about completing their Christmas shopping early Saturday, especially since she had a hot date for the opera that night. She then thought, "What in the hell do you wear to the opera?" She decided that she would have to purchase a new outfit as well, she smiled. As she picked up the phone, she noted there was no dial tone. "Hello?" she questioned.

Surprised that she had a return response, "Cassandra?"

"Oh, mom, I was about to use the phone so it hadn't even rung yet. How are you?"

"I'm fine, dear. I was just calling to find out if there was some little trinket you wanted mama to buy you on my fixed retirement income for Christmas. You know I can't buy any of that fancy stuff you like."

"Ma, I told you that you don't have to worry about getting me anything. On the other hand," she paused, "I could use a nice black and silver belt."

"A belt, Cass" her mom laughed, "I think I should be able to handle that. Hold on." As Cass waited, she heard her father's voice on the line, "Hello," he said. Cass hated when her mom just without notice put him on the line.

"Hi, dad. How are you?"

"Fine. How are things there?"

"Just fine," Cass stated while quickly moving into sports which was about the only thing she and her father could talk about honestly and unrestrained, "How about those Saints?"

"With that black quarterback this year we should get into the playoffs. He's pretty good."

"I hope that they do well."

"Yep. So you gonna be here next week, eh?"

"Yes I will, dad."

"Okay then. Well, here's your mama." She then heard fumbling on the phone and her father's voice yet again, "Love you."

"Love you too dad," Cass responded.

"Cass."

"Yes, mom."

"Have you picked up some of that weight you had lost? Stephanie told me you were looking a bit thin."

"Ma, I'm fine. And I'll save that for when I get to N'awlins. I will be grubbing there."

"Alright, then. When will you be here next week?"

"Probably early Thursday. Who else is coming?"

"I believe Casey and her little boyfriend and your brother said he may fly in, but you know he never knows until the last minute. I wish Stephanie would come, but she said she has to start her own Christmas tradition at home with her kids. They might come for New Year's though."

"Oh, okay. Well I'll see you Thursday. Oh and mom, would you make some bread pudding?"

"I'll see what I can do," her mom replied, "Love you baby. Bye bye."

After hanging up with her mom, Cass still was feeling particularly gregarious. But none of her tried and true crew was available. Both Stephanie and Keisha were out, and she couldn't even reach lil' sis. So, she whipped out her little black book. She laughed at all of the stars beside each of the names denoting whether they were good lovers or not. She came upon Langston with his five plus stars. He was particularly good in bed, she smiled while slamming her leg shut, but he had an even better sense of humor. So she decided to give him a call.

"Hello," she heard a woman's voice on the line. Caught off guard instead of hanging up, her first inclination, she asked, "Is Langston available?" The woman simply hung up on her with no response. Cass was tempted to call back, but figured her attempt would be futile. Defeatedly, she put her black book away and instead decided to do something she hadn't done in a long while. She would get on the computer and check out one of her used to be favorite chat rooms; Black voices over thirty. She decided to shower first and get her clothes ready for work and then she would sit down to the computer before she went to bed. Besides which, she remembered that usually the fun crowd didn't usually show up until the later hours anyway. As Cass was getting things in order, she looked through her closet and fell upon Zac's sweater. She wondered how he was doing. She remembered that their last encounter was very painful. She did miss him though, she thought as she snuggled his sweater, trying to catch a whiff of his scent. But to no avail, it smelled like her with not even sour remnants of the Safari cologne he always wore. She picked up the phone and quickly hung it up stating, "I have come too far to go back there." She laughed stating, "I am at least on the first floor, and don't need to go back into the basement. Been there. Done that." With that said, she hopped up to take her shower and found herself getting excited about checking out her old hang out buddies from online.

After Cass showered and put on her flannel pajamas, she sat down with a glass of milk and cookies at her computer. She figured she could cheat a little on her diet tonight, considering her recent weight loss. When her modem finally connected she went straight to her Favorites and clicked on BV 30. The room was full and therefore she was unable to get in. She tried several times but without success. She then decided to check her mail instead. Most of it was stupid little sex sites which she readily deleted. She did however have mail from a friend or rather an acquaintance, she corrected, that she had gotten to know while she was in business school. His name was Brian. Brian was a good looking guy who tried to get with Cass on several occasions, but Cass just was not attracted to his personality. He was ridiculously arrogant and pompous and thought his shit didn't stink, and Cass shared too many of those characteristics at the time to give him joint control. By the looks of his letter, he seemed to have come down to earth a bit. He was living in Seattle and was planning on marrying his high school sweetheart who supported him through business school. "Poor girl," Cass laughed, "unless friendboy has undergone a major metamorphosis." She tried the room again only to read the same redundant message, so she decided she was going to do some surfing.

Cass looked down the list of chat rooms and first surfed into a room called, "Black Power". This was a room full of militants who believed that blacks in America should go back to the Motherland and build a new and vibrant economy. Cass thought some reasonable points were being made and that African Americans should do all they could to help advance the conditions of many countries in Africa, but the entire African American population moving there was hardly the most viable solution. Since the room was getting a little too deep for her thoughts tonight, she continued looking down the list and came across a black lesbian room. She double clicked her mouse there and decided out of curiosity she would check it out. She was surprised at the number of women there. She just sat there momentarily reading the dialogue. They were talking about how relationships with women started fast and ended slow because of all of the emotion involved. Cass found that rather interesting. Someone then IMed her. "Hi," was typed on the screen. Cass figured it might be best that she not respond. Then typed across the screen was, "Why so quiet?" Cass inquisitively pulled up the person's profile.

"Interesting," she thought as she read that this woman lived in North Carolina and was a published poet and aspiring novelist. Cass not being entirely naïve knew that people online could be whatever fictional character they wanted and all that is written could very well be entirely fabricated. She finally typed, "Not quiet, just pensive," she had learned to extend her vocabulary online which tended to quickly uncover the uneducated folks. She laughed. "Oh I see," was the response. Cass mused, "Well that is a vague enough response." Then across the screen was typed, "I find the computer not a particularly appropriate instrument to use when I am being reflective."

Cass smiled, "Okay, so she knew what that meant or she had dictionary nearby." They continued to talk about everyday things not inclusive of sexuality, with her spelling and grammar remaining very correct and appropriate, which made Cass feel comfortable for a little while at least.

But then the question arose, "So are you gay?"

Cass responded, "No," with several o's behind it.

"So why are you here?"

Cass thought about that for a second and then questioned herself, "Why am I here?" She simply responded, "I don't know. I guess I just happened to surf in."

"LOL. OK"

Cass then realized how ridiculous that response was and typed back, "I guess I was just curious to see what you ladies talk about, assuming you are gay."

"Yes, I am a lesbian, and that statement implies that as lesbians we talk about things other than what you straight ladies talk about, that is, assuming you are straight."

"Yes I am straight and of course the context of your discussions is different."

"Not necessarily. The only thing different about us is who we sleep with. So are you suggesting that all we talk about is sex and sleeping with women?"

Cass then tried to mentally reason her argument and realized to take this any further would ultimately put her foot more down her throat. "I guess you are right," she typed back. "My assumptions are off base."

"Thank you," she typed back. "And next time you just happen to surf in, try to bring your brain with you."

Cass stunned by her response replied, "I'm sorry, you're right," as she did feel somewhat embarrassed by her ignorance. At that moment another IM popped onto the screen. It was Brian. Cass signed off abruptly thinking, "Oh shit, did he see what room I was in. Damn." Cass decided that she was through with the computer for the night and found she was acting like her friend Keisha, creating drama all by the work of her own hands. She quickly jumped into her bed and found herself thinking about and eagerly awaiting her Saturday evening with Harrison. She fell asleep with thoughts of Leontyne Price, the only authentic opera singer she could think of. As she drifted off to sleep, Cass figured since Leontyne Price had been out of the scene for a while she might want to surf into an opera room next time and get a little educated before Saturday.

Twenty-Eight

*C*ass was so glad that it was already Friday. She was concerned since she hadn't spoken with Harrison to confirm their outing on Saturday. "Did he misplace my number?" she wondered. She decided then and there that she would call him as soon as she got home that afternoon, because she was fervently anticipating their evening together. That day Cass was distracted by all the buzz around the office. Apparently, Blake, the only upper level black guy at their firm, was going through a very messy divorce. His lilly white wife had supposedly had an affair and was leaving him for another affluent black guy in the city. She wondered why his sorry ass had been staying late so often and had been uncharacteristically silent. She was starting to feel halfway sorry for him, then she silently chuckled, "That's why he should have married a sister in the first place." Linda apparently knew all the gossip around the office and was now willing to share it with her since they had become office buddies under somewhat false pretenses. Cass's day finally ended after what felt like an eternity. She picked up her things quickly and on her way out saw that Blake was still sitting in his office. Cass subtly knocked and opened his door, "Blake, if what I hear around the office is true, I'm sorry."

Blake gently smiled and said, "Thanks Cassandra. I appreciate that." Cassandra shut his door feeling like maybe she would somehow be able to close the gap that lingered between them. Feeling proud of herself, she decided that she should take advantage of her positive vibes and call Harrison from her cell. She heard his deep and vibrant voice on the line. "Hello."

"Harrison?"

"Yes, Cassandra, Hi. How are you? I was planning on calling you this evening to confirm our plans for tomorrow, that is if you haven't changed your mind."

"No, Harrison, not at all. I told you that I was looking forward to seeing you."

"Well how about we do an early dinner tomorrow at about five and then head to the opera which begins at seven."

"Okay. I guess I need to give you my address."

"I believe that would be a good start, Cassandra." She proceeded to give him her address and he confirmed and stated, "I am truly looking forward to seeing you. On time," he politely added.

"Me too, Harrison. I'll be down in the lobby at four thirty, is that sufficient time?" she sarcastically retorted.

"I believe that would be perfect. Do you prefer any particular cuisine?"

"I am a N'awlins gal, so I eat most anything. I do have a predilection for spicy foods."

"Oh do you? Well, I think I have the perfect place in mind. Bring your appetite because their servings are substantial."

"There is no problem there," she laughed, "I have plenty of that. I have never been to the opera before so bear with me if I seem somewhat slow."

"You should definitely be in for a treat, young lady, and I'll guide you through it all. I will see you tomorrow then." He then emphasized, "Promptly at four thirty."

"Yes, sir," Cassandra teased. He stoically laughed, "Okay then. Good-bye."

Cassandra was taken aback by his blunt manner and his directness. She figured maybe he had a tough day and would lighten up by Saturday, she hoped. "I guess he is a man of few words," she thought as she too hung up the phone curious about what their date would reveal.

Cassandra then called Keisha to possibly meet for an happy hour. Something that used to be their weekly ritual until they both recognized that they were seeing the same ole' tired faces week after week.

Keisha answered, "Hello," curtly.

Cass was not in the mood to deal with someone else with an attitude so she inquired, "What's wrong with you?"

"This man is just getting on my ever lasting nerves. Nothing new, chile."

"How 'bout getting a drink for happy hour?" Cass recommended now establishing that she had a new motive— to get her friend in better spirits.

"Sure. I need to get my ass up outta here for a minute. Swing by and pick me up."

"I'll be there in a few." As Cass approached Keisha's house, she did not have to get out, as Keisha was on the front porch smoking. She hopped up and put out her cigarette as Cass pulled up.

"I thought you had stopped smoking," Cass chastised.

"I did, but every now and then, I need one, and trust me this was one of those days."

"What happened?"

"First, I get off from work and I am wondering why my garage is not going up when I press the button. I say to myself, these damn batteries. I hop out of the car in the damn cold with the opener and go in through the front door. I notice that the house is fucking freezing, is unusually quiet, and Hank is sitting on the sofa with a damn wool coat on. I then ask, 'What's going on?' He says, 'Oh, the electricity was turned off about four hours ago.' I then say, 'What the hell you mean the electricity was cut off. You did pay the bill last month didn't you?' He then tells me 'Of course I did. But last month I told you that funds were short since I had to give Taylor some spending money for Christmas. You disregarded me and apparently the account was overdrafted. Now you are feeling the end results. The check bounced.' Girl, something had to stop me from hurting him. That little spoiled brat of his is going to be the death of us. What eight year old do you know that needs two hundred dollars for a fucking shopping spree? You know I could have killed him."

Cass tried to be sensitive to her friend, but couldn't help but laugh. "Girl, you know you can sleep by me if you need to. Hank is a good guy though woman. Don't you lose sight of that. They have plenty of deadbeat dads who hardly accept responsibility for their kids."

"Whatever. All I know right now is that I want a nice stiff drink," while briskly rubbing her hands together to generate some heat.

Cass quickly found a space and touched up her make up before they entered the club. They both ordered Long Island iced teas and had a seat at the bar. It had been so long since either of them had been to an happy hour they were surprised to see the abundance of people there. Of course, again the women far outnumbered the men.

Keisha then commented, "You know it is hard to find a man these days. Do you see these women? They don't leave anything to the imagination any more. A man doesn't have to do a damn thing."

Cass looked at her friend dressed in her very low cut blouse, with her tight capri pants on and responded, "And where do you fit in?"

"Chile, if you can't beat em, you join em," she laughed as she started to light another cigarette. Cass just shook her head as a gentleman approached her with business card in hand, "Hi, my name is Tony Bridges, Esquire or Attorney at Law," while handing over his card. Cass could not believe that this was common etiquette these days to exchange job descriptions in your initial introduction. Cass blandly responded, "Hi."

"So you're not going to share your name and business affiliation?" he panted.

"Oh I'm sorry," she said as she looked the ugly brother up and down. He must have been five foot two and two hundred fifty pounds she guessed. "My name is Michele."

"How you doing, Michele?" he smiled revealing his underbite which made his bottom lip look as though it protruded out more than his already thick lips could handle. She politely smiled back, as he sat down next to her, breathing heavily. His shirt clung to his perspiring body and moved in and out with each breath.

"You go girl," Keisha whispered, blowing her smoke directly into her face. Cass then turned to Tony and said, "This is my friend, Keisha." Keisha gave her a grimace and smiled without extending her hand, "Hey." Cass tried to keep the conversation light. She noticed his eyes continually focusing on her breasts as he spoke to her. She thought his ass must be desperate, as she knew that her miniscule breasts were some of her less than ample assets. She then felt his sweaty palm touch hers as he asked, "Can I buy you a drink?"

"No thank you." She had no interest in prolonging the conversation and she turned back to face Keisha, figuring he would certainly get the message. Eventually, he left the seat and headed to focus his attentions on someone else.

Keisha laughed, "I was wondering when you were going to get rid of him."

"Girl and he had that smell of a brother who puts cologne on top of a funky body. Girl, look at that fine man over there. I think I might try and talk to him." Cass looked and as usual their taste in men was vastly different because Cass would not have looked at him if she did not point him out. He was a yellow guy, thick but not fat with an afro and long sideburns which seemed to meet his chin.

"I'll be right back." Keisha sashayed over to him and eventually got his number on the match book she was carrying. On her return, she said, "Girl he wears a size twelve shoe."

Cass laughed while gathering her things and said, "Now how in the world did you find out his shoe size in that brief talk?"

Keisha winked and suggested, "You have to find out the pertinent information early."

Cass stopped immediately in her tracks as they were leaving stating aloud, "I know that isn't who I think it is."

"Who are you looking at?"

"Ain't this some shit," as she stared at a handsome man sliding in a booth next to a woman where the relationship appeared to be far more than just casual, as she saw him slide his hand up her bare leg.

"You see that guy in that booth over there?"

"The one kissing that red bone?"

"Yes. His ass! That is Richard, my brother in law."

"Oh, Lawd," Keisha bellowed, "what are you going to do?"

"I don't know what I should do," Cass responded still staring at the couple.

"Well, if it were my brother in law with some other woman I would go over there and kick his ass."

"No. I'm not going to make a scene, but friend boy is going to know I am here." Cass went over to the bar and purchased a Bloody Mary, Stephanie's favorite drink, and asked the waiter to take it to Richard and point her out as the buyer. Cass stared at him the entire time while he was all over this woman. He then received the drink and looked up in a panic towards Cassandra. He promptly hopped out of the seat and ran over to Cassandra who was leaving out of the door, having made her point.

He caught her and grabbed her arm. "Cassandra please. It's not what you think. Please don't tell your sister that you saw me here. This is just a standard business meeting."

"So do you put your tongue down all your client's mouths Richard?"

"No, No. It's not like that at all. I promise this will never happen again. Just don't tell Stephanie," he begged.

"Let me go Richard. And I thought that you were different from the rest."

"I am Cassandra. I am. That's why you have to give me another chance."

"Save your groveling and begging for Stephanie. That's when you're going to need it, Richard. Spare me all the fuckin' bullshit." And with that she met Keisha at her car and in silence they headed home.

Cass dropped Keisha off at her house after again offering her the invitation to stay at her home, but she declined. Cass eventually arrived home to her condo and called her mom.

"Mom. You are not going to believe this. I am so upset?"

"What's wrong, baby?"

"I just saw Richard with another woman."

Her mom hesitantly responded, "Maybe it was a business meeting. You know Richard being a divorce lawyer and all. You're likely to see him with lots of women. That doesn't mean a thing, Cass."

"Mom. I'm not stupid. But you do not grope and kiss all of your clients."

"Did you see it with your own eyes?"

"Of course I did," Cass exasperatedly replied.

"Cass, I think you need to stay out of this. There's no need to get Stephanie all wound up."

"Wound up! We are talking about adultery here. Not a damn missed bill."

"You watch your language young lady."

"I'm sorry mom. I'm just tired of women letting men get away with this sh… I mean this type of behavior."

"Men will be men Cass, and that is something you need to understand."

"I refuse to accept that and I will tell Stephanie. She deserves to know."

"I think you're wrong Cass. Let it go."

"Bye mom. I need to go."

"I'm serious, Cassandra."

"Good-bye," Cass persisted.

"Bye," her mom finally stated after a long pause, recognizing that her daughter was not going to give in."

She did not know how to tell Stephanie, but she knew she had to. She also knew that her sister's pride would not let her stay with Richard. Divorce is imminent, she thought. Shaking her head she tried to dismiss the entire incident thinking about it's affect on the kids, but she could not stand by and watch some man getting over on her sister. She also figured it was almost Christmas and that as a family she should at least let them get through the holiday without having it be ruined annually for years to come by the reality of their father's indiscretions. That was it. She would tell Stephanie but after the New Year, when things would be back to normal and less hectic. She just had to make sure she held her tongue the next day when she was shopping with her. She was convinced that her plan would be the next best route and she would leave that issue alone until the New Year. She then decided that before she got into bed that she would go online to find out some information about the current opera queens so as not to appear entirely ignorant to Harrison. She took a nice warm shower and put on her terry cloth robe to help supplement the heat in her cold home. She plopped in front of the computer and signed on. She looked up opera and found a list of multiple sights. She eventually found the sight which discussed the production which they were to attend and Cass, as if studying for an exam, read the names and rehearsed them in her head with her eyes closed. Shortly thereafter she heard the ringing of an IM. It was Brian who typed in, "Hello Cass."

"Hi Brian. How are you?" as she quickly tried to concoct some excuse to account for the lesbian room which she was sure he had seen her in on the previous night.

"I always knew you were a little freak, that's why you were always able to reject my advances."

"First of all, my cousin who happens to be gay was online yesterday using my name," Cass lied, "and did it ever occur to you that I rejected your advances because I simply was not interested in you?"

"I would love to have you in a threesome. Why don't you hook me up with one of my fantasies?"

"I have no interest in a threesome, Brian."

"Okay, well why don't you let me see you make love to a woman?"

"I told you I am not gay."

"Yeah, okay. Whatever. You probably couldn't handle this dick anyway."

"Brian please. And the word out is that you have nothing to

handle."

"Yeah right, who told you that?"

"Don't worry about it, I am not going to get into a trivial conversation with you."

"Okay cool. Well, I just wanted to tell you hello. Seriously, who told you that?" he repeatedly questioned.

"You are so insecure," Cass typed back. "Good-bye." She guessed the fact that he was going to be marrying soon did not change his conniving ways at all. He was a dog and destined to always be one. Just as Cass had figured she had learned all there was to know about octaves and opera, she received an instant message from *Redvelvet*, the woman she had spoken to the previous night.

"I didn't mean to scare you off. I just get pissed when people expect that lesbians are so damn different," she typed.

"You did not scare me off. My computer just happened to log me off at that moment when my phone rang," she lied.

"Well, I just wanted to say if you ever want to chat or something just email me."

"Okay thanks. Will do. Good night."

"Good night to you too, and pleasant dreams." Cass smiled at the nice gesture, signed off and went to bed.

Twenty-Nine

Saturday morning needed to start early because Cass needed to finish her Christmas shopping with Stephanie, buy a formal dress for the opera, and get her hair done. She knew she had to be ready by four-thirty promptly or Harrison might leave her tardy ass. She quickly hopped up and showered before throwing on a pair of jeans, boots and sweater. She called Stephanie who stated she would be ready when Cass arrived. Cass hastily went to Stephanie's' house and hopped out to greet her niece and nephew. She was disappointed because they had apparently spent the night at their grandparent's house and were not there. Instead, she was greeted by Richard who hugged her as if he were so grateful that she hadn't spoken a word.

"Hi, Cassandra. Great seeing you. Can I get you something to drink?" Trying not to appear too obviously hostile she stated, "No, but thank you for offering."

Stephanie then came out fully dressed with a glow stating, "I'm ready," while leaning to kiss Richard and saying, "See you later, baby. Don't forget that your plate of food is all ready for you in the oven."

Cass couldn't help but notice Richard lightly tap her on the ass as Stephanie laughed and escaped out of the door. Cass quickly left out of the house annoyed as they both hopped into the car. Cass was scared to ask why her sister appeared to be glowing, but since Stephanie was volunteering she didn't have to. Stephanie smiled and exclaimed, "Richard arranged for the kids to go to his parent's house last night and he planned the most romantic evening." As she continued, Cassandra tried to refrain from sharing the real reason for his transition into "Prince charming."

"He had dozens of roses scattered about and candles set up throughout the house. Girl," she excitedly shared, "he even had rose petals leading into the tub. After the candlelit catered dinner, he massaged me and we made the most passionate love that we have ever made in years," she blushed. "I don't know what got into him, but whatever it was needs to continue."

Cass then counter thought, "Yeah, I know what got into his ass." Stephanie then blushed and said, "Don't tell anyone this, but we even made love in the kitchen, we hadn't behaved like that since our college years. It was great," she motioned with her hands and squirmed with her body expressing her sheer enthusiasm. Cass faked happiness for her sister, but couldn't help but feel sad for what she ultimately would have to share with her. She then tried changing the subject, "You know I have a big date tonight?"

"Did you hear anything I just said?"

"Yes, and that's all great," she feigned excitement.

"I thought you would have a little more to say since you always comment about marriage losing it's flair after so long. We are proof that is indeed a fallacy. Not bad after twelve years of marriage, huh?"

"Yes, wonderful," Cassandra moved on into her story. "It's with that professor that I met at the bookstore. We're going to the opera."

"The opera? So, now you have moved from married men to jumping over the color barriers," she scorned, "but that is better than a married man, I guess."

"For your information. He is black."

"Oh really, well we will have to get you looking good, so you can maybe join us in the circle of old married folks," she stated while playing with her wedding band on her finger.

Eddra Marchand

"Whatever," Cass rudely asserted as they approached the mall. They shopped throughout the mall. Cass focused on things she liked while her frugal sister Stephanie searched strictly for bargains for herself and the kids but not for her devoted husband who only wore the best designer clothes. Cass looked in disgust at the sacrifices which her sister made to accommodate his expensive tastes. Cass had to ignore her sister's purchases for her own sanity and instead began looking for her dress for the opera. She eventually found a beautiful black velvet dress that appeared to be most appropriate for the formal engagement, because it was elegant and sexy. She knew it's deep plunge down the back would be particularly intriguing, and Stephanie agreed. As Stephanie was pointing out a beautiful cashmere sweater that she wanted to purchase for Richard, Cass quickly interrupted, "Listen, we need to go, because I have a hair appointment." She did not want her sister spending excessive amounts of money on him for him to look good for his mistress. She ended up purchasing the almost two hundred dollar sweater any way to Cass's dismay. At least, Cass was glad, she had succeeded in stopping her from buying those gorgeous two hundred-fifty dollar brown shoes for him. They finally left the mall and Cass dropped Stephanie off at home en route to the hair dresser.

Stephanie looked surprised when she did not see Richard's car in the driveway. "I wonder where he is?" she questioned while getting out of the car. "Probably buying me another little trinket for Christmas," she smiled. Cass alternately thought, "probably out trying to buy his mistress a nice little trinket," as she forced a smile while waving good-bye to her sister.

Cass rushed over to Leo's place. She always went to Leo when she wanted her hair done for special occasions. Leo was flaming and kept her laughing every time she went to have her hair done, despite his slow pace. He knew that she had a strict deadline to adhere to and promised that he would get her out on time. He hugged her as soon as she entered screaming in his effeminate voice, "Cassandra, girl. It has been so long. You should at least come by and visit sometimes, even if you are not going to have your hair done. Now sit

253

down and tell me about this hot new hunk you're seeing," he smiled as he slapped the chair for her to take a seat.

"Leo. This is only our second date and he is a mature fellow."

"Mature," he laughed, "you are going out with an older man? Well, just make sure he has money, chile. Usually that's the best thing they have to offer." Cass just shook her head at Leo who never openly admitted to being gay, but who would comment on men in such a way that you knew he'd been there and done that. Leo stuck to his promise and had Cass out of there by three forty-five giving Cass only enough time to shower and dress. Her hair was of course flawless as it encircled her face in layers with a hint of light brown streaks which Leo convinced Cass to put in to give her hair a little more lift and life. She had to admit it looked good as she hopped in her car holding her head at a slightly different tilt, which she tended to do when she knew she was looking good. She sped off quickly to head home and do the finishing touches on her make up and get dressed for her early evening with Harrison.

Harrison was promptly there at four-thirty Cass noticed as the concierge desk called up. Cass quickly hobbled out of the door trying to place her shoe on as she did. She was feeling nervous, which she rarely experienced on any normal date. She was curious as to why Harrison had this effect on her. She felt like she needed to be perfect for him, and with everything in its place, she figured she was as close to perfect that evening as she could get. As she exited the elevator there was Harrison looking extremely debonair in his black tuxedo. He smiled at her and hugged her as she reached him, "You smell great."

"Thanks," she smiled as he escorted her out the door arm in arm to the waiting cadillac. He opened her door and shut it once she was settled. Cass sat there feeling very good about the way this night was beginning until Harrison entered the car stating, "You know I think a woman is most beautiful in her natural state. Do you always wear so much make-up or is it just on special occasions?"

"It depends on the event and setting. Usually at formal events, I do wear some," Cass responded feeling belittled.

254

"Oh, I see. You look beautiful nevertheless," he quickly added to hopefully minimize the insult's effects.

"Thanks" she said snidely.

"That is a beautiful gown."

"Thank you, Harrison," she still inexpressively responded.

"Is there something wrong?"

"Not at all," she chided.

He then gently squeezed her hand and continued, "I'm sorry if I offended you, but I will not hesitate to tell you what I am feeling, and I expect you to do the same. That's the way you keep good, honest communication. Isn't that what all the experts say is the key to a successful relationship? To be honest, I know this is only officially our first date but I feel good about you and I want to really start things out on the right foot."

She looked at him feeling that he had slightly vindicated himself but still spitefully responded, "Well, communication is important, but there is such a word as tact. Being tactful is what help's relationships to be healthy as opposed to degrading, Mr. Chauncey. So you might want to work on your tact," she sarcastically added.

"Oh, so now we are getting formal, are we?" he smiled and squeezed her hand. Cass was still irritated but was not going to let his comment ruin her evening, afterall she paid too much for the dress. She was going to enjoy dinner and the opera she told herself, even if this would be the last time she saw him as they pulled into the valet parking of the restaurant. He again opened her door and took her hand as they walked into the restaurant. "Wow! It is a bit nippy out here," as he snuggled her closer to his body. She could feel his firm grasp and his strong hands taking charge. As they entered he gave them his name and they were immediately escorted to a seat in a nice secluded area. He slid off her coat and placed it on the back of her chair revealing her plunging back line which Cass thought made the dress. He quickly looked and frowned in dismay at her choice of dresses as he sat down into his seat. Cassandra didn't notice and figured he must be admiring her sexy elegance. He chose not to mention at that point the fact that her dress was lacking in the area of the type of simple elegance which he favored. He just smiled and said, "I figured you might like this restaurant. Have you been here before?"

"No, never," as Cass began to loosen up.

He then glanced up at her hair and noticed the highlights there and questioned, "Is your hair different?"

"Yes, I recently had it done," she boasted.

"Looks great," he lied and forced a smile as again he rather preferred her more conservative look that she exhibited when they first met at the book store. Cassandra felt his response was contrived and blatantly ignored his smile and slid her hand away from his lightly resting on hers. Just as rapidly as the tension that appeared to at once be dissipating, it returned instantaneously. The dinner turned out to be delicious while the conversation remained light as they both were trying to avoid any further conflicts because they had an entire evening before them. She actually daydreamed a few times wondering what exactly it was that initially attracted her to him as none of those characteristics had apparently shown up that evening. He attempted some playful banter to help try to ease the mounting tensions but at that point Cassandra was hardly moved or motivated. She would have been fine with calling it a night at that juncture. As the waiter returned with his card he stood and sweetly took her hand in his and kissed it, then smoothly transitioned it into his own as they silently walked to the car. Cassandra miffed, still thought he was pretty smooth, sexy and classy which might possibly be his only redeeming qualities; The only thing keeping her from asking him to bring her home.

They arrived at the opera presentation with a significant amount of time to spare. They were escorted to their balcony seats and sat there quietly awaiting the start. Cass could not help but notice the bougie people entering the place. Few were black and the blacks who were in attendance were the ones who tended to forget where they had come from. Cass could see it fully in their mannerisms and in their diction. She turned to look at Harrison and she saw the same attributes in him. She wondered how she overlooked them before. Her thoughts were quickly shifted from him as the curtain rose. Cass was initially intrigued by the story being told in such a unique fashion but soon its novelty began to wear thin as she found herself checking her watch, eager for intermission. At intermission they bought drinks and were being sociable again to one another. Harrison even bought her a rose and apologized again for any insults he had made earlier in the evening. Cass found herself dreading going back in after intermission as she had a profound headache compounded by the fact that Harrison had pissed her off. As they entered into the last act she found herself dozing off, and was terribly embarrassed, but no matter how hard she tried, her eyelids continued to find themselves closed. Cass was relieved when she awakened to thunderous applauding and the sound of Harrison's voice exclaiming, "Bravo. Bravo." He leaned over to Cass and said, "Wasn't that great?" Cass smiled broadly and began clapping without responding to his question, and rather chose to chime in with him, "Bravo. Bravo." However, her Bravo was more in acclaim of the show being over. She laughed at herself for lacking culture.

The ride home was pleasant and fortunately nonconfrontational, as Cass had determined that if he dared to say anything else demeaning to her she would let him have it. Harrison spoke about his summation of the love story sung so eloquently to them. Cass had hardly discerned the same but could care less.

As he pulled up to her place he stated, "Well, Cassandra I did enjoy being with you tonight, despite the fact that you appeared annoyed the entire evening. Maybe we can do something again, on your terms."

"That would be fine Harrison," Cass lied doubting that she would ever see him again. With that he leaned over and kissed her softly on the lips which was nice until he made the mistake of sliding his tongue into her mouth and continued to kiss her with an over abundance of saliva. At that moment, she observed that he continued to single-handedly erase any progress which possibly could coerce her into giving him another chance. He couldn't even kiss and therefore, it was truly time to end the kiss as she closed her mouth and the door to what she at one time believed was going to be a budding romance. "Thank you Harrison for the evening. We'll talk again soon I'm sure."

He hopped out of the car opened her door and escorted her into the lobby. "I hope so Cassandra. You take care. Goodnight," as he leaned again to kiss her on her cheek. Cassandra rode up the elevator to her floor pondering whether she would be able to take the dress back and how Harrison could have turned from such a sweet man to the toad who took her out that evening. She just shook her head as she opened the door to her condo. She was glad to be home and alone.

She was disappointed that the evening was such a disaster. She had cleaned her house specifically believing that Harrison might have charmed his way up, but by the looks of it he would likely not ever get to see the inside of her home and she wasn't in the least bit fazed by it.

Harrison drove in silence and could not believe the awful transition which Cassandra had made. He thought she looked like a high priced whore with all the make-up and that hideous dress as opposed to an elegant woman. He liked his women to be beautiful and subdued. He thought she encompassed those characteristics when he first met her but was totally turned off by her that evening. He thought that he would have slept there tonight and made love to her, but not the way she was looking. He figured if he wanted a whore he could buy one as he pulled up to the curve.

"How much?"

"What do you want daddy?" the woman dressed in tight and revealing shorts and high heeled boots with a fur coat over her outfit.

"I just want a blow job."

"That will be fifty dollars." Harrison leaned over and opened the door letting the woman into the car. He drove down the secluded street which she suggested. She then pulled down his zipper and began sucking him until he exploded into her mouth. She moaned and called him daddy like he always requested and then hopped out of the car. He then drove home saying to himself, "I can buy me a whore, but I want a lady at home," as he shook his head wondering if he would ever speak to Cassandra again.

Thirty

The next morning, Cassandra could hardly wait to call Keisha and share the opera saga. "Hello," Keisha jovially answered the phone.

"Hey girl, wassup?"

"Chile, I'm just sitting here glad to feel the warmth up in this mother for a change," she laughed. "How was your date last night?"

"Don't even ask. I was ready to come home before the night officially began. You know he had the nerve to tell me basically that I wore too much make-up. He indirectly insulted my hair and his ass can't even kiss. He's a slobber," she laughed.

"Girl, usually them guys with juicy mouths like that are good at eating, if you know what I mean."

"Well, Harrison surely will not be having the opportunity to eat anything of mine," she giggled.

"Well then chile," Keisha bragged, "you don't want to know about my evening. Basically I got my brains fucked out and it was all good."

"So you and Hank are still hanging in there with that vitamin V eh."

"Hank. Chile please. I spent the night with Curtis and he rocked my world."

"Who in the hell is Curtis?"

"You remember the guy I told you about who wore a size twelve shoe at that bar the other night. That is Curtis LeJon Jackson who knows how to give mama some good action." Cass was not surprised that her friend had already slept with someone else, and thus the vicious cycle was beginning again.

"He must be good if you know his full name."

"I told you those young boys is where the getting is good. He is twenty-six. Truth be told he is hardly accounting for that size twelve shoe. His ass must be a mutant, but where he's lacking he makes up for it by his vigorous movements and shear force of it all. He gets you where you want to go. Do you hear me chile," she screamed as if she were preaching.

"Enough already," Cass found herself becoming a tad envious.

"Well, he has a friend his age you know. I could hook you up."

"No thanks. I've had my share of your fixing up. I'd rather stick with my old pal, buster."

"You can go on playing with those artificial devices if you want, I just don't want to come and find your ass electrocuted from using that shit."

"Honey, buster and I are beyond that, he is battery operated and is there whenever I want him. Thank you very much."

"So, have you told your sister yet?"

"No," Cass frowned, "I was going to wait until after the holidays, but you know he has become the perfect husband now. So it will make it so much harder for me to tell her about his affair."

"Well, all I know is if you catch Hank, you better tell me as soon as, do not spare me for the holidays. I wants to know."

"How can you be so judgemental with all of the screwing around that you do?"

"Mama bear has to be satisfied to give him what he needs at home. My screwing around is basically helping him out."

"Girl go somewhere with that. I will talk with you later."

"Okay. Bye," she chuckled as she hung up the phone.

Cass felt like she needed to get to church that day. A habit which she had gotten used to and enjoyed when Robert was alive. She sat down in her papasan chair and began hugging herself and out of nowhere began to cry uncontrollably. She began whispering repetitiously, "Robert, why did you leave me?" Cass was feeling like she was truly fooling everyone around her into thinking that she was okay. In reality she was a basket case. Her life had taken a downward spiral since Robert died and she didn't know how to pull her true self back. She was so lonely and desperate for the touch of a man. Right now Harrison was the only dismal prospect and for some reason she was drawn to his fatherly take charge attitude. For a change she felt like she needed someone to take charge of her life until she could get her head on straight. She then considered that maybe that was why God had put Harrison into her life, so someone else could take the lead while she struggled to find herself and restructure her life. On the other hand, maybe she should just try the damn prozac, she silently laughed as she regained her composure.

She then laughed out loud and said, "I just need to get my trifling black ass back to church." With that being said, she slowly got up and dressed quite casually and headed off to church, arriving just in time for the homily. She looked around the church as usual and saw one of her old friends from high school. She also was shocked to see Brian, who was supposed to be moving to Seattle and getting married soon. She noticed that his fiance' was big and pregnant. She wondered if that was what was provoking him to tie the knot. As she stared thinking about that, she was sure of it. Brian caught her gazing at him and winked in her direction. Cass smiled slightly and quickly turned her head. He still was looking very handsome. "If I were a hoochie, I would probably sleep with him," Cass thought to herself. She then remembered where she was and silently admonished herself for having such thoughts while in church. She did decide to have communion and headed out to the church foyer directly after. Brian was standing just beyond the doors and slyly grimacing. "Damn, he looks good," Cass thought.

He opened the door for her, "Cassandra, hey how are you?"

"Fine. I thought you were in Seattle."

"I will be moving there within the next couple of weeks. I have to tie up some loose ends here first," he stated with mischief in his eyes.

"So, now I see why you are getting married. Your soon to be wife is big and pregnant."

"No, you got it wrong. That is not Paula, who I will be marrying next month. That is Jennifer, she just gonna be one of my baby's mamas," he laughed as if it were all a joke. She looked at him in disbelief, wondering how an educated man could not recognize the responsibility that went along with having kids.

"How many kids do you have now, Brian?" He began counting on his fingers.

"Only four. This is going to be my second boy with Jennifer, and I have two others," he proudly shared. As Cass was overcome with disgust at his nonchalance, Jennifer came wobbling out with his three year old son in tow. "Jennifer, sweetheart, this is Cassandra, one of my old business school buddies." Jennifer smiled softly and averted her eyes quietly saying ,"Hi."

He handed her the keys and said, "Here are the keys. Why don't you all get situated in the car and I will be right there." She quickly turned to go to the car without saying anything further. Cass thought, poor woman with not an ounce of self esteem. He quickly distracted her saying, "So are you going to satisfy my fantasy?" walking out of the church. "I know a woman who is truly beautiful and sweet and I'm sure would be happy to join us. I could get Jennifer too, if you are one of those who like sleeping with pregnant women," he boldly offered.

Cass looked at Brian in abhorrence, "I wouldn't even consider sleeping with you alone let alone with someone else. I am not gay and have no interest in being with a woman in the least. How could you be so callous?" Ignoring her words, he looked deep into her eyes making Cass uncomfortable. She turned her eyes away and he laughed, "You have been with a woman. I would never have thought," he laughed.

"Believe what you want Brian. Congratulations on your upcoming marriage," she sarcastically stated.

He smiled while waving, "Let me know if you change your mind. The offer is always open." Cass walked to her car wondering if he could really see something in her eyes. She abruptly hopped in her car while peering through her rearview mirror wondering if something was revealed in her eyes. She laughed, started her ignition and headed home as she realized how ludicrous that was. She turned on her gospel music feeling rejuvenated and ready to enjoy some football, as her Saints were playing the Falcons.

Cass arrived home and promptly hopped out of her clothes putting on a warm up suit. She then began popping some popcorn and ordered some hot wings for delivery. She was watching the pregame predictions as the phone rang. Cass knew it was the concierge with her food delivery so she simply answered the phone, "Let em up," and Sam did as she requested. Cass sat there impatiently awaiting the delivery person as she was starving. She went to get her money and an appropriate tip to offer. With the knock on her door, she was distracted as they were scrutinizing the Saints at that moment. She opened the door and blindly handed him the money while watching the television.

He said, "Thanks ma'am." Cass turned in shock as the voice sounded vaguely familiar. It was Harrison carrying grocery bags and her box of chicken wings.

"Harrison," she surprisingly stated, "What are you doing here?" He let himself in and laid the groceries on her kitchen countertop and said, "I thought I would give you a chance to redeem yourself," he laughed. Cass couldn't help but notice how sexy he looked in his close fitting jeans, sweater, and boots. She was still incensed by his behavior the previous night which he noticed by the look on her face.

"Come on. Let me fix this, the only meal that I can make legitimately for you, and if you still find yourself detesting me, then I will leave never to show up again." He extended his hand and questioned, "Deal?" Cass concealed a smile and shook his hand saying, "Deal, only if you don't mind watching the football game with me."

"Not at all," he teased, "the Falcons are going to kick some butt."

"You are already starting off on a bad foot. My Saints are going to win."

"Okay," he agreed and said, "Now just point out a few pots and pans and then you go on and have a seat." She showed him where all of the essential things were, and then curiously asked, "How'd you get a hold of my wings?"

"At the same time I arrived at the concierge desk the delivery guy had informed the desk that he had a delivery for Cassandra Nicholas. I overheard him and basically paid him a hefty tip to allow me to deliver it to you.

"Oh I see," as she went to take a seat in front of the TV for kick off. She had to admit that she liked his tenacity and decided that maybe she could try to be patient and see how things went.

Harrison had thought about Cassandra all night after he arrived home. He believed once she understood the things he appreciated in his women, she would try to conform to most of his ideals. He might have to give in to a few inconsequential things like highlights or the rare inappropriate attire, but for the most part his women enjoyed catering to him and loved to have a man take control. He could tell from his experience that while she was not desperate for a man, that she was fighting a biological clock which sometimes tended to make these women more flexible. He believed with the appropriate training that she could be his perfect prey. She was beautiful, intelligent and had a sense of humor, all characteristics which were a must in his book. He carefully cooked the stir fried vegetables with shrimp he had marinated in a spicy sweet and sour sauce and finished up the rice. It was basically the only meal he ever cooked. Being a traditionalist, he never cooked or cleaned as those were the duties of the woman and other than rare occasions like a birthday or trying to impress did he ever expect less. He brought in the plates and laid them on the table.

He pulled out Cass's chair, "Dinner is served. What would you like to drink? I brought some White Zinfandel which I recall is your favorite," he smiled.

Cass blushed enamored by the royal treatment and said, "That would be great Harrison." He poured them both a glass as they sat down to enjoy the meal. "I will say grace." Cass embarrassed chugged down the few bites that were already in her mouth and said, "Yes, please." After grace they had pleasant conversation over the food amidst yelps and screams by Cassandra regarding the game. Harrison observed her and believed that he had his work cut out for him trying to refine Cassandra. That day, however, he was going to hold his tongue as he did not want to distance her any further than he already had. He felt a good chemistry between them and wanted to at least give them a chance.

"This is truly delicious, Harrison. Do you have any other hidden talents up your sleeve?"

He flirted, "Indeed I do, but not necessarily in the kitchen." She laughed as it was the first time that he had overtly flirted with her implying something sexual. Harrison loved her smile and the way she appeared that day with no makeup and no flashy attire. He waited for her to clear the dishes from the table and he slid onto the sofa to watch the remainder of the game. She then joined him there where he pulled her close to his body and she didn't resist the closeness, as she felt that he had come a long way to redeem himself and it just plain felt good to be held by a man.

Once the game ended Harrison became more comfortable as he asked Cass to help him with removing his boots, and she did. She could tell that he was making himself more at home and she liked that. She pulled out the board game of scrabble and challenged him. He accepted the challenge and he won both games rather convincingly and had no qualms about implying that his wisdom and knowledge exceeded hers both because of age and his educational background. She gave him his props and instinctively laid a soft kiss on his lips. As he began trying to pull her closer into him, the phone intruded. Cass scampered to the phone, "Hello."

"What you doing girl? I was going to call you earlier but I knew your Saints were playing. Did they win?"

"No they didn't," Cass disappointedly responded.

"I was calling to see if you wanted some company, because Hank is working tonight and Curtis is nowhere to be found."

"Oh, so I am your last resort. Well, as it happens, I have company," she smiled, "and I will tell you all about it later. Bye."

"I know you not gonna leave me hanging. Who is it?"

"Bye, I'll talk to you later," and hung up the phone. "Now where were we?" she flirted as she approached Harrison.

"I believe you were sitting right here," he slapped his lap, "and you were begging me to kiss you."

"Is that right?" she played along sitting on his lap and giving him a soft tender kiss saying, "Is it okay if I kiss you, sir?" This turned him on more and he returned her kiss more fervently as Cass prepared herself to deal with the excess saliva, but this time it didn't feel half as bad. They kissed passionately for a while and Cass could sense that they were both getting excited as he leaned over to kiss her on her neck and then to the cleavage of her bosom.

He then stopped abruptly, "I don't think we are ready to take this any further just yet."

"But why? We are both consenting adults last time I checked?" questioned Cassandra who was now aching for the closeness.

"I know," he smiled, "but I just prefer to take things slower just because I expect alot out of relationships and I would want you to have a full understanding of that before we take things any further," he stated while pulling on his boots. She, totally dissatisfied with that response, resigned to the fact that he could be raising a valid point since just the day before she vowed she was never going to see him again. "Okay then. It's your loss," she teased.

"I guess we'll see about that, but I figured you would come around to seeing things my way," he confidently stated as he kissed her softly on her lips. "Goodnight, and next time you have to prepare the meal."

"That is not a problem." Cass felt like she had gotten to know Harrison quite a bit more and understood his controlling nature. She figured this was one of the situations where, as her mom taught her, you have to make them think they've made the final decision when in actuality you have. Cass had mastered a lot of quirks dealing with a variety of men with different personality traits and figured Harrison would definitely be a challenge, but she was going to try to have fun while breaking down his rigid barriers.

Harrison entered his car in the chill of the night thinking that Cassandra still needed a lot of work. The fact that she would have even considered sleeping with him that night disturbed him. He felt a true lady would hardly consent to such without a more solid commitment. Nevertheless, he knew that young ladies these days did not follow the same rules as they did when he was younger, which he felt was morally detestable, but he realized that he had to conform to the idea of getting the milk before buying the cow. He thought, "Young men today have no reason to get married," shaking his head while pulling up to his usual corner rolling his window down. "What do you want me to do for you tonight, Daddy?"

"I want to fuck you tonight," he told the whore gesturing her to open the door. "No the back door," he corrected.

"Okay. Where are we going?"

"Down the street. I want to do it here in the car." He pulled over, slid into the back seat, positioned her on all fours and silently screwed her from behind in her ass, like he usually did. She recited all the lines which he routinely wanted to hear until he came. He then promptly paid her and rushed her out of the car partially clad and headed home. Harrison had begun justifying his rendezvous with whores early on in his marriage. He believed that as a husband and a provider that his role was to treat his wife like a queen and in the process keep her purity intact aside from her occasional mandatory participation in her wifely duties. Therefore, anything that he considered lewd sexual behavior he left to his incorrigible select set of whores and by doing so preserved his wife's honor. Something for which he thought his wife should be grateful. He in turn instilled in his sons this same ideal of respect for the women who would someday be the mother of their children. In fact, on each of his son's sixteenth birthdays, he hired a prostitute to initiate their transition into manhood, so they could become accustomed early on to their role as sexual dominators at home and thereby upholders of strength and respectability in their families, which would ultimately transform them into successful men. As proprietors of strong family values and the protector of the matriarch therein, he reinforced that they would be great assets to an elite society. He quoted his father, "A man who is always prepared to fight for and protect his family is the man who will remain a steadfast force in life while all others fail," and he genuinely believed it. Though, he arrogantly admitted he may have modified its meaning somewhat to suit his needs, everyone seemed happy which made that fact a moot point.

He didn't understand why more people, particularly women, were not in favor of legalized prostitution. He figured the legalization of this type of activity would encourage more men to treat their women like real women, and alternately their whores like whores. Although he had only been arrested by the police once several years ago, he was fortunate because the arresting officer was the son of one of his good friends, therefore the charges were dropped without incident and since that time he had mastered the rules of the game. He knew to stick to the same group of hookers, who learned to know what he desired and respected his manhood. Rarely, he would be attracted to a new girl on the streets and would ingratiate her into his small circle of whores. He was proud of his ability to coordinate these women into his life without being stigmatized as a menace, but rather a respectable member of society doing his part to uphold family mores. To add to that, he mused, he knew that his girls appreciated his services. He did pay them, but in doing so they all shared the primary goal of providing him with sexual satisfaction, which is how he expected things to be prioritized in any setting. With that he smiled and headed home feeling gratified and wondering at the same time if Cassandra would be the right woman for him.

Thirty-One

*C*assandra went to take a shower and felt that Harrison had quite possibly redeemed himself from his ridiculous behavior the previous evening. She also in the little time which they had spent together realized that he was ridiculously conservative and wondered if she would be able to transform him into a slightly more progressive individual. At the moment she relished his company in lieu of being lonely and was willing to try and compromise until he was successfully molded, she laughed. She wasn't going to become plain Jane Susie Homemaker to appease him nor was she going to alter her way of doing things. She then reasoned that if he was half the man he claimed to be he would be willing to compromise. She then while turning off the shower talked to herself out loud, which she had been doing more of since Robert had died, "I am getting way too deep here. Harrison is a nice guy. I know he is probably not the man for me, but for now he is filling my void." She laughed while drying off and surmised that at least seeing him for a while might help cultivate her social life, if nothing else. She also wondered while laying in bed what sort of time frame he thought was needed for them to move on to the next level. Because she truly had no use for him if she had to use Buster when she felt like being fucked.

Cass had dismantled her innocently warped system of intimacy requirements to which she had once religiously adhered as she entered her early twenties. Prior to that, she had to have had dinner at least three times with the guy, not inclusive of home cooked meals. In other words, brother had to spend some money on her. He would have had to have shared his feelings for her uniquely by either cards, flowers, or some genuine act of sincerity, and last but not least they had to have been seeing each other steadily for at least three months. Cass laughed as she recalled, "Those were the days of very scant dick action." As she reached her mid twenties she began experiencing various flavors of dick as her rigid scale had dwindled down to a mere dinner and old fashioned chemistry as the standard criteria. She didn't consider herself promiscuous, just well rounded, she laughed. Ultimately, when she reached thirty her system had undergone a significant transformation as pure fucking had lost it's novelty and she had basically grown up and sought more substance out of life. Though she still sometimes enjoyed just a good fuck, as evidenced by her encounter with Trey, that was no longer the norm. Her current requirements included a man who possessed character, stability, a job, and could be prospective husband material. According to her calculations, Harrison had all of these attributes except one, he was not husband material but as far as she was concerned he had passed go and was approved to move on to the next level of intimacy. She only hoped that his scale was comparable to hers and that it would not take long for him to reach that same endpoint, because she was ready to sexually experience Mr. Harrison Chauncey she thought as she turned over to sleep fantasizing briefly about what she hoped would be their first sexual encounter in her favorite doggy style position.

Monday turned out to be a classic Monday full of deadlines and phone callbacks. The only thing that helped Cass keep her head above water was knowing that her work week would be ending Wednesday as she had taken a full vacation day on Thursday to get home for the Christmas holidays. Cass however couldn't help being consumed by thoughts of all the work she had to complete prior to her departure. Fortunately Linda helped alleviate some of her stress by inviting her to lunch and sharing with her all the inside gossip on all of their co workers. Cass usually didn't partake of such hearsay, but found that it didn't hurt to be on the listening end of the gossip. Linda confessed that Cass was the only person who had any knowledge of her alternative lifestyle and that she wanted it to remain that way which is why she brought a male escort, John, to the company Christmas gala. She confided that John was truly a dear friend of hers who himself was gay. They frequently returned alternating favors at each of their job functions in hopes of keeping their private lives private. She also confided that she had once been married and had one child, but that three years into the marriage she realized that something was missing in her life. Later, that missing link was filled by a woman named Sheila, who was a fellow tennis player at a local fitness center. Sheila had helped her realize her true identity and helped her in her transition from mother and wife to lover and friend. Her eyes became misty as she talked about this woman, because she admitted that she was her first love and had broken her heart by leaving her for one of her best friends. She still felt immense pain every time she thought about it.

As they walked back to the office after lunch, Linda tried to expel some information from Cass about her personal life, but at that time she was able to evade her queries. She figured soon enough Linda would become aware of Cass's fully heterosexual lifestyle, and she wondered what type of impact that would have on their new found casual friendship. After successfully keeping her personal business personal, Cass finally began the task of completing the immense work before her. However, after two hours of intensity, Cass had reached her breaking point and decided a cup of coffee was definitely in order. Before she could force herself to her feet, a delivery boy knocked on her door with a beautiful bouquet of red roses. Excitedly she pulled out the card, but refrained from opening it immediately and rather took a deep breath and closed her eyes praying that this was not another one of Tanya's ploys. She then opened the card and read, "I enjoyed spending the day with you. I look forward to the day we meet again, Harrison." Cass closed her eyes and smiled pulling the card to her chest and now feeling a new energy which no amount of caffeine could imitate. Linda, passing by, saw the flowers and said, "A gift from your significant other, huh?" she smiled.

Without any references to gender, Cass replied, "Well, we are still at the very early stages and taking things a day at a time," she smiled.

"Well just don't let her move in on the second date," she joked assuming it was a woman. "When you guys get things settled maybe we all can go out sometime."

"Maybe so." The rest of the day went by fast as Cass had a new motivation to get her work done and get home. She wanted to call Harrison where she could be relaxed and talk to him with her undivided attention. Cass finally finished everything for the day and rushed home. Immediately after getting out of her clothes and sitting down to relax with a cooler she called Harrison.

"Hello," he answered amongst several voices in the background.

"Hi Harrison, this is Cassandra."

"Hello Cassandra. How are you?"

"Fine. Actually great. I was just calling to thank you for the flowers."

"It was my pleasure. I wanted to make sure you knew that I enjoy your company, despite my sometimes overbearing personality. You're not the first woman to run from me because I believe in truly honest communication and not euphemizing things. Anyway. Was there anything else?" he abruptly interceded.

Cass, caught off guard, responded, "No, I guess not." She then chose to hastily inquire, "Yes, what is all that noise in the background?"

He sternly responded, "Not that it is any of your business, but every other Monday some pals and I get together to play some poker. I should go now, but we should see each other soon, I hope. "

"Yeah. Okay," she bewilderedly responded while hanging up the phone. Cass could not believe his Jekyll and Hyde personality. Especially during the same conversation. He seemed to always take three steps forward and then five steps back. She had never encountered a man so moody before and she wasn't so sure she could tolerate anyone who shared so many of her own impetuous traits. She then laughed it off and speculated, "we would truly clash when I am PMSing." She then totally out of her seductive frame of mind now, decided that she would get comfortable, and maybe try getting online to check out some of her old buddies.

Cass after having bathed had not found the Monday night football game exciting in the least and chose to sit down in front of her computer and try her luck at getting into her favorite room. This time it worked, but she realized that none of the names looked familiar. She waited for a while, but nothing changed and there were no interesting conversations being initiated. She then thought, "Has it really been that long?" Disappointed she started to sign off but was greeted with a "Hello," in IM land.

"Hi."

"It has been a long time since I saw you online."

"I have been very busy."

"Have you analyzed your reason for coming into the lesbian room last time?"

"There was nothing to analyze," she hastily typed back. "I guess I was just curious."

"Are you saying that you are bicurious?"

"Bicurious?"

"Yes bicurious. Meaning that you have intimate relations with men but want to experience what intimacy would be like with a woman."

"Not at all," Cass honestly responded. "I have never desired to be with a woman intimately."

"Oh I see. Let me put it this way, have you ever been intimate with a woman?"

"Well sort of, but it was all a big mistake and an error in judgement."

"LOL. A mistake. Sorry my dear, it doesn't quite work like that. Taking a wrong turn is a mistake. Buying the wrong detergent is a mistake, but getting intimate with a woman, if it is a mistake, it is a planned one."

"Seriously. It was a moment influenced by wine and a very vulnerable period in my life."

"You need to grow up and come full circle with your sexuality. I have seen your kind before. You are the type that gets married and has children and has that whole nuclear white fence family thing going on. Then one day you wake up and think, I have all this but I am still not happy. You then go to a therapist who gives you antidepressants to help conceal what you already know and are afraid to accept –your true identity."

Cass was appalled by this woman who knew nothing about her reprimanding her about her concept of reality. She angrily typed, "Look, I am a thirty-four year old woman and I am well aware of who I am and don't need you trying to tell me that I have an identity problem. You don't know me like that."

"Age doesn't matter in this equation, dear. I have seen very old women go through life purely miserable trying to conceal their perceived shameful reality, I just don't want to see you endure that same fate."

"You do not know me like that, and I resent your implying that you do."

"I see your kind all the time. You need to keep it real."

"I have to go," Cass angrily replied.

"Running from the truth again, huh. You will learn."

"Whatever," Cass brazenly typed back.

"In case you want me to enlighten you again sometime, my name is Kristina. E mail me if you like."

Cass intentionally withheld her name and responded, "Yeah right, goodnight." Exasperated she signed off.

She flopped down into her bed and lay there angry about an interaction with someone who knew nothing about her. She had always been interested in men and did not foresee any signs of that interest changing any time in the near or far future. She thought back, and the only time she was intrigued by a woman was that most recent incident with Tanya that got too out of hand and was totally misconstrued. She then more insightfully thought and realized in shock that there was one other time during high school in which her feelings could have come into question. She and Stephanie went to spend a summer in Maryland with some cousins, one of whom was a blatant dyke. She invited them to join her at a gay club, and teenage curiosities were peeked and prompted them to agree. Once there, Cass was scared to death and stayed close to Stephanie who was to be her dance partner all night, so as not to suggest to anyone a hint of availability. She and Stephanie danced together the entire night and had a good time. However, at one point Cass did notice an attractive woman trying to catch her eye, she did not know how she was feeling about it, but she was captivated by her. Cass then abruptly turned over, opened her eyes and looked at herself in the mirror above. "Oh my God, I have not only been intrigued by one woman but two, Does that mean that I am gay?" Cass was somewhat disconcerted that a stranger could cause her to question her own innate sexuality. She then hesitated and laughed thinking that the entire concept was entirely ludicrous. She then repetitively stated, "I have no sexual interest in women, I am heterosexual," a fact which she believed steadfastly but needed some self affirmation. She repeated that statement until she dozed off to sleep. While she believed in her heart that she was totally heterosexual, she didn't want any subliminal messages disrupting her sleep and casting any level of doubt on her sexuality, especially since this Kristina woman was so emphatic.

Thirty-Two

The next two days went by fast and Cass was getting more excited about heading home to some good cooking and escaping her mundane life for a minute. She needed a positive diversion about now. She was surprised that Harrison had not called her, but had decided that she was not going to be the aggressor, especially after their recent interchange. She figured the ball was in his court. She was through with it. Before she left the office she wanted to call Keisha to make sure things were in order for their departure the next day.

"Hello," Keisha quickly picked up the phone.

"Hey girl. Are you going to be ready to leave at noon tomorrow?"

"Yes," she hastily whispered, "I am almost totally packed."

"Why are you whispering and trying to rush me off of the phone?"

"I am supposed to be meeting Curtis, and since Hank is here I have to look out for him and get up outta here without waking him up. Girl you know I gotta get me some before I leave for this long weekend. Oh, girl that's him gotta go. See you tomorrow."

Cass shook her head in dismay thinking, "One of these days she is going to get busted." She picked up her briefcase and began to head out of the door and as soon as her hand encircled the knob, her phone rang. She pondered whether she should answer it or not as it was a rare client that called this late in the evening, and her secretary was gone for the day and not able to screen the call. She figured it was likely a personal call and finally decided to put down her brief case and try her luck. "Cassandra Nicholas," she answered.

"Hi Cassandra, this is Harrison."

She nonchalantly responded, "Harrison, hi. How are you?"

"Fine. Since I haven't heard from you, I presumed that my tactless mouth got me into trouble again. Listen. All I can say is I'm sorry about my rude behavior. Well, let's not say rude, because rude I am not. Rather, abrupt behavior."

"I think keeping it at rude would have been appropriate," Cass blandly responded.

He continued without pause, "But what can I say, I am set in my ways and am not used to being questioned or interrupted for that matter. That being said, I have some food on order and it is too much for me to eat alone. Why don't you come by and help me with it?"

Cassandra pissed off that yet again he had waited until the last minute responded, "Harrison, this last minute routine is getting old too and you need to start giving me some advance notice."

Harrison enthralled and simultaneously appalled by her feistiness replied, "Okay. Look I realize I might have to work on some things but I am not going to dissect everything I want to say before I call you. Now this invite was just a truthful offer because I wanted to see you. I will totally understand if you can't."

Cassandra, realizing they were too much alike, lightly laughed and replied, "I want to hear you tell me that you really want to see me and mean it."

Harrison hesitated, being reluctant to concede any power, "Cassandra, I would be most honored if you would join me for dinner this evening." Harrison willingly admitted that he liked Cassandra, but he would not tolerate much more of this blatant insubordination. He was reared in an era in which women did not second guess any man. He did however enjoy the challenge of these "new world" women who were essentially the same but needed the appropriate guidance and the validation to accept their God-given subservient roles. He laughed as he figured Cass would understand that reality soon enough.

He laughed and Cass continued, "I will be coming straight from work because if I go home, I will be too pressured to pack for my trip tomorrow."

He promptly responded, "If you need to go pack, by all means we can take a raincheck."

"Harrison, please shut up."

"Okay then," he laughed "Here are the directions." She copied down the directions and decided that she would try to make the best of the evening even though Harrison's attitude consistently annoyed her. She felt like she needed a diversion then more than ever because as the holidays were approaching, she found herself thinking more of Robert.

There was not a night that passed since Cass had seen the first house adorned with white sparkling Christmas lights and red wreaths on the double doors that she had not reminisced about how she and Robert's house would have been. She had been literally crying herself to sleep every night with thoughts of how her life should have been and becoming angry about how cheated she felt. She now knew what people meant when they described the holidays as the most lonely time of the year for those who had lost a loved one. She had never in her life felt such despair and it took every ounce of energy she could muster not to let herself fall into a deep and unrelenting depression. She found herself always welcoming any detour to keep her from being home only to wallow in self-pity. Since the holiday season began, Cass had been trying to get home strictly in time for bed and to prepare for the next day, which had significantly impacted her wallet as the only thing she had found to do was shop. If anything good had come out of all of this, it was the fact that she now had a pair of shoes for any imaginable occasion.

As Cass got closer and closer to Harrison's home, she questioned her motives and whether she should even exit the car. She had two primary motives. One being a selfish diversion from her mundane existence and two, she wanted a good old fashioned fucking. What better way to accomplish the latter than with a fucking old ass man. She again had to laugh at her ridiculous behavior as she finally exited her car. At that moment Cass firmly decided that she was going to relax and have a good time no matter what. She only hoped that Harrison could hold his tongue long enough to have the opportunity to place it where she desired it. With that erotic thought in mind she smiled and quickly ran through the cold to his door.

Harrison lived in a refined older model home bearing a simple southern elegance. It was painted a pale green with steps leading up to the large porch surrounding the house. It was beautiful, she thought. Cass rang the bell and Harrison appeared shortly looking very cute in his army green shorts and Yale sweatshirt. He opened the screen door smiling, "Cassandra come on in," as he gave her a warm hug. "The food hasn't arrived yet, so just make yourself at home. Would you care for something to drink?"

"Do you have any wine, Harrison. It has been a long week and I would like to wind down a bit."

"Hmmmm," he sighed, "well I do have some Merlot, but other than that, just rum and coke which the fellas had here on Monday." Cass had never acquired a taste for Merlot, and was not a rum drinker so she responded, "How about some bottled water?"

"Now that I can definitely handle." Cass looked around at his home which hardly appeared to be lived in by a bachelor. Everything was neatly in its place and was so quaint and homey. She thought, "I certainly hope this brother is not swinging both ways," she grimaced as she knew that was truly a dilemma so many women faced in Atlanta, the Bisexual Capitol of the South. She left that issue alone and rather continued to observe her surroundings. The house was all hard wood with an Oriental rug in the living room beneath the antique sofa complemented perfectly by two formal chairs. She wondered who decorated his home because it definitely appeared to have had a woman's touch. Harrison then returned with her water and sat down next to her. "So you are heading to New Orleans for the holidays?"

"Yes, I am and I am ready to just get out of Atlanta for a while. Are you doing anything special?"

"Two of my sons will be coming to visit me. The youngest is in Europe on a student exchange program."

"That's great. You must be proud."

"Indeed I am. They all have turned out to be respectable men. My eldest will be getting married next month."

"Wow! I guess you will be very busy, Mr. Chauncey."

"I guess so," he apathetically responded. He then stood and lowered the volume on his stereo which he had set to a classical music station. Cass quietly laughed and thought, what a refined man. As he began to sit, the doorbell rang and he bellowed out, "Alas, the food has arrived." Cass was glad that there was a distraction, as she found herself becoming aroused by Harrison and sensed that he was feeling the sexual tension amidst as well. Cass had found their conversation relatively monotonous and benign, it was simply his quiet arrogance and sexy demeanor that was increasingly turning her on coupled with the fact that she hadn't fucked for damn near five months. She silently smirked, this Buster shit is getting old, I sure hope he is ready to move forward in this. She then smiled as he pulled out her chair for her to sit. It was a large formal dining area with a piano sitting in the far corner.

"Harrison, do you play the piano?"

"I'm a man with many talents, my dear. Playing the piano is merely one of them," he egotistically shared.

Cass sometimes welcomed his domineering presence and flirted, "Well, maybe I will learn more about some of your other talents later."

He sat there smugly and did not respond in the affirmative by gesture or verbally to her last comment. Harrison was not particularly moved by Cass's overt forwardness. He quickly changed the subject as he did not approve of the unbecoming behavior which she readily displayed. Cass again placed a fork full of food in her mouth as Harrison reached for her hand and said grace over their food. She felt so embarrassed as she removed her hand and continued to eat afterwards. They shared light conversation over the delicious Thai food while Cass tried to retain some degree of dignity after Harrison had silently reprimanded her by his lack of comment and by the stinging look in his eyes. Cass decided to break the silence which abounded by doing as Keisha suggested and discretely find out about his medical history, which might help determine if he was even capable of sexually satisfying her. She then shared that her sister was a doctor, purposely neglecting to say what type, and cunningly asked if he was seeing a doctor regularly. He confided that he had some problems with kidney stones in the past, but was otherwise in perfect health. Cass mentally placed a check in the health section of her application for perspective other and silently smiled to herself thinking, "If he gets his personality in check he might be alright." After dinner, Harrison offered to play a classical piece for her. She moved to the sofa and listened intently as she closed her eyes to the smooth yet intricate sound which appeased her auditory senses.

Harrison was always pleased when his listeners felt his music, and it was evident to him that Cass was an appreciative audience. He always liked to play the piano to set the mood for his first sexual encounter with a woman, which was why he had invited Cass over to his place. In his past experiences he had learned that if a woman can venerate classical music, then she was salvageable and would more likely be able to conform to the ideals which he relished in his women. He had concluded in his maturity that all women whether career oriented or not wanted to be taken care of by their man and that once they recognized that he was willing and able to do so, they typically would become his perfect prey. He had seen several women since his divorce and had gotten very close to remarrying on more than one occasion, but something always halted the progress. However, it had been a while since he had placed himself back out into the market of single men. He had become preoccupied by his work and had no sufficient time for developing a relationship. Therefore, during the foregoing several months he had relied on his whores for sexual gratification. He did note before his hiatus that he incurred difficulties in his relationships more related to age differences than anything else. Since he had been dating women usually at least fifteen to twenty years his junior, his most common problems occurred when he requested that they quit their jobs to let him be their provider and he, in turn, would become their full time job. Since women in that age range who intrigued him were usually very independent, most would be opposed moreso because of the principal of the matter rather than the idea of not being officially and gainfully employed.

Harrison hoped Cass was different as he stood up from the piano bench and laid a kiss on her neck while her eyes were still closed and her head lay comfortably back on his sofa. Cass was definitely aroused and was eager to feel the closeness of this man. He sat down next to her and pulled her body closely next to his and began to softly kiss her and then more firmly as his mouth encircled hers and their tongues began to gently intertwine. He then slowly unbuttoned her blouse and began caressing her breast with her bra in place. As Cass reached back to unsnap her bra, Harrison stopped her and said, "I will handle that." He then lay her down on her stomach and began lightly licking and kissing her back and while doing so he unsnapped her bra, releasing her breast from their unwanted captivity. He then brashly turned her over and began biting her nipples firmly while pulling her breast together and taunting each almost simultaneously with his tongue. Harrison was surprised that his manhood had not yet risen to the occasion. He slid his tongue from her breast to her navel, repetitively which really turned her on and made Cass desire either penetration or some other form of direct stimulation. She then began to grab for his penis and he pulled away as he did not want her to be aware that he had no erection. He continued to tease her, so Cass gently nudged him on his shoulders so that he would catch the hint that it was okay for him to eat her. He then abruptly sat up and said, "I'm sorry Cassandra, but I have never and have no plans of performing oral sex."

Cass lay there in shock as her body was still tingling and needing some degree of closeness. She ignored that statement at the moment and again began to reach for his penis. He then pulled entirely away and stated, "I'm sorry, but I still don't believe that we are ready for this," he lied as he did not want to share the real reason, being that he had become so accustomed to the rugged and rough sex with his whores, that sex in this most normal of settings was not arousing to him. This had occurred on a few previous encounters and when it did he had to force himself to stay away from his circle of prostitutes for at least a seven to ten day period. And lately since his sexual drive had been so pronounced with them, he had been seeing one of them almost daily. Cass sat there almost wanting to cry because she was at that point of ultimate arousal. All he probably had to do was penetrate her once or even lick her a few times before she would reach orgasm. Cass wasn't too proud to beg and said, "Harrison, please."

"Cassandra, it is very unbecoming for you to beg. So please stop it," he snapped and turned away nonchalantly Appalled by his insensitive behavior, Cassandra promptly excused herself to the bathroom in an attempt to try to temper her anger and humiliation. When she finally exited the bathroom, Harrison met her in the hallway and grabbed her hand saying, "Let's talk for a minute okay. I think we need to get the record straight. I don't want you to go out of town harboring any negative feelings about us."

"Us? There is no us Harrison."

"Cassandra. Listen. I care for you a lot. Let that be no question. I have never been intimidated by a woman like I have been by you. When I care about someone, I want things to be perfect."

She began pulling away from him while walking to the door, "Let me get out of here. I need to go."

"Cassandra," he inadvertently yelled and then regained his composure. "I think I love you. Please think about that while you're in New Orleans," as he grasped the doorknob tightly and kissed her on her cheek.

Ignoring his plea, Cass removed his hand from the knob and angrily retorted, "Goodnight Harrison."

Cass had become so annoyed by his rude behavior that she felt Harrison had certainly worn out his welcome. His personality stunk and apparently she couldn't even get a fuckin' fuck from him. By all accounts, Buster won out over him. She could not believe that for the first time she thought she might have felt like the men who claim they have blue balls. She had decided in her mind that she was never going to see him again, as she turned up her music to help deter her thoughts from her reprehensible evening and her insatiable horniness. Plus, her decision was made all that much easier as she remembered that he confided that he didn't eat coochie, and if nothing else she needed a man that was willing to gratify her, and in her book there was no better way than by eating the pussy. Harrison left shortly after Cass and drove to his usual corner. As he drove, he conceded by his behavior that he was truly captivated by Cass with her bad attitude and her diffident independence. He laughed as he thought of his totally contrived attempt to assure that he at least had one last chance to gain her trust. "Love," he laughed out loud. "The only woman I have ever loved is my dear old departed mother." He circled the corner a few times debating as to whether he should just go home and save himself for Cass in the upcoming week. He then ran across Lisa, at which point he knew he was going to succumb to his weakness. She was one of his favorite young white bitches, who was beautiful, clean, and tight. As he called her, he decided that it would be his last time for a while because he knew if he did not make love to Cass soon that he could lose her forever if he had not successfully done so already. He shook his head disgusted with himself as he leaned to open the door for Lisa. He brazenly smiled as he was immediately aroused by her and was pleased to know that there was nothing functionally wrong with his equipment as he forcefully fucked her. After releasing himself, he headed home to his empty bed, which he expected would soon be filled with the sweet smell of a woman, his perfect prey. And he secretly hoped that it would be Mrs. Cassandra Chauncey, eventually.

Thirty-Three

Cassandra awakened Thursday morning still pissed, because buster was not what she needed the night before. Buster couldn't hold her and make her feel the closeness that she desired with a man. Cass then laughed, "but she had to give old tried and true buster his props cause he did make a sister come." She then dismally thought, "It might be just buster and me for a while," as she had realized that she and Harrison were definitely not the love connection, or for that matter the like connection. She had categorically deleted him from her short list of available others. She rolled out of bed and was glad that her anger from the previous evening at least helped her accomplish something productive. It gave her the motivation to get all packed when she got home as opposed to at the last minute in which she would have inevitably forgotten some vital things. She just had to pack a few last things like her toothbrush and curling irons after she got ready. As she was brushing her teeth the phone rang. She answered with a full mouth of toothpaste and in a muffled tone said, "Hello."

"Hey, girl," Keisha sounded energized, "Are we going to be leaving on time?"

Cass spit out her toothpaste and wiping her mouth said, "I guess so. You are coming here right, since I am closer to the highway."

"Yeah, Hanky is going to drop me off. I'll be there at twelve noon on the dot, 'cause I'm ready for some good eating."

"Alright then. See ya."

Cass was sitting down in the lobby at twelve noon sharp, and of course there was no Keisha. Keisha did not arrive until almost one, as the concierge had to call Cass back down since she had become restless waiting for her friend.

Keisha hugged Cass apologetically and said, "I'm sorry. You know how men get at the last minute when you are leaving town," she said while putting her luggage into Cass's trunk. "They want to put a claim on your stuff, and it was all good. But I'm here now," she yelled, "So let's hit the road," while shutting the door. Cass had no idea where her friend got the energy to screw damn near everyday, but she was becoming jealous of her friend's easy accessibility to a warm dick. They laughed and blasted the music singing their old jams of Earth, Wind and Fire and Stevie Wonder. Then Keisha had to pull out the Isley brothers, at which point they both became quiet and nostalgic. Cass was thinking of her high school sweetheart, Glenn, who she made love to for the first time in the back of his father's van listening to an eight track tape of the Isleys. Keisha on the other hand abruptly removed the tape as an awful memory had escaped her subconscious mind. She thought that she had successfully dislodged that entire incident from her memory for good, as she tried to hide the tears which were rolling down her face. She looked out of the window trying to avoid Cass's eyes. Cass had been enjoying the music and admonished her friend, "Girl, I was jamming." Cass turned to look and was shocked to see that Keisha was crying. "Oh, honey," she reached out to grab her hand, "I'm sorry, what's wrong?"

Keisha began sobbing more uncontrollably as Cass displayed concern. "I'm sorry," Keisha lied in between sniffles, "I don't know what got into me. Girl I'm just tripping," she tried to hide her pain.

Cass sincerely replied, "I don't know who you think you are dealing with but this is your old friend, Cassandra. You can share it with me. What's going on?"

Keisha then confided, "I have never shared this with anyone because it has been very painful for me." She shrugged her shoulders and said, "Never mind."

"Keisha, tell me," Cass consoled. The tears again began to silently roll.

"When I was twelve years old, you know my mom was still alive." Cass shook her head in the affirmative.

"Well, this one particular day, I stayed home from school because I truly was not feeling well. Mom had gone to work, and dad didn't go in until the evening shift. I just remember one of my favorite Isley Brother's songs came on the radio and I began singing the words to myself. I vividly remember my father coming into the room and saying, "Oh, so you think you are woman enough to sing those kind of songs, huh." He had been drinking which was a habit he had started doing regularly and excessively when we learned that my mother had breast cancer. I just ignored him as I usually did when he was like that."

The tears began again, as she stopped momentarily to compose her thoughts, and then she continued, her words alternating with sobs, "He then jumped on top of me and ripped off my gown and said, "Let's see if you are woman enough for this." He tried to rape me Cassandra, my own father tried to rape me while I was listening to the fucking Isley brothers. All I remember is fighting for dear life. I beat at him and scratched him in his face. That is when he slapped me so hard that I thought I was surely dead. All I could think was, oh my God, don't let my mom see me like this. As I begged and pleaded, 'Daddy please.' It was as if all the drunkenness escaped from all of his pores as he sobbed and tried to hug me. I was hurting so bad. All I did was lay there in his arms like a wet rag. I couldn't move. He never touched me again. But I can remember it like it was yesterday. It was the worst day of my life." She then abruptly got quiet and sat there as if almost in a trance.

Cassandra pulled off the road at the next exit and just hugged her friend, rubbing her back repeatedly saying, "Everything's alright now." Keisha then looked endearingly at her friend and said, "Thank you for listening," and as only Keisha could do, she yelled, "Pull up into that damn McDonald's. A sister is starving." Keisha had learned years back how to shut off her feelings. She always sought relationships to validate her womanhood. She needed to feel worthy of love. In high school, the only boys who professed their love for her were the ones she screwed, so soon screwing became her love refuge. Eventually she ended up with an STD which was probably the reason why she and Hank could never have kids, after having tried for several years. Since she could not have kids and because somehow the words "I Love You," no matter how insincere they were spoken always made her feel special, she continued her dangerous lifestyle. However, HIV quickly made her revise her outlook. While she still screwed around, she now at least made sure a condom was used—most of the time. She longed to hear those three words but didn't want to die for them. She shook her head out of her introspection and screamed into the speaker, "A number one please."

Leaving McDonald's, Keisha took over the driving. Cass looked at her friend and wondered how she could still be sane after the trauma she had endured. She knew that she had read that one in three women were somehow affected by incest, which was a startling statistic to her. "We live in such a fucked up world," she thought before the road tranquilized her into a hard sleep. She awakened to Keisha tapping her leg and saying, "Which exit do we get off of for your house?"

Cass lowered the Anita Baker CD and looked up saying, "Damn, we're already here. Not this one but the next one."

"Girl, you better make sure that whatever man you end up with goes to sleep before you because you snore. I mean you really snore. That's why the music was so damn loud."

"Shut up," Cass laughed. They pulled up to Cassandra's house, and Cass snuck in and could smell the aroma of fresh bread pudding cooking." Her mom was there in the kitchen with flour on her forehead making "beucoup" food.

"Cass," she smiled. "Why didn't you call me before you left? You know I was worried."

"That's exactly why I didn't call. What you don't know can't hurt you," as she circled her arms around her mother's neck who stood six inches shorter than she.

"Keisha, you come here too and give me a hug." Keisha sauntered over and said, "It sure smells good in here, Mrs. Nicholas." Cass grabbed herself a piece of fresh bread pudding and some milk and sat down to eat. Cass's mom looked at her daughter disappointingly and said, "Now I know I taught you better manners than that. Did you ask Keisha if she wanted some?"

"Keisha is no guest, if she wants some she'll get it," Cass responded with a full mouth.

"I'm fine Mrs. Nicholas. I'm waiting to get some of your gumbo."

"Well sit down baby. I have a batch that is ready. I'll fix you some." She looked at Cass and stuck out her tongue, "Thank you, Mrs. Nicholas."

After satisfying their stomachs, they had to do their rounds to see all the relatives. Since they were going to midnight mass, they had to try and get most everyone in by nine or ten o'clock because Christmas day they weren't planning on leaving the house. They left Cass's house and went over by Keisha's parents house. Cass did not know if she could look Keisha's father in the eye after learning of his past. Keisha's mother had died several years before of breast cancer and he remarried when Keisha was fourteen. Keisha's stepmom had successfully helped her father kick his drinking habit by the time Keisha was sixteen, and since that time she no longer had to endure the repercussions of his episodic drunken behavior. And for that, Keisha was forever grateful to her step mom. They pulled up into the driveway of her house in the old lower nine. She looked in amazement at the house which seemed to be so small and in an almost dilapidated state with the blue paint hanging onto the wood in sparse areas. The grass looked like it hadn't been cut since last Christmas. Keisha opened the screen door which was only hinged at the bottom, and knocked .

Her father, who was looking much older than his sixty-eight years, opened the door exclaiming, "Keisha, baby. Come on in." Keisha lightly hugged her father and walked into the disheveled foyer. Cass followed suit and begrudgingly hugged her father saying, "Hi, Mr. Johnson." Keisha quickly went into the bedroom where her stepmom was resting in the reclining chair with her swollen feet elevated. She excitedly said, "Come give me a hug, girl. The doctor told me I weigh too much and eat too much salt. They told me I need to keep my feet up as much as possible to get rid of all this swelling, that's why I am not getting up," as she wiped off the remnants of potato chips surrounding her mouth with the back of her hand. Keisha sarcastically stated while picked up the Lay's potato chips, "And I can see that you are following all of his orders."

"Her, child. My doctor is a woman," she proudly corrected as she chucked down the corner of the beer that remained.

Keisha smiled, "Oh, sorry." They remained there chatting mostly with her mom for nearly an hour and then decided they would head back to Cass's house to maybe get a little nap in before mass.

On their arrival to Cass's house, Cass was surprised to see that her brother had made it into town afterall. He opened the door looking as handsome as ever and hugged his sister warmly.

"Cass, long time no see. You looking good."

"Thank you, my brother, you don't look so bad yourself. You remember Keisha, right?"

Keisha walked in and hugged David, "Hey there." He remembered, "Aren't you the one who used to always come and get our left over pickle juice to drink with your potato chips." She laughed thinking of all the things to remember, and responded, "The one and only."

"Good to see you." Cass had always tried to set up her brother, now divorced and looking very good at almost forty. He and his wife of only three years had no children and he never spoke of the divorce or what lead to it. He just had vowed to his family that he had no plans of ever getting married again, and for the last eight years, he had held true to that. Cass figured her brother was an excellent catch, being a well established electrical engineer, added to the fact that he was very handsome with all of his dark features atop his Indian olive complexion and perfect teeth. He was getting a little scant in the hair department directly at the top, but otherwise his five foot eleven frame appeared to be that of a twenty year old. Cass then questioned, "Boy, are you still living that bachelor lifestyle?"

"That's the only way to be."

Keisha whispered in Cass's ear, "Can you hook a sister up?"

"Girl, that's my brother. Hell no." She loved her friend dearly, but she had been with too many men and she didn't want her brother to become one of her casualties.

"Mom, is Casey coming home?"

"She's supposed to with that fellow Jarred. Have you met him yet?"

"I have not. Are they supposed to be here for mass?"

"She told me that they wouldn't be able to leave Atlanta until Christmas day. So no."

After a brief nap, as usual, they were all rushing to get dressed so that they could arrive at church in time enough to not be forced to stand throughout the mass. Her dad then screamed upstairs, "Alright, everybody. Let's go." Like children they all hastily finished their last touches and marched down the stairs in single file. The five of them squeezed into their parents cadillac and headed to church. Fortunately, they were all able to sit together. Cass did her usual gawking around the room, her eyes resting on several people who she had grown up with. As mass began, Cass felt sleep starting to descend on her. She felt her head bob several times at which point her eyes popped open wide and she glanced around to see if anyone else had noticed, and of course David sat there silently chuckling. Cass eventually was awakened at communion time to the all too familiar pinch on the thigh by her mother. "Ouch," Cass quietly yelled while giving her mom an evil eye, who in turn politely smiled back. It was at communion that Cass saw her high school sweetheart sitting up front with his wife and three children. He looked so happy and content, she thought. She then felt a twinge of jealousy as she passed them thinking, "That should have been me." Glenn caught her staring and smiled at her as he sat back in his pew holding his youngest daughter who was fast asleep. Mass finally ended and Cass wanted to talk with Glenn before he left.

Cass casually snuck away from her family over to him and

said, "Glenn, hi how are you?" extending her hand for him to shake. "I am married now, but I still think we are beyond that," as he pulled her in for a hug. Cass felt so comfortable there as she remembered his strong arms and smelled his same Drakar cologne, with its masculine scent. He then turned and introduced her to Cheryl, his wife, and pointed out his three children who now were all asleep in their strollers. Cass was very curious as to what he was doing these days. They had broken up during her sophomore year of college because of his lack of ambition and his tendency to be slovenly. "So what are you up to these days?"

"Basically, I am enjoying raising my family. A couple of years ago, I got my real estate license and the business has been doing so well that almost a year ago, I resigned from my position at UPS and I am doing my real estate full time. You always told me that I had more potential than I gave myself credit for, and now I believe you. Thanks. You look like you're doing well, Cassandra. Still in Philly?"

Now feeling a very strong sense of resentment, Cass decided she needed to cut this conversation short and responded, "No. I'm now in Atlanta. Loving it. You take care and have a Merry Christmas."

He smiled and said, "You too." Cass felt horrible for herself but happy for Glenn. Well, sort of. She had built Glenn into the man he had become, and someone else was reaping the benefits. He even looked more confident, Cass thought as she felt lonesome and like she was missing out on something. She then somberly resigned, as everyone jovially chatted while driving home, "Maybe someday I'll meet the right person and get rid of this 'Alone' tattoo which must be branded on my head."

Once home her mom made some fresh egg nog with rum and they sat around opening gifts until the wee hours of the morning. Finally, they all found their way into their respective beds. Cass fell asleep still feeling dejected and very single. She bribed herself to sleep by giving herself a deadline. "By next year this time I will be married or engaged to be," as she slowly drifted off to sleep with thoughts of Robert. Christmas morning no one awakened, besides her mom, who was busy cooking until early afternoon. Cassandra awakened to her little sister rubbing her nose with a kleenex to which Cass swatted her hand to presumably move the pestering creature. Eventually she opened her eyes to see Casey standing over her.

"Hey sis," she smiled.

"Girl what are you doing disrupting my sleep?" she laughed giving her sister a hug. Casey tugged at her arm, "Come on, get up. You have to come down and meet Jarred."

"Okay. Okay. Just let me pull myself together a little and I'll be right down. Have you seen Keisha?"

"Yeah she's downstairs already, stuffing her face." Figures, Cass thought as she slowly got ready.

Cass finally made her way downstairs and was shocked to see a white punk rock looking boy sitting on her mother's sofa. He quickly stood up with his hair down to his shoulders and extended his hand, "Hi, you must be Cassandra. I've heard a lot about you." Cass extended her hand in disbelief especially when she saw the tongue ring when he spoke and said absolutely nothing. She turned and said, "This is a joke right?" Cass turned to Casey who she realized had also invested in some body piercing as her cut off shirt revealed her navel ring.

"Do you always have to be so mean? This is Jarred, the man I have been telling you about," she walked over and hugged him.

Cass could see the despair blatantly revealed on her mother's face and slowly said, "Oh. Okay. Nice to meet you then. Sorry." Cass couldn't believe that first of all her sister had crossed the color lines and had done so with a guy who looked like he could be legitimately crazy. Cass held her tongue, but figured she would have to definitely make more time to spend with her sister when she returned to Atlanta, and get her head screwed on tight.

Christmas day went by fast as it was a continuous cycle of eating then sleeping. Keisha had left for a while to hook up with an old boyfriend from back in the day, and Cass stayed home and talked with her mom about Casey amongst other things, who had taken Jarred to the French Quarters. David had not been seen or heard of since much earlier that day, which was his usual disappearing act. Once

Keisha eventually returned with her ever familiar glow, she begged Cass to go to their class reunion which was to be held that Saturday night. Kevin, the guy she had hooked up with, said that their whole entire hanging crew was planning on being there. Cass finally against all her wishes, gave in and decided she would go to appease her friend. Keisha was ecstatic and said, "It will be fun, I promise." Cass then reflected on Keisha's overdriven sexual behavior and wondered if it was precipitated by the incest. She then thought that would explain why she slept around so much, because she felt a need to have total control over what she did with her body. Cass then laughed at herself trying to play psychologist, and thought if she knew the reason for everybody's actions, she wouldn't be the alone, single and bordering on depressed person she was.

Saturday came and still no one had heard or seen David until late that evening when he came in looking fresh and happy.

"Hey there everyone," he exclaimed. Their mom chastised him for not at least calling. His response to that was, "I am a grown man, and I haven't punched a clock for anyone in eight years, and don't plan to now. If you have a problem with that, I will stay at a hotel next time I am here."

His mom ignored his smart comments as usual and said, "You still should at least call. Period." Cass amidst all of the chatter found herself daydreaming about Harrison, and wondered if she should reinstate his name on her list. She couldn't figure out what it was that kept drawing her to this man despite his overtly rude and obnoxious behavior. When she had asked Keisha earlier after having told her about their last date she boldly insisted that she not even consider his old ass. Cass laughed and thought she was probably right, but still kept him on the list albeit at the very bottom. She was feeling rather needy, and going to her damn class reunion party was likely not going to help her. Keisha came down the stairs spry and ready with her too tight black leather pants on, a black sweater revealing her cleavage, and her high heeled leather boots. "Girl, you better get ready, it starts at nine o' clock."

"You got nerve to be telling me about time," as she got up to go upstairs. Cass decided that she would wear her beige pants suit with her cream turtle neck. She at least wanted to look successful and attractive as she applied a little make up and curled the ends of her hair, even if it was faking the funk. She then decided she was going to stop beating herself down and being so pessimistic, as she was successful in many aspects of her life, just not her personal life at the moment. She then looked at herself in the mirror and reaffirmed that she didn't need a man to make her life complete. With that, she confidently strode out of the bathroom with a new attitude, at least on the surface.

Thirty-Four

There were so many people at the class reunion she noticed as she attempted to apply her name tag. People were already drinking and dancing by the time they had finally arrived at ten-thirty. Keisha had of course gotten the wrong directions. Keisha smiled, "I look better than three-fourths of these heifers in here." Cass looked around and had to agree as she saw that a countless number of the women had lost their shapes, likely after having had their kids she presumed. She then walked even moreso with a certain arrogance as she knew her body was tight. As she worked the room, she was asked to dance by Greg, who used to be one of the best looking guys in the class and one of the varsity football players. Cass thought the operative three words were used to be, as he now had a major receding hairline, a beer belly, and knees which must have been hurting by the looks of the way he was dancing. She spoke lightly about what she was doing in Atlanta and opted not to give him her number which he asked for repeatedly since he travelled a lot to that area and was newly divorced. Cass was glad to have been saved by another one of the former football players who interrupted their dance. When he came to dap Greg up, Cass used that moment to escape. She eventually found a seat and then felt a tap on her shoulder and turned to see that it was her old friend, Erika who had not spoken with her since Cass had exposed Dwayne's indiscretions during their senior year.

She held out her arms and said, "Cassandra, I have missed you so much. I know it has been a long time, but I wondered if you would forgive me for my juvenile behavior back then. I have tried to find you to formally apologize, but I was unsuccessful. Once I discovered where you were I figured you probably didn't care at that point and had basically forgotten about it." Cass smiled and sincerely returned the hug, because they truly had gotten close when they were on the cheer leading squad together.

"Whatever happened to that jerk anyway?"

Erika told half of the story, "Well, after we married, I found out that he was continuously having affairs on me and I had decided that once I finished law school that I would divorce him. So I did."

Cass embarrassingly responded, "I'm sorry, I didn't know that you all had gotten married."

Erika, chuckled, "That's fine. What have you been up to looking all good?" Cass went on to explain what she was doing in Atlanta and they sat down and began talking like old times. She learned that she had been a practicing attorney for five years now working with mostly civil cases in New Jersey. She and Dwayne had no children and she was now single going on five years and loving it. Cass couldn't get over how good she looked with her short naturally curly well manicured hairdo, her golden complexion, and her hazel green eyes which Cass always admired. Cass exclaimed, "You're looking good yourself, have you been working out?"

"Yes I have. Check this out, I was surfing the web and ran into a page called Sisters in Shape. This sister, Melanie, gave me an exercise curriculum, some nutritional counseling and a lot of motivation and got me in the groove."

Cassandra interrupted, "You have got to be kidding. Talk about a small world. Melanie was my personal trainer when I lived in Philly. That's why I am looking so good," Cassandra playfully flexed her biceps.

"Wow! That is truly a trip. Small world, huh? Well, I better work myself around to see some other folks, but here is my card and I am going to write my home number on the back. Be sure to call me.

Eddra Marchand

And, one of my firm's primary clients is in Atlanta, so I frequent there. We'll have to hook up when I'm in town." Cass simultaneously gave Erika her card with her home number and they hugged and Cass said, "Most definitely." At that moment, Keisha ran over and pulled Cass out onto the floor as everyone was assembling to do the bus stop. Cass readily joined and danced, laughing at how some things just never go out of style. That was apparently the close out song as the lights were then turned up and everyone started to retrieve last hugs, kisses and memorabilia. Cass smiled as they walked to the car glad that Keisha had convinced her to come, if for nothing else than to rekindle an old friendship.

Cassandra awakened early Sunday morning eager to get back to her life, mundane though it was. Nevertheless, it was hers, and not being interfered with by other people. Cass had become aggravated by her mother's constant meddling into her business, as she only reinforced Cass's desolation. Her mom seemed to believe that the only reason that she was still single was because she was selfish and had too much pride to legitimately and sincerely show a man that she needed him in some way. She said, "Every man needs to feel like he is needed and is making the decisions," she added "even if you really are." Cass totally disagreed and figured she did not need a man and was not going to evolve into a submissive and docile woman because her man was insecure. She told her, "If he is that shallow and insecure, I don't want him anyway." Her mom sighed as if to imply, "My child is a hopeless case." Cass didn't want to remind her mother that she was hardly speaking from experience, as her marriage was a farce, based upon codependence, infidelity, and dishonesty. Cass kept that to herself and promised that she would leave as soon as she got up. She turned over and nudged Keisha, who was in a dead sleep since she had gone back out with Kevin after the party and returned just a few hours ago. Keisha angrily turned over pulling her pillow over her head and begged, "Let me just get a few more hours, please. I'm tired." Cass somewhat envious that she wasn't getting any action, "Look, we need to go. You can sleep in the car," while pulling the covers off of her. "Nobody told you to be screwing around all night."

Keisha flung her pillow angrily in Cass's direction. Cass barely avoided it and warned, "You better be ready to leave when I'm dressed, or you gonna find your ass flying back to Atlanta." Keisha rolled her eyes at her and turned over in disgust.

Cass went to the bathroom and put on her warm up suit and whipped her hair up into a pony tail. As she exited she reminded Keisha who was still soundly asleep in the bed, "I'm not going to tell you again," as she slammed the door behind her. Cass walked into the room where Casey was supposed to be sleeping alone, and found her wrapped in the arms of Jarred who was totally nude as displayed by the covers exposing one half of his skinny body. She lightly tapped on Casey's leg who sat up straight into attention as she thought it was her mother. When she noticed it was Cass, she flopped right back down into Jarred's arms while pulling the covers up to conceal his body. "Oh, it's you," she calmly responded. "Wassup?"

Cass was annoyed that her baby sister no longer showed her the respect of an older sister. She chose to avoid a confrontation though and said, "Just wanted to tell you bye before we leave."

"Oh, okay. Bye," she hoarsely whispered still with her eyes closed and remaining reclined. Cass promptly kicked her and said, "Girl you better sit up and give me a hug." She lazily sat up while holding the sheet above her bare torso and hugged her sister saying, "Be safe." Cass could not help but notice the tattoo on her arm with the name Jarred inscribed on a red heart.

"Girl, why are you mutilating your body with that nonsense." She ignored Cass and laid back down as Jarred exclaimed, "Yeah be safe and nice meeting you, sis." Cass looked at him in obvious aversion and left without saying anything further. As her mom always said, "If you don't have anything good to say, don't say anything at all."

Cass was pleased to see that on her return to her old room, Keisha was up and dressed albeit with a major frown on her face. Cass walked up to her friend and hugged her saying, "I knew you didn't want me driving back all by myself," she smiled.

"Shut up, bitch," she jokingly responded.

"Let's go." They flounced downstairs suitcases in tow and of course mom was up preparing breakfast for them. Cass could never stay mad at her mother. She had a heart of gold. Cass just wished that she protected it like it was a rare element, having been hurt so much in the past by being so giving. They sat and ate the grits, egg whites, and turkey bacon. Her mom had made a special effort to make things the way she knew that Cass would only eat them. Keisha looked at the food and playfully commented, "I never thought I would see the day when a pig was spared in the south, a place where no part of the pig ever goes untouched." She ate it nevertheless and they hit the road, headed back to the black mecca of the south.

Thirty-Five

When Cassandra arrived at her condo for some reason she expected something to be different. She expected to feel excited and care free coming back to the place she now considered home. Strangely enough, Cass felt confined by the walls. She felt trapped by all the things that had happened in her life, which made her not open to a true committed relationship. She didn't know if it was the fact that she had seen her father continuously have affair after affair, or was it that she had become so independent that it cast a formidable character that intimidated men. She just knew that something had to change, if she didn't want to follow in the footsteps of Sallie Mae. She wanted to have someone to come home to, someone who could welcome her unlike the cold walls which had greeted her that night, and many nights for years. She pensively reflected on her life and the many relationships that she had allowed to consume her but ultimately without any sustaining effects. She thought, "Maybe mom is right, but if she is, how do I correct it?" She knew that she had to be more receptive to men and become maybe slightly more flexible with her requirements. She got out of her clothes, slid into her bed and thought out loud, "Maybe I have been attracting the wrong men. I will have to be more open to change and risks, I guess." On that note Cassandra cajoled herself into sleep, which didn't take much after that seven hour drive.

The next week went by fast especially since it was a short week ending early on Thursday for New Year's Eve and not to resume again until Tuesday for Cass, since she had taken a personal day Monday for a visit to her doctor and dentist. As New Year's was approaching, Cass became more concerned about having to tell her sister about Richard. Richard had actually called her at work Monday and asked, "Did Stepphie tell you what I got her for Christmas?"

"No," Cass uninterestingly had responded, "I have been trying to evade her for now until I am prepared to tell her about your affair."

"Cassandra, it was not an affair, it was just a one night stand kind of deal. I love Stepphie and it makes no since for you to destroy her happiness or our happiness for that matter. We have been together for twelve years and add four to that if you include college. I love your sister," he continued to profess, "It was just a big mistake on my part. I bought your sister a new diamond wedding ring and asked if we could repeat our vows. I'm telling you I am a changed man after being faced with all that I could lose." Cass rolling her eyes responded, "What would have happened if I hadn't busted your ass, Richard? You would still be out there screwing around."

"No, Cassandra, that's just it. I was going to be ending it any way."

"Richard please, the way you were groping that woman, you were not trying to end a damn thing," she whispered remembering she was at her office.

"Cass, listen. You have to believe me, I am begging you, if not for me, for the children."

"You are scum," she stated and hung up the phone. "How could he go so low as to bring up the children?" Cass was in a huge dilemma, but she still felt that her sister had the right to know and could make her own decisions after that. She had decided that she would tell her sister after New years, period.

Several days throughout the week, Cass found herself staring at Harrison's number and debating whether she should call him. She was drawn to him for some undisclosed reason which she could not explain, but she did refrain from calling him, until she was essentially coerced to call him when she received three dozen red roses at her office with a card signed, "Remember me? Harrison Chauncey. The man who loves you." Now she remembered partially why she was drawn to him. It was his pure chivalry of old. He knew how to romance her unlike so many younger men she had dated in the past. She had decided she would finally give him a call when she left the office that evening. As her day was finally coming to an end, she received a call on her direct line. "Hmmm," she thought, "only a select few people ever dial that number. Maybe he beat me to the punch." She secretly was hoping it was Harrison as she picked up the phone.

"Cassandra Nicholas."

"Hi Cassandra," she heard a female voice which she did not recognize,

"Hi," Cass hesitantly responded.

"Cassandra, this is Erika girl."

"Oh," she rang out. "Hey."

"How are you lady?"

"Fine and you?"

"Very well. You have any big plans for New Year's eve?"

"None at all. I do have some Champagne chilling in my freezer to pop tonight."

"You mean you don't have a man," Erika shocked inquired.

"Nope, but if you know of any eligible bachelors, give them my number."

"Sure thing."

"How about you?"

"Well I will be spending tonight with someone special, but we have been on shaky ground for a while. I just don't know, girl. Listen, the reason I am calling is that I will be coming there week after next and I wondered if I could stay over at your pad and we could catch up on old times."

Cass smiled, "Oh that would be great. I could use some company in that lonely house of mine. Just call me a little closer to that time so we can coordinate schedules and such. How many days?"

"Three."

"Cool, well you have a Happy New Year and I will see you

then."

"Cool," Erika smiled. "See ya."

Cass left the office somewhat disappointed that she had no plans for the evening and that no one had called to suggest anything. She somberly went home and figured she would probably sleep into the New Year after saying a prayer of thanks but also a prayer for love to reenter into her life. She decided that she would not call Harrison. Three dozen roses didn't mean a damn thing coupled with his piss poor personality. She figured she should just start anew.

Cass arrived home and called Keisha, but there was no answer. She refused to call Stephanie because there was going to be nothing happy about her New Year and Cass would find it hard to hide that, but she did call her sister Casey, hoping that maybe she could help her get out of her funk. "Hello," Casey spryly answered the phone.

"Hey, little woman."

"Cassandra, hey. Happy New Year's. I am on my way out with Jarred to go see the fireworks. It's almost nine o' clock and we probably already will have to walk miles to get to the sight. So I gotta go. Bye." Cass hung up the phone and thought, "Well that was no help. Even Little Bit has plans," as she lay in bed drinking her second glass of champagne, figuring she would probably not be awake for the actual ascension into the new year. She then called her mom who always found a way to uplift her.

"Happy New Year," her mom answered the phone.

"Same to you," Cass feigned excitement.

"Hey there, Cass dear. Are you about to head out to celebrate?"

"No mom I will be staying in."

"Oh well that's good. You are having some folks over?"

"No mom, I am bringing in this New Year alone."

"Well it's good that you won't be out there. It is too dangerous with people firing those guns and things. I hate that you are bringing it in alone though, but you are just going to have listen to your mama's advice. Anyway, your father and I are about to head to that party which we always attend. So you take care. I would put your father on the line, but he is in the tub. We'll call you tomorrow. Happy New Year, baby. Love you."

"Love you too mom," Cass replied almost on the verge of tears. "Oh well," she turned over after finishing her last glass of champagne and fell asleep thinking that next year had to be better. Cass was awakened by the phone at eleven thirty.

"Hello," she barely alert answered after finally getting the phone to her ear.

"Cassandra, Hi." She instantly knew it was Harrison by his distinguished voice.

"I'm so glad you're home. Do you care to bring in the New Year with an old man?"

Cass hesitated, "Harrison. I don't know," she whined.

"I have been thinking of you and figured you were still in New Orleans. I know you must have received my flowers. Are you still not going to forgive me? Why don't we start the New Year together with new and refreshing attitudes. Myself included."

"I'm not so sure that's a good idea."

"You need to answer quickly so that I can make it there before the clock strikes midnight. I love you, Cassandra."

"Where did that come from?" Cass sat straight up in bed and hesitantly responded remembering what she had said about being more receptive and changing some of her rules.

"I felt it so much while you were gone," he lied. "I felt like something was missing. After reflecting for a while, I realized that it was you that was missing." Harrison was so horny he didn't care what it took. He had avoided his whores for over a week and knew he was certainly ready to make love to Cassandra. If not her, he knew he was going to be fucking somebody that night.

After all of that how could she say anything but, "Yes, Harrison. Let's bring in the New Year together." She was not sure as to why she agreed but she felt that if nothing else she wouldn't be bringing in the New Year alone.

"On my way. Good-bye, my love." Cassandra quickly got up and tidied up her place. She kept her hair in its pony tail and just as she was about to apply a tad of make up, she remembered that Harrison preferred her without it. So she smiled thinking, "If plain is what you want, plain is what you will get," as she was just feeling a temporary reprieve from her personal tribulations. Cass thought if nothing else, maybe this visit could abate her horniness and desire to be close with someone after so long.

Harrison arrived just about five minutes before midnight, and Cass opened her door to his radiant smile, his delicious smell, and his arrogant air. All of which were tantalizing to her that night. She lightly hugged him upon his entrance as he exclaimed, "You look beautiful." Harrison truly believed that Cass did look great without any falsifying features. Just her and her silk lounge wear, nothing more and nothing less. Harrison already was feeling aroused after not having had one of his hookers in the past eight days and twelve hours, but he wasn't counting of course. He knew that he was horny and that he would be able to perform optimally that night. They sat before the television and watched the peach begin to drop in Lenox Square starting at ten seconds. They began counting backwards, ten, nine, eight until they reached one, both yearning for the closeness that was shortly to come to ease the sexual tension so prevalent in the room. At the stroke of midnight Harrison passionately kissed Cassandra who willingly gave into him, not caring at all about the fact that she had promised that she would never see him again. She longed for a man's touch and she was glad on many accounts that it was him. She let him have all the control he desired as he carefully unbuttoned her silk blouse exposing her breasts. He looked at them for a few seconds and then vigorously began kissing them both as Cass moaned in excitement. He quickly then picked her up in the darkness and carried her to her bedroom where he commanded her to take off all of her clothes for him, slowly. Cass did as he asked as he lay in bed admiring her perfections. He pulled off his shirt and slid off his pants and patted the bed next to him requesting that she join him there. She lay down on her back and Harrison again began to kiss her and slid his tongue down her stomach. He gently began penetrating her with his fingers, but then he could hold back no more. He spread her legs apart and entered her continuing in a slow rhythmic pattern. Cass moaned in delight as he was being so gentle with her. It was not long before he came and lay there atop of her panting loudly. Cass felt wonderful despite the fact that she had not had an orgasm, which she rarely did during intercourse any way.

Cass was touched by the closeness and the gentleness which encompassed their lovemaking. He fell asleep on top of her and Cass let him lay there to his heart's content, because she felt like their relationship might have turned a crucial corner, and maybe now they could get past the petty attitudes and begin developing a special bond that might pull them closer together and eradicate some of their more obvious differences. Cass kept her arms around him as if she were afraid for him to move too far away and make the night become a memory sooner than she wished.

The next morning Cassandra awakened with Harrison laying close beside her. The glimmer of the sun on his face made him appear older than forty but still much younger than his fifty six years. She smiled as she lightly lifted the covers to see his body which she did not see fully on the previous night. She thought, "Not hardly bad for a man his age," as his manhood was perfectly erect and beckoning her mouth. She was so glad to see a warm dick for a change, she slowly brought the wetness of her mouth to meet it. She let her mouth encircle it and gently moved up and down. Slowly without opening his eyes, his hips instinctively began to move back and forth in sync with her mouth, and then abruptly out of nowhere he pulled back and yelled, "No don't do that. Why don't you go fix breakfast or something," as he turned out of the bed letting his feet hit the floor and pulling on his boxers. Cassandra somewhat taken aback by his abrupt response, promptly headed to the kitchen to get some breakfast going and to avoid any further embarrassment. Harrison sat there on the side of the bed thinking of how she almost ruined his perception of her. "Only whores suck fucking dicks," as he desperately tried to erase the picture of her doing just that. No woman of his would engage in such behavior. She had to at least maintain an image of purity for him to be committed to her in any form. He shook his head again wondering if he would be able to perform with her again. He really liked her and figured he would try everything to make it work, he just needed her to be ready and able to always be a lady and never a whore, at least never again.

Cassandra decided to fix whole wheat pancakes with turkey bacon. She was trying to get over that very embarrassing exchange with Harrison. She usually did not go down on men, but figured it's a New Year and why not, maybe it would give him some incentive to do the same for her, she had to selfishly admit. She heard that he had taken a shower and she was glad that she had placed the necessary towels out just in case he decided to do so.

He came into the kitchen displaying his usual temperament and asked, "Do you get the *Atlanta Journal and Constitution*?"

"I do but it would be downstairs at the concierge. It's one of the rare things that we get free."

As he poured himself a cup of the coffee he requested, "Be a dear and fetch it for me," slapping her lightly on the butt. Cass raised her eyebrows and thought, "Fetch, who the hell does he think he's talking to? A damn dog." Cass then thought of her mother's comments and placed on her warm up bottoms and went to "fetch" the paper. She laughed as she rode the elevator down thinking, "This is totally against my nature, but I'll try this bullshit for a minute." She returned and he was sitting watching the Nature Channel and held out his hand as she entered the door. She brought him over the paper as he did not look her directly in her eyes and said, "Thank you, dear. Is that breakfast almost ready?"

"Yep, any minute," as she tossed the pancakes one last time. She brought the breakfast over to the table and they sat initially quiet eating their breakfast while he continued to peruse the paper. She decided to break the silence and said, "So Harrison," and she was promptly told to shut up just by the simple gesture of his hand and the bland stare over his bifocals.

She continued to eat and focused her attentions on the TV for the moment because she was intrigued by the gorgeous home displayed on the screen. He finally looked up and said, "This breakfast is delicious. Now what were you about to interrupt me for?"

"Interrupt? Apparently, you have lapsed back into the old Harrison. You are supposed to be trying to be more compromising as am I, since we did just bring whatever this is that we have to a new level."

He smiled and said, "Indeed we did. I am very glad that I chose to bring in the New Year with you."

Cass abruptly responded, "I believe it was a mutual decision that I was very tempted to decline."

He then grabbed her hand and said, "Cassandra, I really do like you. Well, to be honest, I love you. I believe with a little more time together and your learning my likes and dislikes, we could probably be a good team."

"Why do you have to be so damn obnoxious?" she replied while abruptly standing. "Everything is not about you Harrison. If that is what you expect from me, we can nip this New Year shit in the bud right now. Pardon my French."

"Relax sweetheart. Relax," he said while beckoning her to sit on his lap. She did so and he pulled her chin to look at him in his eyes while laying the paper to the side, "My sweet Cassandra. I mean no harm by my most innocent of comments." He gently kissed her cheek. "I know that I too must learn the same from you, but I thought that was understood. Any woman that I love, I will always put her interest before my own. Don't ever mistake that." As she stood, he returned to his paper and indicated that it was time again for her to be silent. She picked up both their plates and quickly cleaned the kitchen while he sat on her sofa enjoying National Geographic. She eventually joined him as he stated, "Are we okay now?"

"For the moment," she said sarcastically.

"Good," as he hugged her and kissed her on her cheek, "Don't you think it's about time you take a shower? Especially after the night we had," he winked.

"Again, Harrison. You need to stop treating me like a child. I was just thinking that, but I don't need you to tell me," honestly feeling a bit sticky and grimy. He shook his head in agreement as he tapped her ass again when she hopped up to do so. She thought, "If you tap my damn ass one more damn time I will break every finger on your damn hand." She took a shower and freshened up a bit, refraining from putting on any distinct make up and walked out to Harrison reading the book on her nightstand which she had never been able to get through, because it would always put her to sleep.

"This is a great book, I have read it about three times. I'm sure you will enjoy it." They talked for a while embracing one another and sharing some gentle kisses and they appeared to be an old happy couple. Harrison finally stood to leave stating, "I must be going now, but we will talk very soon. I promise," as he leaned over and kissed her softly on her lips. She walked him to the door and very willingly responded, "Okay see you later."

Cass could not wait for him to leave. She could not believe how different they were and their lack of similar interests, as she wondered whether the age difference was playing a huge role or if it was just his conservative upbringing. She had never in her life met a man who refused a blow job. She shrugged and thought, maybe the opposites attract thing will prove to be true but she also knew that she would not be able to hold her tongue for much longer especially after all of the chauvinistic and antifeminist things he had said. She was especially glad that he had left because she was feeling particularly horny and wanted to gratify herself since he didn't eat coochie—yet. She promptly hopped into bed pulled the covers over her head and let her fingers do the walking until she shuddered in delight. She resolved that she had to get him somehow to be more open minded about oral sex, because on her list of prospective other's must do's, number two was eat pussy, a close second to must have a job. She laughed at herself though she was quite serious. She did have to admit that in some weird kind of self-punishing way she enjoyed Harrison's company, because she had no idea what to expect from him, which was a challenge, and if there was anything that kept Cass's egotistical interest it was a challenge.

Harrison, too could not wait to leave Cassandra's home. While he enjoyed her company, he realized that he had more work to do with her than he imagined. He could not believe that she was going to actually go down on him. Once he arrived home he reluctantly picked up his cell phone.

"Catch a cab here. I'll pay for it. But I need you right now." He quickly hung up and thirty minutes later his doorbell rang.

"Ahh, Lisa. My little sweety," without letting her get into the door good he pushed her down onto her knees and unzipped his pants. She eagerly took him into her mouth as he pulled her head forcefully to meet his groin until he exploded. He threw $200.00 on the floor and turned to go take his shower while saying, "Lock the door when you leave." While washing the remnants of his abhorrent refuge, he sighed and stated, "You've got a lot to learn Cass. Sucking head is strictly for the whores," as he smiled feeling totally gratified.

Thirty-Six

*N*ew Year's day was full of the typical college bowl games in which Cass had no particular interest. She only liked watching the pros at work. After awakening from the sleep induced by her orgasm, Cass did feel rejuvenated. She lay there for a bit before the phone rang.

"Hey girl, this is Keisha."

"I know."

"I saw your number on my caller ID. Wassup? Happy New Year. How'd you bring it in?"

"Don't get mad at me," Cass implored.

"You brought it in with that old fart didn't you?" Keisha intuitively remarked.

"Yes, I brought it in with Harrison. And contrary to what you so readily implied, he does not have a small dick and he made me feel good."

"So he got you there, huh?" Keisha laughed.

"Well, not exactly."

"Oh Lord. You mean you didn't bring in the New Year with an orgasm?" as if that fact were the end of the world.

"We still have some work to do to understand our sexual likes and dislikes."

"Did he go down on you?"

"Nope, but the sex was good."

"Girl you know you can't teach them old dogs new tricks. Is he at least open to it?" Cass hesitated and Keisha continued, "Well you better school him or boot him. I truly brought in the New Year with a bang." Cass was scared to inquire exactly what that meant, especially knowing Keisha.

"Well," Keisha continued, though Cass chose not to question her, "Are you sitting down?"

"Yes."

"Last night, I lived my fantasy."

"Your fantasy?"

"Yes child, I brought in the New Year with a threesome. Curtis was eating me and his very large partner was."

Cass cut her off and said, "You whore. Spare me the details please." Keisha exclaimed, "Girl you better open your mind. Life is too short."

"Where was Hank?"

"Girl, my Hanky did a double last night because he can't pass up no money, chile, especially getting paid double overtime. That shit don't matter to me because his lil' brat takes it all anyway. So I had to do something."

"Yeah whatever. I enjoyed Harrison and we'll just see what happens."

Cass's line then clicked and she promptly hung up with Keisha and laughing answered, "Hello."

"What's so funny?" Harrison questioned.

"Oh nothing, I was just talking to a good friend."

"And who might that be?"

"A girlfriend of mine."

"Oh I see," now feeling satisfied with her response. "I am watching the college games with some friends. I would very much like it if we could spend the evening together and share a bite to eat. I'll be back there at say seven sharp. Are you going to cook something or shall I pick up something on my way?"

"I'll take care of things. I'll see you later." Cassandra definitely was not going to be ordering in because while she rarely did cook, she cooked on every New Year's the green cabbage and black eyed peas for the superstitious myths of money and good luck respectively. Lord knows that she needed any extra help she could get for money to pay down her school loan debt and some luck in love.

Harrison arrived of course punctually at seven. Cass let him up and opened the door to her delicious black eyed peas, while she lit a candle to lessen the awful scent which cabbages always emit.

He smiled and kissed her saying, "It smells good in here," as he tapped her butt and said, "Good girl."

"I got your good girl. The cornbread is almost ready." He sat down while ignoring her last comment and began taking off his shoes and then commanded her to come to him. He lay one of his sloppy kisses on her lips while he groped her bosom. "I'll get some of this later too." They sat and ate while Harrison did his breakdown of the college football teams, in which Cass feigned interest, but actually was bored to tears.

"Harrison," Cass interrupted, "Listen, I think there are some things you need to know about me too. If we are going to try to take this to a new level. You need to understand my likes and dislikes." He straightened his body in his chair, and looked her in her eyes and questioned, "What might that be?" Cass felt like a kid about to tell her parents about her awful report card.

"Well," she stuttered, "Sexually."

He stopped her in her tracks, "Listen, I don't need any lessons on how to satisfy my woman," as he began eating again. Cass wondered if he thought the fact that she had slept with him on one occasion made her his woman.

"Well, I am going to tell you that all women are different and like different things. You said before that you were going to tell me how you feel and I trust that you will respect the same in me."

He cleared his throat and said, "Go on."

"Well, sexually, I like for a man to, well, I,"

"Go on," he demanded, "Spit it out."

"I like for a man to go down on me. Period that's it. It's said."

He looked at her in the eyes and responded, "I told you that I don't do this going down on people, as you call it. Trust me. You will become adjusted to the sex and it will satisfy you, I promise," he said while tapping her on her leg.

She sighed in frustration and continued, "I'm serious Harrison. I am a grown woman and I know what I like. I'm not going to just sit around and pretend that I get off on making love. It's good, most definitely, but I need more. I won't say anymore about it. You know where I stand on the issue."

Later that evening she lay under Harrison as he gently made love to her. She wanted it to be from behind but as she attempted to turn over into the position, he lightly pushed her down and said, "I like it like this, baby," as he continued in missionary style. She lay there enjoying the closeness but wishing for more force and creativity until he came whispering in her ear, "Oh, Cassandra. You are the one who makes papa happy." Cassandra turned over as he hugged her and went to sleep. She lay there awake for hours contemplating if she could endure the effort needed to conform him. She was alone but not so desperate to tolerate his conservative and rigid views much longer. She laughed, "I like challenges, but come on."

She believed that this relationship was certainly on its last legs as almost everything about him was beginning to aggravate her. Even the "chivalry" shit couldn't make up for that. His personality was making him hardly as attractive as one might think looking from the outside. He awakened Saturday morning refreshed and walking around openly nude revealing his more obvious gray pubic hairs. Cass thought, "Gross," as all of his flaws seemed to be so pronounced as she also noticed his balls hanging lower than any she had ever seen. She prepared a small breakfast of coffee and toast and once he left to play golf with some buddies she decided she would screen her calls for the remainder of the weekend, because she had no plans of playing house for the rest of her weekend. She needed to decide how far she was willing to go to not be alone without compromising the essence of her being.

Cassandra enjoyed the rest of her weekend doing whatever

she liked without Harrison trying to order her around. She believed for the right man she probably could give a little and be less domineering, but he certainly was losing the battle in the solo competition. She was surprised however, that it was already Monday and she had not heard from him and was irrationally angered by that fact. She admitted that her anger was misplaced and that she should save her energies for the right and prospective husband material. She figured that she would hang onto Harrison to basically fill a void for the time being. As she sat there continually bashing Harrison, there was a knock at her door. Cassandra thought, "If Sam let someone up again with out ringing me, his ass will be gone by tomorrow." She opened the door to a dozen red roses. She read the card as she closed the door, which read "Missing you. Let's do dinner. Will pick you up at six. Harrison." Cass snickered and thought, "He must have a revolving account with the florist." She then decided she would engage him for a little while in this love-hate thing they had going on as she watered them and placed them on her countertop. She did acknowledge that it was nice to be courted and to be exposed to some of the finer things which so many guys she had dated in the past did not appreciate. She smiled and headed out to her appointments early so that she could be ready for dinner.

Harrison had thought of Cassandra all weekend, but decided that he should let her miss him for a while. He was proud that he had still not gone to a hooker for sexual favors since he had started to prioritize grooming Cassandra to be the next Mrs. Chauncey. He was definitely getting the urge for some rough sex and knew that the time for one of his girls was quickly approaching. He still couldn't fathom that Cassandra wanted him to "go down" on her. He grimaced as he thought about the entire concept. He did give it some thought, however, over the weekend and in fact looked at a few videos displaying such activity and figured that maybe if she took a bath and soaked a little immediately beforehand he might give it a try. He desperately wanted to keep Cassandra because she did bear all of the characteristics he favored and was slowly conforming to his way of thinking. He smiled as he thought of their making love and the way she so willingly received him and desired him. He thought as he fixed his tie and flickered his tongue albeit particularly slow in the mirror, "maybe I will try this cunnilingus thing tonight. Just for you."

After dinner, which was surprisingly pleasant, Cassandra was shocked that Harrison was not being particularly demanding or condescending as usual. She still would hardly be offended if he decided not to come up to her condo as he was dropping her off as she exaggerated a yawn and described what a long day she had upcoming. Apparently that fact did not faze him as he readily parked his car and escorted her up. Cass was going to fake a headache or something because she was not in the mood for his routine missionary sex cadence. Cassandra stated as she walked into her house, "I need to take a few ibuprofen for this splitting headache," she lied as she popped the two tablets and drank water behind them.

"I know just what will make that feel better," as he followed her into her bedroom and tapped her on her ass.

"Why don't you let me fix you a nice warm bath and then we'll go to sleep." Cass looked at him capriciously as he began running her bath water for her.

"Well I would rather just take a shower to be honest Harrison."

"No, you must take a bath. It will make you feel better," he insisted. Cassandra did enjoy the warm bath and found it quite soothing but was curious as to what Harrison's ulterior motives were. She quickly dried off and put on a very boring nightgown and hopped into bed where Harrison was already laying. He initially began kissing her on her lips and neck, and Cassandra in turn faked interest as she quietly looked at the news. He licked down her stomach with his tongue as usual and Cass instinctively opened her legs for him to enter her, the usual scenario. She was surprised when his tongue did not stop at her belly button but rather continued down and rested at her favorite spot, and her body jolted from the unsuspecting sensation. She then smiled, closed her eyes, eased her head back, and let Harrison do what she had been wanting all along. Cassandra's eyes popped open wide as his teeth began biting her there as if he were truly eating something edible. She moved her hips away from his dangerous teeth and tried to push his shoulders a bit for him to catch a hint that he needed to pull up a bit. Cassandra's ploys did not work however, so she decided that she needed to fake an orgasm quickly before she ended up without a clit. She began moaning loudly and called out his name, "Oh Harrison, sweetheart. Yes. Yes." And she finally felt relief from his teeth gnawing her. He immediately got up without a word and went to brush his teeth, thinking "that wasn't too bad." He walked out of the bathroom with his chest sticking further out walking a confident stride, "You liked that huh?"

Cass lied, "Oh yes Harrison. It was great." He then put on his clothes and said, "Well, I have an early morning too. I'll maybe see you later this week," he smiled as he kissed her and let himself out.

Harrison quickly got into his car feeling rather manly and rugged and decided that night was the night for him to retrieve his reward for being so good. He rounded the corner and picked up one of his girls. "Hey daddy. Where you been?"

"So you have been missing me?"

"Of course, daddy." He leaned over and opened the door and said, "Since you've been missing me, let's go to your place so you can give me a special treat."

"Anything you say daddy, but you know it's gonna cost you."

"I know," he smiled as he was very aroused. He went into her apartment and first made her kneel before him and start licking him to arousal. Once he was fully erect, he lay down on the bed and ordered, "Come here bitch and ride me." She did as he demanded until he was finished. He left the money on the dresser and headed home thinking about Cassandra and how he probably had definitely won her over now. He figured he could perform cunnilingus sometimes if she continued to be a loyal and obeying woman and made sure that things were thoroughly cleaned beforehand. He smiled, "Shucks, I might even make you my wife sooner than later."

Cassandra quickly went to get her hand mirror to look down there and make sure the vital things were still intact. "Ouch," she winced as she gently rubbed the affected area. I have got to call

Keisha on this one. Keisha answered the phone on the first ring sounding as if she had been sleeping. "Girl, wake up. I got to tell you this," she said now able to laugh about the incident.

"What?"

"Girl, Harrison went down on me."

"Congratulations," Keisha boringly responded.

"Wait," Cass barely containing her laughter, "that's not it. He almost bit off my clit in the process. I had to fake an orgasm to get him off of my shit."

Keisha burst out laughing and said, "You have got to be kidding."

"Nope," she laughed, "I have some KY jelly there trying to soothe my damn abrasions."

Keisha couldn't stop laughing, "Well at least he tried. That says something for the old man."

"You know he drew sister a bath before hand and I didn't know what he was up to. Now I know. The question is what am I going to do if he tries that shit again. I might not be so lucky next time."

"Well, you just better become allergic to baths. He's one of those who you got to soak it before he sucks it." They laughed and got off the phone shortly thereafter. But not before Keisha raised an issue which Cassandra was not quite ready to face. Cassandra knew that she had to though. She had to set up lunch and tell her sister about Richard. She promised that she would call before the week's end to get the issue finally over and done with.

Thirty-Seven

The week went by at an accelerated pace as Cassandra so diligently tried to catch up. She had met with Harrison Wednesday to see the Atlanta Symphony Orchestra perform, and was surprised how the music had given her a better appreciation of that art form. Harrison sat there throughout smugly proclaiming his favorite pieces beforehand. All of which Cass had never heard before. She was impressed by his expansive knowledge base and knew that she could learn a lot from him in general, she just wished that he were more open to learning some things from her as well. She finally had coerced him into attending a recent black musical in town, but after moaning through the entire show that such productions were a waste of his time and beneath him, she made him leave at intermission while she stayed to the end. She had said she would take a cab home, but of course he was there to pick her up. She resigned that this whole relationship thing would be a slow process and was going to take work, but they had both talked extensively and had decided that they were going to try to transform their relationship into a coupleship. Cass, despite all her misgivings felt good to be a part of a "U'" and "S". It was good to know that she could count on him to be there for her, which was something he definitely enjoyed. Sometimes Cass would just call him for little bits of advice when she already had decided her course, just so he could envision the perceived power which he so desired. He had plans of coming by that evening after work so that they could spend most of the weekend together. She had left him a key at the desk just in case he arrived before she finished dinner with Stephanie.

Cass found herself with mixed emotions about the weekend together simply because Harrison seemed to revert back to his demanding self when they shared too much time together, and she knew she would have to break it to him gently that the submissive mentality shit was not her thing. He would just have to get over it or get to stepping, basically, she decided. Cass rationalized that it did feel good to be needed sometimes and enjoyed the companionship which seemed to be tearing down the walls of isolation which surrounded her for so long. She believed she may have finally begun erasing the negative aspects of her grandmother's life that had plagued her for most of her own. Her present concern was getting through her dinner with Stephanie and not letting Harrison mutilate her with his teeth. She laughed as she headed out to meet her sister.

Stephanie sat at the restaurant well aware that her sister was going to be at least her usual ten minutes late. She was concerned as to what the dinner was regarding because while she loved her sister dearly, they never saw eye to eye on most issues and therefore rarely got together socially unless prompted by some underlying factor. As Cass walked up to the table Stephanie stood and hugged her.

"Hey, lady. What's going on?"

Cass took her seat nervously and said, "Just haven't seen you for a while, and it is the New Year and all."

"Right, Cassandra," in total disbelief as she ordered a virgin strawberry daiquiri and Cass ordered a Long Island Iced tea. Stephanie sat there smiling broadly as she described the transition which Richard had made.

"Things have been so great lately. He has lightened his work load in order to spend more time with us as a family. You would think he's trying to make up for some ridiculous affair or something."

Then Cass looked at her sister seriously and said, "Have you thought about that as being a possibility?"

"Richard," she screamed. "Girl please, he is not the type and plus he hardly has the time. I know where he is practically every minute of the day," she laughed as if the entire concept was absurd. Cass nervously laughed back thinking, "I need my drink. Fast." Stephanie then went on, "Besides which," she outstretched her hand so that Cass could see the magnificent diamond on her finger, "we have decided that we are going to repeat our vows on this Valentine's Day for our thirteenth wedding anniversary."

By then the drinks had come and Cass took a big swig and said, "Listen, I have something to tell you."

Stephanie looked up seriously and said, "Are you alright? Is something wrong?"

"Yes I'm fine. What I have to tell you is about Richard."

Stephanie looked Cassandra in her eyes while drinking from her daiquiri and questioned, "About Richard?"

Cass decided that she just had to blurt it out, "He has been having an affair." Stephanie looked and began to anxiously laugh, "That is totally preposterous."

"I was out at a happy hour the other day and saw him having way more than casual conversation with a woman."

She nervously smiled, "Girl that's just Richard. He's so personable and it might appear that way."

Cass persisted and insensitively said, "It is far more than being personable when you have your tongue down someone's throat." Stephanie then sat there entirely silent. Cass could see her eyes redden as she looked her in the eye.

"I don't believe you. You have always envied me for being better at everything than you. And now when it is obvious that I have the perfect relationship, you bring this bullshit up to tear me down. You are about to turn thirty-five and be a fucking old maid and you decide to take it out on me. That's just not fair for you to be so selfish," she hissed with her voice cracking while standing up and throwing her money on the table. "You need to grow up Cassandra and until you do, I would ask that you leave me and my family the hell alone," as she angrily exited out of the restaurant. Cassandra sat there totally incredulous. She did not expect their exchange to end like that. She had just alienated her sister from her life for simply telling the truth. Cass downed her drink and then also chose to pick up her things and leave the restaurant without eating and feeling entirely drained. She hoped that Harrison was in a good mood, because that night she needed some TLC and some reassurance that she had done the right thing by her sister.

Stephanie sat in her car silently crying with her hands firmly glued to the steering wheel. She knew that in recent months Richard had been slightly more distant and aloof, but she thought nothing of it. He had been working later many more nights, she remembered as she began to seethe with anger. He had explained to her when she noticed lipstick on his collar that it was from the hug of one of his clients that was so pleased with the work he had done for her. "Could Cass be telling the truth?" she worried. Stephanie then started the car and headed home thinking, "I am a professional and smart woman, there is no way that I could have missed all the signs." Her mind then began racing about what she should do. She considered throwing him out immediately and seeking a divorce, she thought of seeing a marriage counselor and she thought of fucking his brains out so that he would not even think of another woman. As she pulled into the driveway she was initially greeted by her children. She hugged them tighter than she had in a long while and told them how she loved them as tears began to roll down her face. Her kids then unendingly questioned, "What's wrong mommy? What's wrong?" She just shook her head in the negative to imply nothing, knowing that if she spoke at all she would probably be unable to hide her pain. She immediately walked into her bedroom and sat on her bed in the darkness. Soon as Richard entered the room and turned on the light, he knew that his infidelity was no longer a secret as he fell to his knees begging for her forgiveness. She knew as soon as she looked into his eyes, that Cass had been telling the truth. She just sat there emotionless in immense agony holding onto him tightly as he sobbed uncontrollably with his arms encircling her waist while kneeling pitifully before her.

Cass drove home and tried to call both her mom and Keisha but was unfortunately greeted by both of their answering machines. She felt that not only was her life in shambles but she had succeeded in creating a similar circumstance for her sister. She drove into her parking space wondering if she should have kept Richard's affair a secret and let Stephanie live her life in denial. She knew that her sister was a strong woman and at least now had the chance to get all the facts and make an informed and appropriate decision, and she reasoned that if she had not shared his indiscretions she would not have the opportunity to reevaluate her marriage and play an active role in its course. As she rode the elevator up she found herself becoming excited about coming home to a warm body for a change.

She entered and heard classical music playing and the water of the shower. Cass, feeling ready to introduce Harrison to a more adventurous type of lovemaking, decided she would quickly undress and sneak into the shower with him, and maybe they could explore one another. Cass quietly opened the door of the bathroom to Harrison humming the classical music playing on the radio. She began to take her jewelry off and lay it on the countertop next to the glass sitting there. But almost instantly she lost her sexual appetite as she saw what was soaking in the glass. Teeth. Not a bridge, but a full set of fucking teeth. Cass quietly almost tripping over herself ran out of the bathroom, as she heard Harrison shout, "Cassandra, dear is that you?" She said nothing initially as she rummaged around for her clothes and tried to put them back on as the shower was silenced. Cass had no idea that Harrison wore dentures. She was turned off and faced by the reality that she truly was dating an older man who had no fucking teeth. She quickly regained her composure as Harrison exited the bathroom with his robe open exposing his entire body as he came towards her for a kiss, teeth now in place. She saw him now in a totally different perspective and found it hard to overlook the teeth thing, together with the gray pubic hairs and the sagging balls now all facing her head on simultaneously. She hid her laughter and disappointment as he closed his robe snugly, "So how was dinner?"

"It was," she stopped and reflected trying to determine the most appropriate verb, "Upsetting," she finally stated. He smiled and said, "Well that doesn't sound good," as he winked at her and returned to the bathroom to start some bath water going. She then quickly interrupted, "No, Harrison dear, I will be taking a shower tonight." He looked up at her mischievously and said, "Suit yourself," as if to imply that she were going to be missing out on something. As she showered, she chuckled silently thinking, "The only thing I'm missing out on is not having my clit ripped off by some fake ass teeth."

Thirty-Eight

They awakened the next morning feeling energized after making gentle love throughout the night alternating with furious fucking. They were only awakened by the abrupt knocking on their door and their children yelling, "Mom, dad. Unlock the door. What's going on in there?" Stephanie sighed and stretched smiling at the wonderful night which they shared. She felt that it was good that Cass had told her about Richard's mistakes, because now she and Richard had developed a new appreciation for one another and a new respect for what they had created over the years. Yes, she realized that the trust was destroyed and that he would have to work to rebuild it, but they were going to take things one day at a time. She had chosen to forgive him as he lay in her arms and repeated, "I'm so sorry. I will make this all up to you. I will never do this again. Never. I promise," while making gentle love to her. For now she knew the repeating of their vows was definitely on hold until they reconstituted within themselves what the vows actually meant. She knew that she had to call Cassandra and apologize, but for the weekend she was going to enjoy spending time with her family, which she cherished more than ever before. She did vow that she would no longer take her husband or her children for granted.

Cassandra, on the other hand, awakened on the other side of town feeling horny. She had slept with a warm body who believed that missionary style was the only appropriate method of screwing.

Finally Harrison prepared breakfast after Cass had shared some of her innermost feelings about that subservient shit. Although only toast and eggs, it was a big step for him and she knew it and appreciated his efforts.   After breakfast, Harrison left to tend to some business and Cass could not wait to share with Keisha her evening, as she again began to boisterously laugh uncontrollably at her most recent discoveries. The answering machine picked up and she screamed, "Keisha, if you are there, pick up. Pick up the phone." She then heard a fumbling and Keisha on the other end, "Hey chic, wassup?"

"Girl, listen to this. My sister is no longer talking to me, and Harrison is edentulous."

"Edencha who?"

"Basically I told Stephanie about Richard and she accused me of being jealous of her and making up stories and she is not speaking to me. And I come home to get some TLC and run into a glass of teeth. Harrison wears a full set of dentures."

Keisha laughed, "Damn girl. But you know that's the ticket to your problem."

"What problem?"

"Girl ain't nothing like a man gumming you. You need to use that shit to your advantage. Next time he tries to go down on you, whip them damn teeth out of his mouth and you will find ecstasy child. Mark my word." Cassandra hysterically laughed and ignored her friend's remarks, because she didn't think she could fathom looking at Harrison without teeth in his mouth even for some good head.

"I need to go girl."

"Don't forget about what I told you. You won't regret it my sistah. Bye," she laughed.

Cass and Harrison had been spending a lot of time together going to the museum, and various cultural affairs throughout the week and just relaxing together, which Cass begrudgingly admitted she enjoyed despite his sometimes controlling demands, but she could deal with him more now since he had also been attempting to make some positive changes. Cass had still been avoiding taking a bath like the plague and figured that soon she would have to come clean with him. She couldn't believe that it was already almost the end of the week. She knew that she had plans to do something but could not remember what they were until she received a call at lunch time.

"Hey Cassandra, this is Erika."

"Erika, Hey girl," as she remembered that she was to be coming up that weekend through to Monday for business.

"Are you still letting me shack up at your place?"

"Sure thing," Cass excitedly responded, "We will have a good time. Do I need to pick you up from the airport or anything?"

"No, I will be using a rental car since I will be in and out on business. I just need the directions to your house." Cass gave her friend the directions who in turn described that she would be in town early on Friday but would likely not arrive to her place until later that evening after attending some meetings.

"Looking forward to hanging with ya girlfriend."

"Me too," Erika sincerely replied, "Maybe we can catch up on all the things which that nigga made us miss out on over the years."

"Sure thing," Cass said while hanging up the phone. She thought it was perfect timing since Harrison was going to be out of town for his son's wedding. She had gotten pissed off with him when he basically insinuated that he thought it was not appropriate for her to be there. He was leaving that day, Thursday, and would not return until after the festivities the next week. He had called several times prior to his departure but Cass avoided his calls. She knew he would be pissed, but he would get over it. She was actually getting accustomed to his being around and was appreciating the attention which he readily was giving her. But, she was less aggravated now because she knew she would have a fun girly kind of weekend, and she could now focus her attentions on getting her condo neatly arranged for company. She also figured that she still needed to talk to Stephanie, because it had been almost a week since their talk and they had not yet spoken. Stephanie evidently had not thrown Richard out according to their mother, who still insisted that Cass should never have said anything about it. Cass argued that it would be a relationship based upon deceit and her mom simply reiterated, "Welcome to the real world Cassandra. Nothing is perfect. Marriages take work and understanding."

"What ever happened to fidelity in a marriage?" Exasperated they again both hung up the phone agreeing that they were perpetually at an impasse. Cass headed out of the office still not believing that women were giving men excuses for their meandering behavior and she could not believe that Stephanie knew the truth and was doing absolutely nothing about it. "Whatever happened to self esteem and self respect?" she thought as she headed home.

Cassandra ran into answer her phone which she heard as she exited the elevator. She answered out of breath, "Hello."

"Cassandra, Hi."

"Stephanie?"

"Yes, listen I'm sorry I haven't called, but I have been very busy. I wanted to apologize for my behavior the other day. I know you were only trying to protect me."

"Well, you still got that dog living in your house."

"Cassandra," Stephanie sighed, "everything doesn't fit into a perfect little black or white square as they seem to in your world. There are gray areas and other things that go into decisions than just hurt feelings or bruised egos. I was hurt by Richard, but we are working through this because he loves me and we have produced two wonderful children together. We cannot just throw that away. Do you understand?"

"You have to do what you feel is best. My opinion is irrelevant, but you can rest assured that I have no desire to talk to him and he better stay out of my way."

"Cassandra, do you hear how irrational you're being? If I can find it in my heart to forgive him, you should be able to respect that and follow suit."

"Listen, Stephanie, I am happy for you and I hope things work out, but you better tell him to stay the hell away from me."

Stephanie exasperated said, "Okay Cassandra, but when you find the man for you, you will understand. I was just calling to apologize. We'll talk soon okay?"

Eddra Marchand

"Sure. Good-bye." Cass hung up the phone still bewildered and concerned about the plight of women who continuously place themselves in predicaments to be hurt. She then sighed, "If this is the way we are dealing with things, I likely will never get married."

Thirty-Nine

ass was greeted Friday by a bouquet of flowers from Harrison. The card said, "Missing you already. Love, Harrison." Cass was hardly fazed by his flowers because she was excited about her weekend and was looking forward to some down time. Plus the whole flower routine was getting old. She was looking forward to just hanging out on the weekend with Erika and reminiscing over old times. Hardly anyone was in the office. Conveniently, Sharon and Ted went to a business meeting together, and poor Blake had taken some sick days, likely induced by the settlement war going on between he and his wife. Linda had come in early and left early because of some guests coming into town. So Cass took the opportunity to handle personal business. She balanced her check book, scheduled appointments to get her hair and nails done and she rescheduled her appointment with her ob/gyn for an abnormal pap, which reminded her that she needed to call Stephanie and find out what ASCUS meant. She called the office and asked to speak to Dr. Jordan. Her receptionist informed her that she had not come in. Cass hung up and tried her at home.

"Hello," Richard answered the phone. Cass remained silent for a while as she was debating as to whether she would hang up or not. He repeated himself, "Hello."

"Would you please put Stephanie on the phone?" Cassandra requested in a monotone voice.

"Cassandra. Listen we have always liked each other. You might as well get used to it. I am going to be a permanent fixture in your life whether you like it or not. Anyway, Stepphie is at the office."

"Okay, bye," she smiled. "Hmmm, I wonder what she is up to," as Cass knew she had to find out where Stephanie was spending her Friday without her husband's knowledge. After finishing up some official work Cassandra also left the office a tad early. She decided that she would pick up some groceries to possibly cook something over the weekend for she and Erika.

Cass fell asleep on the sofa while watching television. She had expected Erika to be there by ten, but was surprised that she had not heard from her. Finally she was awakened by concierge at two thirty in the morning. "I'm sorry to awaken you Ms. Nicholas, but an Erika is down here for you."

"Send her up," Cass yawned and sleepily responded. She opened the door and hugged her friend telling her to come in and make herself at home.

Erika apologized, "I am so sorry for being so late, but I did run into some friends down here who insisted on taking me out."

"That's fine," yawning again, "if you want to take a shower there are some clean towels laid out there for you and the second bedroom is all ready for you here," as Cass indicated that she should place her luggage in there.

"Again, I'm sorry for waking you up, girl. I will see you in the morning."

"Okay," Cass slowly spoke as she walked into her bedroom with her warm up bottoms and tank top on.

The next morning, Cass lightly knocked on the door of her second bedroom with no response so she then quietly opened the door and saw that Erika was soundly sleeping. As she apparently slept in the nude, Cass could not help but notice and admire her muscle tone, as part of her body lay above the blanket. She began to stir so Cass quickly closed the door and figured that the aroma of breakfast would likely awaken her. She began fixing grits, egg whites and multigrain toast. As she predicted, Erika walked out in a bathrobe and yawned, "Good morning".

"Good morning," Cass turned to greet her friend. "If Melanie has gotten to you we should be eating egg white omelettes," Erika laughed. Cass flipped the omelettes for her to see and assuredly stated, "You know it."

"This is so weird that we have not talked in years, and now it seems like old times."

"I know," Erika agreed. They sat to breakfast and ate and talked and laughed. Cass told her of her love, Robert who was killed in a car accident and the tumultuous events in her personal life since that time, including Harrison and his conservative nature, to put it mildly. Erika told Cass of her on again off again relationship for the past two years with Sidney and how she believed the end was inevitable because of Sidney's possessiveness together with obvious insecurities. She described that they had been shacking up for almost that same amount of time and that it was doomed from the beginning. Cass inquired, "Well, why are you hanging on?"

"You know how you get used to companionship and you want to hold on until you know that something better is coming along. I think we both are in that same dilemma right now. We both know we need to let go, but no one is willing to take that first terminal step."

"I know what you mean," Cass agreed, "because I'm pretty sure Harrison is not the man for me, but he is a warm body and someone to come home to, which becomes addictive. Although, I must admit he is doing a much better job of controlling that egomaniacal shit." They decided to go out and exercise at the gym in her building and after showering they went out to eat and returned to watch some movies they had rented. As the night came to an end, they both were feeling so good about the resurfacing of a genuine friendship and vowed that no one would ever come between them again.

Sunday morning, Cass was awakened to a delicious aroma in the kitchen. "What's going on?"

Erika smiled, "You know I am a gourmet cook. I took classes so I have cooked a simple breakfast with oatmeal and fruit and I have begun making a delectable classic Sunday dinner of shrimp etoufee with a fresh spinach salad, and delicious bread pudding with bourbon sauce for dessert."

"Damn," Cass laughed, "My kitchen has never seen good cooking like that."

"I figured that's the least I could do for your hospitality."

"Anytime. What do you say I invite Keisha over to join us?"

"That would be cool I guess, but you know I always felt that she didn't like me."

"Who Keisha? Girl Keisha didn't like anyone who had a man that she wanted. So join the crowd," they laughed. Keisha arrived on CP time as usual but they ate and laughed about the past. Soon as they completed dinner at six, Erika had an engagement with one of her clients for seven so she left. Keisha stayed for a bit and stated, "You know I never have liked her ass and still don't."

Cass surprised said, "What, why?"

"She just always seemed so phony to me with her perfect body and perfect teeth. I didn't vote for her for homecoming queen, but a lot of good that did. I was practically the only one who voted against her."

"Keisha, that's called jealousy. She is pretty and she's nice, you can't fault her for that."

"Whatever," Keisha stated, adding, "And the bitch can cook too." They laughed and then Keisha left to go spend some time with Hank before he left for the road again. Erika arrived late at about eleven and her flight was leaving bright and early Monday morning. So they talked until the wee hours of the morning and agreed that they would make plans for doing something again soon. Erika awakened before daybreak and chose not to arouse Cassandra and snuck out leaving a note next to a bouquet of fresh flowers, "Thanks again for everything." Cassandra was roused awake by her alarm clock and she immediately walked into the second bedroom to assure that Erika was up so as not to miss her flight. She was shocked and disappointed that there were no signs of her and that she had left without saying good-bye. She then saw the note sitting next to the flowers and thought, "What a sweetheart. I hope that this Sidney guy realizes what he is about to lose."

Erika was very tired as she sat there awaiting take off. She really had enjoyed spending time with Cassandra and rekindling their old friendship. Her weekend reaffirmed for her that she had to end the relationship with Sidney, because feelings that she once thought were dead had resurfaced within her over the weekend. She was no longer feeling the closeness which their relationship had at one time wholeheartedly defined, and hadn't felt it for almost a full year. She still had not shared the full story with Cass as to why she and Dwayne had divorced. It was not only his infidelity but hers as well. When she met Sidney at the book store roughly almost three years ago she was immediately attracted. They had seen one another at some night clubs in passing and they both thought it was fate that had brought them together finally. They both, involved in other relationships at the time, began sneaking around until they realized that they yearned to be together. They then agreed to set a finite date to end their then current relationships and shortly thereafter moved in together. After that everything was history. Things were great initially and seemed almost too perfect, then Sidney's possessiveness and vulnerabilities began to affect them. She had to admit that she was not perfect and may have incited some of the problems but the bottomline was that they had grown apart. Period. As she thought of their good times together she fell asleep and was awakened by the tires of the plane hitting the surface of the cement as they were landing. She certainly hoped Sidney was on time, because she had some unfinished business to tend to at work before she could slumber comfortably in her own bed.

Erika was surprised to see Sidney waiting at the gate with flowers in hand and open arms. "Oh goodness," she thought, as she knew that her determination to end things would diminish the longer she procrastinated. She would break the news that night, she thought as she walked over to hug her.

"Hey sweetheart," she exclaimed while extending her the flowers.

"Hey," she softly responded while lightly hugging her.

"Did you have a good time?"

"Well, you do remember this was mostly business."

"Yeah, I know. But you didn't call me at all and you left me no way to contact you."

"Sydney, you know this was also supposed to be some separation time for us to figure out where things are going with us."

"I know," she solemnly responded. "I know how I feel," she stated as she grabbed her hand once they were sitting in the car. "I love you, Erika, and I don't want to lose you. I need you," as she leaned to kiss her. Erika turned her head and stated, "Let's go. I still have some work to do. We'll talk about us this evening." With that Sydney started the car and headed to their home without further discussion feeling her eyes mist with tears as she already knew what her decision was.

Forty

Cassandra entered the office Tuesday feeling good, having enjoyed some innocent girlfriend time for the past three days that was long overdue. Harrison had called a few times over the weekend when she was out and about and had readily reprimanded her for her childish behavior. He informed her that he was returning that day and was expecting her to eagerly welcome him when he arrived at her condo the minute his plane touched ground. Cass had to laugh as he tried to be controlling even through the phone lines. She did miss him though and was looking forward to seeing him. She would prepare a special dinner for him, even though she thought he hardly deserved it. As she thought about her day ahead with Harrison, her secretary chimed in with a call from a Ms. Dobson. Cass answered, "Hey Erika. Sorry I was not up when you left. Did you have a decent flight?"

"Yeah, it was fine. I'm just tired since you kept me up all night."

"Yeah right! You are as guilty of being loquacious as I am."

"I know," she laughed. "I just called to thank you again for your hospitality as well as giving me the courage I need to break things off with Sydney."

"So you are planning on going through with it?"

"Yes, I believe the time has come. Plus my interest has been peeked elsewhere."

"Oh really, you'll have to tell me all about him when you have the chance."

"Sure thing. I need to go, but thanks again," she sat there thinking. "I will let you know all about "her" next time Cassandra, because it is you who has peeked my interest and rekindled a flame that I forgot existed."

Cassandra decided to greet Harrison with a sexy piece of lingerie on his return. She had already finished cooking the red beans and rice with some turkey sausage mixed in and could not wait to dig into them and into him. It was getting later and later and she became concerned because it was not like him to be late. His flight was scheduled to arrive at five and it was now already eight o'clock and she hadn't heard a word. She decided to call the airport and verify that there were no delays and there weren't. So she waited until finally the phone rang at ten o'clock.

"Hello, Cassandra."

"Hello. What do you mean hello. I have been waiting for you all evening. I even cooked something special and all you have to say is hello."

"Now Cassandra calm down. I did arrive on time but an unexpected buddy picked me up and we ended up having some drinks, and time got away from me. How about we take a raincheck until tomorrow. I love you, Cassandra," he stated while hanging up the phone as he turned over in the bed and smiled at Lisa. "That should take care of that. Now tell me where were we?" as he turned her onto all fours and entered her again from behind in her ass.

"Harder, daddy harder." Harrison smiled as he obliged her. Harrison felt no remorse for his behavior because he felt as a man it was his innate right and in fact a duty to protect his woman from this lurid type of behavior. He did, however, have all intentions of going straight to Cass's but he rounded the corner just out of curiosity and saw one of his favorite girls out. She was available and he was hard, so he opted instead to spend the greater part of the evening with her and figured he would indulge Cassandra the next day, who no doubt was missing daddy too, he smiled.

Cassandra sat there pissed off that a buddy could take precedence over her. She promptly took off her lingerie and put on a duster and decided she would sit down and grub on her beans. They were delicious she thought as she obeyed her stomach and retrieved a second helping. Now feeling guilty for her veracious appetite, she decided to call Erika who would at least reassure her and let her know that it was okay to splurge on occasion. The phone rang three times before someone answered.

"Hello."

"Erika, hey."

"No this is not Erika," Sydney responded, "but hold on a minute." Erika came to the phone, "Hello."

"Hey, I'm sorry I thought that was you. Girl I am feeling as guilty as all outdoors."

"Guilty about what?"

"I just ate two full plates of beans, with bread and it is after ten."

Erika laughed, "As long as you are not making this a habit, you'll be okay."

"Just what I needed to hear," as she gulped down the last bit of her wine. "So did you do it, did you give him the boot?"

Erika could not yet find the nerve to tell Cass that Sydney was a woman. "Well, not exactly," as she tried to move out of an earshot's distance of Sydney. "You know how you haven't seen each other in a long while and you have all this sexual tension built up."

"You're kidding. I know you didn't sleep with him." She just sighed and covered the phone as Sydney yelled in the background, "Come on baby. Let me finish giving you that massage. I'm going to count to ten and then it's your loss. One, two."

Erika then quickly stated, "Something like that. Let me call you back later, okay."

"Ten," Sydney shouted as she grabbed and kissed Erika from behind while she hung up the phone. Cass smiled and thought, "At least somebody is getting some tonight."

Cass heard from Harrison bright and early at work Wednesday, but she had a conference all evening and told him that she would not be able to see him until Thursday, which was not entirely true, but she wanted to make him wait.

"Okay, well you could leave the key at the desk and just meet me there."

"No, Harrison. I don't think so."

He laughed, "Are you still pouting because I did not see you yesterday?"

"I am not pouting at all," she lied.

"Okay then. Thursday it will be. Take care, love."

"Goodbye." Cass decided that it was a good time to call Stephanie before she left the office for her all afternoon conference dinner. "Dr Jordan, please. This is Dr. Nicholas."

She came to the phone, "Cassandra, hey how can I help you?" Cassandra shrewdly replied, "You can start by telling me about where you were on Friday that your husband thought you were at work."

"Girl, I had business to handle, that's all."

"Now I know why you didn't send his ass packing, because you are guilty of having your own little lunchtime rendezvous," she teased.

"Girl, please. Is this what you called me for? I don't have time to play games, and I don't have time for any lunchtime affairs. Get your head out of the gutter. I have patients to see. I will talk to you later."

Cass laughed, "Well, I learned nothing on that exchange. I'm losing my touch." Stephanie was not ready to share that ever since she became aware of Richard's affair, she began seeing a counselor alone and had been started on very high doses of antidepressants. She felt like she was getting better until she followed Richard that Thursday and witnessed him with her own eyes kissing the other woman, after he vowed that he would no longer see her. She held back her tears as she thought about how strong everyone thought she was, but honestly she felt like she was falling apart more every day. "This courage and strength bullshit," she thought while slumping into her chair, "is just a façade. I need someone to talk to who will not judge me," she cried while holding the small razor blade in her hand.

Thursday finally came around and Harrison could not wait to see Cassandra. He did miss her and wanted to make passionate love to her. He decided that he would surprise her at work with a nice trinket and then escort her home so that she could give herself to him. It was just before lunch and everyone was preparing for their breaks, and Cass looked up and saw Harrison standing there looking so debonair in his suit and tie holding a small red box. He walked into her office and laid a big kiss on her lips.

He then pulled her out into the main office hallway, knelt on his knee in front of everyone and said, "We have been seeing one another for a while now, and my love is growing everyday for you. My son's wedding reinforced my love for you and my desire to be with you forever as my wife. Will you marry me?" Cass's eyes welled with tears as she looked at him on his knees in front of everyone professing his love for her. Cass entranced by the moment, looked at him and just openly kissed him without daring to give a response, yet. She was moved when she saw the large rock sitting in the gold ban. As he took her hand to place the ring on her left fourth finger she allowed him to as he then stood up and hugged her. Cass looked around and it seemed as though the only person she could see clearly in the crowd was Linda peering at her as if she had broken a secret trust. When their eyes met, Linda abruptly turned around to leave. Cass then knew that she was leaving the office for the day and that no one would protest after what had just happened. Harrison escorted her out to her car and said, "I love you," while opening her car door. Cass looked at him and responded, "I love you too, Harrison."

Cass secretly did not know how she was feeling. Deep down inside she thought she had established that Harrison was not the man for her but she was selfishly enjoying the attention and was more hesitant about assuming that fact. She relished the thought of erasing the title of "likely old maid" from her personal resume. She liked the idea of commitment and companionship. She also reasoned that her only comparison for a mate was practically perfect but no longer on this earth. She then paused briefly and quietly asked, "Robert, am I supposed to be with him?" Then she became encompassed with guilt and decided that she would not totally abandon the idea of marrying Harrison but rather would pray on whether this was truly God's plan since her true soulmate was gone. She then hopped in her car looking at her very traditional ring which she certainly would not have chosen and started the car. She turned on her gospel station hoping to get some sign or enlightenment about why God had placed Harrison into her life.

Harrison smugly walked to his car knowing that she was the one he was going to finally make Mrs. Harrison Chauncey. He followed her to her condo and immediately on their entrance into her condo he demanded that she take off all of her clothes and take a bath. She obliged him and timidly returned afraid of what was to come next. Harrison laid her on the bed and went down on her, but this time he was not biting and choppy but smooth and slow. For the first time ever, Cassandra had an orgasm with him as she shuddered uncontrollably. He then gracefully stood, washed his mouth and came back without skipping a beat to enter her. Cass figured they had yet again moved their relationship to another level as she silently whispered, "Harder, Harrison," and he ignored her request and continued at his slow gentle pace until he came. They slept through the night and Cassandra took a personal day on Friday and they spent the entire day just enjoying one another. Cassandra then honestly contemplated while looking at the ring on her finger, "Maybe he is the man for me. Maybe I will be Mrs. Cassandra Chauncey after all, especially since brother had some coochie eating lessons," she silently chuckled. "Cassandra Chauncey," she repeated. That even has a nice ring to it," as she turned over and fell asleep in his arms.

Cassandra prepared a delicious breakfast and chilled out all day Saturday, relishing the idea of erasing the brand of being alone in the very real future. She raised her hands with her palms faced up like the kids do and smiled saying, "Grandma, I did it. It is finally going to happen." Harrison had left to play golf with his buddies. As soon as he left she picked up the phone to share her news.

"Keisha, girl," she screamed. "I may not be an old maid after all. Harrison asked me to marry him."

Keisha began choking on her orange juice and replied, "I know you are not considering it. You just finished dogging him out about his being a control freak, and to add to that he can't eat coochie."

"Girl, he made up for that Thursday night. He was so gentle and he didn't bite. He took it nice and slow, and I came girl. I came," she screamed. "So why shouldn't I marry him. He matches all my criteria, now."

Keisha boldly responded, "Maybe because you don't love him. Hello," she screamed back.

"I do love him. And he is transforming into a less dominant creature these days. I feel like he has come a long way and the best is yet to come."

"Girl, you need to backup and take your head out of the clouds. He is not the one."

"We'll see. I haven't really officially answered him yet."

"Are you wearing the ring?"

"Yes."

"Well, in essence you have officially agreed to marry him. We need to talk in person child. Bye." Cass hung up the phone and smiled deciding that she would tell her mom and family once things were more confirmed.

Cassandra continued floating around the house feeling like a weight had been lifted off of her shoulders. The feeling only being disrupted when the phone rang.

"Guess who?" Erika prodded.

"Hey Erika," Cass gleefully shouted. Just as she started to share her news, she decided against it for now since she knew that Erika was going through some major relationship problems.

"Wassup?"

"Guess who will be coming into town at the end of this week again?"

"Girl, I know you don't have another deposition here in Atlanta so soon."

"Yes, I do. Now you know I can easily stay in a hotel, but

since we had such a good time last time I was there, I figured I'd ask how you felt about seeing my face so soon, again."

"Girl, you are always welcome here. I will leave a key at the concierge for Friday if I am not here."

"Okay, great. I'll see you then." Erika hung up the phone very eager to begin letting Cass know more about her. Since she had put Sydney out just a couple of days ago, she figured she needed to initiate telling Cass about her lifestyle and about her more than friendly feelings for her. "Maybe this weekend," she thought as she looked around at her very empty house since Sydney had taken mostly everything while she was not there. She then smiled again hardly fazed only thinking about reigniting the flame which now lay dormant inside of her.

Forty-One

The week went by fast as Cass was getting used to Harrison being around all the time. He had practically moved in earlier that week after she subtly implied that she would become the next Mrs. Harrison Chauncey. Since he had put a lot of his domineering ways into remission, most of his character flaws had become acceptable and simplistic. Although sometimes his desire to keep chivalry alive became overbearing, his intent was always well-meaning. She couldn't fault him for that, as long as he respected her independence and did not become totally consumed by his conservative lifestyle. Finally Friday had arrived and Cassandra had gone to the office early and finished early. She wanted to be home when Harrison arrived. She received a call from the concierge desk and wondered why Harrison was calling up when he had a key. She then remembered that it was Erika. Cass readily opened her door and hugged Erika saying, "Girl come on in. Have a seat. You can place your luggage in the second bedroom."

"Sure thing. Wassup woman?" Cass decided she would tell Erika after she found out the status of her relationship with Sydney.

"So," Cassandra offered as Erika sat on the sofa openly admiring her, "Can I get you something to drink?"

Erika needed to acquire the courage to tell Cass so she stated, "How about a beer?"

"Sure. I'll have one too." As she walked over from the kitchen with the drinks in hand, she inquired, "So, how are you and Sydney doing?"

"We are no longer."

"Oh, I am so sorry," Cass sorrowfully responded while grabbing her hand.

"No don't be," she replied feeling more compelled to talk after feeling Cassandra's electrifying touch. She took a big gulp of the beer and said, "I want to share something with you."

As Cass responded, "Go right ahead," there was the sound of keys opening the door.

Cass hopped up, "Harrison, hi sweetheart. This is Erika. Erika," she looked away from her and bashfully announced, "This is my fiance' Harrison."

Erika, flushing, promptly stood up and shook his hand totally feeling like a fool. "Nice to meet you," she lied. "Likewise" he sang back while kissing Cassandra on her lips and tapping her on the ass saying, "I'd like a beer also."

"Sure," Cass replied while returning to the kitchen. He sat down and could not help but recognize Erika's stunning beauty. "You are a very beautiful woman," he winked, as Cass made her way back, beer in hand. Erika ignored his callous behavior, unable and unwilling to conceive that he was blatantly hitting on her.

Cassandra then continued, "You said you wanted to share something with me?" Erika had forgotten all about that, and certainly was not going to profess her desire to be a part of her life in all aspects in his presence and for that matter probably never, now. She responded, "Oh. That can wait." They continued some small talk for the remainder of the evening and Erika couldn't help but observe the weird dynamics of Cass and Harrison's relationship. She was dumbfounded by Cass's attraction to this man who she literally felt hardly deserved her. He was definitely handsome, but his arrogance seemed to overshadow his looks by far and she recognized this fact in only the first few minutes in which she had made his acquaintance. She thought, "I cannot believe she is marrying this jerk," as she realized that some of her feelings were definitely biased. She didn't know if she could pretend to be happy about her friend's impending marriage, and she had thought about going to a hotel several times but felt that her leaving now might be a little too obvious. They finally said their goodnights and went to their respective bedrooms. That night Harrison wanted Cassandra and Cass was a willing participant. She hoped that he would comply with some of her sexual wishes for a change though. They were making quiet gentle love as usual, and Cass wanted him to be less gentle and more forceful.

So she quietly whispered, "Harder, Harrison, Harder."

He then angrily chided, "If it's hard you want,(you obscene whore, he thought) hard you'll get," as he began forcibly fucking her and her bed posts began hitting the wall loudly in a continuous rhythmic pattern.

It was then that Cass pleaded, "That's enough, Harrison, shhh!" as she didn't want to wake Erika. Her wishes fell on deaf ears as he began to perspire profusely while continuing to forcefully thrust into her. Erika at that point decided, "I couldn't care less how this is perceived. I cannot sit here and listen to this bullshit." She quickly packed up her bags and left without a word. She had decided that she definitely didn't need to reveal her news to Cass afterall, because from the looks of things she wouldn't be particularly receptive anyway. She sat sulking in her hotel room until it was time for her deposition the next morning. She couldn't consider sleeping because every time she closed her eyes all she would envision was Harrison screwing Cssandra and she could not tolerate that reality. She had decided that instead of staying until Sunday as planned, she would leave after her deposition because there was no longer anything keeping her in Atlanta.

Cassandra awakened the next morning and was too embarrassed to face Erika. She didn't know what had gotten into Harrison, but of course the night that he decided to comply with her wishes was when she had company. She lightly laughed, "But it was all good," she thought. But she didn't understand his behavior afterwards. She wanted to cuddle but he was very distant and cold and the very same attitude persisted into the morning. As evidenced by the fact that he left exceptionally early without as much as a kiss or the "I love you" which had become routine in the previous weeks since their engagement. She began fixing breakfast and hoped that again the aroma would awaken Erika. When it was noon and there were no signs of Erika, Cass went to her room and knocked on the door, but to no avail. She finally entered and realized that there was no indication that the bed had been slept in and no signs of Erika. She then wondered if something had happened. Cass decided to call and leave a message on her answering machine in New Jersey and hoped she checked her messages, or that she would call her. Cass called her house and the answering machine picked up as she expected, "Hey, Erika what happened? Did you have to leave early for an emergency or something? Please call me. I am worried. Bye." Cass stayed around the house all day but heard no word from Erika or Harrison. She then watched a pay per view movie and drifted off to sleep concerned about two of the newly meaningful people in her life.

Harrison left early in the morning because he was unable to sleep well next to Cassandra that night. He began criticizing his decision to take her as his wife, because he felt like he could just pay for her services if she was just going to be a high priced whore. He didn't like his women, at least the ones he hadn't paid for, to be aggressive at all in bed. He was to be the sole aggressor. They were not to speak unless spoken to. They were not to question the way he makes love. What she had done was an abomination and a disrespect of his manhood, he thought, as he sat at his piano harshly banging the keys. He did care for her deeply and while he had fictitiously professed his love for her in the foregoing weeks, he truly was beginning to believe that he did. In fact, he hoped that indirectly she had learned her lesson for trying to enforce her way of thinking upon him, because he felt stronger for her than any other woman in a long time. His goal that night was to hurt her just a little for her overt insolence so that maybe she would not be so tempted to make a similar request in the future. He had stressed to her time and time again that he wanted a woman who was a lady at all times, no matter what the situation. She apparently was not as refined as he thought. He would continue to work with her, but if anything more tantalizing came along in the meantime, he would be open to making a change. His thoughts then moved to her friend Erika, who he wished he had the pleasure of meeting before Cass. He then silently sighed, "What will be will be," as he slammed the door to his home heading to his favorite corner. As he fucked the prostitute this time, he had visions of Erika and immediately came.

Sunday and Monday passed still with no response from either Harrison or Erika. She then began to wonder if the two of them hooked up and eloped somewhere. She found herself becoming more disconcerted every minute. She finally decided to try calling Erika once again. She was so pleased to here a human voice as opposed to the answering machine, "Hello."

"Erika, this is Cassandra. Did you not get any of my messages?"

"Yes, I did, but I have just been so busy," she lied.

"Well what happened, I thought you were supposed to be staying the whole weekend?"

"Cassandra I was supposed to but once I learned of your engagement, I felt like I was truly intruding on your space, so I decided it would be best if I leave and give you all your privacy."

Cass then embarrassingly questioned, "You heard us didn't you?" Erika tried to hide that fact. "You heard us that night. I am so sorry."

"No problem. I understand being all newly engaged and stuff. I wish you all the best. I should be going now," she decided there was no need to further prolong any discussions between the two of them.

Cassandra then acknowledged, "You wanted to share something with me. You can tell me now."

"You know what Cassandra. All that is now very irrelevant. Good luck to you and congratulations," she hung up the phone and did not give Cass an opportunity to reply. Cass held the phone for a minute and thought, "Are all of my friends freaking out on me or something?" as she hung up the phone totally bewildered. She then decided to call her sister Stephanie and finally share her news. She had tried reaching her several times during the week, but without any luck.

"Hello," Richard answered.

"You again. Please put Stephanie on the phone."

He hesitated, "Uhhh, she is not here."

"Richard, what is going on? I have been calling there at all hours at which she should normally be home and she is never there and never at work. What the fuck is going on?"

He then sighed and said, "She didn't want me to tell you."

"She didn't want you to tell me what?" she responded anxious and concerned.

"Come on Richard. Spit it out."

"Stephanie is at the hospital."

"Okay. That's nothing new. She's on call. What about it?"

"No she is not in the hospital as a physician but rather as a patient."

"What are you talking about Richard?"

"The other day while she was at her office, her nurse walked in and caught her holding a razor blade as if she were going to slit her wrists. She was then voluntarily admitted to a psychiatric unit for treatment and observation."

"You son of a bitch. You caused all this. Where is my sister?" as she began to audibly cry.

"Now that I will not tell you. I know she would not want you to see her in this state. I will tell you that she is doing much better and will probably be out by Thursday." Cassandra just hung up the phone in total disbelief feeling guilty for telling her sister about Richard. She figured that her sister's blood was on both her hands and Richard's. She would let things go until Thursday, but if there was no word at that point she was going to force him to give her the information. She also would wait until she knew more before alarming her mother.

Harrison, finally by late Wednesday decided that he would call Cassandra because afterall communication is important, especially with the woman who was to be his wife, so the books claim. He had received her countless messages and decided that she wasn't worthy of a response until he deemed it appropriate. "Hello," he said as he heard her answer the phone.

"Harrison, what's going on? Where have you been?" still very preoccupied by the circumstances surrounding her sister's hospitalization.

"Well, my dear Cassandra, I was contemplating whether we should continue this engagement, to be honest. Some of your recent behavior has been of concern to me. I can't have you trying to tell me what to do. You must always respect me and know that everything I do is in your best interest. Under no circumstances are you to denounce my actions or decisions. Is that understood?"

"Harrison. What in the hell are you talking about? I told you that I will not be your fucking puppet," she angrily responded prepared to hang up the phone.

"Cassandra. You really need to calm down," he anxiously responded as he was not ready to lose Cass and readily gave in this time, "It's just that I love you and I want us to make this work."

She had already succeeded in almost losing her sister to nonsense and she was not mentally prepared to lose him too. "Okay Harrison. Come on over. Let's talk, because I too would like to make us work."

"I'm on my way sweetheart and I'll pick up something for us to eat. I'll see you momentarily." She hung up the phone feeling mentally and physically drained. She needed to feel his body next to hers and feel like she was loved, because lately all of her substantial relationships had seemed to be bordering on becoming old memories. She had yet to figure out what was going on with Erika, but she was going to hold up her end of the deal, and not let anyone come between their friendship again.

Forty-Two

The ensuing weeks went by fast and Cass's thirty-fifth birthday was not far off. She had finally spoken with Stephanie, who was released in good condition and had decided to separate from Richard for a while and then determine where to go from there. Her counselors helped her to realize that she had been trying to live her life for others, and it was time to think of herself, and her children. Cass had to admit that since Richard was currently out of the picture, their bond had grown stronger and more sisterly. Stephanie had moved into a smaller house, cut her work load down, and was obviously happier than she had been in a while. Cass's life continued to smoothly flow as she and Harrison had actually set a tentative wedding date for the Fourth of July weekend. By that time they would have officially been together for eight months. Their relationship still had its ups and downs, Cass recognized, but surmised that their relationship would be abnormal if it didn't. She had learned years ago from observing her parent's marriage and then her sister's that fairy tale romances are just that, fairy tales. She loved him and was willing to accept his faults as was he hers. They were growing each day and readily communicating about ways to make their union better. She was planning on marrying this man and getting rid of Grandma Sallie Mae's shadow for good, despite all of her family's misgivings.

Her mom had met Harrison once when she had come down

after learning of Stephanie's clinical depression. She immediately expressed her disdain for him and stated that she thought he was too old for Cass and she didn't like the way she behaved when she was in his presence. Cassandra basically explained to her mom that she had just done what she had herself advised and became more flexible and available. Her mother knew that her daughter was recalcitrant, and that any efforts to disuade her would probably result in her distancing Cass, so she instead opted to pray for guidance and support of her daughter's decision. Stephanie also shared the same feelings as her mother, but figured that she was hardly in a position to be giving advice on marriage. She therefore began supporting her sister since she seemed to be content with the relationship and it was what she desired. Casey had only spoken to him on the phone once and was too preoccupied with her own relationship woes to care. She and Jarred had broken up and she was having a hard time reverting back to a normal black college student trying to reclaim her African American heritage. She only expressed happiness for her sister and hoped someday she would find a similar love and commitment with the right man. Unfortunately, Erika had continued to evade Cass's calls and Cass remained in the dark as to the reasons behind her erratic behavior. Cass just continued to find solace and happiness in the well defined path that her life was on. There were no questions, no inconsistencies, and no tribulations. She for a change knew where her life was going and was enjoying the transition from infinite chaos to such stability.

It was only two weeks from her birthday on March fourteenth and Harrison had catered a wonderful dinner at his home and told her that the best was yet to come. He promised that he would do something special every day leading up to her birthday and Cass relished all the attention. Cass was no longer privy to the gossip at the office, because Linda had reverted back to the cold and indignant person of before since Cass's true sexuality was exposed. Cass didn't care, however, because she was too distracted by all the wonderful things happening in her life and did not need to live her life any longer vicariously through others.

That Friday, after a long week at work, Cass noticed that

Harrison had a card poised in her car atop a rose describing a weekend get away in Hilton Head. They were to fly there bright and early Saturday morning. Cass drove home enamored by his incessant romanticism, wondering if it could get any better than that. She immediately hugged Harrison as she walked into their condo, and told him she loved him. He responded, "I love you too." That evening Cass decided that she would seduce Harrison and teach him discretely that there were other ways of making love to your woman than missionary style, which was the only position they had experienced since the inception of their relationship. Missionary was fine but she needed a man at least open to a little sexual adventure. He had already used his money to replace the mirrored ceiling in her bedroom because he believed that it was an unbecoming accent. Cass decided she would modify some of his views that night as she put on a sexy negligee and eased over to him while he was reading a book and gently tugged it away and removed his glasses. He placed his arm around her and pulled her body close to his and smiled saying, "You want Mr. Chauncey to make love to the future Mrs. Harrison Chauncey, eh?"

She began kissing him fervently everywhere her mouth could touch with ease replying, "Yes," with each kiss and he was finding delight in her teasing. As he began to place her in standard position she stopped him and sat on top of him. She then smiled at him cunningly and began to seductively slide her thong underwear aside and began placing his penis inside of her. She began writhing up and down on him with her eyes closed and was pleased that he was receptive to relinquishing some of his control for a change until moments later when she found herself in a blinding daze after she had been slapped so hard by the back of his hand that she was flung onto the floor. She sat there immobile, distraught, and confused, holding her throbbing face while trying to decipher what had happened and why.

He shouted, "You fucking whore. I can pay for this bullshit. I told you to always be a lady, not a fucking whore. You want to be a whore, I'll treat you like a fucking whore," as he roughly turned her over and began trying to fuck her from behind. She flipped out of his grasp, threw the ring at him, and yelled, "Get the fuck out of my house." He then spit on her.

"You are nothing but a whore." As if hit by a jolt of energy, Cass almost immediately jumped to her feet and kneed him in his balls causing him to fall to the floor in pain.

"You bitch." She then reciprocated his own action and spit on him. "You crazy mother fucker! Get the fuck out of my house now before I kill you. You pervert," as she reached into her drawer for her scissors. He slowly stood and began picking up his clothes piece by piece. He began to back away from her, afraid of the rage in her eyes. It wasn't until he was in the hallway that he was able to clothe himself at all. He quickly dressed and limped to the elevator, never to return.

On Harrison's drive home, he wondered if there were no longer any decent women in the world as he gently rubbed his painful groin. He had placed the exact same ring on three other women's finger only to have to take it back because of something inappropriate they had done. He thought he understood women's needs and desires, but then surmised that he was too good for all of them. "How is a good respectable man ever going to get a woman in a society which has lost all morals and decency?" he thought. He figured he would have to take himself off the market again for a while and just screw his whores, who at least did what they were expected to. He shook his head in disbelief thinking, "She forced me to treat her like a whore. She could have been such a good wife too," he thought while enjoying his classical music. He then smiled and said out loud, "But I'm sure I gave her what she wanted. She was a high priced whore all along, just like the rest of them." He turned into his driveway, nonchalantly limped into his home and slept peacefully deciding that he would reinstate his frequent flyer miles which he had used for the flight to South Carolina and save them for his deserving perfect prey.

Cass could not believe that yet again she was back at square one—alone with no prospect of available other. What type of vicious cycle was she establishing? The big difference being that she was a year older with an even more bleak prospective outcome by all statistics. She slowly walked into her bathroom noticing the swelling beneath her left eye together with the emotional pain which seemed to be embedded deep within her soul as well as a physical pain searing like a flaming torch from her pelvis to her head.   She then decided that no one could know about the incident and that it would forever remain inside those walls. It would join the web of other secrets which had become a part of her reality within her home's confines. "Where will I go from here? I need a break, a diversion so that I can get my life in some order." She would tell everyone that she simply realized that they all had made valid points and that she inevitably decided to slow things down and revisit the simpler side of life. She realized that in the past year she had experienced a series of dead end relationships and apparently had not learned from her mistakes. She believed that she needed to come to terms with the very real possiblity of being alone and being okay with that very theme. She then quickly took a shower and washed off any remnants of her relationship with Harrison and her previous self-destructive existence and hoped that it would all one day become a distant figment of her imagination.

Forty-Three

Keisha was the first person she called the next morning while placing ice onto her swollen left eye. "Hey Keisha. Wassup?"

"Hey there. How's my soon to be out of the single pool friend?"

"Well," Cass shuttered trying not to cry, "That's what I was calling about. I called the wedding off. I realized that if I get married it needs to be for all of the right reasons."

"Wait a minute. What is wrong? Did something happen, because I have been trying to tell you that for ages and now out of the blue you agree. I'm on my way over."

"No Keisha please," Cass begged, but realized that she was basically talking to a dial tone at that point. Cass got dressed and tried to apply make up to conceal her swollen face, but was not terribly successful because as soon as she opened her door for Keisha she exclaimed, "Oh my God. What happened to your face?" Cass just began crying and was holding her friend tightly. She went on to share the events of the evening and Keisha became irate. "Cass. I know some people. Let me get them to beat him down. That asshole."

"No. I'm not going out like that. He's out of my life and I need to move on. I realize how foolish I had been for trying to marry for the wrong reasons. Moments like this," she began to cry again, "I wish Robert were here."

Keisha hugged her friend stating, "I know. But we still have to get things going for the birthday girl. It's less than two weeks and we are going to party and have fun despite this crazy bullshit. He didn't deserve you any way." Keisha then added, "Did you think at all about having him arrested for rape?"

Cass just vigorously shook her head in the negative, "That will just draw more attention to the entire situation, and I was not really raped. He tried but I was able to wrestle away from him. I just want to forget that it all ever happened." Keisha hugged her friend and kept her company all night hoping that evil would come to Harrison Chauncey for what he had done.

Cass's birthday was quickly approaching and she allowed herself to readily become consumed by her work, in hopes that it would somehow be overlooked. She doctored on her eye enough that by the time she went back to work it appeared to be almost back to normal. Keisha wanted to set her up on a date for her birthday, but she didn't feel ready to go there just yet. She just wanted to embrace her friendships and not think about relationship issues. She still had not heard a word from Erika and all of her calls continued to go unanswered, but she was not going to let that deter her from discovering what was behind all of her irrational behavior. She figured she would become tired of her badgering calls almost daily and eventually be forced to respond. Finally, on the weekend of her birthday, Keisha put together a small birthday bash at the clubhouse where she lived. Cass was so surprised to see the number of friends who had shown up, and for the first time in the past two weeks it didn't take an effort to smile, she was smiling of her own volition and it felt good. As Cass was sitting enjoying a glass of wine, someone came up behind her and covered her eyes, "Guess who?"

Cass almost instantly knew the voice. She turned around and simultaneously exclaimed, "Erika!"

They hugged, and Erika looked at her with heartfelt sympathy and said, "I know Keisha was not supposed to say anything, but she told me some of what happened, and I am so sorry."

Cass's eyes welled as she responded, "I know, but that's all over now, and I am ready to move on." Erika was glad that Keisha had confided in her otherwise she would not have been present and she would not have been aware of what had happened. After having received so many calls from Cass in the previous weeks, she had planned to change her number and be done with the whole thing. But something told her not to and she was glad that she hadn't.

"Well, since you being all nice, a sister made reservations to fly here at the last minute and I need a place to stay."

"You have one." As the party ended Cass sat down and observed Keisha and Erika cleaning up and told them, "Thanks you guys so much. I cannot think of a better way to have celebrated my birthday. I love you both."

Cass slept peacefully on her birthday night, not being plagued with the recurrent memories of the events of that horrific night that Harrison had essentially raped her. The next morning she awakened to Erika singing Anita Baker, *Giving You The Best That I Got*, and the aroma of some good food cooking. She stretched and hopped out of bed feeling good physically, mentally, and spiritually. She was exercising, becoming at peace with herself, and attending church regularly. As she brushed her teeth bouncing to Janet Jackson, she remembered that Erika still had neglected to share with her the reason behind her abrupt change in behavior and attitude since they last saw one another and resolved that she would get to the bottom of it. Cass walked out and Erika had fixed a delectable plate of regular pancakes with regular syrup and scrambled eggs and regular bacon.

"Stop frowning, you deserve this at least today. You have been good and hell, it's your birthday weekend." Cass reluctantly sat down and ate.

"So Erika now that I have you face to face and you can no longer evade my calls, you need to tell me what happened."

Erika looked up at Cass, knowing that this moment was going to come up responded, "It's not important, really."

"You need to come clean. For real, especially if we are to keep this feeble friendship hanging on a thread growing."

"This is not very easy for me to say, but I have been dishonest with you all along, in a matter of sorts."

Cass deciding not to be judgemental said smoothly, "Go on."

"Well, I told you that Sydney and I broke up, which is true. But I allowed you to maintain your assumption that Sydney,uhhh...." Cass beckoned her with her hand to continue. "Okay, I'm just going to say it, Sydney is a woman. We had been lovers for the past two years."

Cass's eyes got wide and she said, "Are you saying that you are bi?"

"No, Cassandra, I am a lesbian. Growing up I always felt a little different, but was coaxed into believing that was all a normal part of growing up. Then I got preoccupied with law school and life and did the only reasonable next thing, which was in my mind to get married to the person I believed to be the love of my life." She continued with Cassandra's full attention, "I knew it was wrong as I was walking down the aisle, but I continued because it was supposed to be right. It is true that Dwayne was having affairs but I was no saint and once my feelings were substantiated with Sydney, I filed for divorce. That's the story."

Cass sat there absorbing things for a while and then responded, "That still does not account for your behavior with me. Why did you close yourself off to me?"

"I knew you would go there. Well here it goes. You remember when I told you that someone else peeked my interest?"

Cass shook her head, "Yes."

"That person was you." She then quickly interjected, "I don't want you to feel like I am putting you on the spot or anything, I am just speaking the truth." Cass sat there mortified thinking, "Not again."

"Well, Erika I am flattered that you thought of me, but as you know, I am not gay, but I don't see any reason why that fact should affect our friendship. You can be friends with a straight woman, can't you?" she teasingly smiled.

"Well I am a little dissappointed, but of course I can." They spent the remainder of the weekend getting to know one another better and developed a new respect for each other and their individual choices in life. Once Erika left, Cass wondered if she had a gay meter on her somewhere which attracted lesbians to her. Whatever the case she was glad that she and Erika could be friends despite that revelation.

Forty-Four

Weeks went by as Cass worked continuously and dated occassionally, but she never felt any sparks and was very content with that fact. Cass was okay with not becoming consumed by any one particular person because after her recent experiences, she was in no rush to get into a relationship. She was learning more about herself and becoming comfortable with the skin she was in. She realized that she was guilty of living the life which others expected and not necessarily what she wanted. She had become consumed by the material things which she had ample money to buy and in doing so lost the essential qualities that made her unique. Cass had finally come to grips with the fact that being alone was fine and instead she focused her attentions on appreciating the things which she was fortunate to have in her life—like her friendships. She and Erika were keeping in touch regularly and apparently the dating scene was similarly as dismal in the lesbian zone. They shared the horror stories of each of their dating experiences and laughed about both of their abilities to consistently attract the wrong person. Cass was getting excited because as they had planned, Cass was going to spend some time in New Jersey with Erika during the summer, and the time had finally come. She was ready for a change of pace, especially since her work had begun to define her entire life. Once Cass arrived in New Jersey, Erika had an entire itinerary planned including driving to New York to see some Broadway plays and partaking of the multiple cultural events occurring that week. Cass was awestruck by all the things happening in the night life there that she had missed on her previous visit to New York. They club hopped all over and even went to a few gay clubs to appease Erika. So much had encompassed her days there that the days seemed to run into one another and it was already time for her to return home. The last night there Erika prepared one of her gourmet meals with a very light wine to carry the taste.

Cass looked at Erika while they were watching a movie on the tube and said, "I have not had such a good time in a long while."

"Me too," Erika announced. "Isn't it ironic that we both have been out on numerous dates and we only have the best of times with each other?"

"I know. We're just going to have to visit more often to keep our sanity amongst the crazed."

Erika then grabbed Cass's hand and said, "You are a true friend and I appreciate you." Cass stood up to give her a hug, and said "I do too." Erika looked deeply in Cass's eyes and she gently laid a kiss on her lips. Cass initially pulled away, but then she returned the favor and placed a soft kiss on Erika's lips. They continued back and forth until the kisses became longer and more involved. They initially stood there with only their lips meeting, then they began to caress and hold one another passionately.

Erika then pulled away and looked at Cass and said, "Are you sure you want to do this?"

"It feels so right."

Erika pulled Cass into her bedroom and they passionately made love until the sun slowly bellowed through the barely parted curtain. Cass lay there in Erika's arms and smiled looking at the peaceful calm on Erika's face as she quietly slept. Cass had never in her life experienced such oneness created simply by such a genuine closeness and energy felt in each touch and in each kiss. She pensively lay there reflecting on her life and this most recent evolution. Puzzled, she chose not to criticize her decision or doubt her own motives as she had learned the hard way that life is a dramatic process and ever changing. She realized that getting to know oneself is one of the most difficult things to do without reservation and without concern of what that reality might expose. She then smiled and thought, "Wow. This was my first chance to truly let go of all my defenses and succumb to what felt so right. I did it, and it still feels right. To first chances," she clinged an imaginary glass of champagne in the air as she snuggled closer to Erika and watched the sun continue to rise in her unequivocal state of perfect serenity, at least until the alarm rang signaling it was time to go to the airport.

They drove to the airport in a pleasant and reflective silence. And as if they were both suddenly overcome with a desire to speak they in unison spoke each other's names.

"You first," Erika beckoned.

"I don't know what to say, Erika. I am so puzzled and confused."

"Say no more. Take this all at your own pace. I know how I feel and who I am. I will not pressure you at all."

"I will, Erika. I'll be in touch," as she quickly removed her luggage to escape to her gate. She sharply turned and gave Erika a hug. "Later."

"Yeah. Take care."

Sitting on the plane Cass felt like she had come full circle and was unsure whether she wanted to stay along for the ride. She felt a contentment that she had not felt within the past year, but she had felt similar feelings before only to end in disappointment. The difference this time was that she had finally let all of her guards down. She was now determined to deal with the consequences of her choices, good or bad. Cassandra certainly was not prepared to accept that she was a lesbian, but unlike before, she was ready to accept the challenge of looking in the mirror without any boundaries or preconceived notions. She was prepared to search for the true Cassandra Nicholas and willing to accept whatever outcome—man, woman, or alone. She was no longer afraid of dealing with any choice in the triad because she had found a special peace within. She then sighed as the plane took off, as the fear of flying was a challenge she had not yet conquered.

About the Author

Eddra Marchand is a practicing internist in Atlanta, Georgia. She has been practicing medicine since 1994. She completed her undergraduate studies with honors from Xavier University in New Orleans, Louisiana, and subsequently received her Doctor of Medicine degree from Emory University in Atlanta, Georgia. She has long aspired to explore her creative side in the field of literature as this has long been a desire untouched until now.